About Dr. Kowey's Novels:

"Death on the Pole is so different, rich and enjoyable. The plot twists and turns, and we all come away more enlightened in the process. Great formula, Dr. Kowey."

- *John Zogby, author and founder of the Zogby Poll*

"I thoroughly enjoyed the latest book in the Sarkis series. The plot was filled with unexpected twists and turns and the ending left you wondering what is next for Philip?"

- *Robert Hall, Publisher Emeritus, Philadelphia Inquirer*

"Couldn't put it down – great read. Engrossing fast-paced mystery intertwined with cogent medical messages."

- *Ralph Brindis, MD, MPH, MACC, Past President American college of Cardiology*

"Connie and I became fast friends as I watched her life unfold on your pages. I was sad to say goodbye to this remarkable woman."

- *Paula Thomasson, Founder Merevir Strategies, White House Advance Staff, Clinton Administration*

"Peter Kowey again displays his gift for telling tales that ask deeper questions like 'How can love survive deception'?"

- *Richard Verrier, PhD, FACC, Professor of Medicine, Harvard Medical School*

DEATH
ON THE POLE

A Philip Sarkis Mystery

PETER R. KOWEY MD

Sheila,
With fond memories of many years working together

Pavilion Press, Inc.

Philadelphia • New York

Death on the Pole: A Philip Sarkis Mystery
by Peter R. Kowey MD

ISBN:
> Paperback   9 781414507514
> Hard Cover   9 781414507521
> Ebook 9 781414507538

Library of Congress
Cataloging-in-Publication Data
1. Fiction 2. Mystery

Pavilion Press, Inc., Philadelphia, PA
www.pavilionpress.com

Dedication

This book is dedicated to our six gorgeous, brilliant, charming grandchildren, Nell, Norah, Matthew, Amelia, Andrew, and Maeve. I love them all to pieces, and that's all Dorothy and I have to do because we know that their parents are as dedicated to them as Connie was to her babies, Emily and Erin.

Disclaimer

Death on the Pole, as with all of my Philip Sarkis novels, is based on a real case that occurred in Philadelphia many years ago. However, the characters and the institutions in *Death on the Pole* are entirely fictional. Any resemblance any of them have to real people and places is because of my lack of imagination.

Foreword

Death on the Pole is the fourth book in the Philip Sarkis Mystery series. Like its predecessors, this medical mystery novel is based on a real medical malpractice case that occurred several years ago in Philadelphia. As before, I have superimposed a fictional murder to fuel the story, and to attract readers who enjoy this genre. However, my goal here, as in the past, is to educate the public about the terrible consequences that medical malpractice has on patients, doctors, health care providers, and the general public. In this story, Connie Santangelo, a beautiful, talented woman who finally found a somewhat nefarious way to support her babies, died tragically because of the failure of the hospital system, in this case, the electronic medical record. The money that is used to "compensate" the children for their mother's wrongful death is the cheese that attracts the rat who deserted her in the first place. What happens to Sonny Cardinelli is, of course, fictional, as is every character in this book. But the message is clear: the American medical care system is seriously flawed and desperately in need of repair. My fervent hope is that this entertaining story will lead our leaders and the public to bring forward reforms that will improve the way we take care of our patients.

DEATH ON THE POLE

Chapter 1

As she grasped the pole and lifted her body upward and upward, Connie Santangelo began the musing she used to transport herself away from the harsh reality in which she presently found herself. She had discovered, months before when she first took this job, that if she could conjure up memories of her youth, she could block out the mostly drunken men who sat below her at the bar, yearning for a view of her private parts while enjoying the contours of her oscillating naked breasts. In the beginning, it had been difficult to block out their obscene taunts, their ridiculous jokes, their crude observations. Never in her life had Connie heard such things and at times, she couldn't even process what they said. But to have them aimed at her, in this place, at this time of her life, was inconceivable.

Connie tried to piece together the sequence of events that had landed her in this ridiculous place, entertaining men she would never have wanted to meet, let alone expose herself to. But high on the pole, she could escape, her mind transported to happier times, while her body remained in full view and on the job.

What a very special little girl I was. My parents loved me

so much. My earliest memory was playing on the narrow sidewalk outside of our row home on Powell Street in Norristown where I grew up. It was a Saturday afternoon, and my dad was teaching me how to ride my bike. Dad wasn't home very often. He worked three jobs to make ends meet, so having him play with me was a special thing. Dad was a little on the heavy side, so it was hard for him to run. But he did the best he could, jogging along with his hand on the seat of my bike until I had enough momentum to keep my balance, and then he would let me fly. Eventually I would get scared, stop pedaling, slow down, and fall. Funny that I never remember hurting myself. My dad would just laugh as he hurried up behind me, pulling me up to my feet, giving me a kiss on the top of my head, and then setting up my bike for another try. I remember thinking how much I loved my dad when I was a little girl. Why did he change so much and then leave me when I needed him the most?

The Powell Street house wasn't much to look at, that's for sure. Small living room, dining room, and kitchen on the first floor, two bedrooms on the second floor. Everyone had to walk through my bedroom to get to the only bathroom. No shower, just a tub I used for my weekly bath. "Who takes showers?" my father would reply when I asked why we didn't have one. Attic and basement where my friends and I would play endlessly, pretending to be in a submarine, an airplane, a bus, or whatever suited our fantasy of the moment. So many happy hours.

And Mom, the family's glue, who everyone, including me, took for granted. She was like a piece of sturdy furniture, always there when you needed her, reliable to a fault, every meal on time and deliciously prepared, the house in perfect order, clothes cleaned and pressed without ever asking. Her routine was ironclad, including the two hours she gave herself every afternoon to watch her "stories." She was addicted to the soaps but kept it all to herself, not even able to take the time to explain the stories to me on those rare days I watched them with her when I was at home sick from school or in the summer. She sat transfixed, watching the heroes and the villains suffer through life. Could she have known her own story would end as tragically as it did?

The backyard of the Powell Street house was a postage stamp. Dad had put up a small swing set, and in the summer inflated a pool the size of a hoola hoop ring. My friends and I played in that yard for hours in the summer, spilling out into the pothole-riddled back alley for our favorite games, hide-and-seek and stick ball. Out in the morning, a brief respite for lunch, and then out again until the dinner bell my father would ring when he was home. More goings-on and play time after dinner until the stars came out. It must have rained pretty often, because I remember many dreary days with Monopoly and Risk marathons on our back porch, or in our basement or garage.

I don't remember ever having to look for playmates. They were everywhere and they appeared spontaneously. All along my street and our back alley, dozens of kids, boys and girls, my age or close, ready to share a game or an idea. Or maybe an adventure, like a bus ride with one of our parents to downtown Norristown, to see a movie or to shop in the dollar store. And lunch at Lou's, a juicy cheesesteak washed down with a cherry Coke. The adults talked about Norristown's decaying culture—we sure didn't notice it.

Most of the kids in our neighborhood attended the same school. Since most of us were Catholic, and given the fact that none of our families had much money, the only choice was the local parochial school, St. Patrick's. Dad didn't like the idea that we had to pay a small tuition. "What the hell do they do with the money we put in the collection basket every Sunday?" he would grouse. But the fees were small enough that my parents could scrape the money together. I wonder if they didn't have more than one kid because they were so poor. And if so, how did they avoid pregnancies? I remember that they really loved each other a lot and were very affectionate with each other. Did they just give up on sex? Too much to process. Let's move on...

How to describe St. Pat's? The good thing about it is that I could walk there in about fifteen minutes. For the first couple of years, my mom accompanied me, but when I got to third grade, I was on my own. That included crossing streets without an adult to stop traffic for us. One kid was hit, I know, and had a limp for a long time, but the rest of us were unharmed despite our bad habit of running out from between parked cars. My mom let me decide if I wanted to come home for lunch or take food with me in my Disney lunch box. Either way, lunch was good—hot soup in my thermos, and peanut butter and jelly sandwiches on white bread that I can still taste.

It's probably fair to say that we kids didn't attend St. Pat's. We survived St. Pat's. Half of the teachers were Immaculate Heart of Mary sisters. Nuns were a dying breed, even back then, so most of them were old and cranky. Classes were large, and nuns knew they needed to keep discipline, which many of the older ones did the old-fashioned way, with the crack of a ruler on the wrist, or a crisp and well-timed slap to the face. It didn't take much to provoke them, as most of us quickly realized.

But the nuns and the underpaid lay teachers at St. Pat's did know how to drill the basics. We learned how to spell, read, write and do math problems... or else. There wasn't much fluff, but there was a lot of religion. We memorized the Baltimore catechism, attended Mass regularly, and celebrated religious holidays with great fervor. Extracurricular activities were few, especially for the girls. There were no sports, but I was allowed to take piano lessons. My after-school sessions were taught at the convent where I was afforded one of the few glimpses of the inner sanctum. The nuns were mysterious creatures who ventured out rarely. To us, they were endlessly fascinating.

My parents and I discovered I was a smart kid. Schoolwork was easy for me, and I had little trouble getting the best grades. The nuns insisted on seating kids according to their academic performance. I competed successfully for the first seat in the first row of our sixty student classroom, where I was expected to assist the teacher with all tasks like cleaning the chalk board, distributing papers, and answering knocks on our classroom door.

After eight productive years at St. Pat's, it was time for high school. Once again, there was little to decide. Norristown High School was in a neighborhood that my parents considered highly undesirable, even from their perspective, populated mainly by "Negroes," as my father referred to blacks when he was being civil, and thus wholly unacceptable. He would rather shell out a tuition to allow me to attend Bishop Kenrick High School. I took some placement examinations and, to no one's surprise, placed in the top academic group that would have the benefit of the best books and teachers, and the most interesting subjects.

My delight with my new school didn't last very long. Only several weeks into my freshman year, my life foundation, my mom, began to crumble. At first, her deterioration was insidious. Just a few small mental lapses that she passed off as getting a little bit older. But then there were a few more important things, like forgetting to do the laundry or make dinner. I remember coming home late one afternoon to find her staring at the television in the living room, her soaps long over. And then she started dropping things in the kitchen. Dad, the denier, refused to take the incidents seriously until my mom fell in the bathroom one night and couldn't get up. Dad carried her to the car and brought her to the emergency room at Montgomery Hospital, right up the street from our house. That was the last time my mom was home.

They did some tests and told me and my dad that mom had a large brain tumor. Actually, they told us there were a few brain tumors. They said they were metastatic. I had to look that one up in the dictionary. It meant the tumors had spread to multiple places in her brain from somewhere else in her body, but they didn't know where. It didn't take long for them to figure out they had come from my mom's breast. I wonder if that is something I need to worry about? Maybe I should get checked; my mom never did.

Mom went downhill fast. They tried chemotherapy and radiation, but admitted it wasn't going to change the outcome. Actually, it did—she died of an infection shortly after they started because they knocked her blood count down with the drugs that made her last few days miserable.

Mom died pretty quietly, but that didn't matter to me. I was terrified. My major support system was destroyed. I was adrift, and I knew that nothing my father could do would fill the void. The funeral was excruciating. My dad was a zombie, and had no way to reassure or comfort me. I knew he was not going to be there for me ever again, which made my angst tons worse.

I wish I could tell you that someone from our extended family stepped in to take my mom's place. The problem was that there wasn't anyone who could. My parents had siblings, but none of them were local and none of them really cared about us. My four grandparents were all dead and gone. My father turned to our next door neighbors, the Greco's, who gladly offered to make sure I was safely out the door to school and back in the afternoon, until my father got home. I was expected to start my homework, do housework, cook dinner, and keep things in order. I did the best I could, but I could easily see that my father was displeased. There was just too much of Mom to replace.

Here's a big surprise: my schoolwork went downhill that first year of high school. My dad was really unhappy. He said he didn't need my teachers calling him to tell him what a disappointment I was to them. I managed to scrape by and get promoted. As soon as school was over, my father drove me to Florida to spend the summer with his oldest sister, Aunt Daisy.

I have to give Dad credit; somehow he figured out that Daisy and her family were just what I needed. Hard to describe this remarkable woman. Lillian was her real name. She was given the name Daisy by my grandparents when she was a baby. They were migrant workers, and Lillian would be in the field while they worked. She would pick daisies and give the petals to all of the field hands. The name was a natural and it stuck. Like all of her siblings, Daisy dropped out of high school. But she was very attractive, and met a young go-getter who convinced her to move to Florida to start a real estate business.

Joe and Daisy settled on Orlando right around the time Disney arrived. Their business went bonkers and they made more money than they could count. They bought a beautiful lake front property where they raised their two daughters, both about my age, and settled into a comfortable life.

It was a transformative summer for me. I worked in the real estate office with my cousins and aunt and uncle, and found that I enjoyed the intellectual stimulation. Daisy also taught me how to cook and do housework efficiently. She was the master of time management. She gently persuaded me to take school seriously, and to make my dad proud of me again. By the time he came back to get me, I was a different person altogether, now fully prepared to get back to school and my share of the house work. Thinking of my mom still made my stomach hurt, but things improved as her memory faded. Over the summer, Dad had scrubbed our house of all of her stuff. That helped too.

My reentry to high school was not traumatic at all. I was looking forward to proving that I was a smart kid and that I deserved to be in the top academic section. Things fell into place, as I had hoped. My teachers were stimulating, and the courses interesting. I was able to study efficiently, just like Aunt Daisy taught me, and my grades soared. By Christmas break, I felt like I had met expectations and needed new challenges.

When I returned for my second sophomore semester, I discovered that the cheerleading squad was conducting tryouts. The year before, I had scoffed at the notion, dismissing the pep team as fluff. But now it seemed like something I should consider. I liked music and dancing, and I wanted to do something physical. There weren't many girls' sports, so maybe this would be a good way to incorporate all of my interests. I asked a few of my friends and they agreed. Dad was initially opposed, worried that I wouldn't be able to get all of my schoolwork and chores completed. But when he saw my enthusiasm, and when I reassured him that practice would not be a problem for my schedule, he relented.

I made the squad without much of a problem. I was beginning to realize that I was good-looking. My body image, formerly so negative, began to correct itself. I had a good figure, I was athletic and I understood music and rhythm. What I didn't know is that cheerleading is hard work and requires hours of practice. Since I was not a large person, the squad decided I would be a "flyer" or the person tossed high in the air, tumbling and then falling into the arms of the base and back spot girls. It was terrifying at first, but after a while, I started to crave those moments when I would be suspended in the air, all eyes on me as I turned and flipped, confident that I would be kept from smashing onto the ground by a few burly adolescents who hopefully weren't having problems with their concentration.

Cheerleading for the basketball season helped the year fly by. Dad not so gently suggested that I find a summer job. He maintained a small apartment building in nearby Bridgeport that had been willed to him by his parents. One of his tenants managed the Woolworth's in downtown Norristown. My father prevailed on him to give me a job at the check-out counter. The hours were long, but the work was pretty easy, and I was able to save money. My Dad called it my "college fund" and he added a few bucks whenever he could. In his mind, there was no question but that I was going to college. It was just a question of where and for what.

By the time September rolled around, I was more than ready to get back to school. I missed my friends and my favorite teachers, and I was looking forward to my first football cheerleading season. Basketball was okay, but there was nothing like football. The Knights played their Catholic League rivals in a large stadium in Norristown. The Friday night games were always sold out, the crowd an interesting mixture of students, alumni, and Norristonians who were starved for entertainment.

Those fall evenings turned out to be as magical as I had imagined. Cheerleaders provided pre-game entertainment and worked closely with the band at half-time. During the game itself, we set up on the track that surrounded the field and exhorted the fans to cheer for the home team. Halfway through the season, the captain of our cheer squad was caught smoking in the girls' locker room and was expelled. I couldn't believe that the girls voted for me to replace her. Just a year after my mother had passed way, my life was back on the fast track.

What I didn't realize is that I was getting a lot of attention from the boys in our school. It took me a ridiculously long time to notice that the football players would pause as they passed by our squad at practice or on their way to the field on game nights. Or that there was one particularly handsome young man who lingered longer than the rest, eyes firmly on me, a smile forming on his face as he watched us go through our routines. Until someone would yell, "Come on Sonny. Let's get going, man. Time to take a few snaps."

Chapter 2

Pole climbing was something Connie had taken to instinctually. Gus Gouvias, the manager who gave Connie the job, was astounded by how rapidly she had absorbed the lessons the instructors and the other girls at Nightingales had given her. Even the hard-hearted veteran dancers at the club had taken a liking to the rookie. Connie was so innocent and well intentioned. When they saw photos of her two kids, they melted.

But today's climb was not going well at all. Connie's arms felt weak and she was lightheaded. And as frequently happened when this feeling came over her, her heart was racing a mile a minute. Just like it did the first time Sonny Cardinelli had spoken to her.

Our cheerleader practice went overtime that September day. Football practice also broke up around the same time, and the players, helmets removed, streamed toward their locker room. I wasn't paying them any attention, so I was startled when one of the players touched me, ever so gently, on my shoulder. I spun around to see a familiar boy smiling. That's when my heart started palpitating.

"Hello, Connie," he said.

I smiled back. "How you doin' Stephen?"

"Geez, Connie, nobody calls me that, except the teachers."

"Class is the only place I see you."

"Call me Sonny. And that's why I came over. I was wondering if you were planning to go to the homecoming dance next weekend."

I wasn't planning to go, of course, because I didn't want to go alone and I didn't have a date. I wasn't going to admit that to Sonny.

"I was planning to stay at home," I said. "I have a bunch of papers due."

"Would you like to go with me?" Sonny finally asked.

I pointed out to Sonny that he already had a girlfriend. Carol Clarke was a tall and stately blonde all the boys had the hots for, even though she also happened to be one of the brainiest people in our class, and one of the few people who challenged my position as the smartest of all.

"Carol and me broke up," Sonny explained, smiling as if delighted by the development.

"Oh," was about all I could say.

"So what do you say? Wanna be my date?"

"Sure, I guess so," I answered a little too quickly. "I'll check with my dad, but I'm pretty sure it'll be okay."

My dad. What a joke, I thought. He couldn't have cared less about my social life as long as it didn't get in the way of my chores.

"Great. I'll pick you up at about 7:30."

And he was gone, likely to brag to his teammates that Connie Santangelo, ice queen, was Sonny Cardinelli's latest conquest.

For the next week, I did little but obsess about my date with Sonny. What to wear, how to do my hair, what accessories would be just right? It was at times like this that I really missed my mom. She would have known exactly what to recommend. I called Aunt Daisy who gave me some advice on the phone that helped me get over the hump and make some choices.

I managed to put together a fairly nice outfit using some of my mother's jewelry I had squirreled away, and some of my old stuff. I knew better than to ask my father for money for a new dress. I surveyed myself in the mirror when I was finished. Not bad, considering what I had to work with.

Sonny showed up on time, handsome in a dark blue suit, white shirt, and red tie. He certainly was handsome, by anybody's measure. Dark brown hair that he wore as long as the football coach would permit, dark features, and distracting blue eyes. And a good body with just enough muscle to make it interesting. Sonny's dad was a used car dealer who had managed to find a red Mustang at a good price. It was Sonny's baby that he loved to show off. Riding in that car was icing on the cake for me.

The date with Sonny was one of the biggest things that happened to me in high school. It placed me on the arm of the most desirable boy in the school, and elevated me to prominence in the King's court. And the best part was that he chose me.

The dance itself was anti-climactic. Sonny was in demand, and I wasn't. Our classmates came over, one by one, each surprised to see me, followed by questions about Carol. And then the inevitable football talk, all attention on the upcoming game with our archrivals, St. Matt's. What did Sonny think about our chances? How was the team preparing? Even the lay faculty came up to him to get his perspective on the match-up.

I smiled and put up with it as long as I could, but at around 10 PM, I wandered away and went outside to get some fresh air. Lots of kids were already out there, some of them moving far away from the light so they could make out, or try to. Too much for me to take. But as I spun around to go back inside, I bumped right into Sonny who had come out looking for me.

"Geez, Connie, were you bored with all that football talk?"

"It's not the conversation, Sonny. I'm just tired of the dance."

"Then how about if we get out of here?" he asked excitedly.

"It's still pretty early, Sonny. Don't you have to stick around until the team is announced?"

"Nah. By the time they get to that, half the team will be gone. Coach wants us to get home early anyhow, to get a good night's sleep before the game."

So I agreed. Sonny went in to get my sweater, and we walked to the parking lot to his car. He opened the door for me and I settled in. Sonny got into the driver's seat, leaned over toward me and kissed me hard on my lips. I was stunned, but overjoyed. We kissed and petted for the next few minutes, fogging up his windshield, oblivious to being discovered. I began to wonder if and how this was going to end, just as Sonny pulled back, stroked my face, smiled and said, "It's time to get you home."

Neither of us had much to say during the ride to my house. I think I was in shock, and Sonny just smiled and sang along with whatever song came on the radio. He walked me up to my door, gave me a quick peck on my cheek, said good night, and left me on my doorstep, reeling.

I didn't sleep well that night. I re-ran in my head what had happened in Sonny's car several times. It had all come so naturally, but I couldn't figure out if I was capable of stopping. It had been Sonny who had withdrawn, not me. What did that mean, and what would happen the next time we were alone together? Or for Sonny, was it one and done?

I needn't have worried. Sonny strolled over to my locker

on Monday morning, a great big smile on his face. "Did you have a good time on Saturday night?" he asked, obviously knowing the answer.

"Would you like to go to a movie this weekend?" he asked eagerly.

I was hooked and he knew it. Part of me resented his smug confidence, but most of me wanted to say "yes," which I did, trying not to sound too pleased.

We went to see one of the *Dumb and Dumber* movies, something I never would have chosen but I didn't protest. Sonny was every bit the gentleman as he helped me into and out of his car, holding doors, making sure I had the right kind of snacks. He put his arm around me in the theater and held my hand until the sweat made it uncomfortable. Then he took me to a local burger place for fries and a shake before driving me home. We groped each other in his car before he walked me to the door, but he wasn't too handsy and I enjoyed it as much as he did. This time he asked me for another date before he kissed me on the lips and left. It was pretty clear we were getting interested in each other, but as I lay in bed that night, I had a hard time processing why. Was it just physical or was Sonny's persona more fascinating than I had thought?

A week later, Sonny picked me up late on a Sunday morning and told me we were going to take a drive down the shore to his parents' house. I was excited. I love the Jersey beaches but my family hated the crowds in the summer so we rarely had a chance to go there as a family. This was off season, which meant that the beaches would be pretty empty. The weather was perfect that fall day and I enjoyed looking at the trees that had turned all kinds of interesting colors. The family house was in Ventnor. His family owned a small bungalow about two blocks from the beach. He told me that it had been his grandparents' place, in the family for years, and used by all of his cousins and siblings as a get-away year round.

We parked his car in front of the house, and strolled down

to the beach and enjoyed a long walk. We talked about our families, our friends, and our plans after graduation. Sonny wanted to go into business with his father, have a family, and settle in the area. My plans were a good deal more grandiose, envisioning college far away, and a career in medicine.

We talked and walked for almost two hours. Sonny suggested we grab lunch, and we stopped at a burger shack right off the beach. There were few patrons; the enormous deck that overlooked the ocean was all ours. We were comfortable enough in our coats, and enjoyed the bracing breeze coming off the Atlantic. We lingered long past the check, and finally began our walk back to Sonny's house. When we got there, Sonny said he had to use the bathroom, and I agreed it was a good idea, particularly after all of the cola I had consumed. Sonny went first and then waited for me in the hallway.

When I came out, Sonny was all over me. He grabbed me by my coat, and kissed me hard on my lips. I could feel his tongue trying to get into my mouth. He started to take my coat off and unbutton my blouse. I didn't know what to do. I thought I should resist, but I was also excited. Before I knew it, I was helping Sonny take off his clothes. We staggered into the nearest bedroom, fell on the covers and began to explore each other's bodies. Suddenly, Sonny stopped, ran into the hallway, retrieved his coat and pulled a condom out of his side pocket. He smiled while he put it on his engorged penis, jumped back on top of me, and almost immediately tried to insert himself. It was a struggle since it was my first time and I had no idea how to make it easy for either of us. Sonny persisted, gradually inserting his penis into my vagina. Eventually, I felt the glorious sensation of Sonny inside me, moving slowly, giving me pleasure that I had never dreamed could be so powerful. Moments later, I could feel Sonny come as well. He rolled off of me, sweating heavily, both of us giggling at what we had just done.

We lay on the bed for a few minutes, neither of us talking.

My mind was whirling. I hadn't imagined that I would lose my virginity like this, but I was pleased that I had my first sexual encounter with someone I cared about. I finally realized that Sonny had fallen asleep. I rolled over and kissed him, and he woke up, smiled and pulled me close. We talked about nothing important until Sonny said it was time to leave. I scooped up my clothes and headed for the bathroom, holding them close to me, a little embarrassed by my nakedness.

Sonny dressed quickly in the bedroom, and then set about making sure that all signs of our love struggle were removed and the house back in order. "Some of my cousins will be coming down here this evening. I don't want to give them any ammunition to tease me," he explained as I came out of the bathroom.

Our drive home was fun. I was relaxed, feeling positive about our relationship. Neither of us felt the need to talk about the implications of our first sexual encounter, though clearly it had altered my attitude about Sonny. I was now convinced he was not the shallow football player I had assumed, but a sensitive person who cared about me.

To the surprise of every clique at Kenrick, Sonny and I became an item. We were together constantly, before and after class and practice, most evenings and every weekend. And sex became a regular part of our existence. Neither of us thought it was wrong because, as the song says, it felt so right. The tricky part was finding places to do it. I was petrified of being discovered and froze whenever I sensed we might be susceptible. Our usual place was the backseat of Sonny's car. It was anything but roomy, but we figured out how to position each other to maximize our pleasure.

Our favorite parking place was The Bend, a lonely stretch of road a couple of miles outside of Norristown that led to a deserted steel mill. The good news about The Bend is that lots of kids went out there to make out, so it was safe. The cops who patrolled the area knew what was going on, and generally let the kids alone. The bad news was that anybody who recognized Sonny's car and the fogged-up windows would know immediately that we were out there. But true to the unwritten code, no one disturbed us. And with cold weather easing in, we were able to close up the car for more privacy.

I think, in many ways, those were the best months of my life so far. It didn't matter that my father ignored me because now I had Sonny's family. His parents were a lot older, and there was a gap between Sonny and his older siblings. But his parents still managed their home and were active. They hosted the major holidays and made sure that there was plenty of food and drink for the extended family who seemed to enjoy the company. I was welcomed for Sonny's sake and, looking back on it, my acceptance was never complete. Whenever I would point out their aloofness to Sonny, he would reply dismissively, "They're like that because they think we're going to get married eventually, and you'll take me away from them."

As we moved into the second part of our junior year, I started to explore my options for college. I knew my Dad wasn't going to be able to help out, so I was pretty sure I wouldn't be able to afford to go away, and I didn't want to leave Sonny. I took the SATs in the spring and did well. With an excellent GPA, my guidance counselor reassured me that I could get into any of the Big Five Schools, including Penn. The question would be how much aid money I could expect. I started accumulating information from the internet. I determined that I would be a biology major. It was the science I liked the most and understood, and it seemed to be the best way to pursue my dream of going to medical school.

Though I had a lot on my plate, I realized that summer work was a must. I was going to have to save money for college. Even if I got a scholarship and lived at home, I would need money for the commute and food and books. I applied for several kinds of jobs, and was pleased to snag a sales position at the Macy's store in the Plymouth Meeting Mall, just a short bus ride from my house in Norristown. The hourly pay wasn't terrific, but it was mostly day work and there would be a commission if I hit sales targets.

The spring was a whirlwind of cheerleading events for the basketball team, college prep, a lot of schoolwork and tending house. Sonny and I managed to get away on occasion but our trysts became much less frequent, and as they did, I felt like Sonny was beginning to withdraw. I cursed myself for being paranoid, but I couldn't shake the feeling. Whenever I would bring it up, he would wave his hand dismissively. "You know I love you," he would say casually. But I didn't.

As our sex became less frequent, it also intensified. Sonny was wild, coming to orgasm so quickly that I barely had time to react. He was always careful not to hurt me and to help me have an orgasm after him, licking or stroking me, but it wasn't the same.

And then came the night, after a particularly long abstinence, when Sonny and I had our usual foreplay and undressed in his car. He reached for his condom and realized he had forgotten it. "When was your last period?" he gasped, desperately.

"What difference does that make," I answered.

"You know why," he said.

"I don't think this is a good idea, Sonny."

But I was too late. Sonny had his penis inside of me and was moving up and down. The look on his face was demonic. I tried to throw him off, but the more I did, the harder he pushed. I slapped his face, but it had no effect. And when he screamed with his orgasm, I could feel the semen running into my vagina. I finally got him off me, and tried futilely to get the semen to come out. I was frightened because I knew that I was in the middle of my cycle. The nuns, who bashfully conducted our ridiculous sex education courses, had been careful to point out that this was the part of the menstrual period when women were most susceptible to becoming pregnant. This was essential information if one was going to use the "rhythm method," the only non-sinful way to protect against pregnancy, other than abstinence of course.

As I hurriedly put my clothes on, I went from scared to furious. "What is the matter with you? Why did you do that?" I asked.

Sonny lay naked and motionless on the back seat, staring at the ceiling. "I love you very much."

"That's the way you show it? We shouldn't have done that, Sonny. Getting pregnant would be a disaster."

"You'll be fine."

"How do you know that? Get dressed and take me to the drug store right away. I want to see if I can get that morning-after pill that I heard about on the news."

"Yeah, sure. I'll take you," he said. "Keep your pants on."

If it had been another time and place, I would have pointed out the irony of that statement to my clueless boyfriend. But I was so disgusted with him that it would be a long time until we bantered with each other again.

Chapter 3

*As they frequently did, the lightheaded spells and palpi-
tations passed, and Connie was able to do her now-patented
twirl with one hand, head thrown back, as her momentum
took her back to the bottom of the pole. She loved moving
rhythmically to the rock music that Gus, the owner, liked to
play. Music made it much easier to block out the eyes that
were observing her body. It was a slow afternoon, so Connie
was the only dancer, and the extra attention made her embarrassment worse. Fortunately, the place was pretty empty
and a few of the guys looked clean-cut; some even wore uniforms of some kind. Connie could see that they were pretty
distracted with their cell phones and their conversation,
which helped her relax and concentrate on her next excursion
up the pole.*

We did find an open drug store that night. I was frantic
and didn't even think about being embarrassed telling the
pharmacist what I needed and why. He didn't ask my age,
probably because he was anxious to sell me the pill for an
ungodly amount of money that drained my savings account.
As soon as I was out the door, I ripped open the pack and

swallowed the pill without water. It made me sick to my stomach, but I had no way of knowing if that meant it had worked.

The ride home was excruciating. Sonny was oblivious, and made idle conversation as though nothing significant had happened. I douched and cleaned myself thoroughly as soon I got home, got into bed, and tried to sleep. It was a terrible night, fitful sleep filled with nightmares that weren't too difficult to decipher. I had been violated by someone I thought I loved and trusted, and my dreams reflected my indignation and disgust.

I avoided Sonny as much as I could over the next few weeks. We went out to dinner or a movie once or twice, but I warned him not to try to have sex with me. The idea made me nauseous. I could hardly handle my anxiety while I waited to do a pregnancy test. Every time my stomach turned or I had a cramp, I assumed the worst. I knew that my entire future was going to turn on the color of a stick that I was going to pee on.

I tried to keep my career plans on track, while I obsessed about my new problem. I had done well in my SATs so there was every reason to be optimistic that I would get into one of my first college choices. My teachers, oblivious to my social situation or my recent plight, all volunteered to write very strong reference letters on my behalf. I felt like I was leading a double life. Little goody-two-shoes Connie Santangelo, star student, good kid, popular, beautiful, yada, yada, yada. But then there was slut Connie who fucked Sonny Cardinelli regularly enough to get pregnant. Connie the whore who would have to drop out of school and ruin her plans to become the best woman doctor in the history of the world.

One good thing, school was coming to an end and if things went to hell, at least my friends and classmates wouldn't be around to watch my stomach swell. I started my job at Macy's and it helped take my mind off my troubles. The days crept by. I missed my period, but that wasn't the first time it had happened, so even though it increased my angst, I didn't panic. I waited another few weeks, trying to be patient. And then, one morning when sleep was absolutely impossible, I went to my closet and took out the pregnancy kit I had purchased and read the instructions. Hands shaking, I used the cup to collect urine, dipped the stick, and to my horror, watched it turn blue. Fortunately, my father had already left for work, because my hysterical crying would have attracted even his dulled attention. My worst fears had been realized. My life was ruined.

I called Sonny but he didn't answer. I wasn't surprised. Sonny had taken a summer job at his father's agency, driving cars to dealerships all over the Northeast and was frequently on the road. I didn't think this was the kind of news to be delivered by voicemail. I asked him to call me back as soon as possible. I knew I had to pull myself together and get to work. I would have plenty of time to consider my alternatives. The only people I could talk to about this were Sonny, and maybe a few of my close girlfriends. But until I sorted out what I really wanted to do, I didn't want to chance having my news broadcast far and wide.

Sonny finally called me an hour later as I rode the bus to work. It was packed as usual with an assortment of middle- and low- income people who lived in Norristown and worked at the Plymouth Meeting Mall. I told Sonny I couldn't talk but would call him back in a few minutes. This began a fun three hours of phone tag until I finally was able to speak freely during my lunch break. I walked out of the department store and found a deserted corner of the Mall, not hard to do mid-week, mid-day in June.

"What's up Connie?" Sonny asked sounding amazingly care free. "You sound upset."

"I am upset. Perhaps you can take a guess why."

"You're pregnant?"

"Correct, Sonny. You're so smart." I said, doing nothing to hide my sarcasm. "I'm knocked up, thanks to you and your stupidity."

"Wow. That's big news. How do you think we should handle it?"

"We? This is my problem, Sonny, not yours."

"No, Connie. I don't agree. We're in this together, and we'll figure it out together."

I couldn't believe my ears. For the last agonizing weeks, Sonny had never offered solace or reassurance, so I had assumed he wasn't going to be helpful. His response now was totally unexpected. It felt like an enormous weight had been taken off my shoulders, and I began to cry.

"Why are you crying, Connie? You know I love you, and I'm going to take care of you."

I wasn't able to think or speak clearly. I suggested that we get together that evening to talk about our options. "That's fine, honey. I just got back from an overnight, so I'll be around."

We agreed to meet at TGI Fridays, just around the corner from Macy's. Though I didn't appreciate it at the time, that dinner discussion was one of the most important of my life. Sonny arrived on time and was amazingly understanding and comforting. He apologized repeatedly for his behavior, and told me how sorry he was for what he had done. "I would never hurt you, baby," he said repeatedly. He had obviously given much thought to our predicament because, in a very orderly way, he reviewed our options, carefully listing the pros and cons of each.

"I think an abortion is out," he said more definitively than I expected. "My parents would have a fit."

"What are they going to say when they find out I'm pregnant?"

"I think they'll deal with it. My father has assumed all along that I wasn't going to college, that I would drive for a living and maybe even join the family business. It's just going to happen a little earlier than he expected."

"What does that mean?"

"I think we should get married."

"Are you crazy? We haven't even graduated from high school."

"So what? I'll have a good job. Once the kid is a little older, I'll get my GED. You can get your diploma, too, and go to college just like you planned."

"Are we going to have enough money to do all of that?"

"Sure. My dad's business is good. I'll make a lot of money and we'll be able to get some help from my mom to take care of the kid."

"You have thought this all through."

"I want to do the right thing. I know we'll be happy together. I want to spend the rest of my life with you, Connie. Let's use this as an opportunity to get started a little early."

My mind was spinning. I hadn't considered getting married as a realistic option. Sonny not only thought marriage was possible, but he was advocating it. I told him that I would have to think about it, and then I would have to talk to my dad, as much as I dreaded that conversation. Sonny smiled, took my hand, and encouraged me to see things his way. "I know we can make this work, Connie, as long as we love each other enough."

Over the next few days, I began to break the news to a few close friends and cousins. I wanted to see their reaction before I spoke to my father. They were all surprised by the news, but not as much as I had assumed, and almost all were sympathetic. When I told them that Sonny and I were thinking about marriage, they agreed it could be a reasonable option. These were all good Catholic kids who were not going to argue for an abortion.

I eventually got up the nerve to sit my father down and explain the situation to him. Unlike my friends, he went off, cursing and yelling, informing me that everyone would think he had raised a whore. What would people think of him? How could he show his face at church?

His response actually helped me. Since it was obviously all about him, with very little consideration for what was going to happen to my life and plans, I cared much less about his reaction. When he finally stopped screaming, I started to give him the details he had never asked for, like who the boy was, and what we planned to do about it. When he heard we might get married, the first thing he said was, "You can forget about living here. I don't have enough room for the two of us, let alone the cocksucker who knocked up my daughter." Which of course was a lie. We had two bedrooms in our house with adequate living space, especially since my mother passed away. But I chose not to argue. Living in my father's house was not my idea of marital bliss.

As the summer went on, Sonny and I solidified our plans. We both told the administrators at Kenrick that we were going to take a year off from high school for personal reasons. Neither of us told them why. We didn't have to. The word had spread like wildfire among the teachers and students. A few of them contacted me to tell me how sorry they were, and that they would miss me. My guidance counselor assured me that I could come back anytime, and that she would help me get my diploma and apply to colleges, whenever I was ready. Most were silent, choosing to distance themselves from the train wreck my life had become.

I needed a break and got one when Jan, my manager at Macy's, granted my request to stay on after the summer. Fall would be busy, getting ready for the holiday rush, and there would be plenty of work through the winter season. Spring was the quiet part of the year, which was when I was due and likely to quit. Jan confided that her sister had been through a similar experience, which made her more sympathetic, I suspect.

After a good deal of arm twisting and negotiations that would put the Arabs and Israelis to shame, we were finally able to get all of our parents to agree on a wedding plan. It would be family and a few close friends only. No wedding party; just a best man and maid of honor. The priests at St. Pat's elected not to make an issue of my pregnancy. Fortunately, it was early enough that I wouldn't show by our September wedding date, especially if I used my mother's wedding dress that was about three sizes too large for me. Minimal flowers and fluff. Reception at the Local 38 Teamster union hall, no band, but an amateur DJ, bare-bones dinner (literally) and an ice cream wedding cake. If we kept the bill under $10,000, our parents would split the costs. And for a honeymoon, how about a long weekend at Sonny's parents' bungalow in Ventnor, where our affair had taken flight?

Though this was not the wedding of my dreams, I was determined to make the best of it. I did love Sonny, especially the new Sonny who had emerged after I told him I was pregnant. He seemed determined to make me love him, and to stand by me. Looking back, I think he really wanted to do the right thing. At least I wanted to believe that he did.

The wedding itself went well. My father behaved himself at church, agreeing with some coercion to walk me up the aisle with a smile on his face, and to shake hands with Sonny without punching him in the mouth. The ceremony was short. We had elected not to look like total hypocrites by insisting on a mass. The priest who officiated was in a hurry to make his tee time. He sped us through the vows, spun us around to introduce us to the congregation, and was out the door with his golf sticks before a grain of rice had been tossed in our direction.

My father couldn't restrain himself at the reception. Though we only offered beer and wine, he managed to consume enough alcohol to get rip-roaring drunk. This loosened his tongue, and he regaled anyone dumb enough to talk to him with his unhappiness about the wedding, how he didn't give a shit about being a grandparent, and how in the old days the father of a "knocked-up girl" would be within his rights to beat the living daylights out of the boy who had done his daughter wrong. Everyone at the wedding was relieved that my father's tirades were cut short when he finally collapsed into a chair and passed out cold for the balance of the evening. The rest of us treated the reception as an opportunity to have some fun, dance and laugh, and forget the sad events that had brought us to this place, and had caused Sonny and me to squander our bright future.

We used the time at the Jersey shore to relax and recharge. We both knew that when we returned, our lives would be totally different. We were still children who would be forced to live like adults in addition to caring for an infant. We made plans to take childcare courses, and to prepare ourselves, but we both knew we weren't going to be ready. It really didn't matter; the life inside me was growing and there was no turning back.

We managed to find an affordable apartment in East Norriton, just outside Norristown and close to the mall where I would be working, and not far from Sonny's father's car agency. It was advertised as a two-bedroom, but it was really one, with a large closet that would barely fit a crib and changing table. We spent every weekend that fall scrounging around for used furniture to supplement the few things our parents allowed us to bring from our homes. Garage sales were helpful if we arrived early enough. Anyone who visited our place, and there weren't many, would see a menagerie of furnishings assembled solely for function. Sonny would shrug whenever I would point out the meagerness of our surroundings. "Honey, just give it some time and we'll get out of this dump. We just have to get started, is all."

Work was my salvation. It was the best way for me to escape our ugly apartment. I liked Jan and my coworkers, and when I was busy with customers in the lady's accessories department, I frequently forgot that I was pregnant and that I had dropped out of school. To make more money, I begged for overtime, as did Sonny, so we frequently arrived home totally spent and ready to watch a little television before sleep. We had a bit more time on the weekends to be together, and Sonny insisted on one night out for dinner. We had sex once in a while, but it was quick and uninspired. We made excuses about being tired, but we both realized that our relationship had changed.

We were both looking forward to the Christmas holidays. The store was crazy busy so I had arranged with Jan to work lots of double shifts from Thanksgiving to the day after Christmas in exchange for a week off around New Year's. Sonny and I planned to drive up to New York to visit one of his cousins who lived in Manhattan, to do Times Square on New Year's Eve, and to have one last good time before the baby arrived in March.

Sonny's parents invited my father and us to their house for Christmas Eve. When I got off work finally at about 6, Sonny picked me up for the short ride. By the time we got there my father was drunk. Fortunately, this time he was quiet, snoring on the sofa in the living room in front of a gas fireplace. We let him sleep as we enjoyed the traditional seven-fishes dinner his mother had put together. Everyone was in a jolly mood for the occasion. We ate and ate, somehow finding room for the delicious cannoli his mother had purchased at Termini's. "The line was out the door and round the block," she boasted.

"I waited two hours, but I had to have them for my family."

My father finally woke up with a cough and a fart, staggered to the bathroom from which he emerged fifteen minutes later, looking a bit better but still unsteady. "See you folks," he announced. "I have to get home before Santa comes down the chimney. Boy, is he going to be surprised that my daughter isn't there."

I winced at this, his latest barb, determined not to let the bastard ruin the evening more than he already had.

"Maybe you should let one of us drive you home, Mr. Santangelo," Sonny offered.

"Why the hell should I do that? Then I have to come back to get my car."

"One of my brothers can follow us in your car."

"Fuck that," he garbled. "I'm fine to drive. Splashed a little cold water on my face and I'm good to go."

I think every single person at the dinner tried in one way or another to convince my father not to drive that night. No one was successful, and no one had the nerve to try to take his keys away from him. I had seen him get behind the wheel in such a state and manage to get himself home several times. For a variety of reasons, none of us did the right thing, but instead let him lurch though the front door, stagger down the driveway, start his car, and drive away.

I'm sure you can guess the rest. Dad didn't make it home that night. And neither did the family in the mini-van on their way to midnight mass. Dad's car swerved over the center line on DeKalb Pike and hit them head on. One of the kids in the mini-van survived—for a few days. We got the call just as we walked into our apartment, singing Christmas carols, and about as happy as we had been in weeks.

Not only was Christmas totally ruined, but I had lost the only person in my family from whom I had any chance of support, as hard to extract as it was. We spent our time off, not in New York as we had planned, but dealing with the insurance company and making plans for and then attending his funeral. I had maintained some illusion that my father would have put some money away that I might inherit. I was disabused of that notion as soon as I started going through his papers, looking for a will. There was none, of course, which meant his estate would be subject to an enormous tax. But that didn't matter either, because he had almost nothing to pass on. The house still had a mortgage almost as large as its value, and his one bank account had barely enough money to pay for his meager funeral. And any lawsuit brought by the family of the people my father killed on Christmas Eve would be entirely futile.

And meager the funeral was indeed, with a few of his coworkers and drinking buddies skipping the service and making an appearance at the free lunch. If it hadn't been for Sonny's family, the church would have been empty. During the eulogy, the priest did nothing more than illustrate how little he knew about my father, followed by a totally uninspired mass service. It rained all through the burial ceremony, making the priest's perfunctory prayers and remarks even worse.

So now all I had was Sonny. I hated not having options, and now I truly had backed myself into a tight corner. All I could hope was that I, my boy husband, and our baby would all grow up quikly together.

Chapter 4

Connie worried constantly about her girls, even when she was entertaining. Emily and Erin, now two and four, didn't mind daycare. The people who worked there were nice, as was the woman who lived up the hall in her apartment building and occasionally picked them up when Connie got held up at work or in traffic. But Connie always tried to fetch them promptly, or even a little early, to spend as much time with them as she could. This shift at the club was almost over, and traffic on the way out to the day care center in Conshohocken wouldn't slow her down. A few more up-and-downs, and Connie would call it a day.

Our married life got off to a good start. Sonny kept a menial driving job at his father's business with a promise that he would be moved into the office at some point. Our apartment was small but comfortable and convenient to our jobs. We tried to find ways to get out and do things on the weekends. We didn't have much disposable income, I guess you would call it, so we had to be creative. Aside from buzzing yard sales on Saturday mornings, we liked to bike or take long walks on the Schuylkill River trail, or go to free concerts on the Parkway in Philadelphia. We spent a lot of our time talking about the future, the things we might possess, and places we might visit.

The pregnancy went well. I picked a senior obstetrician at Montgomery Hospital, Dr. Carlino, who had been partners with the late Dr. Rubin, the doctor who delivered me. It felt comforting to have that connection with my mother. I wished so much that she could be with me and help me through my ordeal. I was frightened by the idea of childbirth and wasn't sure how much Sonny would help. Sonny's mom was nice to me but we didn't connect. Sometimes I thought she resented the fact that I had ruined her son's life, and that it was somehow my fault that we were in our "situation" as she referred to it. I fantasized about telling her exactly how I had gotten pregnant. I doubted she would believe me.

At the beginning of my second trimester, Dr. Carlino ordered an ultrasound. Our insurance paid for it, and I was anxious to know the sex of the baby growing inside me. It was the one obstetrical visit that Sonny attended, both of us excited to hear the news. I sensed Sonny's disappointment when we learned it was a girl. And looking back, Sonny's enthusiasm about becoming a parent waned progressively from that point onward.

I told Jan that I wanted to work at Macy's as long as I could, and had envisioned going right from the store to the hospital. But my body betrayed me. Seven weeks before my due date, in the middle of the night, I started having contractions. They weren't constant, but they were strong and they scared me. Fortunately, Sonny was home but not pleased when I woke him out of a sound sleep. "Don't worry about it," he scoffed. "Probably false labor."

"What makes you an expert?" I asked.

Sonny had stubbornly refused to go to pre-natal classes with me, claiming that he knew all of that stuff and didn't have the time. "I read about it," he said yawning. "Happens to a lot of pregnant women, especially with their first."

"Really? The instructor said we have to be careful about strong contractions this far ahead of the due date. I think we need to go to the hospital."

"Are you serious? It's 2:00 AM and I have to go to work at 7. Take a pill or something, and give it a few minutes. It'll settle down."

But it didn't, and when the contractions started happening every few minutes, I got out of bed and started getting dressed.

"Where are you going?"

"Where do you think? I have to go to the hospital."

"All right, all right, I'll get up."

"No, Sonny, you just go back to sleep. I'll drive myself or call a taxi."

"Don't be silly."

"Well then, hurry up. I don't want to drop this kid in the driveway."

The closest hospital was Montgomery, and it happened to be Dr. Carlino's principal delivery site. The ER was empty when we arrived. After I was checked in and reported my problem, an elderly nurse appeared with a wheelchair and escorted us back to an examination room. She asked a bunch of questions about my symptoms and pregnancy schedule while she laid out a gown.

"Now just take off all of your clothes, dear, including your underwear, and put this on, opening in the front."

"This" was a cheap paper gown that was about ten sizes too big. The room was freezing, and the gown provided no comfort as I sat on the cold examination table. Sonny slumped into a chair and fell asleep. Meanwhile, the contractions came and went several times while I waited anxiously for someone to tell me what was going on.

An Asian doctor finally appeared, clumping into the examination room, trailing the nurse, wiping sleep from his eyes.

"I'm Dr. Filart. And what's the problem, Mrs…. Cardinelli?" he asked as he walked over to the counter and examined the clipboard that contained my paperwork.

I explained my symptoms once again, trying to keep the impatience out of my voice.

"And you're seven months along?"

"Yes, just about. My due date is March 30."

"I see. And these contractions are coming about every ten minutes?"

"More or less."

"Okay. Let's take a look."

The nurse helped me lie back and put my feet up in stirrups. I knew the man was a doctor, but I was mortified to have to expose myself to a total stranger who had asked me three questions before viewing my privates. Sonny was out cold in the chair, oblivious to my "violation."

Fortunately Dr. Filart was gentle, and went about my examination carefully, explaining what he was doing and looking for. After he was finished, the nurse took my legs out of the stirrups and covered me with a warm blanket. Dr. Filart came over to the side of the bed, held my hand, and talked to me in a soothing, reassuring voice.

"You're fine, Mrs. Cardinelli. Your cervix is minimally dilated and not at all effaced—that means it is not stretched thin. Everything is intact down there. I'm going to ask the obstetric nurse to come down and we'll monitor your baby's heart tones for a little while to make sure your little girl is happy. If so, we'll give you a prescription for a medicine to slow down your contractions and you can go home. I want you to rest in bed until you call Dr. Carlino's office in the morning for further instructions. I'll make sure they know what happened tonight, and what we instructed you to do. Okay?"

I nodded, grateful for Dr. Filart's kindness. He left and I fell asleep for a little while until they came in to attach the device to listen to my baby's heart.

Things went as Dr. Filart had outlined. The fetal heart tones were good and strong, the contractions finally let up, and Sonny drove me home before taking off for work. When I made the call the next day, the instructions were clear. Take the medicine regularly, and remain at bed rest for the remainder of the pregnancy. I was incredulous. What else could happen to make our lives difficult? We needed my salary, but when I informed Sonny that evening, he surprised me again with a positive attitude.

"We'll be okay," he said. "I'll just pick up some more overtime."

"You're working so hard already."

"Don't worry about it. I'll manage. It's not like we have a choice."

I was relieved, but overtime work also increased his time away and my isolation. I lay in bed almost all day long, reading and watching TV, bored out of my mind. Hardly anyone came to visit me, and I had to depend on Sonny for grocery shopping and other chores, which he carried out petulantly.

And now we had the added problem of reduced income. I had accumulated a few sick days, but Macy's didn't pay for pregnancy leave back then, and so the weight fell on Sonny. To his credit, he did take on more work, but I could see he was not used to the stress, and he also didn't like waiting on me. We ate a lot of bad fast food because he refused to learn how to cook. No one in his family offered to help us. I felt like we were on an island.

The pregnancy dragged on to its conclusion and I actually delivered a week before my due date. Sonny was away, of course, so I had to call a cab when I went into labor. I was petrified that I would be like the women on TV who deliver in the back of a car, but Emily was nice enough to wait until we were in the delivery room where Dr. Carlino greeted me with a smile and reassuring words. The staff promised to get hold of Sonny for me, and I was embarrassed when they told me that his mother and father were not available. It was just me and Dr. Carlino and a bunch of really nice nurses who said hello to Emily Mary Cardinelli on that blustery March morning.

It was pretty clear from the beginning that Sonny wasn't cut out to be a father. I remember being furious with myself for not having seen that before we were married. To this day, I can't figure out why he didn't know this about himself, but as soon as Emily came home, Sonny began his evasive behavior. He was working extra shifts, and took on a few odd jobs to pay the bills. Even when he wasn't working, he was looking for ways to be out of the apartment. I compounded the problem by not confronting him or asking him why. I guess I was feeling guilty about how hard he was working, and I was afraid to upset him by restricting what little free time he had.

Our life together just kept getting worse. Emily had colic, and Sonny refused to get out of bed when she awakened in the middle of the night. "What's the point—you have the boobs so go feed her," he would say. I was up with her for hours at a time and never felt like I could catch up on my sleep. That didn't stop him from pestering me about having sex soon after Emily arrived. With all that was happening, it was the last thing I wanted, but Sonny was adamant. I gave in once in a while just to shut him up, deriving no pleasure while he silently and methodically ejaculated inside me. "At least I don't have to worry about getting pregnant while I'm breast feeding," I stupidly thought while he writhed on top of me.

Where I got that idiotic idea, I have no clue. Maybe from one of the ridiculous glamor magazines I read to pass the time

when I was on bed rest. But that little piece of misinforma-
tion became vitally important, because my inattention to birth
control led to the catastrophe named Erin.

That's right, I got knocked up again, with Emily in diapers.
I couldn't believe it when the same stupid strip turned blue
again. I was petrified of telling Sonny. For days, I debated
the best way to do it until the pressure finally got to me, and
I blurted it out one night when he came home from work. The
look on his face was even worse than I had imagined. For a
minute, I thought he was going to hit me. His face was red,
and his mouth contorted into an ugly mask of hate and anger.
It was horrible. He was so angry he couldn't speak. He finally
spun around, stomped out of the apartment and didn't return
for two days. I have no idea where he went and what he did,
and neither did his family. I was getting ready to call the police when he walked in the door about 6 in the evening,
turned on the TV, sat on the sofa, and asked for his dinner, as
if nothing had happened.

The next few months were bizarre. Sonny said nothing
about my pregnancy. I brought it up only when I had to, for
practical reasons. He would listen calmly, and then change
the subject as soon as he could. Eventually I had to start asking tough questions, like how we were going to survive in
our small apartment with two toddlers, and how we were
going to afford daycare or babysitting if I decided to go back
to work. Sonny had no answers to these questions, but didn't
seem to care. "I guess we'll manage somehow," was his only
retort, clearly intending to shut me up.

Nonetheless, the second pregnancy went smoothly. Dr.
Carlino and his staff once again provided kind reassurance. I
decided not to learn the baby's sex. Although Sonny didn't
appear to care, I didn't want to take a chance on getting him
inflamed if he wasn't getting a son—which he didn't. I was
somewhat relieved, because the arrival of a second girl helped
me economize, re-using almost everything we had been given

or purchased for Emily. Sonny's mother begrudgingly arranged a baby shower for me, carping to her daughters that she hoped they wouldn't continue to be annual events. The few people she invited were cordial, but less than enthusiastic, especially Sonny's two sisters, who spoke only to each other while throwing me nasty glances all evening.

Labor this time was not premature. I started having contractions on a Sunday afternoon. Sonny was sitting in front of the TV with a beer, watching a hockey playoff game. He wasn't exactly thrilled when I told him it was time. He did drive me to the hospital, but refused to go into the labor room. "That's why they have doctors and nurses, and besides, that stuff makes me want to throw up." Fortunately, Erin popped out quickly, and I was back in my hospital room three hours after I hit the delivery floor. Sonny was already there, sitting in the bedside chair, feet up, watching another game. He barely looked up when I was wheeled in. He shrugged when I asked him if he wanted to see his new daughter, refusing to hold and cuddle her.

If I try really hard, I can remember maybe a dozen times over the next few weeks when Sonny had physical contact with Erin, or Emily for that matter. He was civil but oblivious to any issues on the home front. He told me he decided to play golf again, and spent almost all of his time at the local golf course and driving range—or so he said. I suspected that he was pursuing other activities since he no longer wanted to have sex with me. The few times I initiated, he backed away and made excuses. By this time, I was so disgusted with him that I was relieved not to have to subject myself to physical contact.

That last summer with Sonny, things just went from bad to worse. Childcare was taking so much of my time that I couldn't think of ways to make Sonny happy. He spent progressively more time away, and it became a vicious cycle.

The funny thing is that I saw it all clearly, but I didn't care. I wasn't resentful of the time Sonny took away from us, I wasn't angry with his family for ignoring us to death, and I didn't feel like my life was coming apart. I had bonded to the girls; they became my total world. The only thing I needed or wanted from Sonny was a few hours of babysitting so I could go out and run errands once a week, which he conceded reluctantly. The rest of my time was baby-centric, and the two girls kept me hopping.

I was never able to figure out his family's behavior, either. In parallel with Sonny, they just kept moving further and further away from us. It was almost as if Sonny had to be around for them to be able to justify spending any time with me or the babies. I had been hoping that grandparenthood would keep his parents engaged, but I was dead wrong. They spent time with their other grandchildren but barely noticed Emily and Erin. I asked them several times if they wanted to come over to visit. They would ask if Sonny would be there and when not, they weren't available. Holidays and birthday parties were just plain weird. They doted on their other grandchildren and moved away from us when we came near.

I guess it shouldn't have been a total shocker the next time that Sonny didn't come home. He went on a three-day work trip but didn't return for a week. He answered my calls and said he was having car problems, but I knew he was lying. I didn't know if there was another woman involved at that point, but in retrospect, I'm pretty sure there was. Sonny wasn't a loner, and he didn't have family or friends he wanted to hang out with for that long.

He repeated the performance a few more times that summer. I have to admit that he was creative with his excuses. He must have spent a lot of time thinking them up or he had a partner with an imagination. Some of the stories were actually laughable, and I started to look forward to hearing them to keep my mind occupied. I could have become depressed, I guess, but the girls were so wonderful that I was actually relieved to have them all to myself.

And then it finally happened. Sonny was preparing for a three-day car delivery trip to New England. He took an unusually large bag with him with more clothes than he would need for a few days on the road, and I noticed that he had packed his golf clubs and shoes. And before he left, he held the girls and said goodbye like he meant it.

I should have been concerned, but it didn't faze me. Either I was in denial, or pleased he was finally exiting my life. For whatever reason, I just let him walk out without confronting him or asking him if he would be back. I closed the door, took a deep breath, and went back to my chores. And that was the last time I saw or spoke with Sonny Cardinelli.

Chapter 5

But as she finished her last climb up the pole, Connie realized, with alarm, that her dizziness was returning and it was worse than ever. She tried to dismiss the symptom as being a result of swinging around the pole too quickly. The fast heartbeats were troubling but the dizziness was intolerable. No matter the cause, she knew she had to respond quickly to keep from hurting herself. She forced herself to descend slowly, chanting while she did, "take your time, Connie."

I wonder in retrospect how I could have been so stupid. My husband had abandoned me with two little babies, I had no one to help me, and I had no job. Maybe it was the exhilaration when I realized that I might finally be shut of that son-of-a-bitch. I didn't have to put on a smile and pretend to be nice to him when he came home, or submit to his clumsy sexual overtures. Taking care of the kids was no worse than before. He hardly lifted a finger to help out when he was home, and he did a sloppy job when he changed a diaper or prepared a bottle. And always the attitude. While I waited that week to see if Sonny would return, I was torn between wanting him back for his support, and hoping he would just stay the hell away.

My father had always taught me to be prepared for an emergency. I guess it had an impact, because from the day we were married, I had worked hard to salt away a few dollars every week. I kept the money in a coffee can in the back of the cupboard, away from Sonny who I knew would gamble it away. The last time I checked, a few days before Sonny left us, there was over a thousand dollars in the can. I figured that would pay the rent and keep the babies in diapers for a few weeks if he were to actually desert us.

So you can imagine the shock when I went to the cupboard and discovered that Sonny, that bastard, had found the money and taken all of it. After I ransacked the entire apartment looking for the money I knew he had stolen, I felt like someone hit me in the stomach. I had to sit down for a few minutes and try to come to terms with what it meant. As the blood finally returned to my brain, I realized I had no choice but to beg from the only "relatives" I had left.

I phoned Gloria, Sonny's mother, and told her what had happened including the money disappearance. She was dismissive. I was clearly over-reacting. Sonny would never do something like that. He was probably just extending his trip, trying to make more money to support the family he was now saddled with.

"Have you called him on his cell, dear?" "Dear" was clearly mother-in-law lingo for "asshole."

"Of course I have, several times."

"Maybe he's just out of cell phone range, dear."

One more "dear" out of you, and I am going to travel through this phone line and strangle your ass. "No, Gloria, I think he's deliberately not picking up. He's been doing that a lot lately."

"I'll tell you what dear, let me check with Michael to see if he can shed some light. He can check the logs to see when

Sonny is due back. I'll call you back as soon as I know something. Now don't you worry your pretty little head."

Why should I worry? The fucker took all of our savings, packed a bag and headed to parts unknown, never to return. Sounds to me like everything is going to be just peachy, fucking dandy.

"Thanks, Gloria," was about all I could manage.

Gloria must have had to contact her husband by pony express, because it took two days for her to call back. "Well, dear, it looks like Sonny's last run took him into New England. He was supposed to drop a car there and come home on the train."

"When was he due back, Gloria?"

"Well, three days ago."

"And..."

"Well, he hasn't come back. I bet he met up with some friends and took a few extra days to blow off some steam."

There is some blowing going on, Gloria, but I doubt steam has anything to do with it.

"What do you suggest we do, Gloria? Should I file a missing person notice?"

"Oh my, no, Connie. I would give this a few more days before we push the panic button."

"Gloria, Sonny took all the money I have. I need to pay the rent and buy groceries and diapers. I don't have several more days."

"Well, Michael and I can help you out a little, dear. I'm sure Sonny will pay us back when he gets back, or maybe you will, when you find that infernal can of money."

"I found the can, Gloria, and it's empty. Your son stole the money."

Hold on, Connie, this is not the way to beg for money from your mother-in-law.

"Okay, okay, I'm sorry, Gloria. Maybe you're right and it

will turn up. But in the meantime, a couple hundred would be terrific."

I had to call a taxi to take me to the dealership to pick up the Mustang that Sonny had left behind, paying the fare with quarters I stole from Emily's piggy bank. The car, reduced to a piece of crap thanks to Sonny's lack of attention, had almost no gas, so I had to white-knuckle over to Gloria's house, praying to every saint I could think of that I would have enough fumes to get to a gas station. Gloria was her usual nurturing self, barely opening her door and thrusting her hand out with the money in a plain white envelope.

I spent the next two days going through the house, reading every legal document we had, trying to understand my alternatives. From everything I discovered, it was clear I was pretty much screwed. Sonny wasn't dead yet, nor was he disabled. We weren't divorced or separated so I had no way to compel him to pay child support unless I found him and literally put a gun to his head. It was fairly clear: find Sonny or get a job and support the kids.

My next call to the Cardinelli household was three days later, and this time Michael answered. "What's up, Connie?"

What's up? You senile prick, I'll tell you what's up. Your fucking good-for-nothing sniveling brat of a child left me high and dry with two infants.

"Michael, have you, by any chance, heard from Sonny?" I said as unctuously as possible.

"Well, sort of…"

Sort of? What the fuck does that mean, you bastard?

"I don't understand."

"He sent a text message to our office manager requesting a leave of absence for a few weeks."

"When?"

"I think it was yesterday."

And you and that miserable bitch of a wife didn't think to

call me to tell me that?

"Oh. And did he happen to say where he was or ask about us?"

"No, I think it was a pretty short message."

FUCK!

"Michael, I'm in a real bind, here. I'm trying to hold our family together, and I'm not getting much help."

"Gloria and I know you're in a fix, Connie. I was going to give you Sonny's next paycheck, but he had the office manager wire him the money in New Hampshire. I guess that's where he and his friends must have gone."

Friends? I doubt that should necessarily be plural.

"Is there some way to give me an advance on his salary? I'm hurting, Michael, and these are your grandchildren."

"Let me talk about this with Gloria, and we'll get back to you..."

"Soon, Michael. Please."

I was finally able to extract a couple grand from the generous grandparents, as a loan of course, but with relatively low interest. Lucky me!

And now came the fun part: job hunting while caring for two babies. With great coercion, I was able to talk Gloria and her sloppy daughters into watching the kids while I ran errands, and tracked down the few job leads that were available to a wretched girl without a high school diploma, never mind a college degree. I tried without success to get my old job back at Macy's, but my luck, the economy was on yet another rollercoaster downturn, and stores weren't hiring. The best offer I got was a waitress job at the local Friendly's. When I did the math, I realized that I wouldn't even be able to cover the cost of the babysitter who lived up the hall. Plus trying to coordinate my hours with hers was going to be a nightmare.

I started to phone the few friends I had left from high school. I couldn't afford the internet so I had no Facebook contacts or ability to access job postings. I got through to a few girls, but most of them didn't have any bright ideas. "Whatever you do, honey, don't get pregnant," one of them advised me, painfully oblivious to my predicament. "Having kids just makes everything in life soooo much more complicated," she opined.

No shit, Sherlock.

And then on a rainy Sunday afternoon, I met Amanda at the Plymouth Meeting Mall. I was trying to quiet the girls while looking for some new outfits in a bargain store. I didn't want to spend the money but I had no choice. Poor Emily was bursting out of her clothes, and the hand-me-downs I was using for Erin were just about threadbare. Amanda was across the clearance table from me, looking for bargains as well when she noticed my predicament.

"Say, honey, would you like me to hold one of your kids while you plow through this garbage?"

I was immediately on guard. Was this person trying to steal one of my kids or was she just being nice? She was dressed a little provocatively, showing a little more cleavage than necessary, but she was attractive in a gross kind of way, and she had an engaging smile. And I was tired of trying to balance the kids to accomplish even the simplest tasks. So, amazing even myself, I gave in.

"Geez, that would be great, if you wouldn't mind."

"No problem. My name is Amanda, by the way. I love kids."

And Amanda obviously did. I could tell by the way she took Erin out of my arms that she was a gentle person with experience. And her face lit up when Erin smiled at her. I was immediately reassured.

I spent the next ten minutes or so looking though the pile, trying clothes on Emily, casting furtive glances in Amanda's direction to make sure Erin wasn't kidnapped. I finally came up with a few things I could throw on the girls without making them look like homeless waifs. I visited a few other sale tables, still paranoid that this woman was going to abscond with my baby, but Amanda followed me around the store, amusing herself, talking baby talk to Erin and chucking her under the chin to make her laugh. When I was finished and ready to take Erin back, Amanda said, "Why don't you go ahead and pay for that stuff. I ain't goin' nowhere."

And so I did. The checkout line took forever, so by the time I was ready to go, I felt enormously indebted. Maybe that's why I offered what I did.

"You have no idea how much I appreciate your help, Amanda. You're so kind. My name is Connie. Can I buy you a cup of coffee?"

And to my further surprise, she replied, "Sure, hon. Like I said, I got nowhere to go and I could use a cup of joe."

And thus began my friendship with Amanda. We found a table in the food court, and ordered our personal Starbucks favorites. The girls cooperated, amusing themselves with their stroller toys and juice boxes, while Amanda and I became acquainted.

We started with small talk but reasonably quickly began to open up. After I finally got around to explaining my predicament, Amanda smiled and said, "That all sounds pretty familiar to me. I went through the same kind of thing a couple of years ago when my asshole husband took off. It was terrible."

"So you have kids?"

"I got one. He's with the babysitter this afternoon. I try to set aside a little time for myself on the weekends, to do something outdoors most of the time. The weather is pretty crummy today, so I thought that some retail therapy was in order."

"I wish I could afford a regular babysitter—it would be

great to have time to myself. You must have a good job."

"You could say that. I have pretty flexible hours, and the money is good. How about you?"

"I've been looking like crazy, but haven't found anything that will pay enough to afford daycare for two kids."

"Yeah, that's a big problem."

"What do you do for a living if I might ask?"

Amanda paused, obviously trying to decide how to answer my question.

"Listen, hon. I like you already, so I'm goin' to tell you the truth. I'm not proud of it, but I'm a hooker."

"Yeah, right."

"No shit. I really am. I never got a chance to go to college, and didn't have any skills. Except one. I happen to like sex and I'm good at it."

"So you became a prostitute?"

"You make it sound like a career choice. I didn't take courses and apply for the job. I did it out of necessity. I needed the money. I was desperate."

"Like me."

"Yeah, maybe even worse. My family wasn't helping me. Truth be told, I didn't want their charity. They asked too much in return. So I was pretty much on my own with a baby to feed."

"How did you get into it?"

"I had a friend who was a 'working girl,' so to speak. She encouraged me to try it. I did, and I haven't looked back. Been doin' it for about four years."

"Aren't you afraid of catching a disease?"

"I work in a clean house. One hundred percent condoms, and no exceptions no matter what the john is willing to pay. And the owner has a doctor come in regularly to do examinations. Any hint of a rule violation, and the girl is streeted immediately. The system works."

"Where do the hookers come from?"

"All over. We've had a run of girls recently coming from the Poconos and Wilkes-Barre/Scranton area. I guess people up there don't get much of an education and jobs aren't plentiful."

"How are they hired?

"It ain't complicated. They show up, the super interviews them, and if they're decent looking... Wait a minute." Amanda paused, sipped her coffee and looked over the rim of the cup. "Are you thinking about trying it out?"

"What do you think?"

"I think you got the looks, but I don't know enough about you to say if you can handle it. It can get pretty ugly."

"How so?"

"The men who come in are not movie stars, hon. And some of them ain't what you want to call hygienic. My place requires that the smelly ones get hosed off before they can lay down with any of the girls, but that doesn't necessarily get the crust off them."

"What else?"

"Some of them are just plain mean and nasty. If they respected women, they probably wouldn't go near our place, so with that as the starting point, you can imagine. Let's just say they tend to be abusive."

"How is that handled?"

"With a couple of very big and very mean bouncers. But if we call them, we may lose the fare and maybe a regular, so most of us suck it up... literally."

I spent the next twenty minutes asking questions, while trying to decide if I was losing my sanity. How could a girl, raised in a Catholic household, educated by priests and nuns, and who still said the rosary at night be contemplating becoming a whore? But for some reason, I didn't stop until I exhausted all my questions. I took down Amanda's number and walked back to my car in a haze.

I spent the next few days plowing through the want ads looking for anything that would pay enough to make it worthwhile, but I couldn't get the prostitute idea out of my head. Finally, after three sleepless nights, I called Amanda.

"Do you think you can arrange a meeting with your... ah, supervisor?"

"Are you sure you want to do this?'

"No, but before I reject the idea, I want to see the place and talk to the people who run it."

"Okay, hon, I'll set it up for you. But remember, I didn't recruit or coerce you. This is your idea, right?"

"Totally."

In retrospect, my first visit to that house was at exactly the wrong time of day. The mistress of the place suggested that I come for lunch so she could get to know me, and I agreed. When I arrived, the house was pretty deserted. And it didn't look like anything I had imagined. It was situated at the end of a cul de sac in Trooper, a very middle class town about ten minutes west of where I grew up in Norristown. There were no homes on the street, just a few empty lots and a seedy-looking strip mall. The house itself looked like a business property, maybe an insurance office. The grounds were well kept, grass carefully mowed, and the driveway and parking lot recently paved.

Pam, the lady in charge, was a tall woman with a big smile, dimpled cheeks, and gigantic breasts. She was wearing a muumuu that hid a multitude of fat. She greeted me warmly, and ushered me into her office where she had set up a small table with a couple of sandwiches and bottled water.

"I hope turkey is okay with you," she offered. "I'm really trying to watch my weight. As you can see, I definitely need to lose a few pounds."

Pam turned out to be as nice as she appeared. Her questions were kind, focusing on my ability to "put up with a lot of nonsense."

"Not many people can do this kind of thing, hon. Amanda has her doubts. She thinks you may be too nice, and so do I."

"How do you know?"

"First of all, we did a background check on you. We have to be sure that people who approach us for jobs have nothing to do with the authorities. As hard as it is to believe, prostitution is illegal, and every once in a while, a politician will get a hair up his ass and decide to 'crack down.' It's actually laughable because half the politicians have been in here as clients. Everybody knows there's no way to stop it. All they do is get in the way, and rarely one or more of our girls ends up doing some soft time, as stupid as that sounds. A lot of them make more money on the inside than they do out here."

"And you think I'm too soft?"

"Wouldn't say that. Just too nice. You know, prim and proper."

"So you don't think I should be here?"

"I didn't say that either. I'm just not sure you can, let's say, adjust."

Pam probably didn't know it, but her attitude was just the thing I needed to embolden myself. I hate it when people tell me I can't do something, and I react by diving in, many times for the wrong reason. Like the time when I was a little kid and jumped into a swimming pool before I had any swimming lessons. Double dare, I guess.

So after we finished our sandwiches, I asked Pam to show me around the place, which wasn't hard because almost no one was "working." I could hear moans and groans behind the few doors that were closed, but I was pleasantly surprised by the facilities. The bedrooms were well appointed, king size beds in all, and each had an adjoining bathroom with a nice shower and bidet. There were lots of windows that let in the light, but each one had a heavy curtain to block out almost all of the sunshine when necessary. The common facilities, kitchen, sitting room, and dining area, were generic but nice. There were a few girls watching TV or reading in the sitting room, lounging in underwear with frilly robes covering very little of what they had to sell. They each said hello, while carefully sizing me up. No one commented on their job or their feelings about it. They didn't have to... they were there and available and not necessarily happy about it.

Pam walked me to the door, gave me her generic business card, and made an impassioned speech about my need to think things over carefully. I nodded and agreed that there was a lot to consider.

"Connie, I like you and I think you could do well here if you can get over the hump. It's going to take a while to get 'plugged in,' so to speak. Don't underestimate that. If you decide to try it out, we can put you on for a few shifts to see what happens. I'll go over the fees with you, but I think you'll find the job to be more lucrative than anything else you can do. There are no benefits or pension, of course; you have to take care of that yourself. But you also won't be paying taxes on what you make, so you and your kids would be comfortable. Just let me know in the next week or so what you decide. I have some other candidates who are not nearly as pretty as you."

What I didn't tell Pam is that I had already thought about it-as much as I could stand. After yet another sleepless night, I called her the next day and told her I wanted the tryout.

Chapter 6

Connie's heart was now racing wildly. She was sick to her stomach and sweat was dripping from her in a torrent. She began to pray, to whom she wasn't sure and didn't particularly care. She just wanted to get off the pole and back to the dressing room. She didn't want to faint in front of all of these people. She couldn't afford to lose her job. Emily and Erin needed her.

"So, Emily, what should Mommy wear to her first session as a prostitute?" I asked my elder daughter who fortunately wasn't paying any attention. She was too busy going through my costume jewelry in the cardboard box on my dresser. I stood in front of the full length mirror I had salvaged out of the trash receptacle in the back of our apartment. The paint was chipping off the wood. The glass was cloudy but usable. The dull patches were a blessing, hiding my imperfections, like my stupid stretch marks. Thanks for that too, Sonny, you miserable prick. Why don't men get scarred from childbirth and have to suffer all of that pain? Maybe they would think twice about sticking it in without any protection.

Erin stood at the edge of her play pen, peering out at me,

watching me put on my make-up and dress. So what should I wear, indeed? I finally decided on some cheap lingerie that Sonny had bought me at a Victoria's Secret clearance sale so he could get off easier. It was in the back of the drawer, of course, but serviceable. At least it covered my ugly abdomen. I went light on the make-up. I was attractive enough, and didn't want to look like the whore I was impersonating.

I took solace in the fact that Pam was clearly going to be nice to me. She promised to bring me in during one of the slow shifts so I wouldn't get overwhelmed. She also told me she would hook me up with somebody decent and clean the first few times until I got the "hang of it." I laughed when she said that. She didn't. I guess once you've been in the whoring business for a while, puns aren't funny anymore, or maybe not so obvious.

I used the last few dollars I had to pay for a babysitter. I couldn't ask my in-laws; too much of a chance they would find out where I was going. The only person I could find to help out that time of the day was the young girl down the hall who seemed very nice but not too smart. I tried to dispel the idea she would tie the girls to a bedpost while she smoked dope and sniffed cocaine with her mass murderer boyfriend. These ruminations will give you some idea of how I think about things these days. Always expecting the best from everyone I meet. How badly had Sonny destroyed my faith in humanity? Something else I had to thank that good-for-nothing asshole for.

It was Friday afternoon, and my route to the whorehouse (I was going to have to come up with a better way to designate my new workplace) took me directly past Bishop Kenrick, my almost alma mater. There were a bunch of kids at gym class, playing soccer on the field behind the school. Though I couldn't see through the filthy windows, I know there were hundreds of kids in the classrooms and labs, none of them particularly happy to be there. If they only knew how good they had it.

Hard to believe that I was a student in that building just a few years ago. I was smart so they put me in the academic track. Lot of good it did me. Maybe I should have taken the pre-whore curriculum instead. The classes would have been a lot more practical. Proper blow-job technique, how to jerk somebody off without getting your hands sticky...that kind of stuff. Stop it, Connie, you're going to drive yourself crazy.

Only a few minutes later, I pulled into the parking lot of the brothel. I could see that Pam was right: not much going on this time of day. I had learned during my brief orientation that the establishment was progressive, and had begun to make appointments rather than depending on off-the-street trade. Appointments made on the internet or a computerized phone system. You know, push one for a blow job, two for a two-on-one, three for a dark passage. Scheduled appointments also made it easier to control the flow and kept the street and parking lot traffic to a minimum, which made it a hell of a lot easier for the cops to ignore the place in exchange for the generous bribes and "parties" that were such an important part of the overhead. It also meant girls didn't have to sit around waiting for a "date" for long hours. Time management in the twenty-first century had come to whoredom. And if it was a massage parlor, as the public was told, why couldn't a busy business person put it on his (or her) calendar? That's right. Female patrons weren't plentiful but were welcome. Customers could arrange for trysts with one or multiple partners of either gender.

I sat in the car for a few minutes and thought seriously about laying rubber and getting the hell out of there. But that double-dare mentality wouldn't let me, especially combined with the stark realization that I was destitute and needed money really bad, and that there was money to be made on my back. But what would happen to the girls if I was caught and jailed? Pam assured me that wouldn't happen; the worst

I could expect was a slap on the wrist and a fine, and that would only occur if the police were forced into it by a busybody or a neighborhood zealot who arbitrarily decided it was time for static. Since the house was tucked out of the way, the chances of that were small.

I took one more deep breath. Let's go, girl. It's party time. I got out of my car, and slammed the door resolutely. The gravel footpath was tough on my strapped, "fuck-me" high heels. I made it to the front door where I was greeted by Pam with a big smile on her face. "I saw you sitting out there in your car and was worried you were going to change your mind." If she only knew the tug of war that was going on in my head.

"I have some good news for you," she continued, "I set you up with one of our regulars. A real nice boy, well man, named Teddy. He had a car accident when he was a child. Went through the windshield. I guess his parents didn't take child safety too seriously. Anyhow, he's not totally right in the head, if you know what I mean, but he's polite and doesn't ask for a whole lot. His older brother brings him in here every month or so 'to let off some steam,' as they call it."

"Sounds good, Pam. Thanks for looking out for me."

"That's okay, honey. The last thing I want to do is scare you off. You seem nice, and you're pretty, so you could become a superstar here."

Yeah, a regular Mickey friggin' Mantle. Pam was a nice person but I could read between the lines: Pam was going to let me have sex with some low-level patrons before exposing me to the higher payers. Then I was going to have to prove myself with the regular scum, who might be disgusting or who might ask me to do things I would find repulsive, but was part of the everyday job description. Only if I passed those tests would I be sent up to the majors.

"All right, honey," Pam said as she led me upstairs. "I

want you to go down the hall to the third door on the right, and get yourself ready. Did you shower before you came over?"

"Yes, and I have clean underwear." This was eerily similar to talking to my mother.

"And you have something provocative to put on?"

"Under my clothing."

"I only ask these questions to optimize the chances for a quick success, which in Teddy's case is going to be one orgasm however you can get him there. Hell, you're so sexy, he may come before you take his clothes off."

I guess in whoredom, that's considered a grand slam home run. "Thanks, again, Pam."

"But remember, he gets no more than an hour of your time. If he doesn't get off, that's his problem. Any questions?"

"Just one. Is there any chance I could be paid for the work I do today? I'm really strapped and I have a million bills to pay."

"Sure honey. Like I told you, we pay immediately, and in cash. Let's see how many tricks you do today and we'll settle up before you leave this evening."

"Thanks, Pam. You've been very kind."

"A lot of people who do my job are actually nice—not the crotchety hags you see in the movies or read about in books. We have to be. After all, this is a service profession, right?" Pam smiled knowingly, and gestured to the room down the hall way. "Time to get to work, girl."

Pam had given me one of the nicer rooms, with decent furniture and a window. I closed the shades and began to undress in the bathroom when I heard the door open. "Hello?" A man's voice, tentative and inquisitive, like he was selling vacuum cleaners door to door.

"Hello," I answered. "I'll be right out."

"Take your time," was the reply. "I'm not in a hurry."

He sounded polite at least.

I finished in the bathroom and opened the door to see a relatively young man in a Villanova sweatshirt, jeans and sneakers sitting on the side of the bed, legs crossed, looking down. He wasn't handsome but had nice features and looked to be pudgy but in pretty good physical shape.

"Hi, my name is Connie. You must be Teddy."

"Yes, that's what my family calls me. I actually prefer Ted."

"Then Ted it will be."

"And what's your name, again?"

"Connie."

"Connie what?"

"Just Connie," I replied, remembering Pam's instructions about personal details.

"You're new here, aren't you? Where did you work before this?"

I had anticipated questions about my experience and I was determined to deliver an honest answer. "This is my first job, Ted. I've never done this before."

"You mean have sex?"

"No, I've had sex, but not for pay. This is my first time... you know, for money."

"Oh, that's okay," Ted managed. "I don't mind. We'll be fine."

"I hope so. I just want you to know that I'm very, very nervous."

"Don't be," Ted answered. "It isn't hard, and I'll be as helpful as I can. You're awfully pretty, Connie."

"Thanks, Ted. That's nice of you to say."

"Connie, how about if I go into the bathroom and brush my teeth and wash up, and you get into bed?"

"Okay, Teddy. That sounds like a real good plan. Why don't you do that?"

Teddy visited the bathroom while I walked across the room to make sure the door was locked. Pam had been adamant about that. "People get drunk and start wandering around and could walk in on you. Sometimes it takes a while to get these guys ready, if you know what I mean. You don't need anything to ruin the mood. If you need help just yell. I have a key and can get in quick."

I got into the bed and pulled the covers up to my throat, hoping against hope that Ted would stay in the bathroom and not come out. I deliberately left my nightie on. I wasn't ready to be naked in bed with a strange man, and I figured the revealing negligee might help Teddy get off, my prime directive.

After several minutes, he walked out completely naked, with a boner and a shit-eating grin on his face.

"Are you all ready, Connie?"

"As ready as I'll ever be. Why don't you get into bed with me, Ted?' I said, trying my best to sound like I was eager.

Ted dashed over to the bed and crawled under the covers. He turned on his side to face me.

"How about if we just cuddle and talk for a few minutes."

"Sure Ted, it's your hour." My way of reminding him that there was a deadline. "We can do whatever you want," I continued, hoping he wouldn't take me literally.

And then Ted began to talk and talk and talk. It was a stream of consciousness, about everything and anything that popped into his head. He told me about his family, his friends, his job as a bus-boy at a fast food restaurant, and his favorite video games. He didn't pause for a minute for a reply or comment. He looked at me across the pillow the entire time, occasionally stroking my face and hair, but touching nothing else. It was pretty bizarre.

I could see the digital alarm clock over his shoulder and I was beginning to believe that I was going to get lucky and wouldn't have to do anything but listen. But then, at the forty-fifth minute, he abruptly stopped talking and said. "It's time, Connie. Would you mind making me have an orgasm?"

A bit flummoxed by the abruptness of the task change, I croaked, "Sure Teddy. How would you like to do it?"

"I would prefer if you would please kiss my penis."

"You mean a blow job?" trying to sound like it was a de-fined menu item. Like a number 33.

"I guess that's right."

"Sure, Teddy. Whatever you want."

I pulled back the covers to see that his penis was still en-gorged. I had performed oral sex with Sonny so I had a pretty good idea of what to do."

"Teddy, you're going to have to put your condom on first."

"I know," he said, and reached behind him to the bedside table in which several of the devices were kept. He had ob-viously done this many times, because in just a few seconds he picked one, took it out of the package, and had it in proper position. He lay back on the pillow, smiled, and waved me in for a landing.

I was fairly confident that I was going to be successful. When I put my head down toward his crotch, I wasn't pre-pared for the odor. It was a terrible stench that started my stomach rumbling.

"Teddy, did you wash up before you came in," I managed.

"I used soap and water, just like I was told."

"Okay," I said, not wanting to upset him so he would lose his hard-on and we would have to start all over again. But this was going to be difficult. I held my breath and put my head back down, but was again repulsed by the odor. By this time, I could feel the bile welling up into my stomach. I knew I was in serious trouble and would have to come up with a solution fast. I remembered that Pam had anticipated this kind of a problem during my orientation and had rendered good advice.

"You know what, Teddy? Let me get some cologne and spray it down there."

"No, Connie. I don't want anything spayed on me. I hate smelling like a faggot. Just do it so I can go home. My brother is waiting for me. And remember what I told you: it's Ted, not Teddy."

"Sure, Ted." I watched in horror as his organ started to deflate. The last thing I wanted was to "blow" my first trick and have to explain my failure to Pam. Come on Connie, you can do this, I said to myself, as I made my third dive.

But it just wasn't going to work. In retrospect, tuna had been a bad choice for the small lunch I had allowed myself before I left home. Pam had advised keeping my stomach as empty as possible the first few times, but hunger had finally overwhelmed me. I could now taste acidy tuna salad in my mouth, and before I could do anything about it, it was all over Teddy's crotch.

"What the fuck?" I heard him scream as he jumped up in the bed. "Did you just throw up on me, Connie?"

I started to answer but was interrupted by a second stream of vomit that pulsed out of my mouth, missed his crotch, and plastered both of his legs and the bedcovers.

"Are you fucking kidding me?" he yelled loudly enough to wake the dead, and sufficient to summon Pam and Teddy's brother who ran noisily down the hall.

"What's the problem in there?" Pam demanded. "Connie, are you all right."

I was still gagging, so Ted answered emphatically.

"The problem is this bitch you gave me. Is this some kind of joke, Tommy? Did you do this to me on purpose because of what I did to your dog?"

"Do what, Teddy. What the fuck just happened in there? Open the door."

"I'll tell you what happened. This cunt just upchucked all over me."

The next and last thing I remember hearing was Ted's brother yelling obscenities and commanding Pam to unlock the door. As I heard the key turning in the lock, I could feel my heart beating a thousand times a minute. And then I collapsed, my face falling into the reservoir of vomit that Ted's crotch had become.

Chapter 7

Connie started to lose her vision, the edges of her visual fields rapidly contracting like the lens of an old movie camera. What she could see in her narrow frame of vision gradually darkened to black. She lost her grip on the pole and started to fall. The patrons, none of whom were astrophysicists, watched and applauded what they thought was a daring part of the act. Connie had just enough consciousness to remind herself to brace for a hard landing. I wish my mom were here, Connie thought as she sailed through the air. And then, amazingly, as she hit the floor Connie saw her beautiful mother standing beside her, arms outstretched.

When I woke up and saw the look on Pam's face, I knew instantly that I wasn't going to work at her place ever again. In fact, I was convinced that my career as a prostitute was over, and I was relieved. I had forced myself to do something I was clearly not capable of on the premise that it was nerves that was holding me back. The truth was that it wasn't in my nature to be intimate with a total stranger, no matter how much money he (or she) paid me. It just wasn't going to work.

Pam used a warm washcloth to clean my face while we listened complacently to Teddy's string of obscenities. He and his brother made it clear they were never returning to her place for anything ever again. They were going to tell all of their friends about what had happened, and all of them would find some other place to get their rocks off.

Pam didn't seem perturbed, whatsoever. I suspect she knew that Teddy and his brother were just blowing smoke. Ted wasn't going to admit that a whore had thrown up on him. Even this village idiot would have to realize that a story like that would make him a laughing stock. And there weren't that many places in the area Ted could be taken to get what his brother thought he needed. Pam just went about cleaning things up, reassuring the brothers she understood their anger and would do everything she could to make it up to them and to guarantee it wouldn't happen again.

I think Pam was more upset because she didn't like things to go wrong. She was a perfectionist who ran a tight ship and was used to having everything just the way she liked it. This episode was a definite curveball. A few of her girls had peeked into the room to see what the commotion was. Fortunately, most of the clientele in the house at the time were in the middle of something they found pleasurable and weren't going to let a frustrated nerd and his brother upset their tryst.

While Teddy ranted and raved, I went into the bathroom, finished cleaning myself up, dressed, and finally screwed up the courage to open the door. I walked through the bedroom past Pam and the brothers and headed for the exit. I said nothing to any of them, and by the time I made it to my car, I figured I had escaped cleanly. But as I started my car and began driving out of the parking lot to the street, Pam came running out the front door, waving her arms, asking me to wait.

I stopped my car and rolled down the window. I braced myself, expecting Pam to issue a stern warning about never coming back again. I was surprised when she started laughing, walked to the passenger side of the car and let herself in.

"Honey, that has to be one of the funniest whorehouse scenes of all time. In all my years, I ain't ever seen or heard anything like it."

"Pam, I feel so terrible…"

"Don't fret about it, Connie. You aren't the first nice girl who found out the hard way that they weren't cut out for this nuttiness. I audition people all the time who crap out. I had my doubts about you, but I have to admit, I've never seen such a clear-cut failure before. Most of the time, girls have a hard time admitting this isn't the job for them or that it makes them sick. In your case, it literally made you vomit, didn't it?"

"I was okay until I got a whiff of his crotch…"

"Then reality set in, I suspect. I should have warned you about that. Teddy ain't the most hygienic person who visits this place. God knows we've asked him a million times to use a little soap and water. His brother should have known better."

"He assured me he had, Pam. That's why I was so surprised."

"He didn't mean no harm, Connie. He just isn't the sharpest tool in the shed. Consider yourself lucky. Some of the girls have complained about finding some critters down there every once in a while."

I gagged with another wave of nausea.

"Sorry, darlin'. That was a little indelicate of me. A lot of this is my fault. I should have given you proper warning. But I guess in a way I did it on purpose. Eventually, I needed to see if you could put up with, shall we call it, unsavory contact."

"I'd say we have our answer."

"Pretty clear cut," Pam agreed.

I lowered my eyes, and could feel the tears welling up.

Pam reached over and stroked my hair. "I'm so scared, Pam. I don't know what I'm going to do. This was my best idea of how to get myself back on my feet."

Pam grinned, "Was that an intentional pun, Connie? Yes, even us hardened veterans enjoy the irony once in a while."

I had to smile.

"Here take this," she said as she handed me an envelope she had carried out with her.

"What's this?"

"Your pay for today's trick."

"There wasn't any 'trick,' Pam. I failed miserably."

"Our clients pay up front. I'll get Teddy taken care of when I go back in there, but you deserve the money for a terrific effort."

"Thanks, Pam. I shouldn't accept this money but I really need it. I'm worried I won't be able to care for my kids."

"I know, sugar." Pam bit her lip. She obviously had something else on her mind.

"You told me that you were a cheerleader in high school, didn't you?" she asked.

"Yes, why?"

"Did your squad do dance routines?"

"Yes, we did them all the time."

"Did you take dance lessons?" she asked. "I need to know if you were good at it. Be honest with me, Connie."

"I was good. Lots of people told me I had talent and that I should try to become a professional dancer. My father thought that was a joke, of course."

"And then 'nature' happened?"

"You could say that. I had lots of big plans that got ruined," I said, trying to keep the tears out of my eyes.

"Look, I can't promise anything, but a few of my girls have branched out into exotic dancing."

"You mean striptease?"

"Of course that's what I mean. Men don't pay big money to watch fully clothed women go up and down a pole."

"Are you asking me if I would consider that kind of work?"

"Yeah. Exactly. You have a killer set of tits and a nice ass, and you have a pretty face. Lots of men would like to see you with your clothes coming off. If you have some coordination and can parade your heinie around a little, you can make some real money."

"But wouldn't I be expected to have sex with guys after the show?"

"Some places make the girls accessible, but it isn't a requirement by any means. Lots of smart owners like to dangle the best stuff in front of the crowd with no extracurriculars unless the girls consent. That's why they call it strip*tease*."

"Keeps the customers on the hook and coming back?"

"Right."

"Until they get frustrated and attack the girls in the alley after the performance."

"What do you want me to tell you, Connie? That there aren't any occupational hazards? Of course there are. It's a seedy business but it beats making minimum wage flipping burgers. You just have to be careful to pick the right job and protect yourself. Come on, Connie. Grow up."

"Sorry, Pam. I appreciate your trying to help me, I really do."

"Here's my suggestion. Why don't you take this money, buy some groceries, and go home to your kids. I'll make a few phone calls and let you know what I find out. You can take it from there if you want to."

The tears came again. "Thanks, Pam. Really."

Pam grabbed my hand and squeezed it and smiled before getting out of the car. I drove off, my head spinning. Not only had I tried to become a prostitute, but now I was going to consider a career as a stripper. And it was all because of that asshole who screwed me and then screwed me again. How could I have been so stupid? Maybe my father was right, and I didn't have any common sense whatsoever. But if that were true, was I going to just keep on making terrible decisions for the rest of my miserable life? And who was going to help me figure things out? I was as alone as anyone could be during that short ride home, and very frightened.

I stopped at the market as Pam had suggested and bought some supplies. I concentrated on anything that would fill my kids up without costing a lot of money. I worried about their nutrition, but starvation was a more imminent danger. I even had a few bucks left over to buy a few treats for myself. I figured I had earned a Tastykake or two.

On an impulse, after the supermarket, I stopped at my old parish church. I made sure my coat was properly buttoned. Victoria's Secret was not usual church wardrobe. The place was empty except for a few old people who were lighting candles. I sat in a pew in front of the Virgin Mary and asked her to give me a sign.

But I guess the Blessed Mother was busy helping out some other poor schmuck. As night fell and I was asked to leave by the caretaker, no epiphany was forthcoming. Nevertheless, I had the distinct feeling someone had been listening to my silent prayers.

"The Lord works in mysterious ways," the nuns used to say all the time. I'm not sure I ever believed it, but I can't discount the idea the BVM to whom I had prayed that late afternoon helped Pam make those phone calls to give me the job lead that would literally change my life. Because two nights later, my phone rang and I recognized her raspy voice immediately.

"I think I have something for you, darlin'," Pam said. "My girls told me that there's a guy named Gus Gouvias who runs a place called Nightingales, down on Delaware Avenue. He's been pretty successful and just expanded his club. They tell me he's auditioning new dancers. Are you interested?"

"But I don't have any experience."

"I know that, Connie. You have to stop being a wimpy girl. Don't you get tired of that crap?"

"Okay, Pam. Sorry. So what do you suggest?"

"From what my girls tell me, Gus is a pretty nice person and is willing to develop talent if you have the goods. And you do. The way it works is that you attend an interview where they look you over. If you pass, they put you through a preliminary session where some of the girls who already work there show you the basic moves. Then you audition for Gus and a few other people. If they like what they see, you get the job."

"That sounds reasonable. What about the prostitute stuff?"

"I asked. My girls tell me that Gus runs a fair place. There are rooms off site for preferred customers, but the girls aren't forced to participate. Up to them entirely."

"That's a relief, Pam."

"Good, a lot better than the whining garbage. You have to take a positive approach, Connie. Remember, there's no guarantee, here. I suspect there will be a lot of girls trying to get one of his jobs. I heard he pays pretty well."

"Do you think I have a chance?"

"Yeah, I do, if you go into it with the right attitude. The big question is whether you can put up with a bunch of guys looking at you naked. Actually, worse than that, naked and seductive. Your job is to give them a hard-on. And these are not necessarily upstanding people. Some are just plain dirt bags who will literally jerk off while they're looking up at you on the pole."

"That creates quite a mental image."

"Although from what I understand, the clientele is changing a bit, now that these clubs have established themselves. Lawyers and business types party there regularly now, and they usually have some cash to put in your G-string."

"That's good."

"Tips are an important part of your income in that business. But I wouldn't plan to meet Mr. Right, hon. Most of the people who go in there are getting their rocks off when their wives or girlfriends are out of town. They just assume that the girls are there for their pleasure, and that they ain't worth a shit."

"Pam, this is all about making money. I don't think I have any hope of gaining fame or self-esteem or finding a husband."

"Good attitude, Connie. Keep thinking that way and you'll do fine. Learn how to do a good job on the pole and you'll be driving a Porsche in no time."

We laughed together before Pam gave me the number to call to arrange my interview. And then Pam said, "I'm really rooting for you, sweetie. You're a nice person, and you're willing to put it all on the line for those kids of yours. I respect that kind of dedication a lot."

"Thanks," I managed, choking back the tears once again.

"Funny, you remind me a lot of me when I was starting out. I had a kid problem, too. Makes it tough."

Silence.

"Let me know how this all works for you, hon. I really want to hear from you. And if this doesn't pan out, we'll look for something else."

So if the BVM was interceding, she was channeling her good works and advice through Pam, a purveyor of whores. You can't make this stuff up.

My call to Nightingales was expected and business-like. I was put through to an assistant manager who took my personal information, asked a few questions about my experience, which was nil, and then instructed me to arrive at the club three days hence at noon for a preliminary "interview."

"Do I need to bring or wear any special clothing?"

A chuckle. "No, honey, just make sure you look as good as you can possibly look naked. That means makeup, hair, nails, and shave off all of your hair. And I mean all of it."

"Okay," I answered, astonishingly not surprised by the requests.

"Oh, yeah, are yours natural?"

"My what?" I asked before realizing how stupid my question was and recovered. "Oh, yeah, they're natural."

"And I hope they're spectacular," she laughed as she hung up, obviously a fellow Seinfeld fan.

I spent the next few days working on my nails and trying to figure out what hairdo would show off my body the best. I finally decided on the wild look. Hair long, hanging down my back with bangs in the front. My hair is blond and fine, so I figured wearing it long would let me flip it around while I gyrated for the judges. That would get their juices going.

So for the second time in two short weeks, I was preparing to do something that was exactly counter to the way I was raised. And once again, I was so riveted on surviving that I was anxious to succeed in making myself a sex object.

I lay in bed the night before my interview, looking up at the ceiling, watching the reflections of the headlights of the cars that passed my apartment continuously. I started to pray.

"Mary, Mother of God, tell St. Peter not to send me to hell when I reach the Pearly Gates. Tell him there was a good reason for me to become an evil woman and do the terrible things I did and am about to do. Blessed Mary, you know how much I need this job. I have nowhere else to go, and I have to take care of my two beautiful daughters. And, Mary, while you're at it, remind your Son that he forgave Mary Magdalene for what she did. Ask Him if I can get that same deal, please."

Chapter 8

When Connie woke up, she was completely disoriented. She couldn't understand why so many people were standing over her. Some of them were touching her, clearly a rule violation. One of them had a uniform and was sticking a needle in her arm while two others held her down. She tried to tell them that her chest hurt like hell and that she was freezing to death. Somebody finally threw a blanket over her naked body. Who were these people? And where had her sweet mother gone?

You probably guessed that I would have the same misgivings and anxiety about my interview at Nightingales as I did at Pam's brothel. But I had no choice. I felt like I was out of options. I desperately needed money and time was running out.

Once again, I had to beg Sonny's parents for food and gas money and to pay a babysitter. The royal couple said they were busy and just couldn't find the time to help me with their adorable grandchildren. That was okay, because the sight of them made me want to puke, just like I did on poor

Teddy. They made sure to remind me that what they were giving me was the last loan, and that they expected all of it to be paid back and soon. I had totally stopped asking their slackjawed, retarded children for help of any kind. They had proven themselves to be more worthless than shit.

Of course I managed to get lost on the way to the Nightingales interview. It wasn't an area of the city I was familiar with, and Philly probably has the worst signage in the universe. I arrived late, and was directed by the bartender to a room in the back of the place reserved for private parties.

I almost lost it when I walked in. Sitting around the table were seven or eight girls, all about my age, and all naked. Well not completely naked, just with their tops off. Most of them were anxiously sitting forward, so their boobs rested on the conference room table like elliptical balloons, each with a slightly different shape and color, with nipples of various sizes. The clothed woman sitting at the head of the table was busy taking notes, conducting what I later learned was a group interview. How bizarre!

I sat down at one of the few empty places and was immediately instructed to take off my blouse and bra. "Nice of you to join us, honey," the woman sitting at the head of the table added sarcastically. "My name is Delores, and I have a few questions. Just relax, and I'll get to each of you eventually. In the meantime, put your personal information on the form in front of you and we'll collect it before you leave."

It's not like I haven't been naked in front of a bunch of women before. But I had hated gym class in high school and this was one of the big reasons. Plus this was so totally out of context. A half-naked group of well-endowed, mostly attractive women having a group job interview? Seriously?

For the next hour, I had to suffer through listening to a bunch of nitwits make up answers to hopelessly pointless questions about her life and background. If a girl was reasonably good looking and willing to take off her clothes in public, what difference did it make where she went to school or what her "ultimate career plans" were? Why would anyone give a crap? The only truly relevant issue was how good a dancer she was, and they weren't going to get that answer sitting around a table in the back of a bar. Nor was anyone going to be forthcoming about the bad things they had done and for which they had been arrested. But I reminded myself to be patient. I tried to remember what Pam had told me and to focus my thoughts on my kids, and how important it would be to get a reasonable job to put food on the table. This was only a means to an end, nothing more.

My turn finally came, and the woman in charge started in. She was middle aged, not too bad looking, but with way too much makeup and I could smell her perfume from across the room. "Your name, honey?"

"Connie Santangelo." I had decided to use my maiden name.

"Any experience?"

"You mean taking my clothes off. I do it a few times a day."

As soon as I said it, I regretted it. Tittering around the table and a frown from Delores.

"I mean with exotic dancing."

"I was a cheerleader and on the dance team in high school."

More snickering around the table.

"Were you now? How very sweet," Delores answered, with just the right dose of sarcasm. "And I bet you were the prom queen too."

"I got knocked up before senior year, so no, that isn't on my resume."

That shut everyone up. I couldn't tell if Delores was impressed with my honesty or getting tired of my crap.

"Any medical problems?"

"No."

"Drug or alcohol addiction?"

As if I would admit it in front of a bunch of strangers. "No."

"Any problem with working nights or weekends?"

"No."

"Kids?"

"Two."

"Stable child care?"

"Yes." If you call a pimply-faced teenager with an idiot boyfriend as stable.

And that was the extent of her questions. Delores came around the table, collected our forms, and told us to put our bras on but to leave our tops off. She said we would be called one by one into another room for an "inspection." I sat nervously, intentionally not participating in the small talk and bantering that the other girls used to break some of the tension. One by one, they were called in and never returned. Once again, as a reward for my tardiness, I was last.

When I entered the room, I was asked by Delores, now sitting at a table in front of a wall-to-wall mirror, to take off my clothes, starting with my bra, and to do so as seductively as I could. This was made even more difficult because also seated behind the table were two fat men, one smoking a cigar. I wondered if they had been chosen for their repulsiveness, because they truly were.

Almost in a daze, I tried to comply. I'm not sure what I did, or how I did it. I do remember one of the ugly guys smiling at me when I was done and standing naked in front of the three. Suddenly, some random music came over two large speakers above the mirror and I was instructed to "dance around." Once again, I had no idea what was expected of me, but I tried to put the situation out of my mind and to just move to the rhythm. That went on for a couple of minutes. The music finally shut down, and I was told to get my clothes on and leave. "We'll be in touch," was all I heard as I left that awful room.

I spent the next day or two at home, anxious for the results of my audition, but not really sure what I wanted to hear. I needed the job, but getting turned down meant I wouldn't have to go back to that terrible place. When the call finally came, I was pretty wired and had a hard time focusing on the words. I did hear, "We were impressed" and "We would like you to meet with our dance instructor" and "Call Janet at our main number to set up a time for your next visit." So this was it. I was on my way to becoming an exotic dancer whether I liked it or not.

My next trip to Nightingales was a lot easier. For one thing, I had figured a good way to get there, avoiding the nightmare of the Schuylkill Expressway. And this time when I walked in, I was greeted by Delores who now had a totally different demeanor. I guess I had made the cut so she could treat me like a human being instead of a piece of flesh.

"Connie, we're so glad you're going to join our team. I think you're going to like it here. We have a lot to do today but first I want you to meet with Gus, the owner."

She escorted me to an office just off the main entrance. Neat but with old furniture, and no decoration to speak of, just an old desk with a couple of cushioned chairs in front of it. Delores let me into the room, took me over to a chair in front of Gus' desk, and then left the room.

Gus sat behind his desk, looking over some papers. I guess I shouldn't have been surprised that he was one of the two ugly fat men I had auditioned for. After all, he was the owner. He had been the one with the cigar, and he had another one, unlit this time, planted in the right corner of his mouth that he kept there even when he was talking. He finally rose from his chair and extended his hand. He wore nice slacks and a turtleneck, had a moustache but was otherwise clean-shaven.

"Your name is Connie Santangelo?"

I nodded, shaking his hand. "That's my maiden name."

"My name is Gus Gouvias. I own the place. Well truth is, I own most of it. I have partners, but they want me to run the joint, and I do."

"Nice to meet you Gus."

"You probably don't mean that, but I do appreciate the politeness, Connie. I just want to spend a few minutes giving you my slant on this place and the job, and what we will expect from you. Is that okay?"

"Absolutely, Gus. I really want to learn as much as I can."

"Good, Connie. First of all, we picked you not only because you have a gorgeous body and can move around pretty good, but we liked the vibes we got from you. A little sarcastic, but that will fit in well around here. And Pam, who I know pretty well, said you're a good kid in a tough spot. I don't mean to pry, but can you tell me a little about your situation?"

I explained what had happened with Sonny, and how I had gotten stuck with two babies to care for. Gus listened attentively, and even nodded a few times in agreement.

"Yeah. And I heard you ain't got no folks to help you out."

"Both of my parents are dead and I'm an only child."

"Should've figured. Else your dad would've kicked that cocksucker's butt for leaving you with them kids. And what about your in-laws?"

"Not much help, I'm afraid."

"Don't they care about their grandkids?"

"They have others. Mine don't seem to count."

I could see that Gus was getting angrier with every answer. He was trying to hold it in, but he had to mutter some obscenities under his breath before he could move on.

"Okay, Connie. Tell you what. Let's get you fixed up and working here and making some good dough, and then you can tell those motherfuckers to go screw themselves. Whadda ya say?"

Probably for the first time since Sonny left, I completely lost it in front of another person. I started to cry and I couldn't stop. Gus reached across the desk and handed me a tissue. "Get it out of your system, Connie. It'll make you feel better, and I ain't got nowhere to go."

So I sat there for several minutes, crying and blubbering, incoherently telling Gus about everything bad that had happened. As my eyes finally cleared and I looked up at him, I realized that Gus wasn't ugly at all. Fat, yes, but when he smiled, he had a pleasant face.

When I was all cried out, Gus came around the desk, sat next to me, and took my hand.

"OK, Connie, let's get down to business. Like I said, we're here to make you successful. We want our girls to be happy and productive. It makes for good dancers, and we don't like a big turnover. The girls who work here are a lot like you, and I think you'll see that they'll be helpful to you as you get started."

I nodded, dabbing my eyes and nose, finally composed.

"We take good care of all of our employees. The benefit package is good, and so is the salary. We provide a $2000 signing bonus that will compensate you while you go through your training and fittings. We pay our rookies $200 per eight-hour shift, plus tips. If the place does real good, you might even get a Christmas bonus, but no promises. You get three weeks' vacation and ten sick days, and you get paid for those days if you don't take them."

"That's very generous, Gus."

"But we do have some rules. There ain't a lot, but I enforce them hard. So please listen to me."

I braced myself, hoping Gus wouldn't ask me to do something I couldn't.

"I expect people to show up, to be on time, and to be completely sober. I don't care if you have a drink once in a while, and I'm okay with grass, but no coke or hard stuff, and I mean never. If we catch you using, you'll be fired. No rehab, no appeals, no suspension. I mean gone. Okay?"

"Gotcha."

"As you'll see, we do relatively short dances. You do an eight-hour shift, and during that shift, you'll do fifteen minutes on and fifteen minutes off, with a thirty-minute lunch that we supply. Hours are a little weird, but we open at noon and close at 2 AM. We usually have three to four girls dancing at any one time, depending on the time of day—more in the evening and night, obviously. You all right with all of this so far?"

"Yep. I have a girl who watches the kids who has a pretty flexible schedule. As long as I can pay her, and I can give her enough notice, I should be fine."

"Good. We set up shifts pretty far in advance, because a lot of the girls have the same problem with childcare. And we don't care if you want to make changes or swap shifts. But like I said, I get a little pissed off if we're short a dancer.

"Now, as for the customers. This is the hard part. We get all kinds of yahoos in here. Fortunately, many of them are regulars and we know their habits, but every once in a while, it can get out of hand. Like a bunch of nerds at a bachelor party. It's what happens when you mix hard-ons with booze. I've been in this business a long time, so I know how to handle it.

"Your job is to ignore them. If you concentrate on dancing on the pole and taking off your clothes as you'll be taught, there'll be nothing to worry about. As you'll see, we have a small army of big guys who work here and who always get their way. I don't have to pay them much because they just enjoy kicking the ass of any rude people who come in here.

Most of the time, the offending douchebags understand and tone it down, but every once in a while, they need to get 'bounced'—and believe me, they are."

"That's good to know."

"I'm not done, Connie. There is never to be any contact between you and a patron. If they want to give you a tip, which you should hope they do, there is a collection basket under your pole, just like at church."

He laughed; I winced.

"No money in your G-string or bra. If they make any move to come up to where you're dancing or if they try to touch you, there is a button at the bottom of the pole that you will push twice that will get you help faster than you can blink."

"That's reassuring. It was something I was worried about. I know a lot of clubs have their girls doing lap dances."

"Not here, Connie. Those things just get people fired up and it causes a mess."

"I'm happy to hear that, too. But doesn't that disadvantage your place? A lot of guys want that stuff, don't they?"

"I don't give a shit what they want. We have great food and music, quality entertainment, and a good reputation. Hell, some men even bring their wives and girlfriends in here. That's what's kept us successful, and I ain't giving that up for a few dry humps. Too complicated.

"But here's something I do worry about. You're going to get hit on like crazy. Not surprising. You're up there sporting your wares and acting sexy and you're a gorgeous woman. And a lot of places like this do a whorehouse business on the side. I don't. Like I said, this place is legit. So no sex with the patrons or any other employees, including the other girls, or the bouncers, or management. Not even me."

Another nervous laugh.

"But I'm not here to be your father, so what you do after hours is entirely up to you. I know some of the girls don't mind giving out their phone numbers to patrons who ask. Some of the guys will try to talk to you after your shift. If you don't want to be bothered, ask any of the bouncers and they'll escort you to your car. It's really your call."

"Did Pam talk to you about my experience at her place?"

"She said you weren't cut out for the working-girl life, but she didn't give me no details."

"If she had, you would know that none of that stuff is going to happen. It literally made me sick to my stomach."

"I know, and a lot of our girls start out that way until they see some cute guy eyeing them up. I'm just here to tell you the ground rules. None of that on our property, including cars in our parking lot. If you decide to get funky, we can get you a room elsewhere."

"Got it, Gus. I promise to be a good girl."

"Not too good. We want our customers to drool over you, remember."

"Approach-avoidance."

"A very fine line, Connie."

"Now what, Gus?"

"It's time to start the process to turn you into a Nightingales dancer. Are you ready for that?"

I couldn't believe it, but I nodded anxiously. At that moment, it was what I wanted more than anything else in the world.

Chapter 9

It turned out that the people in the uniforms were ambulance attendants who had been summoned when Connie passed out and hit the floor. She was now fully conscious, embarrassed by what had happened, and protesting that she was okay. She told them she had fainted and that she did it all the time. She explained that she typically feels her heart beating real fast and then she goes out for a second or two. She said fainting was not a new problem and not a big deal because she could usually find a place to sit or lay down so she didn't hurt herself. It was just bad luck that she happened to be on the pole when it happened this time. The paramedics said they understood, but her heart rhythm problem was very serious and had required emergency treatment. Her EKG was still abnormal, and they had been instructed by their superiors to bring her into the emergency room urgently. Connie didn't give up easily, pointing out that she needed to pick up her kids who were with a babysitter, and that she promised to see a physician the next day. But judging from the look on the faces of the paramedics, Connie realized that the situation

*had escalated way past an outpatient visit. She was going to
the ER.*

Gus had been right: my orientation was an elaborate
"process." There was the usual paperwork, and then a series
of meetings with dance instructors, wardrobe and makeup
people, and managers. I was given a schedule of ten manda-
tory dance classes over the next four weeks during which I
would be taught how to pole dance.

The dance classes were held on the bar stage in the morning before the place officially opened. I was one of four new
girls going through orientation. All of the others appeared to
have more experience including one, Candy, who had worked
at another strip bar. That, by the way, was a term I was dis-
couraged from using in favor of "gentlemen's club," which
was a designation that frankly made me laugh. The good
news was that, in the beginning at least, we would be able to
practice with our clothes on.

The big surprise was how physically demanding pole
dancing can be, especially when it's performed to its highest
quality. The instructor was amazing and made a point of
showing us what we might be able to achieve with practice
and hard work. "It's like anything else, girls; the more you
practice and perform, the better you'll get at it, and the more
tips you'll see in your basket."

Maybe it was that trite little speech, or maybe it was my
sheer determination not to screw up this opportunity, but for
whatever reason, I applied myself and practiced hard and regularly. I even set up a pole in my apartment so I could practice
there, with the shades pulled, of course. Fortunately my
babysitter wasn't the least bit suspicious when I told her the
landlord had installed it to support a weak ceiling.

I was a quick study. With a few lessons, I had caught and
surpassed Candy, and was doing things on the pole that I
couldn't have imagined. The instructor was impressed with

my performance and offered to spend a little extra time with me after the regular lessons to show me things the others wouldn't be expected to take on. I was particularly adept at the upside-down moves the instructor loved because it accentuated our boobs and long hair. "Men go nuts for that stuff, Connie. You'll see."

I also enjoyed the hair and wardrobe sessions. It was all about long hair, apparently a must for pole dancers. The girls with short hair were forced to use a wig to achieve the look. The wilder the better, so my instincts to keep my hair long and unkempt for the audition had been fortunate. And blonde hair was also preferred, no problem in my case, although I was told making it a shade or two lighter would be well received by the clientele.

There wasn't much to the wardrobe as you can imagine. But we did wear a robe when we came out of our dressing rooms and onto our bar stage, and the bikinis we wore in the beginning of the dance were real cute. As Gus had said, the place was legit, and believe it or not, there were city and state laws against complete nudity. So we wore G-strings and had to have pasties on our nipples. That last part wasn't so cool, although I did enjoy some of the more ornate nipple adornments that you could flip around while gyrating your breasts. One of the sets of pasties they gave me had tassels that looked like decorations on my grandmother's lamps.

We finally had a few sessions in which we combined our dancing with stripping. I have to admit that I was so focused on the dance routines I started to forget I was getting naked. The bar was empty except for the four of us and a couple of instructors. I tried not to think how different it would be when a bunch of gnarly men were watching. The rehearsals went well, the instructors calling out instructions constantly as we whirled around the bar, clutching our poles and finding exotic ways to unhook articles of clothing. I know this sounds self-serving, but it was a lot more complicated than you'd think. The day finally arrived when we would put it all together in a dress rehearsal. Gus and his staff parked themselves at a few scattered tables and sat back, arms crossed. The music came on blaring, just as it would one day for real, and out we strutted, smiling as seductively as we could. I was assigned to the pole closest to where Gus was sitting and I decided to watch his reaction carefully. And yes, it was very positive. His face lit up when I took off my robe, and he nodded his encouragement as I began my pole routine. He looked pleasantly surprised to see how advanced I had become in a short period, and how facile I was with not just twirling, but also with maneuvering up and down the pole in time to the music.

Taking off my clothes was another matter. I fumbled with the catches and lost synch with the music several times before I managed to get down to my essentials. Gus frowned a bit and took a few notes. I knew I was going to get dinged for my wardrobe clumsiness.

At the end, the staff came over and congratulated us as we donned our robes. We sat at the bar while they critiqued our performance. Each of us had "passed" and was ready to start work, but we were all required to set up extra time with various instructors to work on our weaknesses. For me, it was all about getting my bikini parts off smoothly while still working the pole. Delores and the wardrobe people came up with larger clasps that I could unhook easily while moving quickly.

They made me perform a few more times for the staff. I think it was also their way of desensitizing me so I would be ready for a crowd of strangers when I finally made my debut. It worked. With each dance, I gained confidence and lost self-awareness.

And so began my career at Nightingales. My first shifts were anti-climactic. I was able to block out the audience and concentrate on my routines. Stage time was short and over before I knew it. Admittedly, my first appearances were in the afternoon, when the place was pretty quiet and the patrons much less rowdy. We got a lot of men who worked downtown and had long lunch breaks or the afternoon off. Most came in groups, but there were a fair number who came in alone, and that always made me wonder. What was their story, and what prompted them to sit alone and watch nearly naked girls dance around? When I shared this concern with Gus, he scoffed. "Don't worry about them. Most of those guys are bored and just want some entertainment while they have a sandwich."

A pretty darn expensive sandwich. When I found out what the club charged for admission, I nearly choked. "Whatever the market will bear, hon," Janet the assistant manager told me with another pun I don't think she realized. Jan was the woman who had spoken to me on the phone the first time I called to inquire about a job. Like many other people in the club, once I got to know her, I discovered she was pretty nice. She seemed to enjoy what she did. Like her colleagues, she had somehow convinced herself that they were performing a service for society. As Gus so eloquently put it, "Men need to get their rocks off one way or another, Connie, and this beats attacking women or kids or beating their wives. And look at them; they're having a real good time."

Once I got all of the logistics worked out, I was able to settle into a pretty nice routine of spending time with the kids and working my shifts. My biggest fear was discovery. I figured it was only a matter of time before I would be recognized by someone who knew me from school. What I didn't anticipate was that it would be one of my brothers-in-law. It was about a month after I started at the club in the late afternoon. I was about half-way through my routine when I heard some guy at the bar yell, "Holy shit. Is that you Connie?" He yelled so loud that it immediately brought Bart the bouncer over to see what was going on. I didn't recognize the voice at first, but when I went up the pole the next time, I sneaked a look at the bar and saw Anthony staring at me. "Oh my God, it is you. Jesus Christ."

Bart moved in closer, touched Anthony on the arm and said something to him. Anthony nodded and Bart went away. From that point on, Anthony said nothing. He just kept watching me. He stayed for another hour or so and watched a couple more of my sets, and then he was gone. When I left that evening, I had Bart walk me out to my car because I was convinced Anthony would be waiting for me. He wasn't.

I spent the next few days waiting for the call from my mother-in-law accusing me of being a bad mother and threatening to take my kids away. It was the only thing I was worried about. Curiously, I didn't care if people knew what I did for a living as long as they just left me and my kids alone. I was so relieved there was good money coming in that I blocked out anything that might influence me to stop. Except for the prospect of losing my kids.

The call never came. And I never saw Anthony at the club again. I concluded that the spineless asshole didn't want his mother to know he had been at Nightingales. He probably had told his brothers but it had not bubbled up to his parents, at least not yet. But the word would inevitably travel to my old friends and classmates, people I didn't care about anymore. None of them had stepped up to help me when I was down and out. Why should I care what they thought of Connie Santangelo, exotic dancer?

Meanwhile, things at the club were going well. I was rapidly gaining proficiency on the pole, and Gus was happy with the warm reception I was getting from the customers, several of whom had become my regulars, guys who asked when I would be performing so they could attend. Gus started to give me extra shifts, and to move me into weekday prime time, between 6 PM and midnight. "You're doing great, kid," he told me one evening as I left the place. "Keep it up, and I'm going to move you to weekend evenings next month."

My success made a few of the other girls jealous and edgy, but most of them were encouraging. It didn't hurt that I tried to be nice to everybody. I complimented the more experienced girls and asked them for advice on how to get better myself. I offered to help girls with their routines and mentored some of the new dancers who started after me. None of this escaped Delores' notice. "I like your style, Connie. You know how to get along with people."

The next few months may have been the happiest of my life. Money was flowing in, we started to fix up the apartment, and I was able to get Sonny's car serviced and running well. I was becoming the go-to girl at work, Gus scheduling me for the busiest nights and special functions. High rollers loved to rent party rooms for bachelor or birthday parties. Gus gave them featured entertainers to make it more likely that invitees who hadn't been to Nightingales previously would become regular customers. And Gus knew that these novices were likely to leave big tips, which is why all of us hoped to be on the select list. It worked great for everybody, especially since I encouraged Gus to spread the good stuff around as much as possible.

Yes, things were going great except for the damn blackouts. I started having them when I was a kid. I would feel my heart start to race for a few seconds and then, if I didn't sit or lie down, and sometimes even if I did, I would pass out for a few seconds. It happened rarely, and I was afraid to tell my parents about them. I had asked a few friends if this ever happened to them, but they all said no, all except one of my cousins, Betty Ann, who passed out at one of my birthday parties. Her mom put a cold washcloth on her face and didn't make a big deal out of it. I never got a chance to find out anything more about her spells. Poor Betty Ann drowned in a swimming pool later that year.

But my mom finally witnessed one of my spells when I was twelve. We were watching television when it started up. I made the mistake of saying "shit." My mom turned to yell at me for using bad language, but by the time she did, I was out cold. I woke quickly, feeling a little groggy, with Mom standing over me, scared to death. "Connie, are you okay?" I heard her ask, "I couldn't wake you up. Your color was terrible, and I couldn't feel a pulse!"

I tried to reassure her, but, as I had feared, she insisted that I see our doctor, a nice woman who didn't impress me as being terribly interested in my problem. She asked me a few questions, examined me, and then sent me off for tests. She called Mom a few days later and told her that everything was fine, including the cardiac tests she had ordered. Apparently, I was just prone to fainting. If the spells became more frequent, she would refer me to a specialist.

Fortunately, it never again happened in front of either of my parents and didn't happen often at all. Until recently. For some reason, I had experienced four of them since I started working at Nightingales. They were just like the blackouts I had as a kid, but now the rapid heart beating went on a lot longer and I had more time to find some place to sit or lie down before I passed out. The one that scared me the most happened one afternoon while I was driving to work. I had enough time to get off the road, and I didn't quite pass all the way out. A cop pulled up while I was sitting there recovering and came over to my car window. Scared the hell out of me. "Are you okay, miss?"

"Uh, yes, officer. Thanks for stopping. I'm fine."

"Are you having car problems?"

Think fast, Connie. "Uh, no. Uh.. uh… I got a call from

one of my kids and I pulled over to take it."

"Very smart of you, miss. Better to do that than get into an accident. But you need to move your car now, please. The shoulder here is very narrow."

"Of course, officer. Right away."

I spent a lot of time after that incident trying to decide if I needed to see a doctor again, maybe somebody with a brain. After all, what would happen if I had my kids with me and I had an accident? I asked around and got the name of an internist near my apartment and called to make an appointment. The receptionist asked me a few questions and gave me a date in six weeks. "Is that the soonest I can see the doctor?"

"I'm afraid so, ma'am. Most of the primary care doctors in this area are booked up and a lot of them aren't taking new patients except for an emergency. Is this urgent?"

"No," I lied. "I'll take the earliest regular appointment you have."

In the meantime, I resolved to do all of the things my childhood doctor had told my mother would prevent or reduce the likelihood of having the spells. Drink lots of water, especially in hot weather to keep well hydrated, and avoid too much caffeine and sugar.

I listened to the receptionist as she recited the usual crap given to patients who need medical help but can't get in to see the doctor for a long time. It was clearly intended to cover the doctor's ass in case something bad happened. "If you have another spell in the meantime, you'll call us immediately or go to the emergency room."

Little did I know that the next spell would be while I was on the pole at work, my worst nightmare, and that the decision to seek medical help would be taken out of my hands entirely. And that the next conversation I would have with a health care provider would be with the paramedics at the club who were summoned when I blacked out and fell off the pole in front of a bunch of customers and co-workers. Shit!

Chapter 10

So despite my resolve to have the problem properly evaluated so it wouldn't happen again, here I was splat on the
floor in front of the bar, looking up at my pole and a bunch
of strangers who kept telling me to lie still and not to worry.
Not worry? Were they serious? I had just blacked out in front
of a crowd of people, and my chest hurt like it was on fire.
They must have summoned emergency help, because among
the large crowd that had gathered were two serious-looking
people in uniform who were crouched down putting in an intravenous line. They had an oxygen mask on me and they
kept asking me questions like my name and where I was. One
of them, the girl who looked like she was young enough to
be a high school student, had a headset on and was talking to
somebody, giving report or getting instructions. She was describing my status and giving them my heart rate and blood
pressure and telling them that I was "stable" and "awake and
alert." I don't know how alert I was, but I was certainly

"awake," and in a lot of pain.

"What's going on?" I must have asked a dozen times.

"Everything is okay," the busy man in the uniform said. He was a little on the pudgy side, but at least it looked like he was old enough to vote.

"I don't think so. Who are you, by the way?"

"I'm James and this is Tricia. We're from Philly Fire Rescue. From what we could see, your heart went out of rhythm, but we were able to fix it, and now we're going to take you to the hospital."

"I don't want to go to the hospital. Just let me rest for a minute or two and I'll be fine."

"I don't think so. You had a heart problem and fell pretty far. We have to make sure you didn't break anything, and we have to get you checked out so this doesn't happen again."

"I have an appointment to see a doctor soon."

"Miss, I'm sorry, but we really don't have a choice. We've been on the radio with our dispatchers, and they agree that you have to go to the hospital and have an evaluation in an emergency room. They'll decide if you need to be admitted, but we have to take you at least that far."

"I have two little kids with a babysitter at home. How long is this going to take?"

It was a question I was going to ask several times over the next three days, always getting the same answer. "Not sure, miss. We'll try to move things along as quickly as we can."

"I'm going to need to make a few phone calls."

"Let us get you to the ER and see if we can do it from there. Things here are a little hectic right now, and we want to get you on your way before something bad happens."

Something bad? What were they implying? And what did they mean by "hectic?" The place had been pretty empty that afternoon. My fall had taken the place down. Music was off, nobody was dancing, and the few customers were milling around. I could see Gus standing in the crowd, wringing his hands with a worried look on his face. Probably concerned about getting sued. I wanted to reassure him that I was going to be all right, but I couldn't pierce the chatter.

The blanket they had thrown over me was beginning to warm me up. They told me they had given me a shot to help with the pain, which it was. The burning in my chest was fading, as was the soreness in my back where I landed. They explained they couldn't give me any more pain medicine until I was evaluated for a concussion, even though my head didn't hurt. To the delight of the perverts standing around, they had to pull back the blankets to put some leads on my chest and make recordings before hooking me up to a portable monitor. The intravenous line was in place and they were running in some kind of fluid from a plastic bag.

After what seemed like several minutes, they loaded me on a stretcher and rolled me out of the bar. I waved at the people I recognized and pretended that I was fine and would be back soon—even though I didn't believe it myself.

They put me in the back of the ambulance. Tricia sat with me while James went around to the front to drive. After checking with their dispatcher, they decided on lights without sirens, thank goodness, for the brief ride to the hospital. "We're going to a real good hospital, Connie," Tricia reassured me. "The Ben is where I would want to go if I had a serious heart problem for sure."

"Serious" and "heart problem." There it was again. All that talk was making me crazy nervous, but I was going to have to wait for an explanation. Tricia wasn't talkative, concentrating on monitoring me as we made the brief trip.

"The Ben" was Benjamin Franklin University Hospital, the principal hospital of the largest medical school in Philadelphia. Situated in the southwest part of the city, it was also the closest hospital, ideally situated to capture business along the waterfront and most of the downtown areas of Philadelphia, as well as South Jersey. And where there had been ample area to grow the campus that now sprawled over several city blocks. Among its many awards, it had been designated a Level I trauma center, so the emergency facilities were always bustling. And since it was the best medical school in the city, and among the most prestigious in the country, it was a magnet for students, residents, fellows, and trainees at all levels.

James expertly maneuvered the ambulance through the traffic that normally choked the streets surrounding the medical center, heading to the entrance reserved for emergency vehicles. There were at least three other ambulances off-loading stretchers when we pulled up, each greeted by a triage nurse who, after receiving a brief report, directed the ambulance personnel to the appropriate area of admittance. Inside the ER, the waiting room was a madhouse of people coming and going, or enduring the inevitable wait that, at the Ben sometimes stretched out for hours, depending on the nature of the medical problem.

It looked like chaos to me, but Tricia reassured me that the system had been designed to keep everything moving. We were directed to an unloading spot where the triage nurse opened the doors, and asked for my name. "Connie Santangelo" from Tricia triggered an immediate response. "Cardiac room 5." How did she react so quickly, I wondered, and then realized that James must have been in touch with the Ben on the phone during our ambulance ride.

I was whisked into a room with a lot of equipment. James and Tricia helped get me over from their stretcher to a rather narrow bed. They said goodbye and good luck, and headed out after handing me over to a sour, elderly nurse who made sure that my IV was working. She hooked me up to assorted monitoring equipment including an EKG that ran continuously on a screen. She helped me get out of my thong and into a hospital gown. I detected a smirk as she put my skimpy underwear and few pieces of costume jewelry into a plastic bag. She murmured a few words of reassurance that didn't sound very sincere, and told me that the doctor would be in to see me soon.

"Is there anything else I can get you, Connie?" she asked, perfunctorily.

"Yeah. How about out of here."

Smile. "Everybody says that. We will, soon," she said.

"I really have to make a phone call to my babysitter."

"We'll do that as soon as the doctor sees you," she said as she left the room and disappeared down the hallway.

I lay on that uncomfortable bed for what seemed like hours before my "doctor" arrived. I knew immediately that he wasn't a fully trained physician. He looked young and rather good looking in a boyish kind of way. But it was his manner that gave him away. He was utterly petrified. I could only guess how few patient encounters he had had before me, but it had to be single digits. He wore a short white coat crammed with manuals and equipment. He had a notebook with him, and after he introduced himself as medical student Mr. Paul Tacon, he stood next to the bed and immediately started in on a litany of questions that he read from a page in his binder, rapid fire, never once looking up at me. He carefully wrote down each of my answers using one of the many Bic pens that filled the breast pocket of his lab coat.

"Do you have a history of any heart problems?"

"No."

"Has anybody in your family ever had a heart problem?"

"Not that I know of."

"Your parents alive?"

"No."

"How did they die and how old were they?"

"My mom had cancer that spread to her brain. She was

pretty young, maybe in her forties. My father died in a car accident in his late fifties."

"Did they do an autopsy on your father?"

"No, why?"

He looked up, stunned that I had asked a question in return. "Uh… he may have had a heart problem that you inherited."

"Like what?"

Now he was screwed. I could tell by the look on his face that he had no idea how to answer the question. Would he make something up or admit he was lost? Medical student humility or wiseass pride?

"There are lots of things it could have been," he tried.

"Really, like what? My father was drunk as a skunk and crashed his car. But you know, Doctor, what happened to him really doesn't matter because there's nothing wrong with my heart. I just fainted."

"You know, I'm not a doctor yet. I'm in my third year of medical school so you don't have to call me Doctor. I hope there isn't anything wrong with your heart, but we have to do some tests to make sure it was just a faint."

"I don't have time for a lot of tests, whatever your name is," I replied, starting to get pretty worked up.

Tacon wasn't ready for a hostile patient, and tried to put the fire out as fast as he could.

"I'll tell the resident that, and we'll do our best. Do you mind if I ask you a few more questions and examine you?"

"Depends on what you mean by examine?"

"Ah, look in your ears and mouth, listen to your heart and lungs, and check out your pulses and do a neurological check."

"I guess that's okay as long as you stay away from my sensitive areas."

He turned beet red. "Of course. I don't want to make you

uncomfortable."

"Too late for that. And you have to promise me that I can make a couple of phone calls as soon as you're done."

"Sure, you can use my cell."

"Is it okay to use cell phones in the hospital?"

"Perfectly fine. We used to think they interfered with medical monitoring equipment, but that turned out to be a load of shit. Uh… sorry."

I laughed. "No worries, Mr. Tacon. I've heard that word before."

His examination was surprisingly facile but not terribly complete. Mr. Tacon had taken my admonition seriously and shied away from anything that could possibly be considered sensitive. He did listen carefully to my heart and pronounced that it sounded okay to him. That was a good thing since no one else, and I mean no one, listened to my heart again during my time in that hospital. In fact, no one interviewed me in depth or examined me fully again. I guess they figured that a young healthy person was going to have a normal examination, so what was the point?

True to his word, Mr. Tacon gave me his cell phone when he was finished with his examination and left the room, promising to return with the team. I called my in-laws first. If I was going to be stuck in the hospital, they were going to have to take the girls from the babysitter. I got a load of crap from Michael. Gloria wasn't home and he didn't want to be bothered. I finally convinced him to go over to pick up the kids. Not once did he ask me what I was doing in the hospital. His only concern was how long I would be there and when they could expect me to pick up Emily and Erin.

I called the babysitter who, unlike my in-laws, was very concerned about me, asked if she could help, and was more than happy to keep the girls for as long as necessary.

And then the real fun started. First, the doctor parade.

Tacon came back with three or four doctors or students and a bunch of nurses who all seemed friendly and nodded or said hello to me as they assembled around my bed.

Tacon started in, presenting my case to the assembled crowd. To his credit, he was very discreet, leaving out the details of my occupation and social situation that he had extracted during his interview, including only the pertinent points of the history. At the end, an older woman with a long white coat began to ask a few questions of Tacon before stepping forward and introducing herself.

"Hello, Ms. Santangelo. I'm Dr. Stephanie Brassell and I will be your doctor while you're here at the Ben."

I nodded hello, intimidated immediately by the stately woman standing in front of me. She had to have been six feet tall, and with one of the most athletic looking bodies I had even seen. She commanded respect by her very presence and her self-confident tone.

"I'm the hospitalist who has been assigned to your case. So Mr. Tacon and my team will be responsible for ordering tests, getting a few consults, and trying to figure out what happened to you and what to do about it."

"I understand, Dr. Brassell. But I think I just fainted."

"That may be, Ms. Santangelo. But we can't make any assumptions. We have to be sure you're going to be okay when you leave the hospital. I understand you have two small children whom you care for."

"I do, and I need to get home to do just that, and to get back to work."

"You're a dancer, Ms. Santangelo, is that right?"

"I am."

"And this happened when you were entertaining earlier today?"

Was this woman being discreet or had Tacon kept her completely at bay?

"Yes, but this has happened to me before. Just not while I was…dancing."

"Well, we'll get to the bottom of this."

"How long do you think I'll be here?"

"I'm guessing a day or two, depending on what we find."

"I'm going to hold you to that, Doctor."

Dr. Brassell flashed an All-American smile and a great set of teeth. "Don't worry, Connie. We'll take good care of you."

And her estimate was pretty accurate as it turned out. They admitted me to a cardiac unit where I was put on a monitor to watch my heart rhythm. I had several electrocardiograms, spine X-rays, cardiac ultrasound, stress test, CAT scan of my brain, and a million blood tests. And a herd of nurses and doctors, including cardiologists, neurologists, and orthopedists.

The most intensive interview was with the cardiology team that specialized in rhythm disorders. They asked me all kinds of questions and seemed to be especially interested in my cousin who had drowned. One of them asked if they could get hold of her medical records. I told them it was okay with me, but that I didn't have any idea where her family lived or how they could contact them. They stood outside my room, analyzing all of the heart tracings, looking for any clue as to what had happened to me.

After each test, Tacon would tell me that they hadn't found anything. He turned out to be very sweet and really concerned with my case. He finally put his infernal notebook down and started to actually talk to me and the more he did, the more I came to like and depend on him. He was the one constant in the hospital chaos.

On the morning of my third day in the hospital, Dr. Brassell came to see me to summarize what they had found so far. "We haven't found anything bad, Connie, and we still can't explain why you passed out. So I would like your permission to do one more test before we cut you loose this afternoon."

"Anything, Doctor, just get me home."

"It's a tilt-table test and it isn't too bad. We just strap you on a table, bring you upright, give you a little medicine and see what happens to your heart rate and blood pressure. It will tell us if you passed out from a faint."

"If it will prove what I think it was, then I'm all for it."

What I learned from that experience, besides the fact that I was right about my diagnosis, is that you should beware when a doctor says a test isn't too bad. It was awful!

It started out innocuously enough. They put me in a wheelchair and brought me into a room where they said they did special procedures. A very nice and reassuring nurse named Ann Marie greeted me and told me that Dr. Siwek would be coming to do the procedure. I knew Siwek. Nice guy who didn't talk much but who had been the rhythm expert who had visited me with his team. He asked me a few questions and then walked out without telling me what he thought I had. This time he came over to me once I was on the tilt table, took my hand, and reassured me that the test was a "big fat nothing" and that we would be done in no time.

They put me upright and after about fifteen minutes of nothing happening, they started to run some medicine through my IV. I started getting dizzy. Ann Marie was standing next to me and I could hear her reading out my blood pressure to Siwek, who stood on my other side watching the screens with his arms folded.

"I don't feel good," I remember saying.

"Everything is fine," I heard Siwek say. "Just hang in there a few more seconds."

Well, I didn't. Not only did I pass out, but I must have thrown up the little amount I had in my stomach because when I woke up, the bed was back down and Ann Marie was cleaning up watery vomit.

"Connie, are you okay?" I heard her ask.

"Peachy," I managed.

"Did you feel the same way before you passed out here as you did at the club?"

"I think so. Same kind of dizziness and things went black."

"I think we have our answer," Siwek said. "Looks like you must have fainted."

"You think? That's what I've been saying all along."

"We needed to make sure, Connie, so we can treat you properly."

They took me back to my room. I felt terrible for several hours afterward. It wasn't until dinner time before I could move around without my head pounding and my knees buckling.

But true to their word, it did get me out of the hospital with reassurance from Dr. Brassell and Tacon that they had confirmed what I had known all along. I was a fainter, and it could happen to me again. They told me I had to avoid alcohol and caffeine, and keep myself well hydrated. They gave me a prescription for a drug they called a beta-blocker and an appointment for a follow-up in the medical clinic. "The most important thing, Connie, is when you feel this coming on, you need to stop what you're doing and sit down or lie down immediately so you don't hurt yourself," Tacon warned me as I prepared to leave.

"What about driving."

"Technically, you are not supposed to drive for six months by state law."

"I have to drive to get to work."

"Nobody here is going to call the Department of Transportation and report you, but you really have to be careful. Anyhow, we gave you medicine that should reduce the chances of it happening again. We'll talk more about this in two weeks when we see you in clinic."

My in-laws were only too happy to pick me up at the hospital entrance so they could deliver me and the kids to our apartment. My babysitter came over to help me get settled that first night at home. She even went out and got us a few groceries so we wouldn't starve.

I was one happy and relieved person that night, reunited with my babies, and reassured that there was nothing seriously wrong with my heart or my brain. And finally given a pill that would keep me from passing out and endangering my life and my children's. It had been a harrowing experience. I sure wasn't feeling all better yet, but I would soon. All told, I was one incredibly lucky girl.

Chapter 11

I called Gus the morning after I arrived home, and gave him an update.

"It was just a fainting spell, Gus. They told me I'm going to be fine. I want to get back to work as soon as I can."

"We want you back, Connie, but are you sure you're okay? Things looked pretty rough when you went out in the bar. The ambulance crew thought you might have a serious heart rhythm problem. They worked on you for a while."

"I'm fine, Gus, really. They checked me out like crazy. I've been fainting my whole life, and I can usually avoid hurting myself. I should have come off the pole that afternoon, but I was embarrassed and thought I could tough it out. I know better now."

"So they said it was just a faint? Are you sure about that? You were out cold for a while and your color was terrible. I wasn't there for the whole thing, but the girls said it was very bad."

"Yes, Gus, I'm all better. I was evaluated at the Ben, for God's sake. It's one of the best hospitals in the world. I should think they know what they're doing."

"All right, Connie. How can I say no to you? But how about if you start with half-shifts and daytime only until you get back into shape?"

"Gus, that sounds perfect," I gushed. "I promise to drink lots of fluids and to lay off the alcohol, just like they told me."

Gus sounded relieved. "I'll have Delores call you with a new schedule and we'll see you soon."

So back to work I went. I was greeted by a cheer from the staff when I walked into the club a couple of days later. They surrounded and hugged me with real affection. I started crying, and pretty soon there wasn't a dry eye in the place.

I couldn't wait to start dancing again, and I really put my heart into it that first day back. I knew everyone was watching and I guess I wanted to show them that I was not only okay, but better than ever. And I was. I think I did some stuff on the pole that afternoon I'd never been able to do before. And the audience appreciated it. They literally gave me a standing ovation when I finished my first set. I was so excited. I was healthy and back doing something I was good at. I had finally made peace with my job. Sure, the nuns who taught me would have had a heart attack if they knew how I was making a living. But I prayed to the Virgin Mary every night for forgiveness. And now, finally, I was surrounded by people who appreciated me and liked me for who I was.

I really enjoyed that next month. The kids were happy with their routine. My babysitter and I settled into a schedule that gave us both what we needed, and I was making enough money to pay her well and even give her a little bonus. I bought a new car, a cute little Nissan coupe. It cost me a lot less money for gas, and I was able to pay to get it properly serviced so I wouldn't have to worry about getting stuck like

I did with Sonny's piece-of-crap Mustang. I bought some stuff to fix up the apartment and had money left over for new clothes. Nothing fancy, but nice jeans and tops I could wear to work without being embarrassed.

I was nervous about it, but my first outpatient clinic visit at the Ben also went well. Mr. Tacon was there with the doctor who supervised the clinic, and whom I had not met before. I told them I hadn't had any spells since I was discharged, not even a light one. Tacon took my blood pressure and measured my heart rate lying down and standing up, did an EKG, and listened to my heart and lungs before telling me that everything looked fine.

"The medicine we gave you seems to be working nicely so far. Any side effects?" Tacon asked.

"Don't think so."

"Work is going good?" he asked, obviously avoiding specific questions about my job description.

"Never better. I'll be going back full time as soon as you give permission."

"I don't see a problem with that," he said. "I'm just curious: do you find yourself less anxious when you're ...uh... dancing?"

"I do, now that you mention it. I thought it was because I was getting used to it."

"I'm sure that's true, but it might also be the medicine. Beta-blockers reduce performance anxiety. A lot of people use them just for that, you know. And they have been proven to work. For example, violinists whose hands shake before a concert play more smoothly when they take this drug."

"Really? Maybe something good has come out of all of this. I'm just grateful that I haven't had that feeling since I went home."

"So am I, Connie. Really happy. But don't be surprised if it comes back. Medicines aren't perfect. What we hope is that it doesn't happen as often, and when you do get symptoms, they won't be as severe as before, and you'll have sufficient time to respond so you don't hurt yourself."

"All good by me, Doc."

"You know I'm not a doctor yet, Connie," Tacon reminded me.

"That's what I call you because that's the way I think of you."

"That's nice, Connie," Tacon said. I could tell he was getting a little uncomfortable and wanted to get back on track. "Just remember to take care of yourself. Get plenty of sleep, keep hydrated, and come back to see me in three months."

"Sleep isn't always easy with two little ones, but I'll do my best. Thanks for all you've done for me. I'm very grateful."

And I was. I wanted to do something to show my appreciation. I actually thought about inviting Tacon down to the club as my guest but thought better of it. Probably better to keep my health care providers in a different part of my life. Besides, he looked to be pretty conservative. Not the type who frequented strip clubs. And when he saw what I did on the pole, he might flip out.

With my new-found confidence and financial security, I even tried to mend fences with my in-laws. They were the only family I had, and I wanted my kids to have the advantage of a good relationship with their grandparents. Since I repaid most of the money they had loaned me, they were at least being civil to me.

I finally sucked it up and invited them over to my apartment for dinner on a Sunday afternoon. I was a little surprised when they accepted, but in retrospect, I wish they hadn't. The afternoon was worse than bad. They showed up late, brought nothing for me or for the kids or to contribute to dinner, plopped themselves on the sofa in front of the TV, and barely talked to us. They gobbled up the spaghetti and meatballs I put in front of them, burped and farted a few times, and left right after coffee, making some excuse about needing to meet one of their sons and his family somewhere or other. I was so angry that I didn't so much wash the dishes as bang them clean, vowing never to put myself through that again. As Tony Soprano liked to say, "They were dead to me."

But this time, I didn't let my rift with my in-laws ruin my mood. The next day, I went right back to my usual routine, now full shifts with a lot of night work, which I liked the most. The crowds were larger, the tips bigger, and the ovations louder. And I was clearly the rising star. I kept after Delores and my instructors to teach me new moves on the pole that I could incorporate into my routine.

I seemed to have a very good sense of rhythm and was able to tailor my dance to the pounding rhythms, and the crowd loved watching me. When I was out there on the bar stage, conversations stopped, heads turned, and the place was more like a theater than a nightclub. And Gus was ecstatic. He knew that I was attracting new business like dancers had never done before.

But Tacon had been right. Although I was generally feeling much better, I started having symptoms again. Every once in a while, without any warning, I would feel palpitations. I would sense a few rapid, skipped beats that would take my breath away for a second or two. I wouldn't get lightheaded with them because they were short, only a few seconds, and I never got dizzy like I did before I passed out. I dutifully called Tacon and told him about the spells. He reassured me that they weren't serious. "I'll check with my attending, Connie, but these things are common. As long as they don't last for more than a few seconds, don't fret about them. If they get longer or you have worse symptoms, call me back right away. We may need to put you on a heart monitor to see what's causing them."

I never did call him back. I had no reason to. The palpitations didn't get worse, and Tacon's reassurance helped me to ignore them. I wasn't enthusiastic about wearing a heart monitor. Not something you usually see on a girl working the pole.

I was determined not to worry about my health. Why should I? Life was good. I had finally made peace with my existence. I even started looking into getting my GED so I could take some community college courses. Much of that would have to wait until the girls were a little bit older and more self-sufficient. But I was determined to make something out of myself. And when I did get that college diploma I dreamed about, I would take it and ram it up Sonny's ass.

And then, it happened. It was going to be a busy Saturday evening. There was a construction convention in town, which meant there would be a lot of horny men in the club looking to have a good time. Gus was excited and greeted me warmly when I arrived at work at about 6 PM.

"Big night, Connie. We're depending on you to lead the way."

"That's great, Gus. I'm ready. I've been working on a few new moves I think you'll like."

I changed into my dance outfit and robe, and sat in my dressing room and had a cheesesteak sandwich and a club soda with the other girls who were on my shift that evening. We were laughing and having fun, talking about anything and everything, and nothing about work. I was amazed sometimes at how normal all of our lives were. It isn't the way most people think about exotic dancers. We're presumed to be sexual perverts and deviants who have sex at the drop of a hat. But most of the girls who worked at our place were anything but. Gus had gone out of his way to hire fairly normal people and had succeeded for the most part. Sure, there were a few who insisted on making extra money "the easy way." But everyone I associated with liked Gus's "hands-off" policy and had chosen to work at Nightingales because they felt safe. The few girls who had worked in places where lap dances were offered and even promoted, tired of the dry hump nonsense and didn't want any part of it. Too weird to think about no matter how much money it generated.

I was to go on at about 7, so after my dinner, I went back to my dressing table, adjusted my makeup and hair, and walked out to the bar stage. When I took off my robe, I was immediately greeted by warm applause, recognized by a number of regulars, many of whom were there specifically to see me perform. The music started. It was one of Robert Palmer's favorites, "Addicted to Love," a tune I favored for its strong back beat. I swung around the pole, enjoying the sensation and in a groove with the music.

I had just started my first climb up the pole when I felt it. My heart started to skip a few beats, and then it just plain went crazy. I could feel myself getting dizzy and things started getting gray. I was so upset I started to cry, but in the middle of my fit of fear and anger, I realized I had to do what Tacon had instructed. So I stopped, came off the pole, climbed off the stage, staggered back to the dressing room, and collapsed on the floor. I could hear the gasps and calls of concern in my wake, but I hardly registered any of them.

Delores and a few of the girls followed me into the dressing room and asked if I was okay. By the time they arrived, I was feeling much better. "I got that same feeling on the pole and I didn't want to crash again. But it seems better now," I said as I sat up gingerly.

"Just take it easy, Connie. We'll call the ambulance."

"I'm okay," I insisted.

"We're calling them," Delores said firmly.

And so they did. In the meantime, they helped me up off the floor and into a chair. They put my feet up and gave me some ice water to drink. I was beginning to feel much better, surrounded by the other dancers. We started talking about what had happened. I was upset and disappointed that the

medicine had failed me, and my friends were trying to con-
sole me the best they could. Gina, who had been a nurse's
aide at one point in her career, said, "You know, Connie,
sometimes doctors have to adjust the dose of medicines before they can get them to work right. You might even need
another medicine. When you get to the hospital, they'll get
things straightened out. I bet they won't even have to admit
you."

I wanted to believe Gina but wasn't so sure. I was dreading
going back to the hospital. And what if Tacon and Brassell
and the other doctors who knew my case weren't on duty?
Would others be able to help me with medication or would
they have to do more tests and procedures?

Delores came over and told me she had called my babysitter and my kids would be okay. But my mind was flooded
with thoughts about how everything I was doing to put my
life back together was being torn down. Would I ever be
healthy enough to dance again? And what would happen to
my kids if I couldn't or if something truly terrible happened
to me?

And then it came back, this time the worst spell of all. I
could feel my heart beating like crazy, and within seconds, I
was unconscious. But this time, it was different. I could feel
myself floating above the scene that was unfolding in that
dressing room. I was an aerial spectator as I watched my body
stop breathing and turn blue. I watched Gina tell everybody
to get back as she started to pump on my chest. One of the
other girls opened my mouth and tried to give me some
breaths, but it didn't look like she was doing a lot of good.
After a minute or two, the EMTs arrived, quickly assessed
what was going on, opened a case, and put paddles on my
chest. They shocked my heart—I know they did because I
watched my limp body jump a few inches in the air. They
looked at their screen, saw that the shock hadn't worked, and
did it again. They did it several times, interspersed with

pumping on my chest and trying to help me breathe with a mask. They started an IV and tried to give me drugs to help the heart go back into rhythm, but that didn't work either.

The whole thing went on for several minutes. Gus who had been out running an errand, returned to see the mayhem in the dressing room. He threw himself down next to my body, sobbing like a baby, exhorting me to wake up. I watched the goings-on while I hovered over the room like a helicopter, looking down dispassionately. It was as though I was watching a TV show or a movie. I was absorbed but strangely unaffected, as if it were happening to someone else.

I watched as the crew became progressively more frustrated and upset, talking with someone at the hospital who was trying to give them instructions. With each unsuccessful attempt to restart my heart, I shook my head in dismay as if I hadn't liked the way the story was unfolding. I watched sadly as the girls became hysterical. Gus and Delores embraced, holding onto each other to keep from becoming completely unglued.

I stayed and watched for a while, and then, as if on a signal, I turned and began to float away into the void. I didn't know where I was going, how I was going to get there, or who was going to take care of my girls. All I knew was that it was going to be someplace better. Someplace where I would see my mom and dad and other people in my family who had gone before me. Someplace where I wouldn't have to worry about making a living or suffering any pain. Someplace where I would be happy all the time.

Chapter 12

Janaye Housling was not a newbie to the hospital risk management world. She was a woman of experience who had come up the hard way. Born in a North Philly ghetto with the liability of a backward city school system, she had to struggle to get into a community college. Fortunately, she managed good enough grades to transfer to Villanova with a partial scholarship. She then had to work a couple of jobs to make her tuition payments. She lived at home to save money, but expected nothing more than room and board from her single mother who had been abandoned by her father when Janaye was a baby. Between Janaye and her mother, who worked in the Temple University cafeteria, they managed to make the mortgage payments and put food on the table, and there was little left over for anything else.

But that was fine with Janaye, who was an absolute study grunt. Janaye preferred hours in the library to a night out with classmates at Kelly's Tavern, the Villanova watering hole. And she didn't want any man issues, so she eschewed advances from men who found her attractive. First of all, Janaye didn't see why. Yes, she had a good figure and dressed well, but she thought her features coarse, and she had never figured out what to do with her hair and makeup. She justified her modesty by insisting to her mother that she simply didn't have time for any of that nonsense.

Janaye had surprised her mother with her decision to go to law school. "How's a black girl gonna make it in that legal world, Janaye? Them's a bunch of honkie white guys who play golf and live in the burbs."

Janaye decided not to try to dissuade her mother of the lawyer stereotype that had been reinforced by years of being disadvantaged. Instead, she decided on the advancement argument. "Momma, that may be true, but black women are making progress. Lots of them are getting into professional schools and doing well. And I don't have to go to take a job with a big law firm where the guys you're talking about usually work. There are other opportunities, and I really want to help people."

Her mother just shook her head, so Janaye added the economic bone: "And I'll be able to make enough money so we can move out of this neighborhood, Momma."

Which was a constant worry for Janaye and her mother after several attempted break-ins and the constant intimidation by gangs that roamed the streets of their North Philadelphia neighborhood, voted each year one of the toughest and most crime-laden in the City of Brotherly Love.

"And how you goin' afford law school, baby girl? Your mama ain't makin' no fortune."

"I've done well at Villanova, Momma, so if I score a good grade in the LSATs, I should be able to get some scholarship money. I'll keep working part time. It'll be fine, Momma, I promise."

And it was. Janaye got into Temple Law with enough grant money that she didn't need to take out too much in loans. She applied herself to her studies, made the Law Review, and established herself as one of the class stars. She liked everything she learned about the law and was having a difficult time deciding on an area of concentration. Though she had no medical background or knowledge, after a med mal elective, she decided to take an internship with the risk management group at Temple University Hospital. This was the group that reviewed cases in which patients may have been harmed, to determine how best to resolve the cases before the hospital was slammed with a lawsuit. It was also their job to look for ways to prevent malpractice cases from being brought by injured and angry patients.

Janaye was particularly intrigued with trying to identify measures that might be put into place to prevent patients from being harmed in the first place. This part of the risk management discipline was still in its infancy, but was drawing increasing attention from Medicare and private payers who were eager to prevent expensive complications. A high-profile Institute of Medicine report added fuel to the initiative, pointing out that thousands of patients were dying or suffering permanent injuries in hospitals, caused by mistakes by health care providers. The report emphasized that these events were completely avoidable and that hospitals that didn't work to reduce them should be punished economically. A sure-fire way to get the attention of hospital administrators and boards.

Once again, Janaye impressed her mentors with her work ethic and enthusiasm and was offered a job with the risk management group pending graduation and passing the Bar examination, which she did easily. As she had hoped, Janaye was placed in the risk mitigation section. Within a few weeks, she began to propose measures that could be easily implemented in the hospital to facilitate patient care while at the same time preventing medical errors. She was particularly proud of her work with the IT department that led directly to new ways to dispense medications on the floors. With the careful audits that Janaye and her team put into place, they were able to show a dramatic reduction in medication mix-ups with excellent staff comprehension and adherence.

Janaye rose quickly in her department to deputy director. Increased earnings helped her to fulfill her promise to her mother with a move to a townhouse in a fashionable and safe part of East Falls. She was also making enough money to allow her mother to retire from her job. This suggestion was quickly rebuffed. "I ain't sitting in this house all the damn day, baby girl, and watching the soaps. I likes what I do, so you just forget about that quittin' stuff. Ain't happenin', no how, no way."

I guess I know where I got my work ethic, Janaye thought with a smile.

The rising importance of risk management in hospital administration provided Janaye many opportunities to speak at educational conferences. National exposure brought new job offers, most of which Janaye rejected. Her mother wasn't going to leave Philadelphia and her siblings, who all lived nearby, and Janaye wasn't leaving Momma.

Until Ben Franklin called. The director of risk management for BFU was nearing retirement age and was recruiting a protégé to be groomed to take over when he departed. They were particularly interested in a woman. And given the recent criticism leveled at BFU about minority hiring, Janaye's race was an added bonus.

The post would be perfect for Janaye, who would be given time to mature and learn the management aspects of her discipline, with the chance to ascend to the post she most wanted. And at one of the most prestigious medical centers in the world. Janaye and her mother could stay put at least for the time being. The salary she would receive as director would also allow another real estate improvement for her mother and herself whenever they wished. After thinking about it for a few weeks and conferring with her mother, Janaye decided to jump.

Janaye quickly learned that the BFU job had complexities. It was a far more elaborate bureaucracy than Temple's, so getting anything accomplished required much more time and effort. And there were many more people with ego issues who had to be assuaged before any proposal had a chance of success. But Janaye was a good judge of character, and quickly learned how to manipulate the many and diverse players she interacted with regularly. Three years after arriving at BFU, the promise was fulfilled and, to the delight of her colleagues and her family, she assumed the directorship.

Now, two years later, the Santangelo file found its way to her desk. She placed it and a pile of other documents in her large briefcase to take home to study over the weekend. She and her mother now had a fieldstone home in West Mount Airy, the most integrated neighborhood in Philadelphia, populated with people like Janaye who were middle class but upwardly mobile, emanating from just about every ethnic minority imaginable. Janaye and her mother loved walking the streets in the evenings, feeling secure as they greeted their neighbors, many with young children who enjoyed the playgrounds and nature trails that dotted the beautiful area.

Janaye woke up early as she always did on Saturdays, made a pot of strong coffee for herself and her mother, and toted her briefcase out to the solarium that she loved so much. The sun was just rising and would warm the day. But now the cool temperatures coaxed Janaye to open the windows to let in the morning breeze. Janaye could savor the honeysuckle her mother had planted in the small garden just outside the windows. It was a moment of perfection that Janaye enjoyed for several minutes, sipping her coffee and reflecting on her successful life before plunging into her work.

The Santangelo file was on the top of the pile. She had to review it before the case conference scheduled for first thing

Monday morning. Janaye's greatest fear was not being prepared. Her most frequent nightmare was walking onto a stage as an actor and not knowing her lines. It didn't take a Freud to interpret that one. Janaye spent an enormous amount of her free time making sure she understood the elements of any issue brought to her department. It was labor intensive, but Janaye's clear imperative.

The file had been prepared by one of the new associates in the department, Olivia Goldberg. Janaye smiled. Olivia reminded Janaye of her younger self. Compulsive and driven, with good attention to detail and a great work habit. The file looked to be in good shape with adequate background, patient information, medical record summary, economic analysis, formulation, and recommendation.

As Janaye read the chart, she became progressively concerned by several aspects of the case. First, this was a young, previously healthy person who had died from a cardiac arrest shortly after having been discharged from BFU. She had originally been admitted for a blackout that may not have been fully explained. But she had not died quickly. After her cardiac arrest, she had suffered major brain damage and it had taken two weeks for her to die in the ICU, during which time she had racked up an enormous hospital bill that would never be fully paid.

But most alarming to Janaye were the details of Connie Santangelo's private life that Olivia had been able to ascertain. She had been raised a Catholic but had dropped out of school when she became pregnant. Her parents were both dead and her husband had deserted her. Connie was a single mother with two very young girls. She would have to confirm with Olivia, but the file seemed to indicate that the father's parents had refused custody of Emily and Erin Cardinelli, who had been placed in foster care by Child Protective Services. These kids were going to need to be cared for. If the hospital and its health care providers were found negligent, the economic recovery could be massive.

Perhaps even worse was Connie's job. Her occupation had been listed as "exotic dancer" and her place of employment "Nightingales." If she had been a stripper, as Janaye surmised, and if the details of the case ever made it to the media, there would be a shit storm. Could there be a story that appealed any more keenly to the public's prurient interests and to their hearts at the same time?

Not surprisingly, Olivia had picked up on several of the red flags, but, with her inexperience, had not followed them to their logical conclusions. Thus, her formulation and plan were inadequate, especially not taking into account the amount of publicity a case of this kind could garner. Janaye scribbled some notes in the margins and then sat looking out to the growing morning light, lost in thought. Her job was supposed to be to mitigate and manage risk to BFU. But increasingly, she was forced to investigate cases not to discover the truth, but to figure out the best strategy to protect BFU against a lawsuit and a massive verdict. If she went into this field to help people, how was she going to reconcile her ideal job mission with what she had to do to mitigate the damages accruing from what had happened to patients like Connie Santangelo?

This question, and the Santangelo case in general, were very much on Janaye's mind while she rode the train on Monday morning, and then began her hike to her office on the BFU campus. By the time she cleared her weekend emails from her computer, it was time for the case conference. The entire risk management team would be present to review active cases and preview the new ones. Janaye still hadn't finalized her recommendations in the Santangelo case. Janaye never liked waiting to the last minute to decide anything, but this one had her stumped... at least for the moment.

Janaye's team assembled in the paneled conference room generously donated by one of the medical school's graduating classes. It seemed that everything at BFU was named for somebody, with a hefty price tag attached. Janaye wondered if they would finally get around to the rest rooms. She and her mother might be able to afford a plaque on one of the toilets.

The group sat around a long oak table that was surrounded by a couple dozen swiveling and cushioned arm chairs, behind which were simpler chairs where the lesser lights were expected to sit. They began with a discussion of cases in progress. Most of them had been shipped to one of the large malpractice defense firms in the city, and the reports merely summarized the case status. For most, it was a litany of depositions and expert reports, all assembled meticulously to marshal the case for the hospital, while also serving to pad the bill that would ultimately be sent to the hospital by the malpractice defense firms.

In her early days, Janaye had railed against the hopelessly redundant tactics of her retained defense firms but had quickly learned that it did little good. If BFU wanted to use the most prestigious firms, someone would have to pay the freight, most of which was accounted for by the impossibly high hourly rates of the multiple lawyers who sat chewing their cuds in endless depositions of people peripheral to the cases.

They finally got around to the new cases. The first two were lawsuits in which the hospital was already named in a formal complaint. Janaye solicited opinions about the best choices for defense firms based on the nature of the cases. Both cases were highly defensible, in Janaye's opinion. A baby had been born with a complex congenital heart defect and had died shortly after birth. The parents had brought a lawsuit contending that the problem should have been diagnosed before birth, as indeed it might have been, had the mother kept her routine prenatal appointments. Hopefully, the fact that she also had a cocaine history would not have to be used to defend the case, but the facts were available if necessary.

The other case was from the orthopedic department. A morbidly obese fifty-year-old man had died during the induction of anesthesia for a total hip replacement. Fortunately, he had been evaluated by an outside cardiologist who had "cleared" him for the surgery. For whatever reason, that cardiologist had failed to find the critical coronary artery disease that killed the man and was clearly demonstrable at his autopsy. BFU's defense would be straightforward, tacitly shifting the blame to another health care provider. Slimy, perhaps, but necessary in the dastardly game of malpractice defense.

"I think the obstetrical case can go to McEwen and the ortho case to Shapiro," Janaye instructed. "I don't see a lot of liability for us in either of them. Any disagreement?"

Lots of head shaking. "Okay, let's move on to Santangelo. I understand that we haven't heard from a law firm yet?"

"And we may not," Olivia Goldberg said. "She didn't have much of a family. Both of her parents are dead and she has no siblings. She did have two young children who are now in foster care. The father apparently took off and hasn't been heard of, and his parents aren't interested in raising the children."

"Olivia, do you want to continue and tell everyone what Connie did for a living?"

"Well, she was an exotic dancer."

"A stripper," Janaye concluded.

"Yeah… I guess you could call her that."

Janaye let up. "Sorry, Olivia, why don't you summarize the case for the group?"

Olivia's distillation was adequate, including the medical facts as they were known, the first hospitalization and disposition, followed by the details of the cardiac arrest, second hospitalization, and her ugly brain death.

"Any questions about the facts?" Olivia asked bravely when she was finished.

Janaye started. "So we don't really know what made this person pass out the first time."

"The doctors said she fainted, based on the results of the tilt-table test."

"How good is that test?"

The answer came from James Luketich, seated halfway down the table, one of the lawyers on the team who had been a doctor before going to law school.

"Unfortunately, there are a lot of false positives. So just because she fainted during the tilt doesn't necessarily mean that was why Ms. Santangelo had passed out at Nightingales."

"And if she had some other reason to lose consciousness that was serious…" Janaye began.

"Her doctors who missed it may then have been misled by a falsely positive tilt-table test," Luketich finished. "There may have been some other tests they should have carried out before they sent her home that they didn't do because they thought they had the answer."

"This case is obviously complicated, and with two small children who do not have caregivers, we have terrible potential exposure," Janaye concluded for the group. "I would hate to see this one make it to the courtroom. The press would have a field day."

Nods around the table.

"Do you want to send it out directly to one of our firms for review?" Olivia asked.

"We haven't received any inquiries from a plaintiff's law firm yet," Luketich said.

"No, but it's early. And it may take some time for the family to realize they have a case," Janaye replied.

"Why don't we have a local expert review the case to see how much liability we have here? What kind of doctor do we need?" Olivia asked.

"We could get a neurologist," Janaye said. "She was seen by our team here at BFU during both of her admissions, and there are lots of neurologic reasons for people to pass out."

"No," Luketich chimed in again. "We're much better off getting a cardiologist to look at it. She died from a cardiac arrest so if she had a serious problem, it was probably heart related."

"What kind of cardiologist?" Janaye asked.

"An electrophysiologist. Somebody who knows a lot about heart rhythm problems. It's a sub-specialty of cardiology. And there are a lot of them in the area."

Janaye nodded. "I remember a guy our defense firms used to favor who was a real hot shot. Had an unusual last name. Circus or something like that."

"I can look him up," Olivia offered. "Should be easy if he's a member of a cardiology group of some kind."

"Try the Heart Rhythm Society," Luketich advised. "They have a full listing."

"If I have the right guy, he should be findable through a Google search," Janaye added. "I'll check my records and see if I have contact information. I'm pretty sure he'll give us an honest appraisal in short order."

Which is exactly what I need before I pull my straggly hair out over this stupid case, Janaye mused, as the next debacle on the seemingly endless case list was brought up for discussion.

Chapter 13

Janaye needn't have worried about finding Philip Sarkis. He was living once again with his long-established girlfriend, Dorothy Deaver, about two miles from Janaye's office in the now-fashionable Fairmount area of Philadelphia. The Bergstrom case in Boston, and his confession to Dorothy about his affair with his best friend's wife, Deb Angelucci, had almost ended their relationship. In fact, Dorothy had left him for several months, changing jobs, and renting the town-house apartment in which he now found himself. But Philip's persistence had paid off, and, after much cajoling, they had finally reconciled. It had taken less convincing than Philip had anticipated. After a few "dates" with Dorothy, he had broached the idea of reuniting and Dorothy had agreed to "try it."

Philip wasn't sure if Dorothy let him move back in with her because she missed him, or Buffy and Meeko. Their precious Portuguese Water Dogs had lived with Philip in the Poconos during their split, and were now joyously reunited with their doggie mom. Except now they were joined by Dorothy's acquisition, an obnoxious but terribly handsome little boy Porty named Rocky, whose mission in life was to pilfer and chew up as many shoes, gloves and hats as he could find unattended.

As much as he had enjoyed the solitude and serenity of the Poconos, Philip fell in love with the idea of living in the city again. Fairmount was in its renaissance, with several restaurants, shops and bars lining the streets now clogged with urban professionals, students, and empty-nesters taking advantage of the area's rich culture and proximity to downtown. And they were only a few blocks north of the Ben Franklin Parkway and the Schuylkill River. The drives that lined the river afforded plenty of grass and foliage to please the hounds. The museum area came alive on weekends with festivals, concerts, and regattas that kept them so busy that they only occasionally retreated to their old Pocono house. Dorothy had encouraged Philip to hold onto the property for its investment value if nothing else. Was she hedging her bets on the reconciliation, Philip wondered, or just making good business sense?

Their work transition was not nearly as easy. Philadelphia was oversupplied with cardiologists and rhythm specialists, so Philip had to give up on his dream of returning to big-time academics. He had burned his bridges at Gladwyne Memorial and didn't even bother to call the chief who had replaced him. Though mired in one of the worst areas of the city, Temple was one of the few places that needed staff doctors, and Philip was attracted to the idea of teaching. The pay was reasonable and Philip was able to negotiate minimal on-call responsibilities. He joined the staff with little fanfare. Only a few of the current young faculty recognized him from his halcyon days at Gladwyne Memorial.

Olivia Goldberg caught up with Philip by phone in his third month at Temple. After summarizing the facts of the

Santangelo case, Olivia made her pitch.

"We need someone with your expertise to look at the case and give us an opinion about the cause of death and the adequacy of the patient's prior evaluation, Dr. Sarkis. We know you're an expert in the field. Would you be willing to look at it for us?"

Philip hesitated. He was in a quandary. Although he was receptive to accepting the engagement and reviewing the case, he had promised Dorothy that his medical-legal consulting days were over, and for obvious reasons. Dorothy told Philip she wanted nothing to do with malpractice cases that had caused them so much grief throughout their relationship.

But Philip was desperate for outside work. His job at Temple was crushingly boring. He rounded on the floors almost every day, seeing patients with the same self-abuse diseases in the units and in the outpatient clinic. The only thing that made it tolerable was teaching the bright residents and fellows who followed him around like puppy dogs. He was so immersed in his clinical responsibilities that he had no time for research, his true love. And after his long absence from academic medicine, consulting opportunities and invitations to lecture were sparse. And so was the revenue those activities could generate. Looking through a legal case for a fee was as good as it was going to get for Philip.

"Let me think it over," Philip said to Olivia, almost surprising himself with his answer.

"That's fine, Dr. Sarkis. If you wouldn't mind sending me your current CV, I'll start to get the paperwork processed. Would an hourly rate of $300 for review be acceptable?"

Acceptable, Philip thought? In his prime he would have scoffed at that amount, but he knew better now. "Sure," he heard himself say a little too eagerly.

"Great. We'll look forward to hearing from you. I hope you can help us."

So do I, Philip mused. But it's kind of out of my hands,

isn't it?

Because it was all going to come down to a conversation with Dorothy. As he drove through the sketchy neighborhoods of North Philadelphia that evening on his way home, he contemplated how he was going to broach the topic with his significant other. Probably a good idea to make sure she was in a decent mood. Her new job was challenging, and she was only now, after a year of hard work, beginning to reestablish the relationships and referral lines that had made her so successful during her first tenure as a health care and personal injury lawyer in Philadelphia. Dorothy was driven to be successful and struggled to make time for her personal life, including weekends with Philip and his two children from his previous marriage. She saw her father Dick for lunch on occasion but worked long hours and frequently missed dinner with Philip. Fortunately they had found a kind Guatemalan woman who lived nearby who looked after the hounds during the day and prepared dinner for them. Her illegal immigrant status didn't bother either of them since they had no designs on political office. Carol was great with the dogs and grateful for the income to help her family.

Philip liked their Philly digs. Dorothy had found a pretty three-story townhouse on the corner of 23rd and Fairmount. They rented the top two floors, the landlord occupying the first floor and basement. He was a good guy who worked part-time as a butcher at the local Whole Foods Market and spent much of the rest of his time woodworking in the basement where he managed to slice off one his fingers shortly after Philip and Dorothy moved in. Philip's quick response getting him to the ER to save his finger, and his love of dogs, allowed him to tolerate the three Porties who made a career of barking at anyone who had the audacity to walk past their apartment, including their landlord.

Their two-bedroom flat had been renovated recently with a modern kitchen, two clean and efficient bathrooms, and a roof deck. What they didn't have was a garage, so Philip was in a constant contest with his neighbors for a parking space. Since he tended to get home a little later than most, it was a challenge that he was gradually mastering. This particular evening, he lucked out with a find only two blocks from their place. Dorothy who was able to bus to work, was already home, in the kitchen, setting the table for dinner.

After being mauled by the hounds, Philip gave Dorothy the perfunctory peck on the cheek, stowed his briefcase and coat, and began to search for a glass to hold the single-malt Scotch whiskey that had become an essential part of his home arrival ritual. Tonight, the selection was Glenfiddich 15-year that he poured over a very large ice cube to chill without diluting the spirit.

Dinner was enchiladas prepared by Carol with authentic ingredients that she was able to gather from local markets. They set the table quickly, filled their plates, and started their customary review of their workday. Dorothy had had a good one, with a new referral from an attorney who had attended law school with her. "Not a great case, but he works for a busy firm and if I handle this one well, I suspect he'll send more."

"Difficult case?"

"They're investigating a security breach at a health care facility. They suspect that a woman administrator copied patient files and made them available to a guy she was having an affair with. They suspended her immediately but they want me to take a look at the case to see if they have enough to start legal proceedings against them. I suspect there could be criminal charges."

"HIPAA?"

"You betcha. I read somewhere recently that there have been more breaches than ever and that the government is really going to be cracking down. We may have to go after this person hard to make an example out of her, and to prove that her employer is taking the regulations seriously. But enough of my day; how about yours?"

"Same shit, warmed over," Philip replied, head in hands. "But I did get an interesting phone call today from the risk management people at BFU."

"What did they want?" Dorothy asked warily.

"They asked me to look at a case. Seems an exotic dancer was doing her thing on her pole when she died suddenly."

"Really? She actually died while performing?"

"Sounds that way."

"That's tragic. But why do they want you to look at it?"

"They're concerned because she had been in their hospital a few weeks before her death after passing out, also while dancing. They worked her up and discharged her on medication."

"Uh-oh," Dorothy muttered. Philip knew he didn't have to explain the importance of the facts to Dorothy, who was very knowledgeable about medicine.

"It gets worse. She was young, in her twenties, and a single mother with two little girls who are now orphaned."

"And no family?"

"I know she didn't have a husband around. Not sure about the rest of it. I didn't get into much detail with the paralegal."

"Did you agree to look at the case?"

"Not yet. I wanted to talk to you about it. What do you think?"

Dorothy hesitated, obviously torn. She knew that Philip didn't like his job and there wasn't a surfeit of opportunities for cardiologists in Philadelphia. She was afraid that if he didn't settle into his job at Temple, he would have to look outside the city, and she didn't want to pull up stakes again. Or worse, be separated from him while he pursued a post in another location. Reviewing a legal case would divert him and help him earn extra money.

On the other hand, Philip had, on several occasions, become immersed in cases so deeply that he had not only dragged her into them, but had placed both of them in legal jeopardy. Not to mention becoming suspects in serious crimes from which they had only narrowly extricated themselves.

"So I take it that this case in not in suit?"

"No. But BFU is pretty sure that it could be, and they want to get out in front of it, for obvious reasons."

"It could turn into a monster settlement."

"Yup."

"What's your inclination?" Dorothy asked.

"I'd like to review it, at least preliminarily. It's possible that it will be so straightforward either way that it will be easy to resolve."

"Agree. But Philip, if it does get contentious, you have to be willing to drop out and let somebody else take it. Neither of us has the emotional energy or the time to go through another complicated case."

"Can't disagree with you there."

"Are you sure, Philip?"

"I understand. You have my word."

Dorothy stared at Philip for several seconds before finally walking away and letting the conversation drop, determined to believe him despite his previous fabrications.

The rest of the evening was quiet and pleasant. After they cleared the table and put the dishes into the dishwasher, they decided to watch an episode of Dexter, the latest serial TV show that captured their interest. There was something about the complexity of the main character, a serial killer with a conscience, that attracted Philip and reminded Dorothy of someone she knew well.

The next day, Philip called Olivia and told her he would be willing to take the case.

"That's excellent. Janaye Housling approved your hourly

rate so we're all set."

Philip had one major question and stipulation. "I assume you're going to send me the electronic medical record?"

"Yes, that's correct. You'll get the full EMR on a couple of CDs."

"I would like you to include any paper records."

"Paper records? I don't understand," Olivia said.

"This has come up when I have looked at other cases. I need to go through everything you have about this patient, including accessory files that may not have been scanned into the EMR. From what I've seen and depending on their SOPs, your medical records department may or may not have left-over paper in a file somewhere. You just need to ask."

"OK, Dr. Sarkis. I will see what I can find and send it all to you soon."

A few days later Philip received a package from the BFU risk management office containing three CD-ROMs, a thin red file folder, and a retainer check for six hours of his time. Philip put it on his desk at home where it sat until Saturday morning.

After a pleasant walk along the river with their pups on a beautiful spring day, Dorothy took her folding grocery chart and ventured out to the local market for some household supplies. Philip returned to his desk with a second cup of coffee. The hounds followed Philip and plopped down on three dog beds of various colors and designs that had been distributed on the floor. Philip was always mystified with the process of how each pup found his or her bed du jour. They had established some kind of rotation but it was not discernible to the mere human mind. Whatever the process, each settled down for a nap while Philip emptied the envelope, inserted one of the CDs into the computer, and started to scroll through the records of the first admission, the most important from the standpoint of causality.

Years of experience provided Philip with an almost instinctual idea of what to look for and where to find it. Connie Santangelo had arrived in the ER, brought in by a Philly Fire-Rescue squad, at about 7 PM. She was evaluated promptly by the ER staff, who confirmed that she was stable. She was awake and alert with normal vital signs, except for her heart rate, which was understandably high, over 100 beats per minute. Her only complaint was mild chest discomfort that was worse when she took a deep breath.

The ER doctor's history was perfunctory but had been expanded upon by the medical student who came down to the ER to admit her. This person, Paul Tacon, had used the standard checklist in the EMR to record the past medical history, family history and review of systems, all of which appeared benign. Connie reported a history of feeling her heart racing and feeling lightheaded, but Tacon had not thought much of it and hadn't probed. There was a mention of a cousin who had drowned, and only a brief description of Connie's prior lightheaded spells.

Tacon's physical examination was limited and didn't disclose any abnormalities. "No murmurs or gallops on auscultation." Philip wondered how carefully he had listened. The electrocardiogram was normal in all respects, even to Philip and the trained eye of the consulting electrophysiologist whom Philip knew well. Not a bad guy really, pretty well-trained but relatively inexperienced and like a lot of docs at BFU, a little full of himself at times. Connie's initial labs were normal except for slightly depressed potassium and magnesium levels. Tacon recommended cardiac monitoring, a bunch of worthless lab tests, and consultations with neurology and electrophysiology.

This initial evaluation by a third-year medical student was signed by his attending physician, and it became the most important part of the chart. The historical details and physical examination were cut and pasted into the notes of just about everybody who saw Connie from that point onward, including the electrophysiology team that came by to consult. Philip shook his head and exclaimed to Rocky, the dog most proximate to his desk. "When are these people going to learn? Copying information without taking the history and doing the examination yourself is dangerous and will come back to bite somebody."

Rocky's head tilted and he growled menacingly. Bite may not have been Philip's best choice of words.

After several expensive tests and three days of observation, Connie had been discharged with the elegant sounding diagnosis of "neurocardiogenic syncope." Which translates to "fainting." The diagnosis had been based on the combination of negative neurological studies and a positive tilt-table test, during which Connie had passed out with the same symptoms she had experienced on the pole and during her previous and less serious spells. With that, Connie had been placed on a beta-blocker and discharged with instructions to return to the medical clinic for follow-up.

After Philip's initial scan of the medical record, he went back to examine every page carefully to confirm that what had been recorded in the progress sheets could be verified. Indeed, the chart had been "buffed and shined" to perfection by the house staff. Philip confirmed that the EKG and telemetry monitoring tracings were indeed normal, that the many tests had been interpreted fairly, and most importantly, that the tilt-table test had been conducted properly and was truly positive.

Philip sat back in his chair, running his hands through his hair. "Looks pretty solid to me, big guy," he remarked to Rocky who was the only conscious dog in the loft. Rocky barked his token agreement then put his chin down on his paws and continued his own musing. "If no treat is involved, you're on your own, Dad," he seemed to say.

Philip took a bathroom break, refilled his coffee cup, and returned to his desk. The other CD in the package contained information from the second admission. The records from BFU were extensive. Connie was brain-dead when she was brought in. She was young and nobody wanted to give up, so the next two weeks were spent with Connie on life-support with no chance of survival. All BFU managed to do was watch every organ fail while building up a hospital bill to rival the GNP of a decent-sized third-world country.

"What I need is the ambulance sheet to see what they saw and what they did on site," he informed the now completely uninterested dogs. After a few seconds, he was able to find it. It had been hand-written on site and subsequently scanned into the end of the electronic medical record of the second admission. Connie was blue when the crew arrived, not breathing, and without a pulse. One of the other dancers was trying to do CPR. They put defibrillator patches on her immediately, but what they observed was ominous: ventricular fibrillation in a very fine pattern. They shocked her heart and did so several times. Each time, her heart rhythm would normalize only to deteriorate a few seconds later. Determined not to let Connie die, they continued CPR, loaded Connie into their ambulance, and brought her, lights flashing and siren blaring, to the BFU ER, where she arrived about ten minutes later. In the ER, they were finally able to shock her heart successfully, but by that time, her brain had been toasted along with several other important organs, such as her kidneys.

Philip read on through the nurses' notes. He learned that the family who had been called after Connie's death was actually her estranged husband's parents. They had to be coerced to come to the hospital to see her, which they did only a few times, making it clear each time to the nurses that Connie was not their real daughter, and that they wouldn't be financially responsible for her hospital bill. When Connie finally died, they reluctantly claimed the body and made funeral arrangements. The case was eventually referred to the coroner who saw no point in an autopsy. Philip shook his head. "What a moron. If this case didn't need an autopsy, when the hell is one indicated? Why did this girl die?"

Philip read the account in sad and silent reflection. And then it hit him.

"Wait a minute. I didn't see the ambulance sheet from the first event. Where the hell is it? It should have been scanned into the EMR."

He went back to the first admission CD and reviewed it thoroughly. "What the fuck?" Philip mumbled, progressively becoming more frustrated. He finally gave up, took the CD out of the computer and closed it down, still murmuring to himself and the dogs, who couldn't have cared less about Philip's frustration. Old story. They had been around Philip long enough to know that he was not a patient person, and frequently interrupted their sleep with his muttering and cursing.

As Philip put the CDs back into the envelope, he looked across his desk and saw the red folder that had been sent from BFU with the CDs. Philip opened the folder, began to flick through the few pages, and found something that immediately riveted his attention.

After he finished reading, Philip exclaimed, "Holy Mother of God!" so loud that he jolted the dogs from their well-earned naps. "You have got to be fucking kidding me!"

Chapter 14

By the time Dorothy arrived home later that afternoon, Philip was pacing back and forth in the living room like a caged lion. He had been unable to concentrate on anything since he discovered the hard-copy ambulance run sheet. Fortunately for the hounds, he had been focused enough to get them out for their constitutional, and to prepare their afternoon meal of kibble mixed with fragrant chicken breast. He also remembered to give Meeko her daily steroid dose to treat the adrenal insufficiency that had nearly killed her a few years before. The three pups lay on the sofas, eyes half open, watching Philip work himself into a frenzy. "Where the hell is she?" they heard him exclaim to exactly no one about every ten minutes.

Buffy raised her head and, with her sad brown eyes, asked Philip the obvious question. "No, Buff," he replied as if her question had been precisely verbalized. "I didn't call her on the phone because I didn't want to talk to her about this case while she's shopping. I need her undivided attention."

Buffy scratched her ear with her hind paw to express the obvious retort. "And the case is confidential, so no emails or texts," Philip went on in explanation.

And for the next full hour, this conversation carried along, the dogs taking turns to raise relevant issues about the case and Philip's impressions of the facts, interspersed with Philip's reasoned answers. Most critical was Meeko, the wiliest of the group, who pilloried Philip with questions about the reliability of the ambulance record he had found in the red folder. "It's clear, pretty girl. I have to believe they did what they said they did." And then, "I know we don't have a record of the rhythm, but it must have been serious." And finally, "I think the case makes sense; it's beginning to fit together. I just need to bounce it off Dorothy before I go back to the risk management people."

Which explained to the dogs why Philip had been a basket case all afternoon. He needed his paramour to provide her customary sage advice and counsel. And so they were all relieved when, at 4 PM they finally heard her key in the lock. Philip sprinted to the entry way and opened the front door just as Dorothy pushed forward, causing her to lose her balance and trip over the threshold.

"What the hell, Philip?" she exclaimed as he caught her and helped her right herself.

"Sorry," he said. "Just trying to be helpful."

"You almost helped me break an arm." Dorothy said as she pulled her shopping cart in behind her and then was assaulted by the dogs, providing their usual enthusiastic greeting. "How did you get to the door so fast?"

"I was lying in wait," Philip said, trying to make a joke.

Dorothy wasn't amused. "I bet you were."

"I was just anxious to talk to you, is all. Where have you been?"

Dorothy took off her coat and hung it on the bronze antique stand she had purchased at a yard sale. "Where do you think? Food shopping. I decided to explore a few new stores. I guess I lost track of time."

"I was anxious to talk to you."

She turned to Philip and asked suspiciously, "Does this have something to do with the legal case you've been reviewing today?"

Even after many years with Dorothy, Philip was still amazed by her instant insight and intuition. He had learned the hard way that obfuscation was useless so he might as well admit it. "Yup. I need your opinion about my findings before I talk to BFU."

Dorothy could tell Philip was anxious, which meant that the discussion would be had soon, and it was just a matter of when. "Okay, Philip. I was going to work on a brief this evening, but I'll put it aside for your discussion. How about if we have a drink, get some dinner, and then have the case review for dessert."

Philip was disappointed but decided to be reasonable. "I can live with that if you promise to give me your undivided attention after dinner."

As it turned out, Dorothy's suggestion was perfect. A vodka martini partially cooled Philip's jets, and dinner provided the respite Dorothy needed before turning on her legal brain. Dinner conversation was small talk centered on their apartment, their families, and Sunday plans.

Philip was looking forward to his visit with his children from his first marriage. Nancy lived in the Philly suburbs with her latest boyfriend, a likeable nerd who was smart enough not to interfere with Philip's fatherly duties. Philip's teenage children liked to see him and Dorothy, but it was becoming progressively more difficult to entertain them away from their friends and their usual social scene, so their visits were infrequent and short. And now there were rumors of a move west that were driving Philip crazy.

"Maybe a museum in the afternoon, and then dinner out?" Dorothy suggested.

"There's a new exhibit at the Franklin Institute they might

like," Philip offered. "They seem to be interested in science and math these days."

The unspoken conversation that evening was Dorothy's desire to have children. Though she enjoyed Philip's kids, they weren't her own. Earlier in their relationship, she and Philip decided to try to conceive and began having sex regularly without contraceptives. When Dorothy didn't become pregnant, they discussed the possibility of having an infertility work-up, but in the end decided they would wait. Dorothy had also begun to look into adoption but hadn't formally applied to any agencies. All efforts had been suspended when they separated, and the subject not pursued since they reunited.

The dialogue meandered to mundane issues: scheduling dog grooming, getting the trash and recycles out, and grocery shopping at the new Whole Foods. Dorothy was secretly impressed that Philip was being cooperative, suppressing his excitement about his case to let a little normalcy into their lives. Perhaps he was finally understanding that a boring lifestyle was just what Dorothy had hoped for. An end to the drama of past cases that had nearly gotten them killed or incarcerated.

They made it all the way to coffee for Dorothy and tea for Philip in front of their gas fireplace before Dorothy gave the "go" signal, and Philip began his dissertation. He rumbled through the facts of the case, intentionally omitting the details of the resuscitation to see if Dorothy arrived at the same conclusion he had. She obviously did. "I don't understand why she died, Philip," was the first thing out of her mouth.

He smiled. "Neither did I until I found... this." And like a proud schoolboy, Philip reached over to the coffee table and extracted the ambulance log sheet from the folder. Without a word, he handed it to Dorothy.

"What's this? I thought you reviewed an electronic record."

"It's the ambulance run sheet. It must have been filed in the medical records department somewhere."

She brought her reading glasses off the top of her head, and began to scan the document. Within a minute, she registered the same reaction. "So what's the big deal, Philip? She was in cardiac arrest and they shocked her."

"Look at the date."

"Okay... what about it."

"Dorothy, that's the ambulance record before she was admitted to BFU the first time."

"I don't understand. I thought she had just passed out."

"That's what I thought, but they actually defibrillated her on site. They got to her so quickly that they were able to restore a normal rhythm and she didn't suffer any organ damage."

"Like brain damage."

"Exactly. Or kidney or liver, or lots of others. And remember, she was young and previously healthy... except for the previous blackout."

"What was the rhythm they shocked?"

"I don't know. They didn't record it. They were obviously in a hurry. I can only assume it was ventricular fibrillation."

"How many times did they shock her heart?"

"It looks like they did it once, but the record is hard to read. Chicken scratch."

"And she didn't know about the shock?"

"Apparently not, or she forgot."

"Forgot. Are you serious? That's a pretty traumatic thing."

"Yeah, but people who have cardiac arrest frequently have retrograde amnesia and can't remember much about the circumstances of the event. And she was out cold when the actual shock was delivered."

"Didn't her chest hurt?"

"Of course, but remember they gave her CPR for a brief time. You get lots of soreness after gorillas pound on your sternum for several minutes."

"And there were no marks from the paddles? Isn't that unusual? Doesn't the electrical shock burn the chest?"

"Two possibilities there. One is that she had a minor burn mark that everybody ignored. Or they were lucky and put the patches on just right so the electrode gel protected her skin. That's the way it's supposed to work. You aren't supposed to get burned."

"There were a lot of people at the club who saw her go down. They must have known that the ambulance crew shocked her heart."

"There weren't that many people there at the time. I can't believe any of them were medically sophisticated, and I doubt any of them were close friends who visited her in the hospital. It's entirely possible that Connie never knew how serious that initial event had been and that nobody told her."

"But correct me if I'm wrong. You still don't know why her heart went out of rhythm in the first place. Was there an autopsy?"

"No. It should have been done, of course, but it is frequently negative in these situations. If there is only an electrical abnormality, there is nothing to find when you look at the heart, even microscopically."

"So you think she had an electrical disease?"

"I do," Philip said confidently. "So tell me, Dr. Sarkis, what led you to your conclusion?"

"She didn't have anything wrong with her heart structurally, so electrical disease is kind of the default diagnosis. But there were a couple of other things that helped. First, I combed through everything, including the nurses' notes..."

"Smart man. Nurses always get it right."

"You betcha. There was a nursing note that corroborates what the medical student obtained in his history. Connie had a cousin who died when she was very young."

"Died how?"

"Found dead at the bottom of a pool."

"So she drowned."

"Or her heart went out of rhythm while she was swimming. That happens to a lot of people with certain forms of electrical disease."

"And what else?"

"Another piece of paper I found in the file. It was stapled to the run sheet."

"Don't torture me. What was it?"

"One of the worst-quality electrocardiograms I've ever seen. From the time stamp at the top, it was recorded by the ambulance crew about five minutes after the shock."

"Doesn't the heart need some time to recover after it gets a high-voltage shock?"

"Good, Dorothy. You do pretty well with medicine. Maybe you missed your calling. Yes, it takes several seconds for the membrane potentials to come back to baseline. Five minutes would be plenty of time."

"You said that the quality was bad. Were you able to get good information?"

"I would say yes, although I suspect I might get an argument about that. The crew recorded only three leads, and Connie was moving around by that time. But even with all of that, it's pretty clear that her QT interval was grossly prolonged."

"Oh my God, the Hamlin case all over again," Dorothy said, harkening back to the case that had ruined Philip's career and had nearly gotten them both prosecuted for murder.

"Not quite. This electrocardiogram, like the run sheet, never made it to Connie's EMR."

"So none of the BFU doctors saw it?"

"I see no mention of it in any of the notes."

"But they must have ordered cardiograms in the hospital. Why didn't they show a long QT?"

"Great question. By the time Connie got to the hospital,

her heart rate had normalized and so had her QT."

"That can happen?"

"It sure can, which is why making the diagnosis can be difficult. A lot of times, we need to put a continuous EKG monitor on patients to find the prolonged QT. In Connie's case, they already had the recording but they didn't know it."

"Who screwed up?"

"Hard to say for sure. I suspect the ambulance crew is not at fault. They couldn't be expected to make the diagnosis from the tracing. Hell, even a trained cardiologist would have trouble with this one. But I would have expected them to give report to the triage nurse at the ER, and it's hard to believe that they wouldn't have told him or her about the defibrillator shock."

"So the triage nurse dropped the ball?"

"Can't say for sure. The problem with medicine these days, and especially ERs, is that everybody works in shifts. That means there has to be multiple hand-offs. If people aren't careful, important data can get lost in the transfer."

"But the log sheet and the EKG tracing were ignored too?"

"They were. I can see nothing in the chart that referred to them, or to their absence. A wet-behind-the-ears med student was the person who did the initial history and never thought to ask for them. And nobody called him on it."

"I'm still having a hard time understanding why the ambulance record was misplaced."

"When hospitals are presented with paper documents, they have to be scanned and then incorporated into the EMR. If that doesn't happen, they're essentially lost."

"These documents weren't lost, though."

"For some reason, the BFU medical records department decided to keep paper files. I didn't know that, of course, but just as a matter of routine, I asked them to send whatever they could find anywhere... and they did."

"How are they going to unravel all of this?" Dorothy asked

warily.

"Not my problem. Dorothy Deaver, I want you to know that I have taken your advice. If you agree with me that someone at BFU screwed the goose, I intend to call the risk management supervisor, tell her what I think, and dump this on her. For once, I'm not going to dive into a mess I didn't make."

Dorothy smiled. "I can't tell you how relieved I am to hear you say that, Philip."

"I'm not saying that I don't want to know what happened, eventually. But it's going to take a lot of detective work. There are a number of people who were at the club when Connie collapsed and who were involved with her care at BFU who have to be questioned. Since this case is not in suit, they haven't been deposed, and I don't have access to them or their stories. I'd be spinning my wheels."

"What you can do is point BFU risk management in the right direction."

"Exactly. I can not only finger the people they need to talk to, but I'll give them a list of questions to be asked and answered. I suspect if they do their job, they'll discover that this was a case that simply fell through the cracks. Connie Santangelo was as much a victim of the system as she was of her disease."

"Because she could have been treated effectively?"

"No doubt about it. If I'm right, her death was completely preventable. She might not have liked the idea of a defibrillator, but it would have been better than the alternative."

"An exotic dancer with a shock box."

"That sounds dirty."

"The thing that's dirty is your mind," Dorothy scolded. "But wouldn't a defibrillator have made it difficult for her to, you know, work?"

"Not really. The devices are pretty small. We have some experience putting them inframammary, under the breast, so they don't show."

"Never mind the cosmetics. How was she going to work if her heart kept going out of rhythm?"

"Most people who have this disease get arrhythmias pretty infrequently. Almost all of them can lead normal lives, work, drive cars, play sports."

"But this girl had two events within a couple of weeks."

"True. They do tend to cluster, so that doesn't mean she'd be getting them all the time. And we sometimes have to add drugs to suppress frequent arrhythmias, especially if they're severe and cause the patient to pass out."

"Because not all patients pass out when their heart goes out of rhythm?"

"Yes, some people don't pass out because the rhythm can be stable enough to get blood to the brain, or because the device shocks the patient before the heart weakens or the blood pressure falls. Each case is a little different."

"But the bottom line here," Dorothy concluded, trying to bring the discussion to a close, "is that this girl had a nasty arrhythmia that was diagnosable, but was discharged from BFU with inadequate therapy to prevent it from happening again."

"In a nutshell, and it happened because the system of care at that hospital broke down. Not because any of the people looking after her were necessarily negligent."

"I know you use that term because it is the legal standard for malpractice. But if you're right about the facts, it doesn't matter. BFU is in big trouble."

"Which is exactly what I'm going to have to tell Janaye Housling when I call her tomorrow."

"Sounds like a good plan, Philip. Do me a favor and stick to it."

Dorothy rose from the sofa, bent over to peck Philip on the cheek, and went to the kitchen to begin her bedtime routine. The doggies needed their short walk to empty their tanks and get treats to entice them to settle down for the night. Philip filled a couple of plastic glasses with ice water for the bedside tables, and each in turn adjourned to the bathroom for teeth flossing and brushing, face washing, pill taking, and toilet attending. They finally settled into bed, Dorothy choosing to read from the fourth book in the *Outlander* series, Philip flicking through a *Sports Illustrated* and the local paper before each turned out their reading lights and quickly lost consciousness.

They slept soundly, undisturbed by the dogs, who, several times through the night, redistributed themselves on their bed, on the floor, or on the sitting chairs next to the gas fireplace. Philip was the first up, as usual, greeting the dogs and attending to their needs before preparing the strong French press coffee that he and Dorothy enjoyed on Sunday morning. Dorothy eventually joined him, prepared oatmeal, and together they sat at the kitchen counter and reviewed their week.

"I'll be in the office shuffling papers all day tomorrow," Dorothy said, trying to sound annoyed when she was actually quite pleased to have some quiet uninterrupted time in the office. "What about you?"

"I need to start rounds about 10, so I can take my time getting in. Do you think Janaye Housling will be in her office early?"

"Worth a try. You really want to get this one off your chest, don't you?"

"Yep. To be honest, it's making me squirm."

"There but for the grace of God?"

"Precisely. Those of us who work in academic places like BFU or Temple are at the mercy of our house staff. We depend on them to get the facts right, and when they don't, we're in trouble. We just don't have the time to go back and double check everything they do."

"I understand. Responsibility without accountability. Always the formula for disaster."

After a pleasant and restful Sunday with Philip's children, Monday, if not depressing enough, presented itself as a cloudy day with the promise of intermittent rain showers. Dorothy prepared for her day while Philip took the hounds for their constitutional. It was a lively walk, the doggies spending a lot of sniffing time on their way to the grassy fields next to the Parkway, where they would be able to do their business. Philip dutifully cleaned up after them under the careful scrutiny of the other dog owners, who clearly regarded poop scooping to be an integral part of dog ownership. Philip paid careful attention to the colonic products knowing that Dorothy would inquire on the principle that healthy dogs make healthy poops.

"The things we do for our pups," Philip remarked to Meeko who panted and cocked her ears in full agreement. "The way it should be, Dad," she clearly opined with an ear flip.

By the time Philip returned to their townhouse, Dorothy had left for the day. Carol wouldn't arrive for the first dog walk for a couple of hours, which left Philip with a half-hour window to review the case with Janaye if she was available. Which she was.

"Dr. Sarkis. Thanks so much for reviewing the case so quickly," Janaye said sincerely, when she got on the phone.

"No worries. Glad to do it. Do you have a few minutes to talk about my findings?"

"Actually, I have a better idea. My team has been deeply concerned about this case, as I'm sure you can imagine, and I'm fairly certain they would enjoy hearing your opinion in person. Plus some of them may have questions I can't anticipate. Would you be willing to come in and meet with us to go over your opinion?"

"Well, it's hard to find the time…"

"You can bill us for your travel, of course and for the time you spend with us. It might help you determine how to structure your written report."

After you hear what I have to tell you, I'm not sure you are going to want a report, Philip thought.

"Okay, I guess we can do that," Philip finally decided, wondering how much the extra money motivated him.

"We have a team conference scheduled for tomorrow afternoon. Can you possibly join us at about 2 PM?"

Philip heard himself saying yes before he intended to.

"Terrific. Our offices are in the Kleinstein Tower, next to the Baker Lobby on the 24th floor."

Philip scribbled down the location and hung up, already considering how he was going to frame the bad news he would deliver to Janaye and her staff the next day.

Chapter 15

Philip awoke early the next day, eager to get to the hospital to make patient rounds before meeting with Janaye and her staff. He had walked the dogs, exercised, and showered before Dorothy appeared in the kitchen looking for coffee.

"You're up early," she said, rubbing her eyes.

"I'm anxious to get this over with. I wish the meeting were this morning."

"I'm sure it will go fine," Dorothy reassured him.

"Yeah. They're going to be really happy to hear the good news," Philip said with a smirk.

"Not your problem, Philip. Deliver the message, give them your invoice, and get out of Dodge."

"You know how much places like BFU like to hear they screwed up. After all, they're the best, right?"

"Everyone makes mistakes."

"I'm just glad I won't have to deal with the fallout."

"I'm sure you are, Philip," Dorothy nodded, hoping to truncate a conversation they had had so many times before.

"I have to get ready for work now."

They left the house together after saying goodbye to the doggies, and went their separate ways, Philip already looking forward to the end of the day and the Scotch that would relieve the tension.

After a mundane set of rounds, patient visits, and a few notes, Philip left Temple and navigated his way to BFU. Though he hated to admit it to himself, Philip missed bigtime academic medicine. He had become addicted to the challenge, the intellectual competition that was at the heart of clinical and basic research. He had selected cardiology and then the study of heart rhythm problems as his specialty because it was one of the most demanding. Electophysiologists, as his colleagues called each other, thought of themselves as the smartest people in medicine, and there was a strong case to be made. The field had grown tremendously in size and complexity over just a few years, and now encompassed not just the use of antiarrhythmic drugs and devices like pacemakers and defibrillators, but had spread into molecular biology and genetics, as the world's best and brightest dove deeper into common rhythm disorders like atrial fibrillation and ventricular tachycardia, to discover their root causes.

And Philip, in his prime, had earned a place in the upper echelons of that fraternity. He had been a regular contributor to the arrhythmia literature, participated in all of the big multi-center clinical trials, and presented at meetings not only in the US, but around the world. He trained young people, authored textbooks, and rubbed elbows with the elite. That is, until the Hamlin case destroyed his career and he nearly killed himself. He had managed to save his sanity and part of his career, but stuck at Temple, he was clearly a bench player, without the time, the resources, or the drive to climb back up the academic mountain.

And BFU represented that mountain, in all of its glory. Its medical school was perennially ranked in the top five nationally, attracting the brightest applicants to all of its training programs. Its scientists garnered millions of dollars of grants from the federal government, foundations and private donors. The area's billionaires vied to endow buildings and programs, ultimately to have their names attached.

In fact, the medical school building had recently been named after the retired president of one of the nation's largest health insurance companies. The price tag had been north of $300 million. Never mind that he and the company he founded had made their millions by slashing fees paid to the doctors and other providers in their system, who were told that if they didn't like it, they could try to practice without having access to the company's five million lives.

"So now he trickles back a small percentage of the money he made by raping our profession, and we're supposed to be thankful?" Philip observed during one of his sofa-based tirades on the topic. "Our state insurance commissioner watched it all happen and did absolutely nothing. Maybe the fact that she used to work for that prick had something to do with it?"

The extra funds that the medical school gained from the naming opportunity did little to aid students whose tuitions rose each year. "If you want the privilege of going to BFU, you're going to have to pay for it," Philip observed to no one in particular as he exited the expressway and began to navigate his way to the BFU campus. While the number of doctors and scientists grew slowly, the staff of administrators increased exponentially, the most senior preferentially housed in palatial offices with magnificent views of the city.

As Philip arrived at BFU, it was easy to see where all of that extra money was going. New towers rose up all around the campus as the hospital and medical school expanded at a mighty pace. Streets closed for construction that spilled into narrow thoroughfares defined the BFU medical campus, making the trip unpleasant at best.

Philip parked and found his way to the Kleinstein Tower that housed several of the administrative offices including the risk management department that now employed twenty attorneys and dozens of support staff.

Philip introduced himself at the registration desk.

"Yes, Dr. Sarkis," the almost too attractive receptionist said. "We were expecting you. Can you please sign in, and may I see a photo ID?"

"Really?" Philip asked incredulously.

"I'm afraid so, Dr. Sarkis. We have a lot of sensitive information up here so we have to be careful about who we let in. Sorry for the inconvenience."

Philip produced his driver's license after which he was issued a visitor pass with bad adhesive, and asked to take a seat until his escort arrived.

Philip looked around as he took a seat on one of the leather sofas. If he didn't know better, he could have been in an upscale center-city law firm, complete with glass partitions, plush carpeting and lots of young people, dressed smartly but casually, bustling through the hallways. A minority wore dresses or suits and ties, obviously preparing for court or a meeting with an important client.

After a few minutes, a petite blonde with a friendly face walked toward Philip and extended her hand. "Hi, I'm Olivia Goldberg. I'll take you back to our conference room. We're just getting everyone together to start our briefing meeting."

Philip followed Olivia down a hallway lined with well-appointed but modest offices with nice views of Center City on one side, and the BFU campus on the other. Most were unoccupied, as Philip followed a parade of people into the conference room. A large boardroom table took up most of the room, with chairs along the walls for underlings and observers. The seats were filling fast.

"Come up to the head of the table, Dr. Sarkis. I have a seat reserved for you next to Janaye."

Janaye herself entered the room just a few seconds after Philip was seated, causing him to rise again to greet her. Pretty much what he expected. Attractive African-American woman, dressed conservatively with a multi-colored scarf, the distinguishing part of her otherwise drab outfit.

"Dr. Sarkis, thanks so much for taking the time to brief us on the Santangelo case. We're enormously grateful," Janaye said, extending her hand.

"I'm glad my schedule allowed me to come over. This is some place you have here."

Janaye looked down, feigning embarrassment. "More than we need. But I don't have to tell you how important risk management has become to the success of any health care organization."

"I guess they come at you from a lot of angles."

"Exactly. There are so many ways for an institution like ours to get into hot water. And it's not all about malpractice, although that does consume a good deal of our time."

"Can you give me a brief idea of what you would like to achieve with this conference and who will be in attendance?" Philip asked.

"This is our weekly conference in which we feature those cases that are developed enough to make decisions about disposition."

"Like settlement."

"Sometimes. We may send a case back to the team for further development. Most of them end up being referred to a law firm."

"Locals?"

"Mostly, but we sometimes go out to national firms if we require special expertise."

"So who will be in the room?"

"The big table will be senior attorneys and some of their staff. The chairs along the wall will be associates, paralegals, student clerks. This is a very popular conference not only because we make decisions, but also because we do a lot of teaching. BFU is an academic institution after all."

Philip nodded.

"We should be starting in a few minutes. Can I get you anything?"

"No. Water should be fine," Philip said gesturing to the pitchers of ice water and glasses on the boardroom table.

Janaye went off to continue her preparations while Philip sat down, opened his valise, and took out a folder with his notes and a few documents. He also pulled out his smartphone and thumbed through the dozen or so useless emails he had received since he left Temple. He really didn't care about them, but flicking through them was part of the corporate pre-meeting ritual that was easily verified as he looked about the room. Nearly everyone not involved in a conversation was using their fingers to flick at a screen that undoubtedly contained information vital to the preservation of the free world.

"How did we get into this predicament," Philip wondered to himself. "What would happen to us if our phones were taken from us tomorrow? Would our civilization collapse?"

His musing was interrupted by Janaye, who was now standing next to him, asking all to have a seat to begin the conclave.

"Thanks, everyone," Janaye said as the staff settled themselves. "We have a rather full agenda this morning." Janaye went on to cover a few housekeeping items for the staff, including seminar announcements and information about pension plans that would be available the following week. She moved quickly through these and then, "We have a special guest with us this morning, Dr. Philip Sarkis, who has graciously agreed to join us today to discuss his impressions of the Santangelo case. Before he reviews his findings, I'm going to ask Olivia Goldberg to give us some background information about the case for those of you not familiar with it."

Olivia rose and went to the podium that had been placed in the front of the room, equipped with a microphone. She asked for the first slide and in the next ten minutes, aided by PowerPoint slides, she reviewed the facts of the case as they were understood by the risk management team. Philip was impressed by her understanding of the medical issues, although most of what she had on her slides had been extracted directly from the electronic medical record. She had elected to leave out details of Connie's employment or social situation. Was she trying to be discreet or was she simply unaware?

"And so," Olivia concluded, "Connie Santangelo had been thoroughly evaluated for syncope that occurred during her, uh, dancing at the Nightingales Club. She was seen by neurology, and cardiology, and had a battery of tests that suggested she had simply fainted. But two weeks later, she had a cardiac arrest from which she was resuscitated. Unfortunately, by the time spontaneous circulation was restored, she suffered irreversible brain damage and died as a direct result. Any questions?"

From the back, a paralegal. "Did she have a tilt-table test?"

"Yes, and it was positive. Her physicians were impressed and that is what led to the beta-blocker prescription."

Same person. "And she had some history of heart symptoms?"

"Nothing nearly as severe," Olivia answered confidently. "Occasionally feeling her heart racing but not usually to the point of losing consciousness. And she had never gone to a doctor for this problem, or been evaluated in any way."

After a few more clarifying questions, Janaye rose again, thanked Olivia and introduced Philip as a distinguished member of the cardiology faculty at Temple with extensive experience in electrophysiology. Philip walked to the podium with his red folder, and looked around the room, enjoying the moment. This was not the first time he held information that when delivered would surprise his audience. At international scientific meetings, he had had the opportunity to report the results of important clinical trials that rendered unexpected results. The thrill was still there and hard to describe.

"Thanks, Janaye, for the opportunity to review the records and to discuss the case with such a learned group. I'm frequently asked why I do legal reviews. There are several reasons but most importantly, I feel I learn from each of them. This case, as you'll see, delivers an important message: to never assume anything, and to be sure to examine every shred of information.

"I will conclude from Olivia's presentation that no one at BFU, either during Connie Santangelo's admission, or with the intensive review you carried out in this department, knew exactly what happened at Nightingales when she had her first spell."

Philip didn't wait for a response. He could tell from the facial expressions of the people in the room that they didn't. "I know that no one from the club came with Connie to the ER. She clearly arrived alone and gave her own history. And apparently none of your attorneys or paralegals called the club to interview the people there, did they?"

Again, a lot of head shaking, eyes staring down at the table. "Don't feel too bad about that," Philip continued. "I didn't either. It's not my place to do something like that. I didn't need to because your medical records department provided me with a document that I bet none of you examined. It was in a paper file. The ambulance run sheet from the first admission."

Murmurs around the room that Philip spoke over. "After Connie collapsed that first time, there was a 911 call. You knew that. The ambulance that was summoned eventually brought Connie in here. What you couldn't have known is that the crew found Connie without a pulse and, after a brief period of CPR, used an AED to shock her out of VF into normal rhythm."

Gasps from the audience.

"She had a cardiac arrest the first time?" Janaye asked incredulously, looking over at Olivia Goldberg, who sat forward, elbows on the table, head in hands.

"Afraid so. Here's a copy of that document. Take a look," Philip said walking over and handing the folder to Janaye. "You'll see that she responded immediately and woke up within seconds. She had no memory of it. She had chest discomfort but thought it was because they had done CPR, which they had, briefly."

"How come the ER staff didn't know about this?"

"The crew said in their report that they gave sign-out to the charge nurse. They didn't name her but I suspect it wasn't the same nurse who supervised Connie's care in the ER. The hand-off failed."

"What happened to the sheet?" Janaye again.

"It was put into a file but it wasn't scanned into the EMR. It was in your medical records department. I suspect this happens to paper records occasionally, but this time it created a major problem."

"This is terrible," Janaye muttered just a little too loud, so that most of the people at the board table heard her, including Philip, who decided to drive in the last nail.

"It's worse than you think. Also in that file, and not in the EMR, was a three-lead EKG taken on site. I have tracings on a flash drive I brought with me. Perhaps it would be instructive to throw them up on the screen. "

This was Philip's chance to play the professor. Olivia recovered quickly, took the drive from Philip, and inserted it into the computer she had used for her presentation. Philip paused until the images were on the screen.

"As you can see, the heart rate on this tracing is slow and

there is a good deal of artifact. Also, only three leads were recorded. But I think you can also see that the QT interval is quite long. And when we go to the next tracing, taken after Connie was admitted to the hospital, the heart rate has come up significantly, and the QT interval is now only minimally prolonged."

"She had long QT syndrome?" Janaye asked.

"Unless she was using a drug that caused this, the answer is yes. And I believe it because Connie told two people here at BFU that she had a cousin who drowned."

"Oh my God," one of the clerks in the back gasped.

"Somebody here knows that patients with long QT syndrome, a familial disease, are disposed to having lethal rhythms when they are swimming," Philip observed.

"But her QT interval was normal here at BFU," Olivia said.

"The prolonged QT interval can be evanescent. There one hour, gone the next."

"This throws a totally different light on this case," Janaye said in a record-setting understatement. "It appears that we missed the diagnosis mostly because of an information lapse."

"Of monumental proportions," Philip finished.

"So if we can't defend the case, we need to talk about settlement," Janaye concluded. "To be honest, I was hoping we wouldn't have to go there."

"Why?" asked one of the staff.

"Connie Santangelo had a tough life," Olivia interjected. "She got pregnant in high school, married the guy who got her pregnant, repeated the mistake, had another kid two years later, and then her husband deserted her."

"Who has custody of the kids now?" Janaye asked.

"Emily and Erin are in a foster home," Olivia answered.

"No grandparents?"

"Connie's parents are both dead, and she's an only child.

The father's parents declined."

"Declined custody?" Janaye asked incredulously.

"Uh, yeah. They've been approached several times by Protective Services and they have been adamant," Olivia answered.

"How old are the girls now?"

"Four and two. Gorgeous kids, by the way, and sharp as tacks. Protective Services doesn't think they'll have a problem placing them.

"But that's exactly the problem," Janaye pointed out. "They're sympathetic. Any good plaintiff firm will make hay over the fact that we turned them into orphans. We're talking at least seven figures," Janaye surmised.

"North of that, I fear," Olivia observed.

"You mean the girls are going to adoption?" Philip interrupted the conversation.

"Yes, that's the end game unless someone from either family steps forward, and so far that hasn't happened. And we're going to have to support the kids even after they're placed. You're right, Olivia, this is going to be expensive."

"Really? The kids will be put up for adoption now?" Philip persisted, his voice raised, drawing stares from the people in the room.

"It's not my specialty, but yes, that's what I understand from the authorities who are supervising the kids," Olivia managed.

"Excuse me, I have to make a call," Philip said as he pushed back from the table and raced out of the room, pulling his cell phone out of his jacket pocket.

"Dorothy, pick up your damn phone for a change," he muttered on his way to the waiting room.

Chapter 16

A few minutes later, Philip was in his car, swerving through Center City traffic, running yellow lights in a gigantic sweat, spooking pedestrians crazy enough to get in his way. Not unexpectedly, Dorothy had not answered her cell phone. After cursing a streak that frightened the receptionist who greeted Philip's call to the main practice, he finally punched in Dorothy's direct office number and was put through to her secretary, Jerina. A North Philly refugee, Jerina was a nice person who greeted everybody with, "How you feelin'," in one of the densest Philly accents Philip had ever heard.

"Feelin' great, Jerina," Philip answered as he usually did, even if he felt like crap. "Where's Dorothy?"

"In a dep, Philip."

"Shit."

"Philip, you don't sound too good. Everythin' okay?"

"Terrific," Philip replied tersely, not wanting to get into a conversation about his state of well-being. "When is she out?"

"I'm guessing soon. They've been in there for about two hours, and the case ain't that complicated, if you know what

I mean."

"Right."

"Do you want me to have her call you back?"

Philip thought for a minute. He didn't have to go back to Temple, and Dorothy's office was not that far away. "Tell her I'm on my way over."

"Uh, okay. She does have a couple of teleconferences on her calendar after the dep."

"Tell her this is very important. I'll be there in about fifteen minutes."

Philip hung up before Jerina could object. He had another call to make on the way that took only a couple of minutes. The person on the other end was quite receptive to the idea of an early dinner at a nice restaurant with Philip and Dorothy. After securing the dinner reservation, Philip was now looking for a place to park during business hours in the densest part of the city. He finally had to give up and jam his car into a crazy tight spot in a lot that charged an outrageous half-hourly rate. He walked briskly to Dorothy's building and soon was in the firm's lobby. Jerina came out to meet him, a look of concern on her face. "Philip, are you sure everything's all right?"

"Never better, Jerina. I have some potentially good news."

Jerina smiled. "That's good, because I don't think Dorothy was too happy about adjustin' her schedule for you."

Philip smiled back and accelerated into Dorothy's office. Though not large or plush, it was well organized and as neat as Dorothy's workspace at home. She was standing behind her clean desk, arms crossed, frowning. "This had better be damned important, Philip. I had to ice a potential client."

"You can decide if this is important or not. Remember the BFU case we discussed?"

"The stripper who died on the pole?"

"Yeah."

"Weren't you supposed to meet with the risk management

people there and dump the bad news on them?"

"Yeah."

"And then walk away and forget the whole thing, right? Philip, please don't tell me that you're going to pull us into another cluster fuck."

"Yes and no."

"Cut the crap, Philip. What's going on? And make it quick. I have work to do."

"Do you remember that I told you the woman who died had two little girls?"

"I remember."

"Nobody wants them."

"What do you mean, 'nobody wants them'? What about her family?"

"Her parents are both dead, and she was an only child. Her former in-laws are out of the picture for some reason. The kids are in foster homes until they're placed permanently."

"All very sad, Philip. What does that have to do... Oh my God, Philip! Adoption?"

"Yep."

"Us?"

"Yep."

"Are you serious?"

"Serious as I can be."

"But we aren't ready. And we don't know anything about the kids. This is so sudden."

"All true. I can't argue. But from what I've gathered, these two girls are gorgeous and cute and bright. I'm afraid that if we don't move quickly we won't have a chance."

"I need time to think."

"What is there to think about? We've discussed it and we've agreed it's something to pursue. This is just a little quicker than we thought."

"What makes you think we have a chance anyway? We haven't had classes, or screening, or home visits. All of that takes time. We won't be able to do it fast enough."

Philip smiled and bit his lip knowingly.

"Okay, out with it. You have something up your sleeve."

"I figured, like you, that we couldn't just get in line and hope for the best. To get these kids, we're going to have to pull some heavy-duty strings."

"That sounds evil, Philip. Why should we be able to get in front of people who've been waiting for an adoption?"

"Well, for one thing, we can afford to take both of them so they aren't split up. Not too many people can do that. And the other reason is that I don't give a shit. We can't afford to play nice if we want kids. Especially American kids. Success often requires a little back-room manipulation."

"Even if I agreed to get into the dirt with you, Philip, I wouldn't know where to start."

"Think, Dorothy. Who in this town knows everybody in the legal system and can fix just about anything? And would do just about anything you asked?"

Dorothy smiled and tears welled up. Philip walked around the desk, put his arms around her, and held on. "Do you think he could pull this off?" she whispered into his ear.

"I spoke with him on my way over here," Philip answered softly. "I didn't tell him what he needed yet, but I know he'll bend over backwards."

Philip pulled back and looked down at his watch. "It's five o'clock. Tell Jerina you're leaving, and get your things together. I told him that we'd meet him for an early dinner in about thirty minutes. Reservation set. Let's go."

They decided to walk to Amis, one of their favorite Italian restaurants in Center City. Good food, informal atmosphere, generous drinks and friendly staff—all the requirements. They arrived a few minutes early and sat at the bar for a cocktail as they chatted nervously about the prospects, each excited but trying not to be too optimistic. "You do realize how crazy this is, Philip."

"It's a little nuts, I agree, but I think this kind of thing happens all the time. We have to take advantage of the opportunity and at least try to make it work."

"We're going to need a lot of help, Philip."

"Which is exactly why you have a wonderful father," said a deep voice coming up behind them.

Philip jumped up and shook hands with the handsome, burly man who then went to the next stool to give Dorothy a hug. When most people met Dick Deaver, they were reminded of the "most interesting man" commercial. A handsome person, with a carefully trimmed gray beard, steely blue eyes, and wonderful wardrobe, Dick attracted attention whenever he entered a room. And his occupation, private detective, didn't do anything to dilute the interest mature women showed in him.

"Dick, thanks for making time," Philip said.

"Anything for my daughter, and her... uh... boyfriend," Dick Deaver replied, doing little to hide his customary disdain for his daughter's living arrangements. "I think our table is ready. I'll get a drink after we sit down. I have a feeling I'm going to need one before I hear the details," Dick continued. "Did I overhear something about an adoption?"

Philip and Dorothy took their drinks and the three were directed to a table in the back of the nearly empty restaurant. After Dick ordered his usual Grey Goose martini, up, with olives and very cold, Philip reviewed the case for Dick, who interrupted him occasionally for clarification. Dick nodded knowingly as Philip finished, looked at Dorothy, and asked the most important question.

"Is this something you want, sweetie pie?"

"I think so, Dad. I mean, I just found out about it myself. I know nothing about the kids or their situation or background. I'm in shock!"

"That's understandable. But Philip is right, if you're going to do this, you have to move fast. These kids are ripe for the picking, especially if they're as cute and as bright as those attorneys suggested. There are literally thousands of people aching to adopt white children. I know that sounds racist, but it's the truth. A lot of them bail out to go to Asia or South America or other places to get kids, but America is everybody's first choice."

"How do you know so much about all of this, Dad?" Dorothy asked warily.

"Guess."

"Girlfriend," Philip laughed.

Sideways glance from Dick. "Bingo. I used to date a woman who's a partner in one of the largest adoption firms in Philly. Nice person, but talks a little too much for my taste, especially business stuff. But at least I am, how you might say, better informed about the topic. We're still good friends. I should be able to persuade her to intervene on your behalf, if you like."

"You mean manipulate the system so we screw somebody in line and get the kids, right?"

"Please, Dorothy, don't be crass," Philip interrupted. "Your father is just trying to be helpful."

"Not so much crass as naïve," Dick said. "Do you think the adoption business is all above-board, daughter? Deals are cut all the time. It usually boils down to who you know and how much money you're willing to spend."

"How much do you think this one will cost, Dick?" Philip asked.

"At least five figures, I'd say. There are two kids, you guys have not been vetted, and it's a rush job. Worst of all, you aren't married," Dick frowned.

"Not much we can do about that, Dad," Dorothy answered quickly but firmly.

"All right, let's not get into that again," Dick continued. "I can call Maggie tonight and she can start exploring this.

As long as you're absolutely convinced this is what you want."

"So it could be a little steep, money wise," Philip returned to the financial question, some of the enthusiasm lost from his voice.

"I suspect you guys aren't sitting on a lot of cash," Dick said.

"That's an understatement."

"Well, let's see. Since this little venture is going to make me a grandfather, I suspect I should be able to help out, right?"

"No, Dad," Dorothy answered before the nodding Philip could get words out of his mouth. "That's out of the question. We'll take out a loan."

"Okay," Dick replied. "We'll call it a loan. You can pay me back with grandchildren time for interest," winking at Philip.

"You two are incorrigible. Why don't we see if this is even possible and how much it's going to cost before we worry about this loan business."

They suspended their conversation as the waiter delivered Dick's drink and explained the specials of the evening. Then Philip hoisted his vodka tonic. "Let's toast the Sarkis-Deaver family. Philip, Dorothy, Emily and Erin. And Grandpop Dick."

Dorothy smiled for the first time, as tears welled up again. "I can't believe this is happening. Oh my God, I don't want to be disappointed."

"Not if I can help it, my girl," Dick said. "I have a good feeling about this. Let's see what Maggie has to say when I call her after dinner. Or maybe I'll just drop by her place and practice a little friendly persuasion."

They chatted casually for the rest of the dinner, trying not to dwell on the adoption prospects. When they parted on the street after dinner, they agreed to conference the next morning. Philip and Dorothy walked to Philip's car, arm-in-arm, each lost in thought. They said little during the brief drive home, where, after some dog and TV time they fell asleep in each other's arms, preparing to dream of children's laughter echoing through the halls of their home.

What neither could ever have imagined that evening was how fast their world would change. Maggie Smart not only agreed to help, but turned out to be a jewel of an advocate. She was tireless, working on their behalf, helping them move step-by-step to navigate through the complex adoption system. She called in favors, and when that didn't work, threatened anyone who created an obstacle. Fortunately, she was experienced and able to avoid many of the pitfalls that stalled adoption proceedings.

One particularly difficult issue was Sonny. He had disappeared, and even his parents didn't know where he was. He hadn't even come back for Connie's funeral. They knew he wasn't dead because of his incessant phone calls, asking for money to be wired to wherever he happened to be at the time. His parents claimed they had spoken with Sonny about the adoption, and that he had insisted he wanted nothing to do with his daughters. They would only remind him of that bitch he had married. Besides, he wanted to be on the road and a free man. The girls would only tie him down. But no, he wouldn't put anything in writing. The lawyers could go screw themselves. He didn't have the time for legal shit... he had places to go and things to do.

Within a month, Philip and Dorothy and their home had been qualified, and they were vetted and in position to take custody of the girls. Maggie had thoughtfully reminded them to keep Carol out of the conversation. An illegal immigrant who helped around the house would only raise red flags with the adoption agency and give them an excuse to reject the application. They met Emily and Erin at their foster home and were immediately captivated. The girls were expectedly bashful, but by the time their hour visit was over, they were sitting next to Philip and Dorothy asking to have their books read to them. Philip was able to steal a look at Dorothy, whose joy was transparent and transcendental.

And whether it was because she was attracted to Dick, Maggie's fees were modest as were the expenditures for the entire process. Philip managed to scrape together all but five thousand dollars, which Dick happily contributed. "That'll cost you five thousand hugs from those beautiful girls," Dick reminded them cheerfully when he handed them the check.

After all of the details had been ironed out, and only a few weeks later, Philip and Dorothy took custody of Emily and Erin, and signed the final papers at Maggie's office. It was a beautiful, sunny day and the collective mood at the meeting couldn't have been more positive. The girls were excited to be going to a place where they could have their own room with constant "parental units." Philip and Dorothy were gentle with them, as their mother had been. The authorities were convinced that the girls were getting a great home, and Philip and Dorothy were over the moon. They had spent the last several days setting up their home to accommodate the girls, right down to the car seats they would use today to transport their precious cargo. They even managed to ignore the stipulations in the adoption papers regarding parental rights. Specifically, the biological parents or first-degree relatives would have the right to change their mind until the adoption was finalized in a year. Maggie had made this clear to both of them at the beginning of the process, but reassured them that the odds of such a thing happening were very low, especially in this case in which the only surviving biological parent had verbally rejected custody.

As they had expected, it took a few weeks for the girls to become acclimated to their new environment. They had no pet experience, so the dogs had frightened them in the beginning. But soon they were rolling around on the floor with the hounds, who were delighted to have humans paying so much attention to them. Dorothy decided to work through the transition, but only part-time. The girls attended a daycare near their townhouse in the mornings, but spent each afternoon with Dorothy and with Philip on the frequent occasions he was able to get out of work early.

Emily slept well, but Erin took longer to adjust, and crawled into bed with Philip and Dorothy most nights. They feigned concern, but each was excited to have her with them, nudging her way past the dogs populating the bottom of the bed, and burrowing under the covers, falling asleep almost instantaneously.

They spent their weekends together, exploring every kid-friendly venue in and around the city, from the zoo to Please Touch to Sesame Place, the adults enjoying the experience perhaps even more than their munchkins. They looked for opportunities to include the doggies, who pranced along on their leashes on long walks, happy to be with their newly expanded family.

Philip and Dorothy's relationship prospered as never before. They were much more patient, easy in each other's company, and gentle in their interactions. It was as if refocusing and expanding their nest helped each of them see the other in a different light. Philip loved watching Dorothy's mothering skills, and she Philip's doting attention.

And Grandpop Dick became a much more frequent visitor, looking for any opportunity to stop by, showering the girls with gifts on each occasion, ignoring Dorothy's admonition about spoiling them.

"That's what grandparents are supposed to do," Dick would answer. And when Maggie came along to join the party, she would agree adamantly. "Enjoy every minute of it. They'll grow up fast," she warned playfully.

And sometimes in the evening, as the girls watched their one hour of television, Philip would sit and observe them with a large measure of joy and satisfaction. "Almost too good to be true," he would say to himself, and, being the considerably skeptical person he was, wonder if this new-found heaven would last.

But last it would, at least for five of the most wonderful months of their lives, until their new, idyllic life began to unravel in a most horrible way.

Chapter 17

It happened during a typical topsy-turvy evening at the Sarkis-Deaver household. Dorothy was late to the daycare center to pick up the girls after their morning session because she was immersed in a silly slip-and-fall case that was taking more time than she had allotted. Seems a friend of one of her good clients decided to try to milk an insurance company for a twisted ankle caused by a loose walkway brick while leaving a dinner party, and succeeded only in infuriating her hosts who now wanted to counter-sue. Dorothy was doing her client a favor and just wanted a settlement for the small amount the case was worth. She had tried to work from home in the afternoon, but only became frustrated with the constant interruptions from Emily and Erin who were intermittently hungry, bored, and belligerent.

Philip had promised to be home early to help out but had been bushwhacked by his house staff and fellows, who had tried mightily to kill an elderly man who had passed out and was found to be in complete heart block. They managed to perforate his right ventricle with a temporary pacemaker wire, and Philip had to rescue the situation by inserting a catheter under the ribs to suck the leaking blood out of the sack around the heart to restore the man's blood pressure. He then took the patient to the electrophysiology laboratory to insert a permanent pacemaker to make sure he would have an adequate heart rate overnight. Naturally, the implant took forever. Philip directed one of his green trainees until his patience was exhausted. To the decided relief of the veteran laboratory staff, Philip finally took over and finished the case. But by the time he spoke with the family, changed into street clothes, and navigated his way home, household pandemonium had set in.

"Now that we're both here, we should go man-to-man," Philip observed whimsically as he bounded in the door. And this time, it worked, Dorothy concentrating on getting the girls fed and bathed while Philip de-cluttered the house, cleaned up the kitchen, and started the adult dinner.

Philip and Dorothy were seated on the sides of the girls' beds finishing up bedtime stories when the phone rang. They decided to let the call go to their voicemail so as not to interrupt the evening ritual that the girls loved so much. They had to be tucked into their beds with their favorite blankets and stuffies, and kissed and hugged. All of the lights in the room and hallway had to be carefully adjusted, and lullabies played softly in their room before they would settle down and agree to close their eyes and surrender to innocent sleep.

Back to the kitchen, where Philip chopped vegetables for their salad. Dorothy headed to the phone. When she heard the message source, she put the phone on speaker so Philip could hear as well. What they heard made dinner preparations moot, the news completely wiping away their appetites.

"Hi, Philip and Dorothy. This is Maggie. Sorry to bother you at this hour, but I thought it was important that I reach you so we can talk tomorrow. There's been a new development in the Cardinelli adoption proceedings. Seems that Sonny Cardinelli has resurfaced. I got a call from an attorney in Norristown representing Sonny, who is interested in getting his kids back. I know this doesn't sound good, but please don't fret too much. The probability is that he won't be able to get custody after all that's happened. Most likely, the worst we're looking at is visitation rights. But we're going to have to come up with a strategy, so call me in the morning at my office and we'll figure this out. Thanks."

Dorothy and Philip looked at each other in stunned silence. Despite Maggie's encouragement, each believed that their worst nightmare was coming true. They knew full well that biological parents always held the upper hand in any scenario, and that the adoption process was not yet final. Worse, during their orientation, they had been regaled with stories of children snatched back by immature parents who had a change of heart. Philip and Dorothy didn't have to say any of this to each other. Their manner and facial expressions for the rest of the evening conveyed their concern and stress better than words. Each managed a few bites of dinner before heading off to their respective space to work, and struggled to quell the sinking feeling in the bottom of their gut.

They called Maggie Smart the next morning and decided that a meeting at her office at lunchtime was preferable to a lengthy phone call. She offered to arrange sandwiches for lunch but each demurred, their appetite still not recovered after the body blow from the night before. Maggie's office was on the eighteenth floor of Two Liberty Place. Though clearly a high-end space, Maggie's office was modest without the ostentatious furnishings that characterized attorneys' digs in other parts of the building. And Maggie fit right in, conservatively dressed with minimal jewelry, a plain hairdo but a warm smile.

"Look, you two," she addressed them from behind her desk, once they were settled in easy chairs, "I know this is a bit of a shock, but it happens all the time in the adoption business. As I suggested in the phone message I left you, there are ways to compromise so everyone gets what they want."

"And what do you think this asshole wants?" Philip asked through gritted teeth.

Dorothy turned to Philip with a frown. "That attitude isn't going to be helpful, Philip."

"I have to agree," Maggie added, less sternly. "We have to engage Mr. Cardinelli and his attorney with compassion. They are his kids, after all. We don't really know what happened to him or what his motivation is now."

Philip was not to be assuaged. "There are about five million reasons why that douchebag is back in the picture."

"You don't know that, Philip."

"Really? I grew up in those neighborhoods. I know guys like him. He knocked Connie up, deserted her, forced her to earn a living demeaning herself, and then refused to come back when she died and the kids needed him. Now he's in the conversation when a huge amount of money is about to be dumped on the kids."

"You don't know they're going to get a lot of money, Philip," Dorothy reminded him. "The settlement isn't official."

"And remember, Philip, that's money you might be getting," Maggie reminded him. "Why wouldn't somebody assume that you're gold digging?"

"Because I'm not, that's why. I don't give a shit about the money. And you know it. And besides, we got into this adoption before BFU offered anything to settle the case."

"You are being disingenuous, Philip," Maggie scolded. "You consulted on that case so you knew it had economic value. But that's not the point of this conversation. Whatever his motivation, we're going to have to deal with Sonny and his attorney. Who I understand isn't a bad guy. At least he has a good reputation in the Norristown area."

"So what do you suggest, Maggie?" Dorothy asked, eager to get the planning conversation back on track.

"We have to meet with them and offer something. Visitation seems the easiest thing to swallow. And along with that, a proportional amount of the settlement funds would go to Sonny for childcare."

"So, if he gets them one weekend a month, he would get a fifteenth of the settlement money."

"Something like that."

"And we would set the ground rules for those visits, right?"

"To some extent. We don't want to make it onerous. We want him to accept our accommodation without demanding full custody."

"How the hell can he do that?" Philip asked.

"Don't know. As far as I can tell, he isn't married, and he doesn't have a job. He's living with his parents presently, but I don't know if that's a temporary arrangement."

"There's a lot we don't know," Dorothy added. "I like the idea of meeting with him to get the facts before we commit to anything."

"Agree. I'll call Doug Kilcoyne, his attorney, and set up a meeting here this week, hopefully. Is that good for you guys?"

"The sooner the better," Philip half barked.

"I suggest you take a valium or something before the meeting," Dorothy said.

"Correct," Maggie nodded. "You can't come into the meeting loaded for bear, Philip."

Philip didn't answer—he didn't have to. It was obvious from his body language that he was angry and not disposed to hiding it. He rose to go, as did Dorothy, while Maggie promised to call them that evening after her conversation with Kilcoyne.

But of course, nothing in the law is ever that easy. It took Maggie three days to get on the phone with Doug Kilcoyne, who was in a trial. Kilcoyne was initially resistant to the idea of a meeting. "What do we have to meet about, Maggie? This is about as clear-cut as it gets. The father of the children had a medical problem that kept him from responding to the custody request, and now he's back and wants his kids."

"Oh, come on, Doug. You know as well as I do what a huge crock of shit that is. Your guy doesn't care about those kids. He wants the money from the malpractice settlement."

"Maggie, I'm going to pretend I didn't hear that. This man has wanted his kids from the get-go. He just had some problems that kept him from accepting the children."

"Then his mother is a liar. We have it down that she said she spoke with him before the placement. She said he wanted no parts of the kids."

"He said, she said," Kilcoyne countered. "It's hearsay and not even in writing. I suspect there was just a misunderstanding. No matter, the adoption isn't finalized, and we're fully inside the window in which parents can change their mind. Sonny has changed his."

"Doug, the adopting parents are good people. They love the kids to death and they have provided a wonderful home for the girls. They're willing to negotiate visitation…"

"My client isn't interested in visitation. He wants the kids full-time."

"And how is he going to manage that?"

"He's living with his parents. His mother is a wonderful person and has agreed to help with childcare while Sonny works."

"Works where?"

"He got a job driving truck… locally. Nothing over the road."

"Wonderful. And I'm sure he'll spend every Sunday in church at Mass."

"As a matter of fact…"

"Save it for the judge, Doug. Because we're going to the mat if we can't resolve this. So how about if we just have the meeting and see if we can meet him half-way. For every-body's sanity and conscience."

"Fine, Maggie. I'll ask my client and get back to you."

"Please do. And before the end of the week?"

"Sure, Maggie. That shouldn't be a problem.

Maggie reported her conversation with Kilcoyne to Philip and Dorothy, softening the blow with reassurances about how difficult it would be for Sonny to convince a judge of his serious intentions.

As she might have expected, Kilcoyne didn't deliver for another ten days while Dorothy and Philip walked on hot coals. When they weren't distracted by work or chores, they were frantic about the adoption. They wanted to bond with the children but were afraid to, since losing them would be all the more difficult. For their part, the kids were clearly thriving in their new environment, becoming more familiar and affectionate with their new parents by the day. The thought of the children leaving was becoming so painful that Philip and Dorothy couldn't even voice their feelings to each other. Neither had gotten a good night's sleep since Maggie's phone call.

Which is why they looked like zombies by the time they marched into Maggie's office for the showdown. Sonny, on the other hand, literally whistled his way into Maggie's con-ference room, looking like the world was his. And he cleaned up well, taking his lawyer's advice to get a haircut, shave his scraggly beard, and wear a conservative suit, white shirt and military striped tie. Philip and Dorothy were already seated across the table next to Maggie, looking like they had a bad case of seasickness. Sonny sat next to Kilcoyne who leaned over and whispered last minute instructions while Sonny nod-ded gravely.

Maggie began the meeting with introductions. "Mr. Car-dinelli, my name is Maggie Smart. I represent Dr. Philip Sarkis seated to my left and Ms. Dorothy Deaver, seated to my right. On behalf of my clients, I want to thank you for coming in today to talk to us."

Sonny started to reply but was halted by Doug Kilcoyne who threw a hand in front of Sonny's face.

"Thank you, Ms. Smart. I'm Doug Kilcoyne and I represent Mr. Stephen Cardinelli who has graciously agreed to talk to your clients today. I want to make a few things clear before we start. This is not a legal proceeding. No one is under oath, although we all agree to be truthful with each other. Nothing we agree to in this room is binding in any way. And there will be no official record of this conversation, not by minutes, summary, or transcript."

"That's fine, Doug," Maggie answered, deliberately using his first name. "May I assume you aren't going to ask for a body search?"

"Sounds like fun, Maggie," Doug retaliated, "but no, I don't think anyone is wearing a wire. Nor will sarcasm be needed. I'm just trying to lay out the ground rules so there is no misunderstanding later."

"I believe we're of similar mind, Doug."

"Good. Having said that, my client wishes to make a brief statement that he believes will help resolve this matter quickly."

"Go ahead, Mr. Cardinelli," Maggie instructed.

"Thank you," Sonny said. He took a stack of index cards out of the breast pocket of his suit and began, referring to his notes as he spoke. His speech was obviously well rehearsed. "First of all, I want to thank Dr. Sarkis and Ms. Deaver for taking care of my kids these last few months," Sonny said with absolutely no feeling. "It has meant a lot to me and my family. You guys are very generous people.

"I also want to apologize for any misunderstandings that may have occurred. My wife's death had a dramatic effect on me, and it has taken me a long time to recover and come to grips with it. I'm happy to say that I'm better now, and I'm ready to assume my parental responsibilities. To that end, I've secured employment with a Mack franchise. I'm driving a truck for that company and have been able to arrange a schedule that will permit me to spend every evening with my children. I'll be living with my parents and my mother will provide daycare for my children. The local kindergarten and grade school that my children will attend is within walking distance of my parent's home, so there will be no problem with arranging for their excellent education.

"You also know that I have a loving extended family. My children's cousins are looking forward to accepting Emily and Erin into our family where we'll spend weekends and holidays. I plan to raise the children as Catholic and take them to religious services regularly. I have given considerable thought to all of these arrangements, and I'm convinced that my children will have a wonderful life with me."

"Amen and hallelujah," Philip said before Maggie realized.

Sonny scowled, but gathered himself quickly and changed his expression to a smile. "Amen is right!" he said, nodding.

Maggie didn't waste any time. "Mr. Cardinelli, thanks for your kind words. However, a number of your statements don't seem credible. For example, when the children were in foster homes, why did no one in your wonderful extended family come forward and offer to take them in?"

"They ain't well off. I suspect it was a money thing."

"Speaking of which," Maggie continued hardly pausing, "Is it merely coincidental that you came forward after you heard about a potential settlement with BFU regarding your deceased wife's wrongful death case?"

"They agreed to some kind of settlement?" Sonny answered, hardly able to suppress a grin.

"Do we look like fucking fools?" Philip half rose from his chair.

"Enough, Philip. I'll ask the questions," Maggie said, her

arm across Philip's chest. "You weren't aware of that matter, Mr. Cardinelli?"

"I heard that they were feeling bad about my wife's death and might try to make it right. I had no idea they were going to give us a lot of money."

"When did you find out about BFU's 'feelings'?"

"When I got home. My mother told me."

"And who told her?" Maggie persisted.

"Beats me."

"Whether or not my client knew about a potential settlement is immaterial to what we're discussing here today," Kilcoyne interjected. "And please remember that there has been no official monetary offer to settle the BFU case."

"Get real!" Philip again. "That case has everything to do with this scum-bag coming out of the slime he lives in!"

"I'm sorry, Dr. Sarkis. You may be a wonderful cardiologist, but you're not a lawyer. The question for us today is who has custody rights. Unless you have some reason to believe that my client can't raise these children, you don't have a cause of action. Nothing about his wife's death is material."

That silenced Philip but not Maggie, who was anxious to find a compromise. "We would like to propose an arrangement by which Mr. Cardinelli can visit his children while my clients house and raise them. If BFU does make a payment in support of the children's rearing, Mr. Cardinelli would be entitled to a proportionate share of that money. Is that acceptable?"

"Allow me to confer with my client," Kilcoyne said. Head to head, they whispered only a few words before Kilcoyne said, "No. That is not acceptable to my client. He believes he's entitled to full custody without any stipulation."

"Then we're going to end up in front of a judge. My clients will not voluntarily surrender custody of the children until the court has ruled on Mr. Cardinelli's previous behavior and his suitability."

"Terrific," answered Kilcoyne in an instant. "You're only delaying the inevitable, Ms. Smart. I believe we're done here." Whereupon he rose and pulled Sonny to his feet. They turned and left the room without another word.

"So what do you think?" Dorothy asked after the room had cleared.

"If they can verify the arrangements he says he has made for those kids, we'll have a tough time in court."

"But what about abandonment? He left that family to fend for themselves. Doesn't that count against him?"

"I wish it did. And it would in a sane society. But in ours, biology trumps almost everything else. We have no evidence that he harmed the children, and we can't dispute his story about his 'disability'. Hell, we can't even prove that he didn't send money back to his family. Connie is gone, she didn't leave a will, and no one else has the details."

"So we're sunk?" Dorothy asked, tears welling up.

"Frankly, I'm at a loss as to what to argue in front of the judge. We'll put something together but I'm not hopeful. I expected him to take the bait and compromise in exchange for some of the money. But he's a greedy little prick and wants all of it."

"You know he'll take the money and leave the kids again," Dorothy concluded.

"High probability, I'm afraid. But you can't arrest a criminal until he does the crime."

Through their distressing debrief, Philip sat silently, biting his lip, deep in thought. If Dorothy had not been so upset by their plight, she would have noticed his stare into the distance, and she would have realized that if anyone could solve their problem, Philip Sarkis would find a way, whether she liked his methods or not.

Chapter 18

You could say that Lee Wallingbird was one unhappy trooper—literally. Lee graduated from a small local college with a major in anthropology in the lower tier of his class without a marketable skill. After a brief but lackluster military career during which he had an opportunity to kill not one enemy of the United States, or to advance in rank from private, he decided to resign and become a policeman. Not just any policeman, but a Pennsylvania State Policeman. There was something about their uniforms or maybe the way they wore their wide-brimmed hats with the straps across their chins that excited Lee so much. He remembered the day when, as a college student, he had been pulled over on Interstate 95 for speeding by a state trooper who looked like he had been chiseled out of a rock of granite. The trooper had been nice to Lee, and had only given him a warning, but succeeded in convincing Lee that traveling at high speeds simply wasn't cool, a lesson Lee had never forgotten.

Lee himself was tall and fit, and he thought he would look terrific in a trooper's outfit. He didn't tell his parents, his friends or the recruiter this, of course. He didn't want to sound like a weirdo. Instead he had made up a story about how he wanted to help his fellow human beings or some such crap. Whatever he had said, combined with a clean military record and honorable discharge, had worked. To his and his family's delight, he was admitted to the state police academy on the first try.

Where once again Lee succeeded in establishing his mediocrity. He graduated by the skin of his teeth and had to beg his way into the assignment he coveted—crime investigation. Lee realized early that he didn't have the brights for the job, but he managed to keep that fact hidden for several weeks until he washed out of the final examination. His supervisors were sympathetic but realistic. They liked his enthusiasm and were able to finally convince Lee that if he had a future in the state police, it was going to be as a patrolman, at least for the next few years. Maturity and study might bring other opportunities, but no promises.

The only consolation was that Lee had managed to guilt his supervisors into assigning him to the Philadelphia barracks, and not some God-forsaken outpost, of which Pennsylvania had many. But patrolling the highways was a thankless task, with few interactions to spell endless hours of isolation, focusing a radar gun from roadside traps on hapless drivers who didn't seem to understand why speed really does kill.

Which is exactly where Lee found himself this particular morning, parked on the side of the Schuylkill Expressway, by all accounts, one of the worst roads in the history of modern civilization.

By the late 1940's, it finally occurred to the corrupt and somewhat dim-witted urban planners of the day that population growth in the Philadelphia metropolitan area was occurring principally to the west, in small towns like Norristown, Conshohocken, and King of Prussia. Many, if not most of the people who built houses and lived in the sprawling western suburbs needed to get into center city to work. The only catch was that there was no direct route. Surface roads built decades before, many for horse and buggy, were simply not able to handle the huge load of cars now being used by the working public. And then there was the truck traffic. As commerce in the region ramped up, so did the number of tractor-trailers that transported every kind of freight across the Delaware Valley.

To make matters worse, the oil barons had been able to persuade politicians years before that building a public transportation system was an inferior option to the mighty automobile that had clearly captured the imagination of the American public. Who needed trains when John Q. Public could simply walk into his garage, start up his car, and motor his way directly to his office? The meager rail system that was eventually developed would never be able to keep pace with the explosive growth of population and commerce.

When it became obvious to the geniuses in public works that something had to be done to accommodate the flood of trucks and automobiles, a decision was finally made in the early 1950s to construct a major highway to run along the Schuylkill River, west to east, to facilitate the movement of workers into Philadelphia. The problem was that the terrain between the river and the steep hills that bordered it meant that the road could be no more than four lanes wide until it wound its way into the city limits, where it might expand to six. Unless, of course, more land was purchased and the surrounding hills blasted. That idea was thoroughly nixed by the people who lived along the proposed route, who threatened the politicians with annihilation if they tried any such thing. The decision to limit the road's capacity was the death knell for the Schuylkill Expressway, the ironic moniker chosen for the new road.

Because by the time it opened a few years later, the road was anything but "express" and essentially obsolete. It has

been said that the first traffic jam on the expressway occurred about 5 minutes after it opened. There were just too
many cars per cubic foot of road surface.

And nobody anticipated that the real estate development
in the western suburbs would lead to a concomitant growth
in businesses that drew almost as many workers wishing to
go west as east to Philadelphia each morning. The weekends
were no better and maybe worse. If you wanted to travel to
the Jersey shore, sporting event, airport, or train station, the
expressway was the most direct and crowded route.

As the volume of cars increased and the situation became
intolerable, the "distressway" became the butt of jokes by
local media personalities and the object of public derision.
Even local singing groups jumped on the bandwagon. The
Soul Survivors fashioned a song called "The Expressway to
Your Heart" in which the "expressway was not the best
way"…because it was "much too crowded." Every day,
radio listeners who bothered to tune into traffic reports heard
the endless litany of delays and jammed traffic at every point
along the road where mergers occurred or available lanes
dwindled.

But the most pitiful part of the story was that after sixty
years, the road was still there, unchanged and unimproved,
a monument to urban planning stupidity. Used by hundreds
of thousands of cars every day, responsible for generations
of lost man-hours and the deaths of hundreds of poor souls
who simply dared to drive the registered speed limit or to
change lanes in front of someone who finally saw some
open road.

Accidents were commonplace and it took only one fender
bender to back traffic up for miles. Lee's job was to patrol
the road and try to keep people from killing themselves with
speed. The problem was that catching the scoundrels who
insisted on weaving through traffic at ninety miles an hour
was dangerous and difficult. The Philly police had all but

given up. But if the state wished to keep their federal high-way dollars, the state police were required to maintain their presence. After all, this death trap had been designated an Interstate Highway (I-76). What a joke, Lee thought. Any-body traveling through Pennsylvania did anything they could to avoid the expressway, since stumbling onto it was a sure-fire way to arrive late wherever you were going.

Lee's boring job this particular morning was to sit on the side of the road on the very narrow shoulder, facing west at Girard Avenue near the zoo with his radar gun hung on the outside of the driver's side to pretend that he was interested in stopping speeders. Fortunately, he had already made his citation quota for the month, mostly capturing idiots who drove their economy cars like maniacs at off-peak hours, when Lee had a chance to track them down. All he hoped to accomplish this particular morning was speed control through intimidation while he slowly sipped his Wawa cof-fee. Two hours left in his shift, and then home for a nap and a walk in the woods with his golden retriever pups. All good.

Unless of course, there was a crash or a disabled vehicle, he thought. And sure enough, just a few minutes later, as the rush hour was coming to a close, the call came through. Three miles further west, a severe truck accident. Trooper needed on site.

Lee put his coffee in the cup holder, buckled up, switched on lights and siren, and began to navigate his way through the traffic. At least an accident investigation will make the time go faster, Lee mused, as he bullied his way up the road, using his fog horn to blow people over who were either ig-noring his siren or just being obstinate assholes.

By the time he arrived at the scene, several cars had pulled over. The drivers had exited their cars and trucks and were looking down into the valley that separated the road from the river beyond and then Manayunk, one of the many areas of the city that was being revitalized. Where just a few years ago there had been smoke-belching factories and low-income housing now stood upscale condominiums, shops, and offices that were taking advantage of a view of the river that was, after years of abuse, clean enough to swim in. In that same river valley, a bicycle path had been built that allowed week-end-warrior bike enthusiasts to travel long distances from the western suburbs into the city on an uninterrupted flat surface.

Lee didn't see the truck until he got out of his car and walked over to the crowd of people peering down the embankment. At the bottom of the steep hill was a white truck lying on its left side. It was demolished, its roof and sides thoroughly pushed in, suggesting that it had rolled down the hill several times before coming to rest. Once on the hill, Lee could hear a man screaming for help from the truck.

Lee knew that the dispatcher who called him would have already summoned an ambulance and fire crew. His priority was to get down to the truck to see if the driver and any passengers were hurt or worse, and if he could extract them safely and administer first aid. Lee knew that doing so was very dangerous. Cars and trucks in this situation may catch fire or just explode. But waiting was only going to increase the risk, and it was the job he had signed up for.

Lee went back to his car and pulled out the emergency pack. It had bandages and tourniquets, and a few vials of medicine that Lee had been taught to administer.

After warning the growing crowd to stay put, he slung the bag over his shoulder and started down. It took him a couple of minutes to reach the truck, gingerly navigating through the dirt and brush. And then there was the trash and garbage that had been thrown from cars by the good citizens of Philadelphia, known around the country for their littering prowess.

As he pushed himself through the weeds and approached the truck, he smelled gasoline and saw its trail as the fluid trickled down the hill below where the truck had come to rest. No fire yet, so Lee climbed up on the passenger side of the truck's cab and peered in. He saw one person who looked to be in his twenties in the driver's seat, awake and in terrible pain. "My legs," the man managed through gritted teeth. "I can't move them, man!"

Lee could see that his legs were pinned and probably crushed under the dashboard, which had been shoved downward as the cab's front end had collapsed. "Get me out, please," the man pleaded pitifully.

Lee pried opened the door and climbed partially across the seat for a better look. It was clear that he wasn't going to be able to get the man out by just pulling. He was going to need an extraction team that should have been summoned with the fire department.

"We'll get you out of here, buddy, I promise," Lee said with as much confidence as he could muster. "But I need to get some help to get your legs free."

"Hurry," the victim cried out in agony. "I don't want to die."

"You aren't going to die. You're going to be fine," Lee answered, having a hard time believing it himself.

Lee lowered himself off the truck and looked up the hill. By this time, the Philadelphia Police had arrived along with one ambulance. "Call Fire Rescue," He called up to the officers. "Tell them we need them here right away and to make sure they have extraction equipment. And we need a tank truck to throw some water on this baby, like right now."

Lee went to the back of the truck to get its license plate number and other identification. Non-descript, painted white with a Mack Truck insignia on the side and back. Straight job, probably on a local delivery, he thought. Important stuff, I guess. Everybody's in a hurry.

"The cavalry is on the way, buddy," Lee hollered into the truck cabin. "Hang on, and we'll get you out of there and on your way to the hospital in no time."

At this point, there was no response—just groaning. The

man was rapidly losing strength and was barely able to speak. In what turned out to be a pivotal decision in his life, Lee decided not to go back up on the truck and instead turned away and started to climb the hill. He was anxious to get the extraction team to the truck so they could get this poor guy out. He also wanted to make sure that witnesses were being interviewed by the other cops who were up on the hill. What had caused the accident and were other cars and people involved? Indeed, those inquiries were in progress, as Lee learned later.

The scene however was transformed when Lee was about half-way back up the hill. From his hospital bed, Lee would later remember hearing a hissing noise, very much like the noise fireworks make when they're first shot into the air, followed by a massive explosion that blew Wallingbird off his feet. Fortunately, Lee was far enough away from the scene to avoid severe injury aside from a minor concussion and a few superficial wounds from the shrapnel that had been launched into the air when the truck exploded.

The people who gathered on the hill were unharmed except for a few who were knocked off their feet and suffered temporary hearing loss. The injured were carted off by the ambulances that had assembled. The rest were encouraged to stick around to be interviewed by the police. Most stayed, but a few wandered off, not wishing to become involved. Other policemen shut down the highway, allowing the last few cars to file by the scene before constructing barriers at the preceding exit.

The ambulance crews ascertained that the truck driver was no longer the person who needed medical attention. Rather the main surviving victim was Lee who was taken on a stretcher up to a waiting ambulance and whisked away to the nearest trauma hospital, BFU.

To the chagrin of every commuter who regularly used the "Surekill" Expressway, the road was closed in both directions for several hours as investigators poured over the scene trying to figure out the identity of the victim and what had caused the accident.

The witnesses who were interviewed reported the Mack Company truck was clearly exceeding the speed limit but was not swerving or at all unstable before they heard a loud crack and the truck veered dramatically to the right. Despite the driver's apparently frantic efforts to steer the truck straight, it had sideswiped two cars before breaking through the right guard rail. Once through the barrier, the truck rolled down the hill, flipping over at least three times before coming to rest. The cars that had been struck were not severely damaged and the drivers unharmed. A few had called 911 on their cell phones. Lee Wallingbird had been the first responder.

As the morning wore on, the site investigation continued. It turned out that identifying the driver was not difficult, even though the explosion and fire had since destroyed the truck and wiped away any identifying information, and Lee Wallingbird was semi-conscious and in no position to answer important questions. It took only one call from the state police to the Mack Truck Company.

The supervisor at their office said that the only driver in the area of the accident that morning had been one of their new people. Today was his first day, making an early morning parts delivery to South Philly, and he should have been on his way back to Norristown.

"His name?" the supervisor repeated. "Wait a minute, I don't remember. I need to go get my clipboard. The guy goes by some kinda nickname. Hold on."

He put the phone down and returned just a few seconds later.

"I can't help you much, officer. Don't know da guy personally. I think he was a big deal football player in high school, but turned out to be kinda a loser, if ya know what I mean? Got dis job cause his father's in da car business and knows somebody, I think. At least that's what the guys in the shop said. What else can I tell yaz?"

"How about his name, buddy," the officer asked impatiently

"Oh, yeah, here you go. Sonny Cardinelli. But I think his real name is Stephen."

Chapter 19

The day that Philip and Dorothy had dreaded was finally upon them. After several sessions with Maggie, some of which Dick attended, they had finally decided not to take the adoption case to court.

"It will be tough on the kids," Maggie argued cogently during their last meeting. "And in the end, you're going to lose."

Maggie based her conclusions on a thorough investigation of Sonny and his family, in which Dick had assisted. Although he had run out on Connie and his children and traveled around the country visiting friends and raising hell, he had not been arrested and had no criminal record. In addition, every element he had promised at their initial meeting three weeks before had been accomplished, and in some cases exceeded. The girls were to be cared for by his mother when he worked. Sonny not only had a job driving a truck, but was able to secure a schedule that would keep him at home almost every night and weekend. The local parochial school was within walking distance of his parents' home, just as Sonny had stated, and everyone in the family who had been interviewed vowed to help out with childcare.

"The only thing we have is his prior abandonment of the

children and non-support. His story is emotional distress caused by his failed relationship with Connie. And now, even if he were to pull the ripcord again and take off, there is a pledged back-up, his family."

"What about allowing us to see the kids once in a while," Dorothy asked pitifully.

"There's no basis for that request, Dorothy. You have no standing. As far as the court is concerned, you have been roughly equivalent to a foster family. A place-holder. Kilcoyne will argue that visitation rights will be a distraction, potentially confusing and therefore harmful to the children."

"So now what?" Philip asked in exasperation.

"You're going to have to pack them up and deliver them to Kilcoyne's office. I managed to get them to agree to wait until Monday morning. You'll have another few days with them, but I can't hold them off much longer."

"And what about the BFU settlement money?" Philip asked.

"I don't know for sure. I don't have the amount. I've been told by the lawyers at BFU that the money, several million I suspect, will be earmarked for the girls and will be placed in a trust administered by their caregivers. That will now be Sonny and his family."

"And he can draw as much as he pleases?" Dorothy asked.

"I don't know that either. I can't believe that BFU cares enough about the children to try to restrict the family's access. They just want to write the check and get the hell out of the case. I do know that they've stipulated no disclosure and no admission of guilt. They want to keep this one out of the media as much as possible."

Silence in the room while Philip and Dorothy gathered their thoughts. "Do you have any more questions?" Maggie asked, trying to be as helpful and sympathetic as possible.

"I can't think of any," Dorothy answered, Philip sitting silently.

"I know this is going to be hard, but try to help the kids understand what is going on and be as supportive and as positive as you can. Whatever you do, don't let your negative feelings make it harder for them."

They nodded their agreement with tears in their eyes.

"See you on Monday at 10 AM," Maggie reminded them as they rose to leave.

"Yeah, can't wait," Philip answered, spitting out the words venomously.

Philip and Dorothy decided to take the rest of the week off to spend as much time as possible with the girls. They wanted to be distracted and they knew that visits to the zoo, kids' museums and playgrounds would help keep their minds off the inevitable. The weather cooperated, featuring beautiful sunny autumn days, gorgeous fall colors against the background of crystal blue skies. Philip was called in for an arrhythmia emergency on Thursday evening but managed to keep his absence relatively short.

Philip and Dorothy also agreed they weren't going to discuss the transfer until Sunday evening, but they would be certain to leave lots of time for the girls to ask questions. They determined they weren't going to close the door on the visitation issue. They would allow the girls to believe they would still be around, even though it would never happen. Hopefully, Emily and Erin would gradually forget about Philip and Dorothy as they were swept up into the Cardinelli clan. Maggie agreed to continue to pressure Kilcoyne and use whatever leverage she could to open the door to occasional weekend visits if Philip and Dorothy insisted. She wasn't optimistic.

Philip's demeanor over the weekend was once again transformed. He had a wonderful time with the kids, playing games, watching TV shows they liked, and playing with the dogs. Dorothy admired his ability to hide his anger and frustration from the children, something that was not so easy for her.

They weren't home to take Maggie's phone call on Sunday afternoon. Nor did Dorothy notice a message on her cell, which had been silenced and sunk to the bottom of her purse. Philip saw the message light on the answering machine when they arrived home from the playground but decided to ignore it while he and Dorothy started what they assumed would be the last dinner with their little family. They were making the girls' favorite dish, spaghetti with meatballs. Dorothy was sipping a glass of wine, preparing a salad while Philip sat at the counter, gulping a single-malt Scotch whiskey. The girls were playing video games, usually restricted to an hour a day but, to their delight, not today.

Philip rose and absent-mindedly went over to the answering machine and pushed the button while he poured a generous whiskey refill. "You have one new message," the disembodied voice advised. "First message: Philip and Dorothy, this is Maggie. I've been trying to reach you for the last two hours. I need to talk to you. Please call me on my cell. It's important."

Startled and worried, Dorothy hurriedly looked up the number, called, and put Maggie on speaker.

"Have you guys seen the news about a truck accident on the expressway on Friday?" Maggie asked. "A delivery truck broke through a guard rail, rolled down an embankment, and eventually caught on fire."

"I heard something on the radio news, KYW I think," Philip answered. "It closed the expressway down for a long time and created a traffic mess. But I didn't pay much attention. Why?"

"I got a call from Kilcoyne this afternoon. Apparently the body of the sole victim was burned beyond recognition, but the police were eventually able to identify the driver and notify his family. It was Sonny Cardinelli."

"What?" Dorothy exclaimed. "Sonny is dead?"

"Yup. Sounded pretty gruesome, too. Apparently he was

alive but trapped in the truck before it exploded a few minutes after the crash. There were a lot of witnesses who heard him screaming that his legs were crushed. The extraction people apparently didn't get there in time."

"Oh my God" is all that Dorothy could manage. She was so upset that she didn't notice that Philip registered little surprise or any emotion for that matter. He leaned on the wall on the other side of the phone, biting his lip.

"So I guess our custody transfer for tomorrow is off?" Philip asked coldly.

"Ah, yeah," Maggie said, somewhat surprised by Philip's initial reaction and his tone. "That's why I was anxious to get ahold of you."

"Permanently?" Philip continued.

"I don't know, Philip. It depends on what the rest of the family wants to do."

"You mean, any of those scumbags could still get custody?"

"Once again, Philip, it's not a particularly good idea to refer to the other side that way. It might slip out at a meeting. Since none of the siblings lifted a finger when Sonny was out of the picture and actively declined custody, they're going to have a hard time convincing a judge they're taking the kids for the right reason. The grandparents have some standing, but I don't think they want the kids. They aren't particularly young or healthy. I guess the money isn't important enough to them. We've been through all of this before, haven't we?"

"So we should be able to keep the children with us?"

"At least for the time being, until Kilcoyne straightens this out with Sonny's family and gets back to me. You can imagine that they're pretty upset right now and in no position to make a big decision about custody."

"Right," Dorothy cut in. "Understandable. So we just sit tight."

"Yes. Kilcoyne said something about a police investigation

of the accident. According to witnesses, the truck went out of control without any provocation. They said the driver appeared to be fighting to keep the truck on the road before it hit the guard rail."

"The police think there was foul play?" Dorothy asked.

"Don't know. Just saying, so you're aware. I doubt the two of you will hear anything about that part of the story."

Dorothy jerked around to look at Philip who at that moment had a quizzical smile on his face. "Yeah, no reason to talk to us," he said as Dorothy stared daggers.

They rang off, promising to keep in touch over the next few days as the situation hopefully became clearer.

"I'm dizzy," Dorothy said. "I can't believe what I just heard."

"Neither can I," Philip agreed.

"Really, Philip?"

"What do you mean by that, Dorothy?"

"Nothing. Forget it."

"No, come on, Dorothy. Tell me what you're thinking."

"I said forget it, Philip."

"You think I had something to do with this?"

"Should I?"

"Of course not. What kind of monster do you think I am?"

"That's enough. We're not going there. Let's get dinner on the table. The girls are hungry. We're done with this subject—for now."

Or so they thought. Or hoped. Or maybe Dorothy's stern reaction to Philip was because she knew it wasn't the end of the story. Maybe she knew that someone else would be thinking the same thoughts and having the same weird suspicions that were rattling around in her brain. And sure enough, the next morning the phone rang again with yet another surprise.

Philip was making coffee in the kitchen and Dorothy was getting ready for work, hoping that her cold shower would help shake out the cobwebs. What could have been a joyous evening, celebrating their reprieve, had instead been tension-filled. Few words had been exchanged over dinner. After the kids were tucked into their beds, Dorothy adjourned to her desk to work long past the time that Philip had fallen into oblivious sleep with Sunday Night Football blaring on the TV in their bedroom.

Dorothy's night was filled with nightmares about thieves breaking into her house and stealing her valuables while she stood by and watched without resistance. It was as if her fears of losing custody of the children had been loaded on her dream projector and, despite the latest news, had to be run on her brain's screen nonetheless, like the old horror movies she loved to watch.

Dorothy had toweled off and was brushing her teeth when she heard the phone ring twice. She assumed Philip had picked up. She couldn't make out what he said over the buzzing of her electric toothbrush, but the conversation was short and a few seconds later, Philip stood in the bathroom doorway.

"Remember Detective Scotty?"

"Yes, why? Was that him on the phone?" Dorothy asked, rinsing her mouth.

"Yup. He's in the neighborhood and wants to come over to ask us a few questions."

Dorothy stopped and looked at Philip in the mirror, mouth agape, toothpaste dripping down her chin.

"Whaaaa?" she gurgled.

Philip, stone-faced, turned and walked away. Hastily drying her mouth, Dorothy chased him down in the kitchen.

"Philip, what the hell is going on? And please spare me the bullshit."

"How the hell should I know?"

"Fuck you, Philip, and stop playing dumb. Maggie told us there was a police investigation. And the victim in the crash just so happened to be in a nasty legal dispute with us. And Scotty knows our, or should I say your background. That alone makes us look guilty. But what I really want to know is if you did something that gives Scotty a special reason to come over and pay us a visit."

"What do you want me to say? Sure I thought about killing the fucker. I bet you did too. But I didn't act on it. I don't know anything about the crash. I swear."

"If I'm having a tough time believing you, I can't wait to hear what Scotty has to say."

"He'll be here any minute so I guess we'll find out."

"You told him to come over now? It might have been a good idea to give ourselves a little time to figure out what to say."

"There's nothing to figure out. We just tell him the truth. We had nothing to do with Sonny's death."

Dorothy's protest was interrupted by the doorbell. "Holy shit," she said as she sprinted for her changing closet. "I need to throw on some clothes. Make sure the girls are settled— let them watch TV—and I'll be out in a minute. Keep your mouth shut until I get there."

Philip went to the door and greeted Scotty with a handshake.

"Detective, nice to see you. You look well."

Scotty smiled. To Philip, he looked exactly as he had the first time they had met after the Hamlin murder. Italian good looks, reasonably well dressed, trench coat over a conservative dark suit. Patterned tie, loose at the neck.

"As do you, Dr. Sarkis. It's nice to have you back in Philly."

"Nice to be here, Detective. The Poconos were fun for a while, but we like being back in civilization. Won't you come in?"

Philip led Scotty to the kitchen and motioned him to one of the chairs. "The girls are watching TV in the living room.

We can talk in here. Can I offer you a cup of coffee?"

"Sure. Cream and sugar would be great."

While Philip poured and arranged the sugar bowl and creamer, Scotty started in.

"I heard about your adventures in the mountains from Lieutenant Detweiler. Sounds like an evil bunch of nurses were doing some really bad things to patients?"

"That's what we heard. A real tragedy."

"And then I heard from a Detective Lentz in Boston about an attorney you knew who was knifed on Harvard Bridge. How did that work out?" Scotty continued, trying to sound like he really didn't know the answer.

"I didn't know the victim, Detective," Philip said, suspecting that Scotty knew the facts and was baiting him. "They arrested some black dude, as I recollect. Didn't find out if they convicted him or not."

"You seem to have an amazing tendency to be in the wrong place at the wrong time, Dr. Sarkis."

"Is that a crime, Detective?" Dorothy asked as she walked into the conversation.

Scotty jumped up and grabbed Dorothy's offered hand. "Certainly not, Ms. Deaver. Just remarking about the situations you and Dr. Sarkis seem to find yourselves in. I must say, you're looking as radiant as usual."

"You're too kind, Lieutenant. I'm afraid that my age is catching up with me. And stress is no help at all."

"And I hear you've had some of that recently."

"You mean the adoption?"

"I mean the revoked adoption," Scotty added, making sure Philip and Dorothy knew he had done his research. "That must have been quite painful for you both."

"Well, Detective…" Philip started, interrupted quickly by Dorothy.

"Let's just say it was very disappointing. But we were warned it might happen, especially since there was a biological father out there."

"Who, by report, said he didn't want the children. And then suddenly reappeared."

"Let's be honest, Detective. We knew that the malpractice settlement might entice him back to his children. And it did. It was all perfectly predictable," Dorothy said.

"You make it sound like it was all so atraumatic."

"It was difficult. But Dr. Sarkis and I have been through worse things. We would have managed."

"How nice that you didn't have to hand over the children. Do you expect to be able to keep the kids now that Mr. Cardinelli is out of the picture?"

"We don't know, Detective. It isn't something we had thought about or researched. Our attorney has some hope, but there are other family members, including grandparents, to deal with," Dorothy replied.

"I'm going to bet they'll be reluctant after they find out that their son may have been murdered."

"And you're basing that conclusion on what?" Dorothy asked pointedly.

"I'm not in a position to provide any details, of course. Let's just say that trucks don't usually fall down embankments for no reason."

"Maybe Mr. Cardinelli was speeding or fell asleep," Philip offered, risking another non-verbal rebuke from Dorothy.

"We have witnesses who passed him before his truck went out of control. They said he was going a little fast, but he had his window open and appeared wide awake, for what that is worth. Then they saw him begin to jerk his wheel like he was losing control of the truck. It just kept veering to the right until it broke through the guard rail and started rolling down the hill."

"Wow, Detective. That's a lot of detail from passing drivers. People usually fly on that road. I'm surprised they were able to give such a good account," Philip chimed in.

"Traffic was not moving that fast, I guess. I can only report what we were told by eye witnesses."

Dorothy decided to bring their conversation to a point. "You haven't told us why you are here, Detective."

"I'm sorry. I thought it was obvious. The man who was going to take away your adopted and suddenly rich children died in a mysterious truck accident. You have had the good fortune of having people you don't like or don't want around turn up dead in one way or another. My coming to see you could not possibly have been a surprise."

"I didn't want to imply we weren't pleased to see you after all of these years. You're always welcome," Dorothy said without conviction. "But unless you have some evidence linking us to that awful accident and Mr. Cardinelli's death, I don't think we need to go on much further."

Scotty looked down at his lap and smiled. "Ms. Deaver, as an experienced investigator yourself, you know that it takes time to piece together such a complicated case. I'm just starting to explore possibilities. You and Dr. Sarkis are the only people who might have been motivated to hurt or kill Sonny Cardinelli. I'm also starting here because you're close by, and I have pleasant memories of our conversations. You always have a perspective that is valuable to me, in one way or another."

"Thank you, Detective. But we have to start getting the kids ready for school. Lunches made, teeth brushed, papers in backpacks, you know the drill. You must have children at home."

"I do but they're much older, in high school, so they can get themselves ready in the morning—under protest, of course. They're teenagers, after all. But I do understand and apologize for getting in the way of your morning routine."

"No worries, Detective," Dorothy replied. "If you have any further questions, just let us know. We want to be helpful to your investigation."

"I'm appreciative, Ms. Deaver. I may take you up on that at some point. You guys have a terrific day."

Dorothy leaned casually on the kitchen counter as Scotty made his way out. The instant the door closed, she twirled and practically ran to the wall phone.

"Who are you calling?" Philip asked.

"Who do you think, Philip? The only person I trust who can find out what really happened to Sonny and keep us out of the fray."

Philip had but a second to contemplate the identity of Dorothy's savior before she said into the handset, "Hi, Dad. Got a minute?"

Chapter 20

Dorothy told her father on the phone that she wanted to pick his brain about a case, deliberately not telling him about Sonny's death or the adoption "reprieve" they had received. Dick was surprised that his daughter was thinking about a case at this most difficult time for Philip and her. When the phone rang, he had assumed she had called to cry on his shoulder about the girls' departure. In any case, he was always pleased to see or hear from his daughter, especially without her boyfriend. He missed the father-daughter time they had had after the untimely death of his wife many years ago. She was his only baby, and he adored her.

They decided to meet for lunch in Center City that day at noon. Dick suggested Vedge, a trendy spot in a part of the city called the gayborhood, so named because of the heavy concentration of gays and lesbians who inhabited the district. It also happened to be about halfway between their offices and an easy walk for each.

"Why a vegetarian place?" Dorothy asked when they met

on the doorstep of the restaurant. "This isn't your style, Dad."

"I have a lady friend who is a health nut. We wagered a hundred bucks that I couldn't abstain from meat for a week, and I plan to win."

"I should have figured there was some angle. She trusts you that much?"

"Yes, my dear. She thinks me an honest man. How about that?"

"That won't last long," Dorothy teased. "Especially after I get a chance to brief her."

Dick was a good guy, but a private detective had to bend the truth once in a while to gather necessary information for clients. And Dick was never averse to that. He knew almost everybody in Philly, including their hot buttons, and he was more than willing to push them whenever necessary.

Dick and Dorothy were greeted by a practically emaciated hostess and promptly seated near a window where they could look out on Locust Street. People watching was one of Dick's favorite past times. He fancied himself a surveyor of humankind and believed he could tell a lot about anybody just by the way they dressed and walked and talked. Dorothy laughed at that notion, informing her father he was merely stereotyping. Dick ignored her comments, pointing out proudly that special skills like those made him an effective private investigator.

As soon as the waiter took their drink order, and as they perused their menus, Dorothy started in. "Dad, I have some big news. We didn't turn the girls over to Sonny Cardinelli this morning."

"I suspected something happened. Why not?"

"He's dead."

"What? Sonny Cardinelli is dead? What the hell happened to him?"

Dorothy went on to explain what she knew of the circum-stances of Sonny's accident and their subsequent conversation with Maggie.

Dick was incredulous and agitated. "This is good but it is not good, Dorothy. I'm elated you have the girls, but the police are going to investigate Sonny's death thoroughly. Given the circumstances you described, they're going to suspect foul play."

"That's the next part of what I wanted to talk to you about. Remember Detective Scotty?"

"Sure, from the Romano case."

"He paid us a visit this morning."

"Shit. He's a smart guy, but that was fast, even for him. What did he have to say?"

"What you would have expected. He's pretty convinced that the accident wasn't an accident."

"You mean that the truck was tampered with?"

"Something like that. I don't think he has a handle on the whole thing yet, but he's snooping around aggressively."

"And your idiot boyfriend has to be a person of interest."

"Oh yeah. That's pretty clear. Dad, should I be worried?"

"I don't know, little girl. If it were anybody else but Philip, I would say no."

"Do you really think he was involved?"

Dick could see that his daughter needed reassurance.

"We have reasons to question his innocence in the other cases, but implicating him here is going to be tough. He would have had to figure out some way to rig a large truck so that it would go out of control at just the right time to do some damage. He's smart, but is he that smart?"

"Not really. He's an idiot when it comes to cars. He has no idea how to add washer fluid, let alone interfere with a steering mechanism. I guess he could have paid someone to do it for him."

"Here we go again. Trying to figure out what your wacko boyfriend did or didn't do."

"I agree he's difficult," Dorothy said, quickly sidestepping

215

the usual criticism. "Don't you think getting someone with the precise skill to rig the truck and kill Sonny would have been expensive?"

"Very."

"I know how much Philip makes, and his salary is a direct deposit."

"Is he doing a lot of work on the outside?"

"He'd like to, but he doesn't get many calls anymore."

"Then it's unlikely he squirreled away enough money to hire a hit man. I suggest you check your bank records to see if there were any large, recent withdrawals or significant payments made to anyone you don't know."

"I pay the bills and we don't keep a large balance in any of our accounts. Especially not with all of the girls' expenses. I'll look as you suggested, but assuming I don't find anything, what do you suggest I do next?"

"I have to find out what Scotty knows," Dick concluded.

"How are you going to do that? He isn't going to volunteer information."

"Of course he won't. But he's a careful cop so I'm sure he's filing reports as he proceeds with his investigation," Dick said, stroking his close-cropped gray beard.

"Those reports are filed on the police system. From what I know, they're essentially unhackable."

"Hacking would be tough, but there's always a way."

"Dad, how about if you don't tell me what you're going to do so I don't have to perjure myself when you end up in jail?"

"Look who's talking. You haven't been above procuring privileged information when you need it, if I remember correctly. You were a good student," Dick said, making reference to the years that Dorothy had worked in his private detective firm, where she acquired a unique set of skills that provided an advantage in her investigations.

"All right, I'll admit I've not been, shall we say, 'conventional' in my investigative approach. But police documents are special. You had better be careful."

"That I shall, my little girl. Now let's move on to more important items. Like my grandchildren. Photos, please."

They spent the rest of lunch on family matters, Dick reveling in news about his newly found and retained grandchildren. He couldn't believe his good luck. His priority now was to keep Philip and Dorothy clear of suspicion so they would have the best chance of holding onto Emily and Erin.

Dick stepped out of his lunch date with Dorothy briefly, during coffee, to call a certain woman at the Center City police district. Dick wanted to make sure Madeline Harvey would be available to meet with him soon. From the sound of her voice, Madeline was happy to hear from her old friend, even though she suspected an ulterior motive. And yes, a drink at the Ritz Carlton bar would be just the thing.

After lunch, Dick returned to his office and pushed papers around his desk until about 4:45 PM when he began his short walk to his favorite bar in Philly. The Ritz stood right next to City Hall, a renovated bank building that contained much of the architecture and furnishings that only a bank could have afforded in the Depression era when it was built.

Dick strolled into the main entrance, and said hello to the doormen who knew him well. The bar was tucked away to the left of the lobby, tastefully furnished with a few small tables scattered across from the ornate bar. On a bar stool sat Madeline Harvey, shapely legs crossed, sitting forward to show the bartender just the right amount of cleavage, already working on her first dirty martini.

Dick sidled up next to Madeline and whispered into her ear, "You have to be the sexiest cop in the world."

"Not a cop, big boy," Madeline oozed. "But sexy, I like."

"Let's not quibble," Dick answered, starting in on the bantering that had been such a normal and fun part of their relationship. "You work in a police station and keep order in the ranks."

"Nobody can do that, darlin'" Madeline answered, exaggerating her authentic Georgia drawl.

It was that Southern accent that had attracted Dick initially, and he had many pleasant memories of their tryst several years ago. He had met Madeline at another Center City bar shortly after Dorothy had departed for college, leaving him alone and vulnerable. Madeline was an immediate turn-on. She was anything but pretty, with rather coarse features and hair that went everywhere. But she had a dynamite body that Dick found irresistible. The sex had been white hot, and Dick literally couldn't get enough. It was Madeline who finally called a halt when it became clear that Dick had no intention of getting serious. Their abrupt parting had been friendly, each confessing what he/she needed in a relationship, finally realizing they weren't going to get it from the other person.

"Madeline, I don't know how you do it. You look terrific."

"Thanks, Dick. That's kind of you to say. You don't look so bad yourself. But you didn't call me up and offer to buy me a drink to tell me how good I look."

"How's your love life these days?" Dick persisted, trying to keep the conversation and small talk going before the grand request.

"Okay, I guess. I have a couple of suitors but I don't believe either one is going to make me an honest woman. How about you, Dick? You look like you've kept yourself in fightin' shape."

"Thanks, Madeline. I work out but it's tough to shave off the spare tire."

"So what can I do you for, Dick?" Madeline said, now very curious to hear Dick's reason for their meeting.

"I need your help with a case."

"Thought so. Just don't tell me you need inside information, Dick. You know how much I hate that."

"Nothin' super-sensitive, Maddy. Just a few facts that one

of your detectives should have in his report. It's almost public information."

"Which detective?" Madeline asked warily.

"Lou Scotty."

"And what case?"

"The Cardinelli truck accident."

"The disaster on the expressway last week? I didn't know they were investigating it as a murder."

"I don't think the investigation has escalated that far yet. But that's pretty much what I want to know. Can you help?" Dick asked, trying not to sound desperate.

"Let me get this straight. All you want is what Scotty has put in his reports about that one case to date?"

"That would be perfect. I just need a starting point."

"I have to admit it sounds pretty bland. And easy to access without a trace back to me. Let me take a look at what he has."

"Thanks, Maddy."

"I have to warn you Dick. Scotty is one of the worst record-keepers in the world. I don't know how much I'm going to find. I'll also do a little discreet asking around and see what the gossip is."

"That's more than I can ask for."

"If the stuff isn't super-sensitive, I'll run it off for you and put in your mailbox. You still at the Riverfront condo?"

"Yup. Why would I move? It's the perfect bachelor pad."

For sure, thought Madeline. Like a spider web for ladies.

"And if and when this blows up, you'll never divulge how you got the information, correct?"

"Lips are sealed."

"Too bad. That tongue of yours should be in the Guinness Book of World Records for endurance."

"It's still available for rent or lease."

"We aren't going back there, honey. As good as it was, I don't need the diversion."

"Understood. How about if I pay off with dinner. Anywhere in town, anytime."

"Deal. We'll talk about that once you have the material. Don't hate me if it isn't what you expect."

"Nothing on earth would make me hate you, Madeline. I should have married you when I had the chance."

"Listen, buster, I suggest you quit while you're ahead."

The bantering continued a while longer until they both tired of the venue and went their separate ways. Two days later, a few computer-printed pages appeared in an unmarked envelope in Dick's mailbox. Dick took the envelope with the rest of his mail to his flat, poured himself a drink, and began to read.

As Madeline summarized in her cover note, there wasn't much. What information there was, was pretty vanilla, and no one at the station knew much about it. Scotty had determined that the parts delivery vehicle had been serviced the day before the accident at the Mack Truck service facility itself. It had received a complete inspection, including the undercarriage and drive train. A senior mechanic had certified that everything was in working order before the truck left the shop. That night, it was parked on the Mack Truck property, protected by barbed wire and patrolled by a guard and a surly German shepherd. Early the next morning, the truck was loaded with truck parts to be taken to a distribution center in South Philadelphia.

Sonny waited at the factory until the forklift transferred the last skid, and off he went. The drop off had gone smoothly and no one at the distribution center had spoken with Sonny, who stood by and smoked cigarettes while the truck was unloaded. Scotty had convinced himself that no one could have tampered with the truck at any time after the inspection. The crash really was an accident, as best he could tell. The truck had been consumed by the explosion and fire, so no further evidence would be forthcoming. He planned to continue to investigate the case, but without a smoking gun, proving foul play was going to be difficult if not impossible.

Dick read through the report and called Dorothy. Dorothy initially seemed pleased to hear the good news. But by the end of the conversation, Dick detected doubt in her voice.

"You aren't ready to give up, are you, little girl?" Dick asked pointedly.

"I don't know, Dad. Are you?"

"Sort of. I guess I'm a little disappointed in Scotty. Maybe he's overworked, but I thought he might do a little more digging into the circumstances and the people involved. Maddy, my friend, said he's a terrible record-keeper. It's possible he knows or suspects a lot more than the skimpy notes we found."

"I agree."

"Let me think about this a little and get back to you."

"Okay, Dad. I appreciate your help. I guess I'll let it simmer for a few days too."

Always looking for an excuse to see Dorothy, Dick said, "We'll do lunch again next week and catch up then. What do you think?"

"Perfect," Dorothy answered, happy that her father had bought her line about letting the case go. Because there were a few things Dorothy wanted to do before throwing in the towel.

One of which was a computer search of the Santangelo and Cardinelli families, once again using the skills that Dorothy had learned when she worked in her father's private detective agency during her summer breaks from high school and college. She felt comfortable with surfing public information, occasionally diving deeper into datasets that were restricted but not terribly difficult to pierce.

That afternoon at work, Dorothy snagged her lunch sandwich from the firm's refrigerator, grabbed a bottled water to wash it down, closed her office door, and began her internet search. She was on a mission so by the time her sandwich was consumed, Dorothy was able to reconstruct most of the

Peter R. Kowey

family trees.

She was amazed at how similar the two families were with regard to lineage and development. Both Sonny and Connie were third-generation Italian, as pure bred as could be certified. All eight of their grandparents had immigrated to the United States from Italy in the early 1900s, and found their way to the Norristown area. Italians had gained a foothold there, and those who succeeded were generous with new immigrants, offering their cousins a temporary place to stay while they looked for work. They formed strong neighborhoods, usually centered around the local church. New Italians met and married, and, like the good Catholics they were, started large families. The kids attended the parish schools staffed by nuns who were paid nothing but knew how to keep order in a grade school classroom.

The Cardinellis were into cars and trucks, establishing several franchises in the Philly region. The Santangelos were more diversified, taking a variety of factory and manufacturing jobs to establish themselves and to provide for their families. In neither family had the second generation advanced. Many had to use Italian in the home and didn't speak English well. Few had pursued higher education and when they did, it was at most a community college degree.

Connie's father Frank was a prime example of the Santangelo clan. His working career, recapped in his obituary, read like a want ad for laborers. Dorothy scrolled though his employment list dismissively until one item caught her eye. In his early life, Frank Santangelo had been employed in the warehouse of a famous furniture store in South Philadelphia. He hadn't been there very long before moving on to a short-lived, family-owned business in Norristown. Nevertheless, Dorothy's heart skipped several beats as she absorbed the names of the owners of the South Philly establishment.

"Please, dear God in heaven," she exclaimed to a deity she didn't believe in. "Don't make me go back to that place and to those people again."

222

Chapter 21

Dorothy gathered herself and managed to get through her afternoon appointments despite being distracted by the prospects of yet another wonderful visit with the brothers Romano. After her secretary departed for the day, Dorothy closed her door and dialed a number she knew by heart, thinking: if someone told you ten years ago that you had memorized the phone number for a couple of Mafia members, you would have immediately declared them insane. But it had come to pass. The phone was ringing on the other end, and Dorothy couldn't decide if she wanted someone to answer or not.

She only had to wait for two rings. "Romano Brothers Appliances. How may I direct your call?"

Another step forward in the technological evolution of the Romano Brothers business. They now had a central switchboard with several extensions and a sweet- sounding receptionist.

"May I please be directed to Roe Wells?" Dorothy asked, hoping that her one connection with sanity still worked there.

"Why certainly. Let me check to see if she has left for the evening."

The muzak started. Something innocuous and inane at the same time. Lawrence Welk-like. Why don't they just get it over with and play the theme from the *The Godfather*?

Dorothy was saved after only a few verses of a Barry Manilow instrumental favorite. "Hello, Roe Wells here. How can I help you?"

"Roe, this is Dorothy Deaver. I'm not sure if you remember…"

"Of course I remember you, Dorothy. How are you?"

Dorothy stammered, somewhat surprised by Roe's ultra-friendly welcome.

"Uh… fine, I guess. Well, not really. I have a problem and need to talk to the Romanos again. Would that be difficult to arrange?"

"I don't believe so, Dorothy. The gentlemen think the world of you, and I'm sure they would love to see you again. Let me take a look at their calendar. Give me a minute. I just shut down my computer and have to log back on."

"I can call back…"

"Nonsense. It will just take a minute. How have you been, Dorothy? And how is Dr. Sarkis?"

"He's fine, Roe. Thanks for asking," Dorothy answered, wondering how she remembered Philip's name so easily. Was it because there had been recent contact, as she feared?

"Let me see. How about tomorrow afternoon, around 2 PM? The gentlemen are having lunch with the mayor, but they should be back by then. Does that work for you?"

Lunch with the mayor. How interesting, Dorothy thought. I'd love to hear that conversation.

"That would be perfect," Dorothy answered mechanically. Truth was any time would have worked for her. She needed to get to the truth as soon as possible, or go crazy with worry.

"And don't forget to arrive just a little bit early."Roe didn't need to explain why. Dorothy was already looking forward to the body search that Roe would conduct as the interesting prelude to her meeting with the gentlemen. The excuse was to exclude wires, but Dorothy suspected that the search was just as much for weapons. Senior Mafia members don't get to be senior without an abundance of caution.

"I will, Roe. Don't you worry," Dorothy answered, trying to keep the sarcasm out of her voice. No need to punish her; Roe was only doing her job, such as it was.

"See you tomorrow, Dorothy," Roe concluded as joyously as if she had just arranged a visit for Dorothy to pick out a wedding dress.

Once again, Dorothy was faced with the prospect of spending an evening with Philip when she was distracted by an impending visit with the Romanos. This time her suspicion didn't focus on Philip specifically. Sure, Philip could have alerted his old friends about Sonny Cardinelli and his evil plan. Maybe Philip knew about the Santangelo connection that Dorothy was going to inquire about. But if the Romanos felt an allegiance to the Santangelo family because of Frank's prior work at their warehouse, they could have stepped in to squash Sonny on their own, without speaking with Philip. They clearly had a wide circle of influence in the Delaware Valley and legions of informants. That didn't exclude the possibility that Philip had been complicit and facilitated the killing, which is what Dorothy wanted to exclude.

Fortunately, Philip arrived home late from the hospital, well after Dorothy and the girls had finished their dinner. A patient transferred from New Jersey had been very sick, and Philip had worked with the house staff to get the person stabilized and "plugged in."

Philip dragged himself in the front door, poured a Scotch over rocks, scarfed down some leftovers from the refrigerator, read a story for the girls, and headed for bed where he read the newspaper and quickly fell to sleep. Dorothy didn't have to worry about being tempted to quiz Philip about the Romanos. They barely spoke, and he was out cold before she even had a chance to brush her teeth.

Dorothy woke early with the girls the next morning, and

got them ready for daycare while Philip slept in. Dorothy had forgotten to ask him what time he was supposed to be up, and by the time he did rise, he was late for rounds at work. He whirled around the bedroom, skipped his shower, threw on some clothes, and headed for the door while he chirped at Dorothy.

"Sorry I didn't have a chance to take the hounds out this morning. I'll be home early for a doggie walk. And I'll pick up the girls at daycare on my way home, and then get dinner started. Send me an email later and let me know what you want me to cook and when you'll be home," he said over his shoulder as he vaulted out the door with a cup of coffee in one hand and car keys in the other.

To Dorothy's relief, she hadn't needed to pretend that everything was fine when her stomach was in a knot. And she didn't have to lie about her afternoon activities. All she had to do was get herself to work, distract herself with a few meetings and teleconferences, and then summon up the courage to visit the Romanos one more time to find out what they knew about Sonny Cardinelli's untimely death.

Dorothy left her office shortly after lunch, deciding to walk from her Center City building to the Romano's place of business on South Broad Street. It was another pleasant fall day, a few clouds limiting the sunshine, but low humidity and comfortable temperatures. Dorothy was able to shed her jacket about half-way there, enjoying the stress-reduction that a little vigorous walk provided. How easy it would be for people to feel better if they just exercised a little more, Dorothy thought. Me included.

It took Dorothy about forty-five minutes to reach the Romano establishment. Though it had only been a couple of years since she had been there, the transformation was striking. The Romanos had purchased and razed two large buildings that had flanked their store, and renovated, and expanded the storefront. They were now able to display dozens of appliance models of all kind, and for the first time, a full line of televisions.

Dorothy entered the showroom and was directed to the offices on the second floor. Whereas previously Roe had been joined by one other secretary, the large room now contained several clerks, some of whom were busy on the phone and the computer dealing with virtual customers. Clearly the electronic era had dawned at the Romano establishment.

The receptionist at the front desk asked Dorothy to wait a moment. She reappeared quickly, leading Dorothy past the counter, through a maze of cubicles to the waiting room in the back where Roe was seated.

"Dorothy, so nice to see you again," Roe gushed. "Come with me and let's get you situated."

Interesting choice of words, Dorothy thought. She wondered how many body searches Roe and her staff carried out in a day. No way was it pleasant, but somehow Roe kept up at least the appearance of job satisfaction.

The search was much more perfunctory than previously, perhaps because Dorothy had been vetted and not considered a threat. Roe was satisfied with a pat-down that was less intense than an airport screen, once again apologizing while making small talk to relieve Dorothy's anxiety.

Roe led Dorothy into a large conference room and asked her to wait. The brothers were on their way back from City Hall and would join her momentarily. The room was simply but nicely furnished. Generic pictures on the walls, and little that pertained to the business conducted there.

Dorothy's wait was short. Within five minutes, the Romano brothers entered, Vincente leading with his hand extended.

"Dorothy, how wonderful to see you," he said, wrapping her hand in both of his and holding on a little too long. "Giancarlo and I were just talking about you last week, wondering how you've been. And Dr. Sarkis."

"We've been fine, Vincente," Dorothy answered, wondering what incident had conjured up her name. "Very busy with our new family."

"New family?" Giancarlo asked, taking his turn at hand shaking and massaging.

"We adopted two little girls," Dorothy informed them, closely watching the brothers for any sign of prior knowledge.

"Really, Dorothy? How wonderful," Vincente exclaimed. "You two must be very happy. Come, let's sit down. Sorry about using the conference room. Our office is being renovated and it's a mess in there," Vincente explained. Dorothy refrained from asking if the mess included blood and brain fragments.

They selected chairs next to each other at the end of the conference table. After they were seated, Dorothy resumed her explanation. "We're okay now, but we had a bit of a bump in the road. The father of the girls had deserted them, and their mother who subsequently died. We assumed he was out of the picture. He insisted he didn't want anything to do with the children, but he suddenly reappeared several months after we took custody."

"And before the adoption was finalized, I bet," Giancarlo observed. "I remember when we adopted our two children. We were on pins and needles that first year. So he tried to take the girls back?"

"Yes," Dorothy answered, choosing not to bring up the fact that the murder of one of Giancarlo's children, John, had been the key to discovering Bonnie Romano's guilt in the Moira Hamlin case.

"What was his reason for returning after he had denied them?"

"That's where the story gets a little complicated."

Dorothy went on to detail the saga of Connie Santangelo,

focusing on her death and the legal case that had produced a windfall for the two girls.

"And that scoundrel wants the money," Vincente concluded before Dorothy had a chance.

"Right conclusion, wrong tense, Vincente. He wanted the money. That much was clear. But he died before he could collect."

"Died?" Giancarlo asked with amazement.

Either this guy is the world's best actor, or he really didn't know what happened, Dorothy thought. Watching the brothers carefully, Dorothy went on to explain the circumstances of Sonny's violent death on the expressway while the gentlemen listened with rapt attention. Dorothy was careful to leave out the part about the criminal investigation although she knew they would assume that the police were interested in the case.

"What about the rest of his family? Will they try for custody?"

"We doubt it. It appears that they don't want to be responsible for the girls' upbringing. I guess they aren't as desperate for the money as Sonny was, or maybe they don't want more kids to raise."

"So you and Philip are in the clear? That's wonderful, Dorothy. I'm sure you're both happy and relieved."

"An understatement, Giancarlo," Dorothy agreed. "Although nothing has been finalized yet."

A prolonged pause in the conversation before Vincente asked the obvious question.

"Dorothy, you didn't come here today just to deliver the good news about your new arrivals. They have Hallmark cards for that purpose, I'm sure."

Dorothy figured it was time to put everything on the table: "The police are concerned that the crash may not have been an accident."

"Do they have physical evidence to prove it wasn't?" Giancarlo asked a bit too quickly.

"I don't think so. The truck was burned to a crisp with the explosion. What concerns them most is the strong motive Philip and I had to kill Sonny."

"Understandable, I would say, given the circumstances and the timing. For all they know, you were interested in the money as well."

When Dorothy's head snapped up, Giancarlo added quickly, "Of course we know you aren't. It's just that the police..."

Vincente, the smoother of the two, took over. "But without some other evidence, they won't be able to go much further. I wouldn't worry too much, Ms. Deaver."

"I can't help it, Giancarlo. I need to know if this was just an accident or if somehow Sonny was killed and Philip had a hand in it."

"And you think we had Sonny killed, Dorothy?" Vincente asked.

"No, Vincente," Dorothy answered. "I don't know if anyone killed him."

"This situation sounds very familiar, doesn't it Dorothy? You've had concerns about Philip in the past and, as you'll recall, he was exonerated each time. However, this time, we really can't help you. We know absolutely nothing about Sonny, his miserable family, or the crash. In fact, I'm having a hard time figuring out why you're even here."

"In my research of Connie's family, I found something that made me want to talk to you."

"Really?"

"Did you know that Connie's father, Frank, worked in your warehouse when he was a young man?"

"Frank Santangelo. That's a pretty common name in these parts, Dorothy. And you must be talking at least thirty or forty years ago," Giancarlo said.

"I don't have any other details. All I know is that he was employed in the Romano appliance warehouse. It said he was partially responsible for setting up a program by which customers who became members of the Romano Club could shop directly at the warehouse and save money."

"Yes, that was our little brain child. I guess you can say it was the birth of wholesale shopping at outlets. We were careful to limit the appliance selection so our main store wouldn't be compromised. We set up that program. Frank Santangelo may have helped out, but it wasn't his creation. And we don't have any reason to be grateful to him."

Another pause in the conversation, both men clearly trying to decide what and how much they could tell her.

"Dorothy, would you mind if we stepped out of the room for a moment?" Vincente asked.

While she waited, Dorothy was left to imagine their conversation. "Shall we let her know that her idiot boyfriend is a cold-hearted killer, or should we keep lying to her so she's reassured?"

When they reentered, the gentlemen flanked Dorothy, each sitting forward and holding her gaze.

"Dorothy, once again I'll assure you that we had nothing to do with Sonny's death."

"Why should I believe you?"

"It's fairly simple, Dorothy. We hated Frank Santangelo. We wouldn't lift a finger to help anyone in his family."

"Why? What did he do to you?"

"When you read about Frank Santangelo, did you find any information about his employment after he left our place?"

"I believe he went on to work in a family-owned business in Norristown."

"Do you know what the business was?"

"No."

"Or what happened to it?"

"Can you please stop asking me questions I can't answer and tell me what happened to make you hate the Santangelo family?" Dorothy asked, unable to hide her uneasiness.

"It's not complicated, Dorothy. It's about stealing an idea. Frank Santangelo and his family decided to replicate the Romano warehouse in Norristown. Except they put all of their appliances up for sale and tried to compete with our store and warehouse on price. Not quality of service, of course, or customer loyalty. But they got a lot of attention up there and were very successful. For a while."

"We warned them, Dorothy," Vincente interjected. "When they promoted the place before it opened, we told them it wasn't a good idea. They went ahead anyway. We met with them several times, and strongly encouraged them not to undercut our prices. We offered to buy them out and turn their place into another Romano warehouse. Our offer was terribly generous. But they were reckless and greedy, and pushed even harder."

"So we had to do what we had to do," Giancarlo concluded.

"Which was...?" Dorothy asked in horror.

"There was a fire. Several alarms, as I recall. A real spectacle. The place burned to the ground very quickly. Ascribed to a faulty gas line. Can you imagine?"

"You burned their warehouse down?"

"Not us personally. It takes quite a bit of skill to set a fire like that and avoid an arson investigation."

Tell me about it, Dorothy thought, recollecting the Adolphus nursing agency blaze, so expertly arranged by the men sitting in front of her.

"The Santangelos must have been furious."

"They were, at first. They even foolishly threatened retaliation until a few visits to their homes by our colleagues convinced them to take the generous insurance settlement and look for something else to do."

"The end of Santanglo Appliance Warehouse," Vincente announced proudly. "And based on that precedent, we were able to convince others to stay out of the wholesale appliance business. It was over two decades before large chains started making inroads. By that time, we were well established with a loyal clientele so it didn't make much difference to us. 'Appliance' in this area is synonymous with Romano."

"We truly like you and Philip, Dorothy," Giancarlo went on. "And of course we would be open to helping you settle difficult family matters. But the very last thing we would ever do is help a Santangelo, especially by committing a crime."

Dorothy was staggered as she tried to take it all in. The Romanos were right. Their killing Sonny made no sense whatsoever. The rest of the conversation was mostly one word answers as the gentlemen made sure Dorothy understood their motives and why their involvement was simply not possible. When they were convinced she had processed all of the information and her questions were answered, they escorted her to the door and asked Roe to accompany her to the street.

"Remember, Dorothy, we are always there if you need us," Vincente said as Dorothy left. "And once again, congratulations on your splendid new family. Please give our very best regards to Philip as well. And remember, if you need an appliance of any kind, let us know. We'll be sure to give you the best deal in town."

Oh yeah, I'm sure you would, and a few bodies thrown in for free, Dorothy thought as she staggered down the steps to the street. She began to walk back to her office but was so distracted that she made multiple wrong turns before she finally gave up and hailed a cab.

As she sat in the back seat, Dorothy processed all she had heard. She couldn't decide if she should be happy to know that Philip and the Romanos had not collaborated on a murder, or concerned that she still didn't know if or how Sonny had been killed. The most important thing she had learned this difficult afternoon was that she needed to find a way forward to a happy family life with her girls... with or without Philip Sarkis.

Chapter 22

It was 9 AM on a cloudy and humid Philadelphia morning. Dick Deaver sat at his office desk, or more precisely leaned back in his plush desk chair with his Gucci-loafered feet up on his desk blotter. This was his best position for "cogitation," as he liked to call it. It was what he did when he needed time to reflect, and now he wanted to process all of the things he had learned about his daughter's recent adoption fiasco.

It wasn't that Dick was unhappy about the adoption. Far from it; he was ecstatic. He had fallen in love with Emily and Erin pretty much at first sight, and was enjoying getting to know them. Not only were they beautiful, with long, silky blonde hair and sparkling blue eyes, but Dick sensed they had good brains. Though they had lost their mother tragically, their good fortune was to have fallen into the competent hands of his daughter, who was going to be a wonderful parent. In moments of weakness, Dick even had to admit that Philip had fatherhood potential if he listened to Dorothy and did what he was told.

No, it wasn't the adoption that was maddening to Dick, but all of the stuff that had happened since Dorothy and Philip had assumed custody of the children. Most disturbing was the reappearance of Sonny Cardinelli, soon followed by his violent death. And then Scotty's appearance, which jarred his daughter into yet another tap dance with the dangerous Romano brothers. In fact, it was Dorothy's phone call the night before in which she related her South Broad Street experience that had kept him up most of the night and led to this morning's brainstorming. By including all of the gory details, like the Santangelo warehouse fire, she had ignited in her father a deep concern for her safety, which was the thing that made Dick the most anxious.

As extremely well timed as it was, could Sonny's death have been an accident, after all? Or was he the victim of foul play? And if it wasn't the Romanos who made the "arrangements," who did? And if Philip had concocted the idea, who helped him? As long as these questions hung out there, his daughter and maybe her bumbling boyfriend were in jeopardy. And that meant that his newly acquired gorgeous granddaughters could be taken away. That was not an alternative, by any stretch of the imagination. It simply wasn't going to happen.

Dick weighed his options carefully and finally decided to confer with the other person investigating the Cardinelli case. If Lou Scotty believed that Dorothy's father really wanted to find out what happened, maybe his suspicion of Dorothy and Philip would wane. Most importantly, Scotty might have information that could put Dick on the right track. If Scotty were willing to share it, of course. Dealing with Scotty was like handling a stick of dynamite that could blow up in Dick's face. After stroking his beard for almost an hour and weighing all of the alternatives, he concluded it had to be done.

Dick had his secretary put a call through to the precinct that housed Scotty's detective unit. Dick got lucky; Scotty was in and taking calls.

"Hello, Lou," Dick started. "This is Dick Deaver, Dorothy's father."

"Hi, Dick. I don't think we've ever met, have we?"

"I don't think we've even spoken directly, but I certainly know of your work. I've seen your name on a lot of cases I've investigated over the years."

"Like the Hamlin murders, for example."

Silence while Dick tried to recover. Scotty had elected to bring up the case that had nearly landed Philip and Dorothy in jail. He had to know it had shock value. Why jolt Dick at this point? Scotty had to have a theory he wanted to test somehow. Dick tried to sound casual.

"Yeah. Quite a case. Those poor people. Nobody deserves to die like that."

"Makes you think someone was really pissed about something they did, doesn't it?"

Can't go there, Dick thought. "Never gave it much thought, Detective."

"You're going to tell me you only know what you read in the papers, right?"

"Look Detective, I know my daughter's boyfriend had an apparent motive. Those people tried to crucify him, and I guess you can say they succeeded in many ways. But there was no way he could have drowned those people in a limo trunk. And as I recollect, his alibi was solid."

"That case is still open, Dick, so I can't really discuss what we know and don't know. I do tend to have a long memory, however, and people who do things like that frequently repeat. It may be a cold case, but it isn't forgotten."

Scotty had just voiced Dick's greatest fear: that another crime in which Philip was involved might drag his daughter back into the conversation about the Hamlin murder. It reinforced Dick's resolve to dig into the Cardinelli case deeper.

"Detective, would you mind if I came down to your office? I'd really like to pick your brain about the Cardinelli case."

"Sure, Dick. I understand you have some skin in that game too, so any light you can shed would be helpful to us. But please realize I can't share too many details with you since that incident is also under active investigation."

"I understand. I have some time later this morning."

"That would work. I'm just pushing papers around my desk most of the day, so come on down. Say about 11?"

Dick spent the next two hours summarizing in writing what he knew about the case, pecking at the word processor with two fingers. He had progressed to the point of knowing how to turn on his office computer and to open a Word document. More sophisticated software, like Excel spreadsheets, although ideally suited to tracking investigations, baffled him beyond belief. Simply not going to happen, Dick concluded.

Dick was relieved when 10:30 AM rolled around and it was time to actually do something. Scotty's precinct office was in North Philly, not far from the Temple campus, an area that Dick usually avoided. As Dick drove up Broad Street, he was surprised to see the area's rejuvenation, at least along Broad Street, where much of the university expansion had occurred. Despite this progress, Philly had a long way to go, Dick thought, still stuck with the highest percentage of people at the poverty level compared with other large metropolitan areas in the US, featuring large blighted areas scattered widely around the city.

The precinct sat in the middle of one such neighborhood, its parking lot surrounded by a high fence topped with barbed wire. The gate was open during business hours and Dick was able to find a visitor space. His 500 series BMW stuck out like a sore thumb among the squad cars and the late-model domestic SUVs and pick-up trucks favored by the police and staff who worked at the precinct.

Dick was greeted at the door by a gruff desk sergeant who directed him up two floors to the detectives' room. It was filled with desks, separated by flimsy partitions that did little to preserve privacy or sanity, for that matter. Dick eventually found his way to Scotty's desk, which, unlike any of those that flanked his, was as clean as a whistle. The few papers on the surface were neatly stacked in front of a few photos of Scotty's family. Scotty was outfitted in a white shirt, sleeves rolled up, with a red and blue striped tie that was loosened at the neck. Dark brown hair carefully combed with just a little bit of product, steel-rimmed glasses, a pleasant smile, showing good teeth. Good-looking guy overall, Dick thought. His mom would be proud.

Two small armchairs sat in front of Scotty's desk. After standing to greet Dick, Scotty invited him to take one of them and to make himself comfortable.

"The coffee's pretty overcooked this time of day, Dick, but I would be happy to get you a cup or something else to drink if you'd like."

"I'm just fine, Detective. By the way, do you mind if I call you Lou?"

"I guess we're kind of in the same business, Dick, so please do."

Dick didn't waste any time with small talk. "Lou, I know you're busy so let me get to the point. I don't want to get in the way of your investigation. My only interest in the Cardinelli case is that I don't want to lose my new granddaughters."

Scotty listened stone-faced, not betraying what he was thinking, expecting Dick to continue.

"You have kids," Dick went on, "and I hope your parents are still around. You know how important grandchildren are. I want to do everything I possibly can to make sure Dorothy and Philip keep those kids, including reassuring you, adoption officials, and everyone else that they had nothing to do with Sonny's death."

Dick sensed he had hit the correct chord because Scotty's expression gradually changed. His features softened with just a hint of a smile. "Family is everything, Dick. I get it. I wish

I could tell you that we've resolved this case and that we know it wasn't a crime. The truth is, I really don't know what happened."

"Nothing you got from the crash site helped you?"

"Let me show you the photos." Scotty swung his chair around, opened the bottom drawer of one of his cabinets, and pulled out a file. On top was a set of photographs taken at the crime scene, featuring what was left of Sonny's truck, taken from several angles.

"Take a look at these, Dick, and tell me if the crime scene people had a chance of figuring out what happened."

Dick flicked through the photos, realizing immediately that it was futile. "Christ, the truck was burned to a crisp."

"As was Sonny. We're as certain as we can be that the explosion was caused by a gas line leak after the crash. If this was a hit, whoever did it was pretty certain that Sonny would be killed simply by losing control of the truck. The fire couldn't have been predicted."

"If you believe that, the accident had to be exactly at the right place and at the right time."

"Otherwise, you would have to say it was the play of chance."

"Bad luck," Dick surmised.

"Or good luck. I guess it depends on how you look at it."

"It's hard to believe that a killer would accept a high probability that the crash would be less than fatal."

"Agree. Because if the truck had not been incinerated, we might have been able to figure out how it had been rigged, which could then have led us to the perp."

"Was the truck old or in bad shape?" Dick asked.

"It was about ten years old and had about 400,000 miles on it."

"When was the last time it was serviced?"

"It had routine service two days before the crash. They put a lot of miles on those trucks, so they get a lube and oil change every month or so."

"Anything else you can tell me, Lou?"

"Not really, Dick."

"What about Sonny? Anything else going on in his private life that might shed some light."

"He apparently had a wild time while he was traveling around the country. He didn't stay anywhere very long, but we haven't come up with anything unusual. Just a bunch of bars, a string of whores, and a lot of gambling houses visited with friends and then left behind."

"So you know of no one who might have been motivated to hurt him?"

"I can't get into specifics, Dick, but we've done the usual interviews, and no one we talked to appeared to be pissed off enough to fry the guy. We have a few more people left on the interview list, but unless something new pops up soon, we may end up concluding this was just another dumb accident."

"I hear you, Lou. I really appreciate your willingness to talk to me."

"I hope you get to keep your grandchildren, Dick. I really do. But I have to finish my investigation, and if anything points to Philip or Dorothy, I'm going to pursue it--hard. Right now, honestly, I got nothing."

As he left the precinct, Dick couldn't decide if he should be worried or reassured after Scotty's last admonition. But he did know he was going to have to keep on digging until he satisfied himself that Dorothy was in the clear.

Dick was preoccupied during his drive back to his office with something Scotty had said. He remembered being disturbed but couldn't put his finger on it. He replayed his conversation in his head over and over before it finally hit him as he was pulling into his office garage. It had to do with planning the accident! Dick needed to talk to someone who knew a lot more than he did about vehicle crashes.

Dick parked, waited impatiently for the elevator, and rushed past his secretary's desk, anxious to pull his previous case files. As he recollected, he had consulted a crash expert during a case he had investigated ten or so years ago. He needed a name and phone number and a little luck that Ray Petri was still around.

Since Dick didn't know the name of the case, it took him almost an hour to find the file. It was a case in which a car mechanic got the hots for a cute young cocktail waitress he met in a Fishtown bar. He convinced himself she was the woman with whom he wanted to spend the rest of his life. The only problem was that he was married to a seriously violent woman who had already been arrested several times for husband abuse. She had informed the man that he was stuck with her, and any attempt to leave or divorce her would be met with a beating from which he would never recover.

The poor schmuck serviced his own cars in the small unattached garage in the back of their row home property, so once he got the idea, it was easy to rig his wife's car brakes. He claimed later, after he was caught, that he was only trying to put a scare into her so she would let him go. Unfortunately for him, when his wife lost control of the car, she was on a steep incline and had not buckled her seat belt. Police who investigated said she had set a new record for distance covered by an adult body in the air after crashing through a windshield on impact. Worse, she had not been killed but severed her spinal cord, rendering her a quadriplegic. The police refused to consider that the car had been rigged, even though the victim's family screamed bloody murder. The irate family hired Dick to investigate the case. Dick took their concerns seriously and brought in Ray Petri.

Ray worked for large automakers and had spent his career designing cars and trucks. He was extremely talented but too outspoken to rise in the corporate ranks. When he finally tired of the politics and of living in Detroit, he took his pension and returned to his native Alabama and became a consultant. To his pleasant surprise, he became instantly busy. Seems that investigating accidents had become a cottage industry, with a considerable dearth of talent in most constabularies.

Dick had been impressed with Ray's common sense approach to the investigation, and with his sense of humor. Ray hadn't charged a ransom for his work, as he easily could. In only a matter of days, he was able to convince the police that the car's brakes had been tampered with. Once they pursued the husband, his motive was easy to unearth.

Dick had been pleased to refer fellow investigators to Ray, but it had been years since they had spoken. Dick retrieved the Alabama phone number, called, and got a mechanical and anonymous voice mail greeting. Was it Ray? How to know? Dick left a message and had to wait only about fifteen minutes before his call was returned. His secretary put the call through, and Dick recognized the voice and the southern drawl immediately.

"Hey, Dick. How y'all doin'?"

"Ray, great to hear your voice. It's been a long time."

"That it has, pardner. How's your family? Everybody okay up there in Philly town?"

For a moment, Dick thought about telling Ray the backstory as to why he was interested in this particular truck accident but then thought better of it. There was no reason to, and he wanted to avoid biasing Ray. He needed a clean answer to a distinct hypothetical.

"We're all good, Ray. Thanks for asking. How about yourself?"

"The little woman died last year of cancer. She suffered a lot—tough to get through. And I do miss her. Been tryin' to keep busy with consultin' to fill the hours."

"I know what you mean, Ray." And Dick did, having lost the love of his life years ago when Dorothy was a toddler. "But there are lots of fish in the sea. I'm sure you'll be back in the game soon."

"Maybe so. Anyway, you didn't call to find out about my personal life. What can I do you for, Dick?"

"Ray, I'm investigating a case in which a truck went through a guardrail on the Schuylkill Expressway about a week ago. People who saw it happen claimed that the driver was awake and working to get control but couldn't."

"What happened to the driver? Did he buy it?"

"Yup. Not right away. When a state trooper arrived, the guy was alive and awake but pinned. Before the extraction crew could get there, the truck exploded and burned like crazy. Nothing much left to analyze."

"What kind of truck was it?"

"Mack, R model. About ten years old."

"Tractor-trailer, I assume," Ray said.

"No. It was a custom-made straight job that the local Mack dealership used to haul heavy-duty truck parts."

"Let me get this straight," Ray said, his southern drawl suddenly much less pronounced as he got into more serious stuff. "This guy is driving along, minding his own business. Sober, right?"

"We think so. The accident occurred about 9 in the morning. And he hadn't been bar hopping."

"Anyhow, this guy is driving along pretty fast?"

"A little above the speed limit, as best we can tell."

"And his truck goes out of control, crashes down an embankment, and is down there for at least a few minutes before it explodes, frying him up in the process."

"Right. Now what I need to know is if someone could have rigged that truck so it would crash."

"Hell yes," Ray answered quickly.

"Is it difficult?"

"Hell no. Any moron could weaken any part of the steering mechanism so it would fail. You could set it up by sawing halfway through the part you wanted to break and then waiting for the inevitable."

"Could somebody set the thing up so the truck would crash at a specific time and place?"

"Setting it up so it would happen at exactly the time you want the dang thing to go haywire? It could be done, I guess, but that would be a remarkable accomplishment."

"Impossible, Ray?"

"I didn't say that, but it gets more interesting, Dick. If someone were to severely damage the truck to get immediate gratification, it would be fairly easy to detect. You would be able to see what part was tampered with, and it wouldn't take a genius investigator like me to figure out who done it."

"So the fire after the crash was essential to covering up the crime?"

"You could say that, and it had to be one hell of a hot fire to melt everything enough to keep a smart person from finding clues."

"So you think foul play is a possibility…"

"Just not particularly likely with all of the stuff that would need to be done correctly. Unless…"

"Unless?"

"Unless you can find someone with a lot of expertise who also happened to be highly motivated to fry your victim while he was still alive. Pretty grizzly, huh?"

"For sure," Dick agreed.

"Hope this was helpful, Dick. I have fond memories of working on cases with you."

"As do I, Ray. This was extremely helpful. I'll stay in touch with you as we proceed on this end. And let me know where to send the check for your time today."

"Hell no, Dick. This was nothin'. And you've steered plenty of business my way. I'm grateful, so this one is on the house."

Dick thanked Ray and they rang off. Though Dick was still mystified about the cause of the crash and the intent, the conversations with Lou Scotty and Ray Petri helped him draw a remarkably straight line to the next step in the investigation, which was a visit to the Mack Truck franchise where Sonny had worked, and where the ill-fated truck had been serviced just a day before the crash.

Chapter 23

Like Kleenex, Mack Truck was a brand name that had become part of the American lexicon.

"He hits ya like a Mack Truck," was a phrase sports announcers were known to use to impress their audience with just how hard a tackle on a football field or a punch in the ring had been. Mack trucks were known for their toughness, symbolized by the iconic bulldog that graced the hoods of their early model tractors and decorated the keychain of not a few proud truckers. Through the latter part of the twentieth century, Mack had been the pre-eminent manufacturer of large trucks intended to pull loads of anything that could be transported on wheels. Franchises proliferated in the United States, and just about any entrepreneur who could come up with the millions required was successful in obtaining a marketing license. Manufacturing plants had a difficult time keeping pace with demand as haulers eagerly scarfed up the new models. Mack was an American success story that politicians embraced and profiled as a shining example of American enterprise and ingenuity.

But as with any successful enterprise, complacency set in. Mack didn't pursue technological improvements as quickly as the burgeoning competition, and before long, European and Asian companies, following on their amazing automobile manufacturing success, began to eat into the Mack-dominated truck market. And the unions didn't help. Whereas their emergence years ago had protected the workers against unfair labor practices, now their unreasonable wage and benefit demands escalated costs, rendering the company even more susceptible to foreign competition. Mack sales declined in the US, and they were unable to sustain any kind of global market. The company retracted and franchises closed. Eventual implementation of new ideas and stubborn brand loyalty by some truck buyers kept the company from folding, but the magic of Mack was no more.

One of the franchises that did survive was Norristown Mack. Tony Palmucci, a successful small businessman, purchased the franchise from a Quaker family in the 1960s and moved it from the small lot on which it had been established in the remote western edge of Norristown to Ridge Pike, in the eastern sector. He had correctly anticipated the establishment and development of a long corridor along which several car and truck dealerships would operate. By the beginning of the 1980s, "dealer's row" included franchises for just about every domestic and foreign car and truck dealership, including the Japanese new kids on the block, Datsun and Honda.

Norristown Mack was a thriving business, and unlike several other franchises, maintained itself for several years based on customer loyalty that Tony and his family encouraged and counted on. Just about every hauler in the region had a fleet of Mack Trucks, and they scoffed at the idea of buying "Jap" or "Kraut" manufactured brands. Through personal relationships, clever advertising, and personal "inducements," Tony was able to sustain his business when many other dealerships were wilting.

"It's all about the personal touch," Tony would tell his son-in-law Milt every chance he found. And if that meant free rounds of golf at Plymouth Country Club, comped dinners with spouses at the Blue Bell Inn, or front-row tickets to see Franki Valli in Atlantic City, Tony was all in. And his beautiful wife Rita was more than happy to co-host, adding her considerable charm to any occasion.

A large part of Norristown's business was truck parts. Many of Tony's customers still operated old Mack models that held up exceedingly well over the years. Given the need for frequent service for high-mileage trucks and their distance from a Mack facility, many of Tony's clients had established their own service departments and hired mechanics who were trained to fix the beasts. To do so, they needed replacement parts in high volume, which Tony was happy to supply. In the recent past, the parts business had eclipsed new truck sales as did in-house servicing, the other cash cow for the franchise.

To keep pace with the demand, Tony had outfitted four trade-in trucks as heavy-duty parts carriers. In addition to a fleet of vans that hustled small parts all over the region, these larger trucks delivered engine and drive train material. It was one such truck that Sonny had been driving the day he was killed.

In his usual methodical way, Dick spent a few days gathering information about Norristown Mack's history and operating practices. Or to be more precise, he commissioned Al Kenworthy, one of his staff, to do it for him. In addition to being a sound investigator, Al was a busybody who liked to gossip, and he had many sources who fed him prime material. He also had a crush on Dorothy that Dick had used in the past to entice Al to garner extra information or to work overtime. On this occasion, Dick decided to omit details about why he needed the report, or any mention of his daughter.

Dick now sat at his desk, feet up once again, flicking through the ten-page, meticulous report Al had generated. As instructed, Al had used whatever source documents he could find on the internet or in the public record before resorting to several secure local informants who knew the Palmucci family well. As usual, the report was filled with details that Al had managed to glean without ever having to contact or disturb the principals.

Al painted a picture of an organization that had been held together with a large dose of micromanagement. Dick paid particular attention to the chain of command. Tony ran the organization with an iron fist, with few others empowered to make any decisions of consequence. He was also a family man. The only individuals who had ascended in the organization to executive level had been members of his family. His son, Len, had died in his twenties in a tragic car accident. Daughter Linda had been Tony's administrative assistant until he realized her only talent was attracting men, one of whom, Milt Belrose, had a reasonably good business mind and a malleable personality.

Milt was a junior college graduate who came to work at Norristown Mack part-time when he was a student. He was a good-looking guy who finally screwed up the courage to ask Linda out for a date. Tony liked Milt from the get-go and encouraged him to pursue Linda. She finally agreed to marry Milt as much out of family loyalty as for love. Though neither was particularly satisfied with "home cooking," their extramarital exploits were carried out discreetly enough to prevent filial erosion. They dutifully produced two less than notable kids, secure in the knowledge that as long as they stayed together, produced grandchildren, and kept their dalliances private, Milt's future in the company was secure.

Currently, Milt Belrose was listed as the general manager of the franchise, reporting directly to Tony. Judging from the corporate reports Al had managed to find, Milt had day-to-day responsibility for the parts and service departments while Tony continued to supervise new truck sales. Old habits die hard, Dick thought to himself. Sales had been the foundation of the franchise for years. It was what Tony was undoubtedly familiar with, so that is where Tony spent his time, no matter the relative size of the revenue streams.

The report was also valuable to Dick because he now had a clear idea of how to focus his investigation. Al Kenworthy recommended an initial interview with Milt Belrose as the person most likely to provide details about the service and parts department, the areas of greatest interest to Dick, who had to hope that Milt was as much of a detail man as his father-in-law wanted him to be. Meeting with Milt in person and getting the lay of the land was a particularly good idea, Kenworthy advised, and Dick agreed.

Dick also decided that obfuscation was not necessary. No need to disguise his identity or to make up any stories about his investigation. He placed a call to Milt's office and asked to speak with him. "May I tell him who is calling?" Milt's polite secretary asked.

"My name is Dick Deaver."

"And is this a business matter, Mr. Deaver?"

"Yes and no. Tell Mr. Belrose that I have questions about a former employee. We're investigating his accidental death."

"You must mean Mr. Cardinelli. We're so sorry for his family."

Dick noticed that the secretary didn't mention that Sonny was a "nice person" or "great guy," the usual drivel that people spewed when somebody, anybody, died young and unexpectedly. Was this on purpose? Or was he reading too much into her reply?

"Yes, a terrible tragedy," Dick said with as much pretended conviction as he could muster.

"Hold on a minute, Mr. Deaver, and I'll page Mr. Belrose. I know he's in the building somewhere."

Dick was treated to an amateurish Norristown Mack commercial while he waited. A shrill female voice extolled the company's wonderful record of service and reputation for high-quality merchandise. Precisely who had conferred these accolades was conveniently unstated. No matter, Dick mused. Messages such as these rarely register. Just another addition to the barrage of advertising all of us are subjected to on a regular basis. He did notice that the person reading the lines eventually identified herself as Linda Belrose. Nepotism or personal touch? Whatever the reason, the woman could clearly benefit from some voice lessons.

His cynical pondering was interrupted by the secretary. "Here he is, Mr. Deaver. Go ahead, Milt... I mean, Mr. Belrose."

Dick smiled. First-name slip. Was the secretary one of Milt's diversions? No time to process. "Hi, how can I help you?"

"Mr. Belrose, I'm a private investigator looking into Mr. Cardinelli's death."

"Yeah, I heard there were some questions about the accident...whether it *was* an accident."

"Exactly."

"I already spoke to the police, Detective Scotty."

"Yes, I chatted with him as well," Dick said.

"Then you know I couldn't help him much."

"I understand. I just have a few more questions. Would it be okay if I came to your office to talk? I won't take long, I promise."

Silence while Milt processed. "You said you were a private investigator. Who hired you to look into this case?"

"I'm afraid I can't disclose that information on the phone. However, I can assure you that you and your company are not in any trouble whatsoever. At least not at this point. The police have been willing to conclude that the crash was accidental, and I'm inclined to agree. I'm simply trying to close the loop for the comfort of the people who hired me."

"His family?"

Dick had gotten the response he expected. He figured that

Milt would assume that Sonny's family was behind his investigation. "Mr. Belrose, I really can't divulge the name of my client at this point."

"All right. I see no harm in a visit. Come over this afternoon, say around 3 PM. I have another meeting at 4 so please be prompt."

"I will, Mr. Belrose. And thanks."

Dick spent the rest of the morning reviewing other files. "I have to make some money once in a while," Dick muttered to himself as he prepared to read reports that had been stacked on his desk by his staff. "Can't spend my whole life bailing out my daughter and that stupid boyfriend of hers."

But now with the beautiful Emily and Erin in jeopardy, the stakes were much higher. He hoped that the interview with Belrose would dismiss the possibility of criminal intent so Philip and Dorothy could maintain custody, and they would all live happily ever after. "No pressure, Deaver," he said to himself as he drove west to Norristown Mack for the pivotal interview.

The ride out to the suburbs was torture. Unscheduled construction on the Schuylkill Expressway had traffic down to a crawl westbound. Dick had to call Milt's office to let them know he would be a little late. Fortunately, his GPS showed him an alternate route that got him to his destination only ten minutes behind schedule.

Dick had little time to survey the neighborhood. Retail suburbs at their best, with car and truck franchises lining the four-lane road interspersed with business offices, small factories and America's best examples of fast-food dining. Boring, Dick the Center City snob thought. Couldn't live out here.

Norristown Mack sat in the middle of it all. The property was dominated by a large fenced-in yard where dozens of recently delivered and non-configured trucks were parked, waiting for preparation and delivery to the thriving businesses in the area that still used the brand. The main building was divided into offices, the parts department, and a large service garage. There were only a few cars in the visitor lot next to the offices where Dick pulled in. The employee lot was rather full, dominated by SUVs and light trucks owned by the mostly men who worked there.

Dick was greeted by a receptionist who escorted him back to Milt's office. Cute little number with a wiggle Dick didn't fail to notice and enjoy. Nothing fancy, facility wise. Not even the owner's quarters that Dick managed to peek into as he was whisked by.

Milt rose from behind his desk to greet Dick with a handshake as he entered. "Mr. Deaver, nice to meet you," Milt opened. "Please have a seat."

"Thanks for seeing me," Dick answered as he took a chair in front of Milt's rather cluttered desk, which included an ashtray full of cigarette butts. "I won't take up much of your time. As I said on the phone, my clients just want to get closure. They were disappointed with the police reports, as you can imagine."

"I guess we all were," Milt agreed. "Do you have a reason to believe that somebody wanted to hurt Sonny?"

"Mr. Belrose, I'm going to have to confide in you, and I hope that whatever we discuss will be kept confidential."

"Sure, Mr. Deaver. I have no reason to be indiscreet."

Dick believed him. There was something about Milt that inspired trust. Maybe the clear blue eyes and friendly face? He decided to parcel out some of the facts, being careful to omit his own personal interest and relationships.

"I'm not here on behalf of Sonny's family. I represent two people who have been brought under suspicion because they were attempting to adopt two children who had lost their mother and been abandoned by Mr. Cardinelli. He came back into the picture to reclaim the children when it was rumored that they were about to be awarded a large settlement in their mother's wrongful death case. Sonny's death naturally led the police to my clients. I'm trying to ascertain, before the police do, if there is a way they could possibly be implicated."

"Wow. That all sounds terribly complicated," Belrose said. "I think I understand, but I have to tell you that we've already assured Detective Scotty that the truck that was involved in the accident had just been serviced and was in perfect running condition, according to the mechanic who did the work. And I have no reason to doubt him. The truck appeared to be working fine when Sonny took it off the lot that morning."

"Yes, of course. And who was the mechanic?" Dick asked.

"It was Jimmy Chamberlain, our assistant shop foreman."

"And how long has he worked here?" Dick asked.

"I'd say close to thirty years. Started here right out of high school. He worked in our parts department for a long time before transitioning over to service. Worked his way up to assistant shop foreman. He could have been the foreman if he wanted the job, but he's been satisfied with second place."

"So there was nothing unusual about the assistant shop foreman doing routine maintenance on a parts hauler."

"Not in Jimmy's case. He likes to work on the trucks in addition to helping out with the administrative stuff."

"Anything else you can tell me about Chamberlain?"

"He isn't married, lives alone, and keeps to himself mostly. Comes by himself to our social functions, but rarely attends. I understand he plays a lot of golf and is pretty good. He's a dependable worker. I don't think the guy has missed a day of work in thirty years."

"And he was the person who worked on Sonny's truck before the accident."

"Yes, we confirmed that when Scotty was here."

"Did Scotty talk to Chamberlain?"

"Sure did," Milt answered quickly.

"And were you present at this interview?"

"No. Scotty asked to speak with him and a couple of other people in the shop privately."

"Did Lou have anything to say after the interview with Chamberlain?"

"He came to my office, thanked me, and told me everything was okay. He said he would get back to me if he needed anything more from us, but he doubted it."

"Would it be all right with you if I talked to Chamberlain as well?" Dick asked as offhandedly as he could.

"That's up to Jimmy. He's off today so you're going to have to call him at home. I'll give you his number."

"Thanks."

"I would ask that you not talk to him at work. Sonny's death was a blow to him as it was to everyone here. I think Jimmy is even more upset because of the possibility he made a mistake when he serviced the truck and that caused the accident. I don't want him embarrassed further in front of the people who work with and for him. Fair enough?"

Dick was impressed with Milt's consideration for his workers. It was a style he himself used that helped him retain good employees.

"Fair enough, Mr. Belrose."

"Is there anything else I can do for you Mr. Deaver?"

"What do you know about Sonny Cardinelli?"

"He had just started with us, so I didn't know him well. Seemed like a friendly kid. I'm sure you know his father asked us to take him on. He drove cars a lot but was new to trucks. The model he was driving that morning wasn't complicated, though. He should have been able to handle it."

Dick nodded and rose from his chair. "I've taken enough of your time, Mr. Belrose."

"I want to get this matter cleared up. This business is my life, Mr. Deaver. I've worked here since I was a Kenrick student and then took a full-time job when I graduated from junior college. I've invested a lot in building our reputation, which I think you'll find is quite good. People like our trucks for their dependability and safety. Something like this is a blow to us, and we want to keep it from ever happening again."

"I understand. I'll be careful not to do anything that needlessly impugns your company. I suspect that when we're all done, it will just be an accident we can't explain and people will forget."

"I hope so, Mr. Deaver," Milt said as he came around his desk. "Let me walk you out to your car. I could use a little air."

They made small talk as they passed through the reception area and walked through the front doors to Dick's car.

"So did I hear you say you went to Kenrick?" Dick asked.

"Yes, graduated in the early eighties. It was a decent place, but I realized I didn't like school so much and knew I didn't want to go to a four-year college. I met the boss's daughter, and we fell in love and got married. I guess you can say the job was part of the dowry."

"My daughter's significant other went to Kenrick about that time," Dick mused. "Guy by the name of Philip Sarkis. Did you know him?"

"Phil!" Milt smiled. "Sure, I knew him. Didn't hang out with him much at school. We ran in different crowds. But he worked here in the parts department one summer, so we got to know each other. Seemed like a reasonable guy, but very quiet. Smart as hell, of course."

Dick was surprised to hear his daughter's boyfriend referred to as "Phil." Philip hated it when people shortened his name. It must have been another era in his life when he wasn't so damn self-important.

"I thought he spent his summers helping his father with the fruit business," Dick continued.

"He did, but this one summer he wanted a second part-time job. He said he needed the extra money for college or something like that. Anyhow, he didn't last long. He quit pretty abruptly after a month or so. Tony was pissed off because it left him short-handed."

"Do you know why he left?"

"Haven't a clue. I don't think it had anything to do with the job. In fact, he seemed happy with the work. He used to hang out with some of the guys after his shift and played golf with a couple of them."

"Was Jimmy Chamberlain working in the parts department back then?" Dick asked, now much more engaged in the previously idle conversation.

"I think so. Must have been. You can ask him if he worked with Phil when you speak to him. He might remember."

"I'll do that, Mr. Belrose," Dick said as he opened his car door. "You can depend on it."

Chapter 24

True to his word, Milt emailed Dick after their meeting and forwarded Jimmy Chamberlain's phone number and address. Milt took the opportunity to emphasize that he wanted to cooperate with the investigation but as far as he was concerned, and according to the last word from the police, Sonny's death had been an accident. Dick understood that Belrose wanted to get past the event, to limit the damage the accident might do to his company's reputation. And without the knowledge as to how enormously Philip and Dorothy had benefitted from Sonny's crash, it was easy for anybody to simply brush off the coincidence. But Dick had learned over his many years of investigating cases that coincidences were rare, and concluding any such thing out of hand was hazardous. He had to push on, and talking to Jimmy Chamberlain was the logical and essential next step.

How best to approach Chamberlain? Dick thought about an introductory phone call, but that would give Chamberlain time to fabricate a story. Better to just show up and start asking questions. Dick decided on the frontal strategy, preceded as usual by an Al Kenworthy exploration of Jimmy Chamberlain's life.

Al's dossier was thin indeed. Jimmy had to be one of the most boring persons in the history of the planet. Graduated from high school, where he devoted most of his time to vocational tech. He loved cars since he was a kid and always wanted to be a mechanic. Took a job at a car dealership after graduation and then at Norristown Mack a few years later. Started in the parts department but moved on to truck service, just as Milt had described. Been there ever since. Seemed reasonably happy at work, was respected by his peers, but didn't hang out with the guys as much as others.

Chamberlain's private life was even more nondescript. He lived alone in a two-bedroom townhouse apartment in Plymouth Meeting. Never married, no kids, one sibling who lived in Montana, parents dead. Played a lot of golf with a couple of friends at local public courses and was an avid reader. Collected baseball cards as a hobby. Didn't venture out much except to a movie once in a while, but usually alone. Neighbors hardly knew him, but a brief surveillance confirmed that he was a homebody for sure. The only curveball was a report from a Dick-mandated five-day stake-out that Jimmy's apartment had been visited on consecutive evenings by a well-dressed middle aged man who appeared to enter without knocking. A license plate check identified the man as Bernie McBride, another single man who lived in neighboring Blue Bell and worked as a floor manager at a department store in the Plymouth Meeting Mall. As of midnight, when the surveillance ended, Bernie had not departed Jimmy's townhouse.

Dick decided to knock on Jimmy's door early one evening after work. Jimmy would have had a chance to have his dinner and unwind. Tired people tend to make mental mistakes and volunteer information they might suppress when more alert. A minor advantage but why not use it, Dick thought as he pulled into the parking lot of the Green Briar Estates apartment complex. Nice place, but hardly "estate" level, Dick mused. He quickly found Jimmy's door and rang the bell.

As the door swung open, Jimmy said laughingly, "Did you forget your key?"

When he saw Dick, his expression changed in a blink from pleased to surprised to wary. "I'm terribly sorry. I thought you were someone else. Can I help you?" Jimmy asked, trying to recover.

"That's perfectly okay, Mr. Chamberlain. My name is Dick Deaver. I'm a private investigator hired to look into the Sonny Cardinelli truck accident. Would you mind if I asked you a few questions?"

"I already spoke with the police. I have nothing more to say."

"I understand. I just have a few questions and won't take much of your time. Do you mind if I come in?"

Chamberlain hesitated and then swung the door open and gestured for Dick to enter. Dick sized up his prey. A tall, almost gangly man, clean-shaven, with thinning gray-brown hair and piercing brown eyes. The kind of person you would pass on the street and never notice.

Jimmy led Dick to the living room. "Sit wherever you like Mr. Deaver. Can I offer you a beverage?"

Dick quickly surveyed the apartment as he followed Jimmy to the sofa. Unremarkable in every respect. Clean, boring furniture, a few bargain-basement paintings on the walls, old-style TV set into a hutch that had a few random knick-knacks on its dusty shelves. The only distinguishing furnishing was a putting green stretched out in the dining room area with several golf balls congregated around what was supposed to be a cup.

"No thanks, Mr. Chamberlain," Dick replied. "And you can call me Dick if you like."

"Well, then, it's Jimmy. Would you mind if I made a brief phone call before we start?" Jimmy asked nervously.

"No, please. I'm in no hurry."

Jimmy headed for his bedroom and closed the door behind him. Dick tip-toed over to see if he could hear Jimmy's half of the conversation, which he did in fragments. It was fairly easy to understand that Jimmy was asking someone to delay his arrival at Jimmy's apartment. He declined to give details, but was able to convince whoever was scheduled to join him later and that he wouldn't be long.

As Jimmy hung up, Dick quickly returned to the sofa and tried to look as bored as possible. Emerging from the bedroom, Jimmy apologized for the interruption. "So what do you want to know, Mr. Deaver?"

"I understand that you serviced the truck that Sonny was driving when he had his accident?"

"Yes, I guess it was a day or so before."

"Right. First of all, do you remember anything unusual about the truck or your service?"

"Nothing at all. Just a routine oil change, lube job, and general inspection."

"I was a little surprised that the assistant shop manager would assign himself to such a mundane job. Is that a common occurrence?"

Chamberlain smiled. "I love working on trucks, Dick. The routine stuff is actually fun for me. I do those tasks all the time. It's also good for the guys to see that the bosses don't mind getting their hands dirty once in a while."

"I agree with that, Jimmy. I have the same philosophy at my agency. Keeps morale high. Just hard to find the time. I assume you went over the truck pretty closely?"

"Yup. I put it up on the lift and got underneath and examined the truck carefully. It's my routine."

"So if there had been anything wrong with the truck to cause the accident, you would have seen it."

"Within reason. Trucks are machines and they break down sometimes without warning. There wasn't anything obvious, but who knows if one of the critical parts failed?"

"I understand. Just trying to be complete. Where did you service the truck?"

"What do you mean? In our shop."

"Was it in any particular part of the shop? Were other people around when you were working?"

"I really don't remember exactly which bay I used. I was working alone as usual, but guys walk by all the time. It's a pretty open environment."

"I remember that you worked on the truck late in the afternoon."

"I think you're right about that. I frequently help my guys mop up work that hasn't been completed through the day so they don't have to stay overtime."

"So you hadn't planned to work on that particular truck?"

"I don't remember if it was on my list. We share the work pretty casually. Like I said, it's all about getting everything done on time."

"What time do most of the mechanics clock out?"

"I'd say around 5 PM. But we do have a few who come in and leave late."

"So there would have been fewer people walking by, as you called it, at that time of day?"

"I guess so. What are you suggesting, Dick?"

"Nothing, Jimmy. I'm just trying to understand the circumstances and how the shop works."

"Bullshit, Dick," Jimmy said, suddenly energized. "You're implying that I tampered with that truck and you're trying to figure out if I could have done it without anybody seeing me."

"You got me, Jimmy," Dick finally admitted. "That's exactly what I need to know."

"Why do you think I would have done that, Dick? What possible motive could I have had?"

"That leads to my second line of questions, Jimmy. How well did you know Sonny?"

"I only met him a few days before he died."

"Did you know he had two kids?"

"I heard that, and his wife had died."

"And that he had abandoned them several months before?"

"No, I didn't know that."

"And then came back to reclaim the children when it was clear they were going to receive an enormous amount of money in their mother's wrongful death lawsuit?"

"No."

"Detective Scotty didn't ask you about any of that?"

"The only questions he asked had to do with the servicing. He seemed satisfied that there was nothing wrong with the truck."

Dick was incredulous. Scotty seemed like a sharp investigator. Not probing Jimmy Chamberlain further seemed like an unlikely error. If Jimmy was lying, he would have to know how easy it would be for Dick to find out. No time to explore that issue right now. Dick pushed on.

"The reason I'm here is that my clients were in the process of adopting Sonny's kids when he reappeared. His unexpected return put them in jeopardy of losing the children. Understand?"

"Which gave them a reason to kill him?"

"I guess you could say that."

"I don't understand how that bit of information brought you to me," Chamberlain said.

"What if I told you that one of my clients is Dr. Philip Sarkis," Dick said, watching Chamberlain carefully.

"Phil, the guy who worked in our parts department?" Jimmy countered, seeming truly surprised.

"Yeah, that guy."

"I haven't seen Phil in years."

"He didn't contact you to tell you about his problem with Sonny?"

"No."

"Are you sure, Jimmy?"

"I think I would remember that conversation."

"Tell me about your relationship with Phil... Dr. Sarkis."

"I heard he went to medical school. What kind of doctor is he?"

"Cardiologist."

Chamberlain smiled. "Glad he made it. He was a pretty motivated guy, as I recollect."

"Again, can you explain your friendship with him?"

"We hung out. Phil and I both liked to play golf. Went out to play nine after work a couple of times."

"And then what?"

"What do you mean?"

"You know, dinner after golf?"

"We might have had a shake and a burger afterward. I don't remember. That was a long time ago."

"Did it ever go any further than a sandwich?"

"I'm sorry, Dick, but this conversation is beginning to make me very uncomfortable."

That's the point, buddy, Dick thought. "Fair enough, Jimmy. Why don't you tell me about Bernie McBride?"

Jimmy finally flinched. Dick could see the wheels turning. Deny Bernie or lie about his relationship?

"Bernie is a golf friend."

"Like Phil?"

"Sort of. I've known Bernie for a long time."

"How did you two meet? What does Bernie do for a living?"

"What does this have to do with Sonny's accident?"

"Why don't you answer the questions?"

"Because I suspect you already know the answers."

"I do. It wasn't hard to find out. And it didn't take me long to find out what Bernie did in the Army either. Pretty interesting set of skills your friend has, Jimmy."

Dick now had Jimmy's full attention. Time for shock treatment.

"Jimmy, are you gay?"

Jimmy's facial expression answered the question. "We're done, Dick. I would appreciate it if you would leave my home."

"I don't think that clamming up is a good idea, Jimmy. Let me explain why. I'm trying to get to the truth of what happened to Sonny. The other person who is also somewhat curious about this case is Detective Scotty. It's only a matter of time until Scotty stumbles onto what I already know about you and Philip Sarkis, and he'll ask the same questions about your relationship. And about Bernie. If you level with me and we get this straightened out now, I'll be able to help deflect Scotty and maybe keep you and your significant other out of harm's way. If you throw me out, you'll be on your own. So if you want my help, answer my questions truthfully. I'll ask you again, are you homosexual?"

Chamberlain looked down at his feet as he contemplated his options.

"I think you know the answer to that question as well, but tell me why my sexual preference has any bearing on this case, Dick."

"Good point," Dick admitted. "Perhaps I need to ask a much more specific question. Did you have a homosexual relationship with Philip Sarkis?"

"No," Chamberlain answered emphatically. "It wasn't like that."

"Were you attracted to him sexually?"

"That's a hard question to answer, Dick. I liked Phil, but he was just a kid and I would never have taken advantage of him. I'm not a child molester."

"So there was never any physical contact between you?"

"Never."

"Just two guys playing golf and hanging out?"

"Yes, I swear."

"Why did Philip leave Norristown Mack that summer?"

"I remember he was feeling stressed. He was putting in a lot of hours at his family's business. I suspect he was overwhelmed."

"It had nothing to do with your relationship with him?"

"I can't imagine why. He never told me he was upset and never acted that way."

"Were you having relationships with other men when you knew Philip?"

"Nothing sustained. I was very much in the closet back then. I guess you can say I still am, in many ways. Anyhow, I went up to New York on weekends and would pick up men at gay bars once in a while. I had a couple of bad experiences and had to stop."

"Did anyone at Norristown know about your homosexual activity?"

"I doubt it, but I'm sure people have been suspicious through the years. As I said, I used to be terrified of being outed, but I don't worry about it as much anymore. People are a lot more accepting. That's not to say I'm ready to make a declaration, so I would be deeply appreciative if you wouldn't share our conversation with anyone."

"Absolutely, Jimmy. I know how devastating that can be. So you're certain that Philip had no way of knowing about your sexual preferences."

"I never brought it up."

"Even after a few holes of golf?"

"Never. As I said, there was too much at stake, and Phil was just a kid."

"Jimmy, I know this is painful, and I'm sorry to probe your personal life. You can't afford to have the police use your relationship with Philip as an explanation as to why you may have set Sonny up to die."

"I understand, and I appreciate your help. I've told you the truth. I haven't talked to Phil for years. I do have fond memories of the time we had together, but it was purely a golf thing. Like I said, he was my friend, and I would never have come on to him. Phil never showed any interest in me, and if he had, I would have put him in his place."

Jimmy stopped and waited for Dick to respond. But Dick just stared at Jimmy, trying hard to decide if he thought the poor guy was on the level.

"You have to believe me, Dick."

"I do, Jimmy. The question is what Detective Scotty will believe."

"What can I do to help myself?"

"If Scotty comes back, just tell him the truth, no matter how painful. Exactly like you did with me. There is no crime in being gay. Lying to keep the world from knowing is only going to make you look guilty."

"Thanks for the advice, Dick."

"Now let me get out of here so you can have some time with Bernie."

"Was I that obvious?"

"Figuring out what's going on is my business, Jimmy."

Dick shook hands with Jimmy as he departed and gave him his card and instructions to call him if he heard from Scotty or if anything else occurred to him about Philip and his time at Norristown Mack that might be useful.

Dick sat in his car for a few minutes before starting the engine and processed what he had learned. Philip had never given any indication that he liked men, but lots of people had dalliances when they were young without enduring effects on their sexuality. He wasn't about to condemn Philip for it, but this was an important point in the development of motive. Imposing on an old golfing buddy to rig a truck to kill somebody was not as plausible as calling on a former lover to do the dirty work.

At this point, it really didn't matter. Dick wasn't going to take the facts he had discovered any further unless Scotty pursued the case, and Dick had no way of knowing how likely that was. Scotty had already interviewed Chamberlain and hadn't made the connection to Philip. Was that sloppiness or was he holding on to it to surprise Jimmy and Philip later?

What to do next? As much as he would have loved to have her perspective, he certainly wasn't going to bring any of what he knew to Dorothy. But Dick needed to have one more difficult conversation before he tucked this one away for good. A heart-to-heart with Philip was going to be necessary. He had to explore the Chamberlain relationship, and, even more importantly, he had to make sure his daughter's idiot boyfriend would know how to react if and when Scotty confronted him with a past he would certainly wish to deny.

Chapter 25

In absolutely no way was Dick looking forward to his confrontation with Philip. To say that they hadn't hit if off was a colossal understatement. Dick did have enough insight to know that a large part of his negative feelings about Philip stemmed from his resentment. How could any other man dare to establish a relationship with his daughter? After his wife had died, Dick made an active decision to dedicate the rest of his life to Dorothy. She was his obsession for years, and to Dick's delight, Dorothy had not shown an active interest in men until well into her twenties. She dated occasionally though college and law school, but she was focused on her career and had little time for anything else. Until Philip. From the way Dorothy looked at Philip, Dick knew, from the first time he had seen them together, that this was a different kind of relationship for his daughter.

And their relationship endured despite several bumps in the road that Dick had been convinced would cool their passion. Serious events that had placed both of them in jeopardy and under suspicion. They had even managed to pull Dick into the muck, always with his best intentions of aiding his daughter, and each time he was forced to bond more firmly with the "son he never had." Ironically, after each crisis,

Philip and Dorothy had not only mended their rifts but seemed to become closer. And now, in the ultimate escalation, they acquired two precious little girls who had stolen Dick's heart and would make it impossible for him to "let nature take its course." He knew he was hopelessly entangled in the new family and was going to have to work hard to protect them.

Dick decided that he needed to catch Philip off guard and without any chance that Dorothy would be present. He decided on an easy ruse. Philip had referred Dick to a senior urologist for urinary symptoms. The first test had been a PSA that was elevated, raising a red flag that Dick might have prostate cancer. After several weeks of trying to decide what to do, Dick had finally assented to a prostate biopsy. Philip had been opposed, arguing that chasing elevated PSAs had never been proven to save anyone's life and that the strategy was built on faulty scientific data at best. Dick didn't care. He wanted to know if he had cancer, the disease that had killed his beautiful wife.

Fortunately, the prostate tissue samples had not contained cancer, which made the procedure-induced infection and profuse bleeding tolerable. Dick was now compelled to schedule regular appointments for rectal examinations that he dreaded and more infernal lab tests to track the possibility of disease missed with the random biopsies. Since Dick had to come to Temple for these visits, it would be relatively easy to suggest to Philip that they meet at the medical center cafeteria for a quick man-lunch. He had to bank on the fact that Philip was not keeping track and wouldn't remember that Dick's actual next visit was still weeks away.

They exchanged text messages and decided to meet in the hospital lobby at 1 PM. Dick arrived first and a few minutes later saw Philip breaking off from his team of residents and students on their way to a scheduled teaching conference. Philip looked the part of a doctor, right down to the slightly wrinkled long white lab coat, natty bow tie, graying temples, and closely cropped beard. He smiled when he saw Dick, looking like he was authentically happy to see Dorothy's father. Was it possible that the arrival of children had finally straightened Philip out? Were Dick's suspicions unfounded after all? Was he making a mistake in confronting Philip about Sonny's accident? Was he about to destroy the goodwill he had finally built up with his daughter?

No, Dick told himself, this is too damn important to sweep away. Maybe I can convince Philip to tell me the truth so we can work together to keep him out of jail and at home to take care of Dick's daughter and new grandchildren.

They shook hands and small-talked as they descended the flight of stairs leading into the monstrous room that functioned as the main eating place for the medical center. Philip briefed Dick on the latest cutest things Emily and Erin had done at home. The girls were adapting to their new home faster than anyone had imagined, including the adoption counselor who visited their home regularly.

After picking up a tray and utensils, they were confronted with the need to choose among the various food courts. Philip headed for the salads, Dick for the deli counter. They made their selections and timed their arrival at the cash register perfectly. Philip insisted on paying for lunch, reminding Dick that he had a faculty value card he rarely used since he usually brought lunch from home. Dick politely acquiesced and preceded Philip into the maze of tables, finally settling on a two-top next to a floor-to-ceiling window. Not much of a view, Dick thought, gazing out at a small, partially landscaped courtyard bordered by another part of the gigantic building complex that was the medical center's main inpatient facility.

"This place just keeps getting bigger," Dick observed as Philip took off his lab coat and draped it over the back of his chair.

"It does. And nobody seems to know where the money is

coming from. The hospital loses revenue every year, but they just keep on hiring and building."

"Our tax dollars at work."

"Yeah, the state does pump a lot of dough into this place."

"It has to," Dick replied. "Without Temple, the people who live in North Philly wouldn't have health care. And that's a lot of folks with some pretty bad diseases."

"I can't help thinking the bubble will burst someday soon," Philip said as he poured copious amounts of ranch dressing onto his salad. "But that's not my headache right now. What is, is taking care of a lot of people who have diseases that could either be prevented or kept under control if they had decent primary care doctors. These poor people can't get in to see doctors unless they're really sick, which is why they end up in the ER half dead."

"Tough job. Is this something you always wanted to do, Philip?"

Philip was stunned. In all the years he had known Dick, this was the first time he could ever remember that Dick had shown any curiosity about his career ambitions or early life. His first thought was that Dick was manipulating the conversation for his own purpose, but there was no harm in playing along.

"As long as I can remember. My parents encouraged me, of course, but they really didn't understand much about education let alone what a medical career would entail."

"And I guess they didn't have a lot of resources."

"That's an understatement."

"You worked a lot of jobs, I suspect, to earn money for school."

"I had scholarships for the tuition part, but I had to work summers and part-time to have enough for room and board and books."

"You helped out with the family business, right?"

"Which paid me exactly nothing. I had to go out to get

other jobs to actually produce money."

"What kind of jobs did you have?"

Philip wasn't sure if it was that specific question or the barrage of inquiries from a usually aloof Dick that finally alerted him to the game. "Geez, Dick, you seem to be awfully curious about my early life. Why the sudden interest?"

Dick had to quickly decide if he wanted to continue the game or just come clean. He looked at Philip and tried in that instant to see what his daughter saw. An earnest doctor who had been unwittingly pulled into cases not perpetrated by him, sucked in by his naiveté? Or, as Dick feared, a conniving, vindictive maniac who took revenge on anyone stupid enough to commit a crime that offended his sensibility or threatened his family? Dick realized in that moment that it didn't matter. What was driving his questions now had little to do with Philip and more with his own primal instinct to protect his daughter and his new family. It was time to be direct.

"Philip, I've been a private detective for a long time. I know a lot about my job, but even more importantly, I've learned a good deal about people. For example, I know that you're a fanatical family person, so it was pretty obvious that you had a strong motivation to stop Sonny Cardinelli from taking Emily and Erin away."

Dick watched carefully; Philip didn't flinch. He just kept shoveling salad into his mouth, occasionally looking up with a stone face.

"Whenever someone has such a strong motivation, a good investigator has to dig a little deeper to determine if that person, no matter who, could have been involved."

Continued silence. Philip's expression hadn't changed nor had he offered a response.

"Philip, I talked to some people at the Mack dealership where the truck was serviced. I didn't know you had worked there when you were in college."

A nod.

"Detective Scotty also made the connection."

"So what?"

"It isn't just the fact that you worked there, Philip. What I also learned, and to my surprise what Scotty apparently doesn't know yet, is that you had a relationship with the guy who serviced Sonny's truck."

"And who might that be?" Philip asked, still looking bored with the conversation.

"You don't know Philip?"

"No, I have no idea," Philip said with apparent sincerity.

"Jimmy Chamberlain."

"Jimmy Chamberlain, eh? And precisely what do you mean by 'relationship'?"

"I don't know, exactly. Which is why I'm asking you."

"What did Jimmy say?"

"He told me you were golfing buddies."

"Sounds about right."

"Did it go further than that?"

Finally, a reaction. "What the hell is that supposed to mean, Dick?"

"Did you know that Jimmy is gay?"

"Answer a question with a question. Brilliant. Interrogation 101. Dick, stop trying to manipulate this conversation and tell me where this is going."

"Come on, Philip. Do I have to paint a picture for you? Let's say Jimmy Chamberlain liked you…a lot. Maybe he's had feelings for you all these years. So when he finds out that your dream of having children with Dorothy is about to get derailed, he steps in to help out."

"And how does old Jimmy find out about my need to get rid of Sonny?" Philip asked, finally engaged.

"That's what I need to know, Philip. And why we're having this lunch."

"That you set up with a phony visit to your urologist."

"Forgive me my duplicity, Philip. Right now, I'm doing exactly what you would have done: trying to protect my family."

"Really? How does that work?"

"I need to know if you went to Jimmy and asked him to kill Sonny for you."

"And because we played a few rounds of golf together when I was in my teens, you seriously think Jimmy would attempt murder at my behest?"

"No, that wouldn't hold water. Jimmy would never have gone out on that limb for a casual friend."

"But he would for..."

"A lover, maybe?"

"So, in order to prove that Jimmy killed Sonny, you want me to cop to the idea that I was Jimmy's boyfriend?"

"Philip, everybody knows that kids experiment. And that it doesn't mean they're homosexual. But I do need to know what kind of relationship you had with Jimmy."

"No, you don't, Dick. All you need to do is ask me if I had anything to do with Sonny's death, directly or indirectly. And the answer is a resounding no."

"You didn't contact Jimmy at any time about Sonny and your adoption problem."

"Absolutely not. I haven't seen or talked to Jimmy for years. I didn't even know he still lived in the area."

"Do you know a person named Bernie McBride?"

"Who the hell is he?"

"A close friend of Jimmy Chamberlain. I believe he might have had some special skills that were relevant to this case."

"What kind of skills?" Philip asked, suddenly more interested.

"I don't want to go into that now. Just tell me if you know who he is."

"No, I never heard of him. I don't hang out with guys who like guys, Dick."

Dick didn't answer, using a big bite of his sandwich as a chance to process what he had heard and decide how much more to push Philip, who was obviously getting more agitated.

"So, in addition to being a faggot, you figured this Bernie guy helped Jimmy kill Sonny, is that right?" Philip continued.

"No, Philip. I'm just trying to piece things together."

"With me as the central puzzle piece. Did you have this mental image of the three of us partying together naked or something? You must think I'm a pervert."

Dick shook his head. "No, Philip. That is not an image I have. This conversation is not about your sexuality. It is about your relationship with a man who had access to a truck that malfunctioned in a bizarre way and led to the death of a bad man who was threatening your family. Why can't you understand that?"

"Dick, this conversation is not going anywhere. I have and will continue to deny that I contacted Jimmy Chamberlain or anyone else about our problem with Sonny. You're going to have to believe me."

"It isn't me who has to believe you. It's the police. If Scotty digs deeper and finds out that you and Jimmy used to 'hang out,' he's going to go at you hard."

Philip nodded. "Yeah, I guess he could. But he's not going to be able to find anything that proves I contacted Chamberlain or McBride or anybody else."

"Are you sure, Philip? It's not easy to completely expunge electronic data. And how do you know that Chamberlain or his man friend won't squeal if they're pressured? Did you threaten to expose their sexual preference?"

Philip chewed on his latest mouthful of salad and used his fork to gesture at Dick emphatically. "Dorothy and I believed you and I were finally getting to know each other better, and that we were going to build a better relationship. Knowing that you suspect me of conspiring to kill Sonny to keep the kids is a real buzz kill, Dick."

"Don't take this so personally, Philip. This is what I do for a living. I'm paid to suspect people of doing all kinds of things. That doesn't mean that I believe they're criminals, I just need to make sure they aren't."

"And how are you going to make good on that proposition in this case, Dick? How are you going to convince yourself that I'm innocent?"

"By examining the facts dispassionately and tracking down every lead. Something you don't seem to be able to comprehend."

"And once you have 'examined the facts,' you believe you'll be able to dispel all questions about my guilt?"

"I think so."

"Forever?"

"Yeah, forever," Dick answered, trying to hide his exasperation.

Philip deliberately lowered his voice to a snarling whisper to contain his anger and to keep the people at neighboring tables from hearing his next remark: "So, next year, when we're sitting across from each other at the Thanksgiving dinner table, you won't look at me and wonder if in exchange for a blow job at age seventeen, Jimmy Chamberlain and his cock sucking friend cooked up a plan at my insistence to blow up Sonny's truck and fry him alive? That thought will never cross your mind?"

"Philip, have you ever treated family or friends for a medical problem?"

"What the hell does that have to do with anything? Of course I have."

"When you see them socially after you treat them, do you focus on what their coronary arteries or their heart valves look like?"

"You know I don't, but your analogy is bullshit. You're

implying that I used a prior sexual relationship to prevail on someone to kill another human being. That's different from ordering and interpreting an exercise test and prescribing medicine."

"You may think so, Philip, but it's not how my mind works. This thing we're discussing is a disease, as far as I'm concerned. It needs to be dealt with and disposed of, just like a heart valve infection. And after it is, I will not let it get in the way of our relationship, I promise."

Maybe it was the tone of Dick's voice or his insistence, but Philip's manner and facial expression changed from agitated to placid.

"Okay, Dick. I'll accept your premise that you're a 'clinician' who is only interested in healing. And that you want to protect your family. All good. Tell me where we go from here."

"Not much of anywhere. I have no leads to pursue, so if you're telling the truth, we sit tight and hope that it all blows over."

"And that Scotty doesn't reopen the investigation."

"Right. And he won't unless he has a reason, like new evidence, which is why it's important for you and me to have an understanding. You have to tell me the truth, Philip, or I'll have no way to protect you against Scotty."

"Let's just say that I admit to you that I contacted Chamberlain. Hypothetically speaking, of course. What would you do with that information, Dick?"

Dick was silent, using a sip of iced tea as an excuse to think about how to respond to Philip's question.

"Come on, Dick. You must have thought about it. Would you turn me in?"

Dick shook his head. "I've always taken pride in cooperating with the police in all of my investigations. This might have to be an exception."

"So maybe we need to end this conversation, Dick," Philip

concluded triumphantly. "Let's get on with making our girls happy, and do exactly what you said: forget about all of this stuff, put it behind us."

Dick nodded, feeling a good bit less convinced than he looked. "Okay, Philip. Let's do that for now. We won't talk of this again. But I think we need to promise each other to keep our ears open and to confer if either of us uncovers anything new that might be helpful or relevant."

"Agreed," Philip said, rising from the table, snatching his lab coat and tray. "I have to get back to work, and I know you're busy."

They dropped their trays on a conveyor belt at the cafeteria exit, and Philip walked Dick back up the stairs to the hospital lobby, bustling with health care providers, patients, and visitors. He grabbed Dick's hand and shook it but held on to look Dick in the eye.

"I don't want Dorothy to know about any of what we talked about today. We've finally gotten our relationship on track. She's deliriously happy about the kids and I'm not about to pull that rug out from under her."

"I understand, Philip. I agree that Dorothy need not be bothered with this stuff... not unless things start coming apart."

"But you and I will decide if that ever becomes necessary, correct?"

"Yes."

"In that case, as far as I'm concerned, we're buddies again," Philip concluded. "I'll check with Dorothy, but we should plan to have you over for dinner on Sunday. The girls will be excited to see you."

Dick smiled and nodded, wondering, as he walked away, if he had just sold out his integrity for a chance to play on the floor with Barbie and Ken dolls with two beautiful little girls who adored him. But maybe that wasn't such a bad trade, in the great big scheme of things.

Chapter 26

Dick didn't sleep soundly the next few nights. This was a distinctly unusual development because Dick had become quite adept at emptying his mind of whatever matters were troubling him at just about the time his head hit the pillow. He regarded this remarkable ability as one of his most important skills, his professional "secret weapon," as he called it. Solving cases was hard enough when your brain was rested, Dick preached, and impossible when it wasn't. He made it a point never to wake up in the morning, at least not on a workday, feeling tired or groggy. After a cup of strong coffee, he was pretty much ready to take on the world, to solve any case that happened to be at the top of his docket.

But not this week. The Sonny matter had somehow wedged itself into Dick's subconscious causing the same bad dream to play over and over in his head, like an old black-and-white movie.

Dick is walking alone along the Schuylkill River when he hears a loud engine noise. He looks up and sees an airplane falling from the sky, engines on fire. The aircraft plunges into the river, just a few yards from where Dick is standing, making a terrible sound. Frozen by fear, Dick stands on the bank of the river. He can hear screams coming from the airplane and then watches as a door on the side of the fuselage pops open. Standing in the threshold are Emily and Erin, all alone, crying hysterically, reaching out to Dick for rescue. Dick gets ready to plunge into the river, to swim to the plane, to save his girls, when he realizes he can't swim. He looks around and discovers that no one else has witnessed the crash or responded to it. It is up to Dick to do something. He runs into the river and forces himself to wade out into deep water, where he begins to sink like a stone. The airplane cabin has now caught fire. As he tries to push himself to the surface, Dick can see the flames sweeping up through the cabin, inching slowly but inexorably toward the emergency door where his granddaughters are standing helplessly, crying piteously. Dick calls out to them to jump into the river but his voice is muffled by the water that has entered his mouth and his airway. His girls will certainly perish and he'll drown unless...

Unless he wakes up, which he does at this point in the nightmare, panting for air, in a cold sweat, heart racing. And the worst part is that the terrible dream starts again every time he falls asleep so he becomes unable, or unwilling, to go back to sleep for hours. His rest ruined, Dick pulls himself out of bed in the morning and attempts to revive himself with gallons of coffee and hot and cold showers, to no avail.

The torture continues for several consecutive nights before Dick seeks counsel. Another one of Dick's traits: don't bother others with problems if it can at all be avoided. But when the night terrors become intolerable, Dick consults Ursula.

Dick had dated dozens of women since his wife's death, none of them seriously. Except for Ursula. She was one of Dick's few regulars, and, as Dick would say, "Ursula is a peach." Memories of meeting her and their early dates were some of Dick's fondest.

It was one of those harsh, cold and damp winter nights that Philadelphia is famous for. A monster nor'easter had worked its way up the east coast, battering the shoreline, bringing buckets of rain to the Carolinas before combining with a cold front to spray what weather forecasters referred to as a "wintry mix" on the Philadelphia region. The storm hit just as rush hour was starting, and the ice and freezing rain paralyzed travel into and out of the city. Dick, oblivious of the weather as usual, walked briskly out of his office building, fell on his butt, and slid across the sidewalk almost to the gutter. Fortunately, he injured only his pride. Three young people maneuvered their way over to get him back on his feet. Dick thanked them profusely, righted himself, and decided that travel, at least until the streets and roads were properly salted, was not on his agenda.

Fortunately, one of Dick's favorite taverns, McGettigan's, was just next door to his office building. Dick decided that a Scotch, a roast beef sandwich, and a Flyers game on the tube would be just the thing to pass the time until it was safe to travel home.

The place was even more packed than usual on a Thursday evening, with dozens of young professionals looking for refuge on a stormy night. Dick maneuvered his way to a seat at the bar, put his wet coat on the back of the bar chair, attracted the bartender's attention, and had a Balvenie on the rocks in front of him within seconds of his arrival. The Flyers game was yet to start. Talking heads mouthed their impressions of the teams, their voices not discernible over the din of the bar. Dick began to look around and noticed a middle-aged woman seated to his left, nursing a bourbon, absorbed in a magazine article.

"Something interesting?" Dick asked randomly.

She slowly rotated her head toward Dick, looking over reading glasses perched perilously at the end of a very cute turned-up nose. But it was her eyes that Dick noticed first. The most interesting shade of blue he had ever seen, contrasting sharply with the dark red hair that she wore up in a petite bun.

The woman merely stared at Dick for several seconds and then wordlessly went back to her reading. Nothing more was said until the second Scotch was delivered and loosened Dick's tongue further.

"Can I buy you another drink?"

After a slow turn. "Is that what you want to ask me or are you just trying to get my attention?"

"Do you really want to know what I was thinking?" Dick asked boldly.

"Yes. I admire honesty above all," she answered flatly.

"I was wondering if you dye your hair, or is that its natural color."

A smile, and then a laugh. "Really? That's what you want to know?"

"I'm a truthful soul."

She hesitated, preparing her response carefully.

"All right, cowboy. I'll play your silly little game. Why don't you guess what I'm thinking?"

"Okay, penny for your thoughts."

"Not enough. I need another drink."

Dick summoned the bartender, who poured another bourbon for the woman. She held the glass to her lips for a second or two after her sip, lost in thought.

"I don't want you to take this the wrong way, but I was wondering what you might look like naked."

Dick tried to hide his surprise and pretend he was accustomed to hearing such candid comments.

"Are you really interested in finding out?" he said, trying to sound casual.

"Not really. There are at least a few other things I need to know in the meantime like…"

"My name?"

"That's a good start."

"Dick Deaver. And yours?"

"Ursula Manchester. And what do you do for a living, Dick Deaver?"

"I'm a private detective."

"Sure you are. And I'm the Queen of the May."

"No, really. That's what I do for a living."

"Interesting. Well, I'm a potter by trade."

"What's that mean?"

"I make pottery and sell it on the internet."

"You must be pretty good to make a living doing that."

"I am. As a matter of fact, I'm here in Philly to do a craft show this week."

"Where're you from?"

"I live in Manhattan."

The rest of the hour-long bar conversation was taken up with the usual get-acquainted stuff. Dick liked the way Ursula looked and her direct manner and knew pretty early in the dialogue that he was going to want to see her again. So when she finished her second bourbon and started to exit, he made his move.

"Can I see you again this week?" he asked. "How about tomorrow for dinner?"

"That would be lovely. These showings are usually pretty lonely. I'm staying at the Sofitel on 17th Street. Let me give you my business card. It has my cell phone number."

"Excellent. I'll text you with a time to pick you up. We'll do something near your hotel."

"Hoping to get lucky?"

Dick didn't get a chance to answer.

"Are you shocked that a woman of my maturity would be so crass?"

"Well... uh... not exactly the words..."

"Save it, Dick. It was a rhetorical question. You don't need to answer. But you do need to listen carefully to what I'm going to tell you. As you'll subsequently learn when you do my background check..."

"I'm not…"

"Shut up and listen. If you really are a private investigator, you're going to look me up. And when you do, if you're any good at what you do, you'll discover that I'm a three time loser."

"You've done jail time?"

"No, dummy, marital loser. One of my exes, the best of the three, died, and two divorced. I'm not looking for number four. So nothing serious is going to happen between us. That doesn't mean I won't jump in the sack with you once in a while. That's possible. But I'm not going to get all mushy and fall in love or some such nonsense. I have too many things to do before I die to take on another old codger."

Dick was speechless. He managed to nod his agreement before Ursula collected her belongings, swung off of her barstool, and headed for the door.

What actually happened over the next several months was just as Ursula had predicted and then prescribed. They saw each other every few weeks, and each meeting was just a lot of fun. They called it "Amtrak Love" because one or the other would take the Acela to spend the weekend in New York or Philadelphia. The usual agenda was a casual Friday evening, a museum, or a long park walk on Saturday afternoon, followed by a nice dinner and a show, pleasant sex Saturday night, and brunch on Sunday before a taxi ride back to the train station for the visiting team. Neither Dick nor Ursula wanted or asked for more than that. They became excellent friends and confidants without strings attached. Most importantly, they agreed not to introduce each other to their children, of which Ursula had two. Just another way to keep the relationship different and fresh and exciting, they decided.

It just so happened that Dick's next rendezvous with Ursula in New York was only a day away. He hadn't seen or spoken with her for weeks. This was not unusual; they had agreed that they would get on the phone only when they had something important to say, not feeling compelled to simply hear each other's voice.

As he packed his bags for the trip, Dick realized how much had happened since the last time he had seen Ursula. He contemplated how he might present the complex story to her to get her opinion and advice. Should he or could he unload the entire story on her? And if so, should he parse it out and deliver small pieces at a time? No, Dick thought. I have to make some tough decisions soon about what to tell Dorothy and Scotty. He didn't have the luxury of rolling it out gradually. And it wasn't a story that would lend itself well to serialization.

Dick's trip to New York was a hassle. The train was packed with business people returning to New York from Philadelphia, college students returning home for a laundry weekend, and tourists on their way to the Big Apple for the usual tour of the city. Dick was able to find a seat at a four-top and bumped knees all the way to New York with a sleeping Jewish rabbi, slumped down in the opposite seat. And no big surprise that the taxi line outside Penn Station wrapped around the corner. Dick also knew that the subway would be a sardine can. He had learned to pack lightly and to take a roller board so he could walk comfortably uptown to Ursula's loft apartment.

Dick arrived tired but instantly rejuvenated by Ursula's warm greeting. She was dressed in a colorful bath robe, her dark red hair down around her shoulders, looking clean and refreshed.

Dick kissed her chastely on the cheek. "You smell good."

"I got home a little early and decided to take a long bath with a cup of tea. Would you like one?"

"Bath or tea?"

"Don't get any big ideas. We're talking herbal tea."

"Not just yet, but thanks."

Ursula sensed immediately that there was something on

Dick's mind. "Okay, buster, do you want to tell me which work problem has you worried?"

Dick would have been surprised by her perspicacity except now he was used to it. "It isn't work, but I have quite a family story to tell you. A lot has happened to Philip and Dorothy since the last time I spoke with you."

"Let's make ourselves comfortable before you start. Come on over here."

Ursula led Dick to her sofa, where they seated themselves far enough apart so they could turn to face each other. Directly in front of them was a pleasant view of a remote portion of Central Park. It was Ursula's favorite perch where she could savor one of the few slices of nature New York City provided.

Dick started off with the good news about the adoption, spending abundant time describing Emily and Erin. He didn't need to tell Ursula they had captured his heart; it was obvious. He moved on to the glitch that threatened custody, the arrival of the villainous father, Sonny, and the nefarious reason for his sudden interest in the children. And finally, the story of Sonny's gory death and the subsequent police investigation. He then focused the briefing on what he had learned from Jimmy Chamberlain and about Chamberlain's lover. He left nothing out of the presentation, including his suspicions about the relationship Philip had had with Jimmy, and his fear it was not all about golf.

Ursula nodded and asked clarification questions intermittently, but mostly remained quiet until he had finished.

"Wow! That's quite a saga, Dick. Kind of puts you in a difficult situation, doesn't it?"

Dick was relieved that Ursula had cut through all of the details and grasped the reason for his recitation and his angst. "It does. It's why I had to tell you the whole story."

"You want my advice?" Ursula said matter-of-factly.

"You're the person I trust the most. I have nowhere else to turn."

"I'm not the person you trust the most, but you can hardly ask Dorothy her opinion, can you? Tell me what you think your options are, Dick."

"Pretty simple. I either keep my mouth shut or I can tell Lou Scotty what I've learned. And if I decide to do the latter, I'll have to tell Dorothy first."

"Okay. Let's consider the implications of talking to the police. They know that the truck was serviced at the Mack Company just before the accident, right?"

"Yes."

"And they know that Chamberlain was the mechanic."

"Correct."

"What you know and they don't is that Chamberlain may have had a motive, based on his previous relationship with Philip, and the means, because of his lover, Bernie, or whatever his name is."

"Right."

"And why do you think this Bernie was an asset?"

"He's a vet who worked on a bomb squad in Iraq."

"So he knows something about explosives."

"He must, don't you think?"

"But you have no proof that he had anything to do with this."

"I don't."

"And Philip denied the whole thing."

"Of course. You don't have institutional memory, but Philip has a propensity to be hanging around when weird stuff happens to people he doesn't like. And he always claims ignorance. I'm not prepared to rely on his veracity."

"From what you told me, Sonny was a bad guy who probably deserved what he got."

"He abandoned his family and then came back like a buzzard to pick over the remains. I'm not sure he deserved to get roasted in his truck."

"But the world is a better place without him?"

"My world certainly is, and so is Philip's."

"And what's the down-side of keeping all of this to yourself?"

"I can't think of one. I'm not obstructing justice or harboring a criminal. Dorothy would be blindsided but not necessarily in harm's way. If I speak up, it would focus the investigation back on Philip for sure."

"Dick, if you're willing to absorb some guilt, I suspect you need to be silent. Let the police do their work and let the chips fall, so to speak."

"Scotty may be working his way through the investigation more slowly than I did, and may circle back to Chamberlain at some point."

"And if he does, you'll have at least forewarned Philip and Chamberlain so they're prepared to answer Scotty's tough questions when he gets to them."

Dick was silent as he processed his next thoughts. "There's another consideration here."

"Dorothy?"

"Yes. If she finds out that Philip may be behind another dark case, she'll freak."

"And you don't want that to happen…"

"For multiple reasons."

"Including keeping your grandchildren near you…"

"And in a stable home environment."

Ursula finally smiled. "See how easy it is when you say it all out loud?"

Dick smiled for the first time since they had begun the conversation. "What did I do for common sense before I met you?"

"It's not just common sense, Dick. This is a difficult decision. You're used to seeking the truth and always being honest. But here you are concealing facts in a potential murder case."

"And from my daughter, with whom I've always tried to be transparent."

"You needed validation that what you're doing is not

crazy. And it isn't. You're making an exception to your normal principles for the sake of your grandchildren. They need to have two parents and you in their lives. They have been through so much, and you need to protect them."

Dick nodded. "When you put it that way, the choice is easy. Thanks, Ursula."

"You're welcome. I'm sure you'll return the favor many times over."

Ursula moved closer to Dick on the sofa. "Enough of this. We can talk about it again, but not this evening. I want you to get a good rest this weekend. I say we start with a good strong vodka martini and then start negotiating what we want to do about dinner."

"Sounds like a great idea."

"There's a new Thai place around the corner that just opened. Their menu looks spectacular, and I've been dying to give it a try. Game?"

"You bet. Do I have to get changed or will what I have on be okay?"

"What you have on is not at all okay," Ursula replied with a giggle.

"Why not?"

"Because what you have on has got to come off."

"Oh…"

"So what do you say we make the martini the second thing we do to start our weekend?" Ursula asked as she grabbed Dick's shirt and pulled him to herself.

"What do you have on under that robe?" Dick asked as he kissed her neck and reached around to grab her bottom.

"Did I say I had anything on?" Ursula laughed as she disengaged herself, took Dick's hand and led him to her bedroom.

"By the way, welcome to New York, sailor."

Chapter 27

Sonny's death, coupled with his family's refusal to take the children, cleared the way for Philip and Dorothy to pursue the adoption process. Maggie Smart was able to petition Children's Court for a hearing to discuss the status of the case and to plan the timing of the actual adoption. She was particularly interested in obtaining a ruling from a judge that would clearly outline the path Philip and Dorothy would have to pursue to retain custody of Emily and Erin and to keep the Cardinelli family from changing their minds and cashing in on the BFU settlement. Given the unusual circumstances of the case, and the fact that Philip and Dorothy had no formal rights of custody, Maggie was convinced it was a necessary step despite the trauma the hearing might cause. Otherwise, Child Protective Services could act on their own discretion and assign custody to foster parents pending a final resolution of Sonny's motion, which had not been officially withdrawn.

Maggie was also concerned that Philip and Dorothy weren't married. She had told them at the beginning of the process that marriage would strengthen and solidify their adoption advantage. Neither had seemed particularly amenable to the idea, although Maggie had the distinct impression that it was Dorothy who had demurred. Her direct questions had been deflected on multiple occasions, and Maggie didn't have the fortitude to insist. There had to be reasons she had met resistance into which she didn't care to delve.

"I was amazed that his parents and siblings backed away," Philip observed during one of their pre-hearing meetings with Maggie. "Even if they don't want the kids, there's a fair amount of money on the table. What was the final settlement from BFU?"

"It will be something like one and a half million after legal fees and taxes," Maggie replied.

"That's a lot of money but they would have to raise two little kids. None of them seem like stellar parental material," Dorothy added.

"True. And each couple who stepped forward would have to be vetted. They may not have been qualified to take the kids or even have something to hide. Who knows what would have come of it?"

"And raising a kid is expensive and hard," Philip agreed.

"I believe the court would have insisted on measures to ensure the money would only be spent on the kids," Maggie pointed out. "I guess when you put it all together, the family's decision to back away may not be so bizarre. Nevertheless, we have to be thoroughly prepared and ready to rebut any arguments put forward in support of their getting the kids. People change their minds all the time. And they have plenty of time to consider their options." Maggie had to notice Dorothy's wince.

One of the most complicated parts of Maggie's job was walking the fine line between full disclosure and worrying adopting parents to death. And this issue was a sure hot button. Biological families hold enormous power in adoption proceedings, and Maggie had seen several decide to take the children back because of guilt or an incidental change in living arrangements. It was the nightmare scenario that Dorothy knew well and feared the most.

Maggie's meticulous preparation for the hearing paid off. Judge Lockhart, a veteran of the Children's Court, was impressed with her thoughtfulness and careful consideration of the details. Even more importantly, he was influenced by the quality of the adopting parents. It would be difficult to question the ability of a doctor and a lawyer to raise two young children, especially since they already had custody and were given high marks by the oversight agencies.

Fortunately for Philip and Dorothy, their previous brushes with the law had not come up. Despite their suspected involvement in a few matters in which scary things had happened and people had been killed, no one had been able to garner enough evidence to file a formal charge. Consequently, they didn't have a criminal record that an opposing attorney would be able to cite. As far as Judge Lockhart knew, the worst thing either of them had been accused of in their lives was ignoring a parking meter.

"I see no reason why Dr. Sarkis and Ms. Deaver can't retain custody of the children while our agencies continue the adoption process," Lockhart pronounced quite anti-climactically. "However, I'm going to reset the clock on this case, Ms. Smart. Finalization of the adoption will not occur until one year from now. I'm going to give the Cardinelli family that much time to reconsider their decision not to assume custody of their flesh and blood. I'm amazed by their lack of interest and their unwillingness to take on this responsibility."

"As are we, Your Honor. We've had several conversations with the family. We agree that the family needs to be given every consideration. I gather that the girls' grandparents are elderly and not capable of chasing after two young children. The siblings already have large families and have no place to house the children."

"Well, the fact that the family is not here and not represented by counsel pretty much tells the story, doesn't it, Ms. Smart? I plan to talk to them myself in the next few weeks so they understand their options clearly, and what their actions mean."

"We appreciate that, but I wouldn't be optimistic, Your Honor."

Dorothy and Philip worked very hard not to show their negative reaction to the judge's presumptions and plans. Maggie watched them out of the corner of her eye, hoping they would remain calm as she tried to put the best face on their position. "On the other hand, Your Honor, we intend to be cooperative with whatever the process. And, most importantly, my clients will take good care of the girls in the meantime."

"Based on what we've seen so far, I'm sure they will," the judge answered as he banged his gavel. "Now go have fun with the kids, you two, and hopefully we'll see all of you here next year to make things final."

And so Philip and Dorothy were able to continue on with the latest phase of their lives together. To start, they agreed that they had to continue to reorder their professional lives. Philip met with the head of cardiology at Temple and informed her that he intended to stay on but had no plans to pursue research opportunities. He wouldn't have time to travel or write grants or manuscripts. He was interested in continuing his patient care and teaching responsibilities but wanted to reduce his on-call responsibilities so he could spend more time with his children.

"You don't have to remind me that I'll need to take a pay cut in exchange for less on-call time. I'm fully aware of that and I understand," Philip offered at the meeting.

"You're seriously handicapping your academic career, Philip," his wet-behind-the-ears chief warned. "Are you sure this is the direction you wish to take?"

Philip shrugged. He didn't want to get into a debate with this nice woman, who had a fraction of his professional experience. His academic career had been ruined by Hugh and Moira Hamlin years before. What was left wasn't worth spending time fretting about. By raising Emily and Erin, he wanted to create a real legacy.

"My family is going to have to come first. I know a lot of people around here say that, but I guess I mean it. I've had enough of writing grants and presenting papers. Time to move on."

Philip was also concerned about the situation with the kids from his first marriage. Nancy had recently hinted that she was going to move to California with her new husband and the kids. Philip had joint custody and warned Nancy that he would initiate legal action to keep his children in Philadelphia. Nancy literally laughed at him. "Go ahead and see how far that gets you," she taunted. In the end, based on Maggie's strong advice, Philip dropped the matter, despite realizing that if Nancy did leave town, he wouldn't be seeing his kids for a while if ever again. He wasn't about to let that happen with his new family.

Likewise, Dorothy set about putting her job in context, informing the partners at her firm that she was no longer interested in extra work or in cases that would involve extended time or traveling. She had decided that a four-day work-week would maintain an adequate income and, like Philip, give her abundant time for children activities.

"This will be my only shot at being a parent, so I want to take advantage of it," she argued to her managing partner, who, being a family man himself, was happy to acquiesce.

Next came the townhouse. Although it had provided more than enough room for Philip, Dorothy and their dogs, the girls made it cramped. In addition, Philadelphia's public school system didn't have a good reputation. If they remained inside the city limits, the girls would have to go to private school, a significant investment. Philly also enforced a city wage tax. Taken all together, it was fairly clear they were going to have to move out of the city eventually, to a suburb with good public schools. Dorothy focused her search on the western side of the city, favoring areas served by good public transportation to limit their commute time.

Philip and Dorothy quickly realized that the real estate search was going to be a time-consuming project with no instant fix. In the meantime, they made the space they had as livable and as much fun for the girls as possible. They gladly gave up office and leisure space to accommodate another sleeping area and turned their TV room into a play area, the wall shelves now populated by stuffed animals and games. They needn't have worried. Compared to the life they had left, Emily and Erin considered their accommodations luxurious.

Philip, who had always been known for his sudden change of moods, was transformed into an entirely optimistic, energetic, and doting father. Though Dorothy had witnessed his chameleon act so many times before, she was, once again, thoroughly amazed. All of the positive attributes that had made Philip into a world class cardiologist--his intellect, perseverance, and time management--were now channeled into parenting. He was a constant presence in the girls' lives, from the time he roused them from sleep in the morning until he tucked them in at night. He dropped them off at daycare and did everything in his power to pick them up in the afternoon, grumpily giving up that chore to Dorothy on those occasions when his patient care schedule was unalterable. He supervised their evening activities, starting with their limited homework to watching an hour of carefully selected television with them on his lap, followed by the reading of as many books as they could possibly squeeze in before lights out.

And the weekends were always a whirlwind, each one

highlighted by a fun trip to someplace like the zoo, Please Touch Museum, Franklin Institute, or a kid movie. They traveled to the mountains, to the house they kept there, at least once a month. The seasons dictated whether they ice skated, boated, swam, fished, or some combination, always accompanied by the hounds. The dogs, sensing Philip's maniacal dedication to Emily and Erin, guarded the girls carefully while making themselves available for amusement and playful abuse. "The doggies have a new pack," Philip loved to point out to any interested party. "As far as the dogs are concerned, it's now seven instead of five."

But in actuality, it was eight. Dick was ever more in the picture, spending time with the kids on the weekend, enjoying himself on every occasion. His favorite activity was board games. With each visit, Dick would bring a new game with which to entertain and delight the girls. Their favorite by far was Operation, in which they would attempt to remove organs using a pair of forceps. Contact with the metallic side of the organ cavity caused a buzz that set the girls to squealing and laughing as Dick muttered to himself, feigning poor manual dexterity.

"Let me show you how to do it, Pop-Pop," Emily the elder would offer. Dick in pretended frustration would hand over the forceps and then observe Emily as she extracted the organ in question. "You're amazing, Emily," Dick would profess, Emily grinning with great pride in her accomplishment.

"It's easy, Pop-Pop," Emily would explain to Dick who simply beamed.

Dick was the perfect grandfather, entertaining the girls, helping them learn, without an ounce of judgment or negativity. And Dick had made a point of keeping his mouth shut, eschewing recommendations as to how Philip and Dorothy could do a better job of raising the girls. He knew to bite his tongue and nod his agreement whenever discipline was required, behavior much appreciated by the parental units.

One spectacularly sunny Saturday afternoon, Philip and Dorothy's constitutional with the dogs and the girls took them to Washington Square Park, a particularly beautiful refuge in the older part of the city. A playground had been constructed at the edge of the park, and as the pups rested their paws, Philip and Dorothy sat on a bench and watched the two girls run from the swings to the sliding board to the monkey bars, enjoying the opportunity to play with other children who had congregated at the playground. They laughed as they watched their kids chase and crash into each other, picking themselves up, turning every collision into a giggle fest.

"They're so happy, Philip. I can't believe how well they've adjusted to their new home."

"Take a little credit, Dorothy. You've done a remarkable job with those kids."

"So have you, Philip. I'm impressed with how much time you spend with them. It has to have made a difference."

"I hope so."

"Do you miss the buzz?"

"What buzz?"

"You know. The buzz you got from being an academic big shot. From being the center of attention."

Philip took Dorothy's hand. "You know, I have thought a lot about that. And the answer is a decided no."

"Why not?" Dorothy asked, staring back into Philip's eyes. "What makes you so happy to give up all of those approbations?"

"Because no matter how much I kidded myself, it was never anything I could truly share with you."

"And this is?" Dorothy asked nodding toward the children.

"For sure. Their success will be our collective accomplishment. I love that idea."

"Did you feel the same way with Nancy and your other kids?"

"I blew it. I was riveted on my career. I didn't spend

enough time with them and I paid the price. I won't repeat that mistake."

"I know you won't, Philip. I have no worries about that."

"You obviously prefer to spend your time worrying about other things."

"Yes."

"Like Sonny's family."

"The Sonny thing freaked me out. I'll admit it."

"It was very scary."

"Philip, I have a confession to make."

"What terrible thing did you do this time, Dorothy, my love?"

"Please don't get upset, but I discovered that Connie Santangelo's father Frank worked for the Romano brothers years ago."

Philip paused, absorbing the meaning of Dorothy's statement. "You suspected they had killed Sonny for what he did to Connie out of loyalty to her father?"

"You have to admit that it's plausible."

"Especially if you assumed that I facilitated their involvement."

"I didn't say that…"

"But you obviously thought it."

"I admit that I did, but the Romanos denied any involvement. They dismissed the possibility entirely, and I believed them."

"You went to see them?"

"Yes. I didn't tell you because nothing came of it, and I didn't want to upset you."

"How did you conclude the Romanos are innocent?"

"Frank screwed them in a business deal. They hated the guy. There's no way they would have done him a favor."

Silence as Philip crossed his arms and looked down at his lap.

"Philip, I'm telling you this because I think we need to be

honest with each other. It isn't just the two of us now. There's a lot more at stake."

Philip grabbed Dorothy's hand and squeezed it hard. "Dorothy, I had no idea that Connie had a connection to the Romanos. And even if I had, I would never have asked those criminals to kill Sonny. No matter how desperate I might have been to keep the girls."

"Do you think Sonny's death was accidental, Philip?"

"I do," he answered without hesitation.

"And what leads you to that firm conclusion."

"Mainly because I can't imagine who might have arranged to kill him and how they could possibly have managed it. Think about it. That truck exploded after it had rolled down the embankment. How on earth could anybody arrange for that to happen?"

"So we're the benefactors of a remarkable coincidence?"

"I think we were due for a break, don't you?" Philip asked quizzically.

"I know. Poor us," Dorothy teased, faking a frown.

"All right. We've been fortunate."

"You're damn right, friend. We found each other, we have these two beautiful children and wonderful dogs, and we have good jobs and financial security. Time to count our blessings, don't you think?"

Philip smiled and put his arm around Dorothy and pulled her close. "Leave it to you to put it all in perspective."

"We have wonderful lives in front of us, Philip. All we have to do is go with the flow, stay out of trouble, and maintain our priorities."

"I agree. And those girls out there have to be at the top of the list."

A few moments of silence. "They aren't going to take the girls away from us, are they, Philip?" Dorothy asked in a trembling voice.

"Never. I promise."

Dorothy pushed herself into Philip's body, warmed as much by his hug as his reassurance. Because no matter how much Dorothy might question his actions, Philip ended up being right about most things.

They sat in silent contemplation for the next few minutes. Dorothy struggled to think good thoughts about Philip. Despite his protestations and her desire to put it all behind them, Dorothy still couldn't be sure if Philip had anything to do with Sonny's death. But given the enormous benefit of Sonny's demise, and what was ultimately at stake, this time she wasn't sure if she really wanted to know the God's honest truth.

Chapter 28

Dick's personal life was now clearly headed in the correct direction. He had managed to focus on his grandchildren and stopped worrying about all of the events that had jeopardized his family life. He rationalized his decision to keep quiet about what he had learned about Chamberlain by remembering what his daughter had been though over the last several months. Anything that might signal a legal impediment to keeping Emily and Erin would throw her into an emotional turmoil from which she might never emerge.

"I'm not taking that risk," Dick said as he peered at himself in the mirror while trimming his beard or brushing his teeth. And to make himself feel better, he reminded himself that oracle Ursula had heartily agreed with his "don't ask, don't tell" attitude about the Cardinelli case. And thankfully, there was radio silence from the police, who didn't seem to be terribly concerned. And as anyone who watched television knows, the longer a case goes cold, the harder it is to resurrect and solve.

So the call from Detective Scotty a few weeks later was a jolt. Dick was noshing on a chicken salad sandwich at his desk when his phone rang. "There's a Detective Lou Scotty on the phone and he said it's important," the secretary informed him.

Instant indigestion. "Put him through," Dick answered reflexively, dreading whatever message Scotty was about to deliver. It wasn't going to be good news.

Scotty sounded unusually chipper, however, raising Dick's hopes for something positive. "Hi, Dick. It's Lou Scotty. Hope I didn't interrupt your lunch."

"Well, as a matter of fact you have, but no big deal. Just working at my desk. What's on your mind, young fellow?"

"I have some new developments in the Cardinelli case I'd like to discuss with you."

"What kind of new developments Lou?"

"I'd rather not get into it on the phone. Do you have some time this afternoon?"

"Sure, I can clear things."

"And how about that son-in-law of yours, son-in-law to be, that is. Is he available as well?"

"Philip?"

"Yeah, Philip. You only have one daughter who, as far as I know, only has one boyfriend."

"Why do you want Philip here?"

"Because these new developments have raised a few more questions that I have to ask Philip, that's why."

"Really?"

"Really, Dick. Come on, man. Are we going to do this the easy way or the hard way?"

Scotty didn't need to spell out what the hard way meant: a trip to police headquarters and several uncomfortable hours of interrogation and intimidation. The threat implied that Scotty had important and relevant information that he needed to vet one way or another. He now had Dick's attention and cooperation.

"I'll call him. He usually leaves the hospital around 4. Can we plan on a 5 PM meeting here? I'll call you back if I have to change the time."

"That would be just ducky."

"I'm not going to ask an attorney to join us, Lou, but I'm going to tell Philip not to answer any questions that might incriminate him in any way."

"That's up to you guys, Dick. No one is going to get charged with anything... at least not yet. Obviously, if Philip clams up it will just take longer for me to figure it all out, and it might get tougher on all parties involved."

"Instead of making threats, Lou, why don't we just sit down like adults and see what you need? It's entirely possible that between Philip and me, we can put your mind at ease."

"I like the way you think, Dick. See you at 5 in your office."

Dick hung up and immediately called Philip on his cell phone.

"What's up, Dick?" Philip asked. "I'm in the middle of CCU rounds with the residents."

"That's okay. I don't want to talk on the phone anyway. I need you to come to my office by about 4:30. Something important has come up in the Cardinelli case."

"Oh, something for me to worry about?"

"I don't think so," Dick lied, not wanting to alarm Philip and extend the conversation. "Can you make it?"

"Sure, if you think it can't wait. I'll call Dorothy and see if she can pick the kids up. I don't think it will be a problem. I believe she said her afternoon was light."

"Don't tell Dorothy you're coming here. I don't want to get her upset."

"Upset about what, Dick?"

"See you at 4:30 and I'll explain then." Dick winced at his gaffe, and hung up before Philip could ask any more questions.

Philip arrived a few minutes late, to Dick's chagrin. He wanted time to discuss possible reasons for Scotty's visit and, most importantly, how Philip should comport himself. Philip was dismissive as usual, minimizing the importance of Scotty's revelations and their implications.

"What could he possibly have discovered that we don't already know?"

"I can't guess, Philip, but Scotty is a serious person. I don't think he would yank our chain for the hell of it. He has something he wants to spring on you. It's important that you not react in any way, positively or negatively."

"I can handle myself, Dick," Philip answered just as Dick's phone rang to announce Lou Scotty's arrival.

Dick answered and put his hand over the phone for final instructions. "Just the same, Philip, it would be better if you just kept quiet and let me do the talking. We'll regroup after he leaves and decide then if we need to do anything."

"Send him in," Dick finally directed his secretary as he seated himself, Philip occupying one of the two arm chairs on the other side of his desk. Scotty entered the room wearing a suit, once again carrying a trench coat, looking not as rumpled as Columbo but vaguely reminiscent of the famous detective.

"Gentlemen, thanks so much for meeting with me on short notice," Scotty announced as he found his way to the armchair next to Philip. "I don't want to take up too much of your time."

"Not at all, Lou," Dick answered, reaching across his desk to shake Scotty's hand. "Happy to help," he said, trying hard to sound like he meant it.

Philip ignored Scotty, choosing to stay seated with his head down, concentrating on the smartphone he had pulled out of his pocket when Scotty entered.

"How are you, Dr. Sarkis?" Scotty asked.

"Fine," Philip grunted, refusing to look up. "Or at least I

was."

Scotty grimaced, finally deciding to ignore Philip's pout.

"Let's get on with this, shall we? You both remember that the guy who worked on Sonny Cardinelli's truck was Jimmy Chamberlain, right?"

"Yeah," Dick replied.

"And I bet you both knew that Jimmy shacked up regularly with a guy named Bernie McBride."

"So what?" Philip spit out, finally looking up.

Scotty refused to be baited, keeping his voice even. "First of all, I suspect you both knew about Jimmy's, shall we call it, sexual proclivity well before I did and chose not to share it with me."

"Is that a crime, Detective?" Philip asked sarcastically.

"Of course not, Dr. Sarkis. I guess I naively assumed that you and Dick were going to play straight with me. But I guess I was wrong about that."

"I'll admit that I did find out that Chamberlain was anything but straight," Dick cut in, hoping to shut Philip up before he pissed Scotty off. "I didn't think it was relevant."

"I also could give a rat's ass about whom he chose to spend time with, Dick. Except for the fact that Bernie's other talents were much more important to this case than his ability to play Jimmy's skin flute."

"And what was that talent, Detective? We're all ears," Philip interjected.

"Explosives."

"Really?" Philip said.

"Yup."

"And where did he acquire that skill set?" Philip asked.

"Iraq. Turns out Bernie is a Desert Storm vet."

"No shit," Philip again.

Dick stared a dagger in Philip's direction, wondering what part of "keep your trap shut" he didn't understand.

"Well, that's what I found out in my research. I wasn't able to confirm anything with Bernie."

"Why not? Did he refuse to speak to you for some reason?" Dick asked.

"Not exactly. I haven't been able to locate him."

"Chamberlain should be able to help you."

"That's why I'm here. Seems Misters Chamberlain and McBride have absconded."

"What?" Dick exclaimed, taking note of what might have been Philip's authentic startle. They both sat forward in their chairs, waiting for Scotty to deliver more.

"Yes, indeed. Gone. Both of them. Packed up some things in the middle of the night and took off for parts unknown."

"Wow. What are the police doing to track them down?" Dick asked.

"Not much. The case hasn't developed much momentum. I don't have enough evidence to tie either one to Sonny's death. Hell, we're not even sure it was a murder. So putting out an APB seems like overkill because if and when we apprehend them, we couldn't hold them for spitting on the sidewalk. Add in that Bernie is a war hero, and you can see why I'm stuck, and why my superiors aren't willing to go out on a limb."

"War hero?" Dick asked.

"You know, Dick, sometimes I wonder if you're a really good investigator who likes to pretend you're not, or if you're just plain untalented. Because it's hard for me to believe you didn't know all about Bernie and hadn't scoped the guy out. It took me no time to find out who he was and a lot of stuff about him. Medal of Honor winners tend to get their names in the newspapers frequently, especially if they also happen to have been wounded four times in the line of duty."

Dick decided to play dumb. "I'll admit I knew that Chamberlain was gay, but I didn't go as far as you did in my background checks. But now I can see why Chamberlain was concerned about being outed. Advertising his boyfriend would have been a real problem for a war hero."

"And you claim that you didn't know any of this? Really, Dick? You can stick to that story, but I'm sure you can see now why I'm here. I need to know if there's any connection between Philip and Dorothy and Chamberlain and his boyfriend."

Philip shook his head. "Detective..."

"And before you start lying, you need to know that I spoke with Milt Belrose at the truck agency. I know you worked there when you were younger, and that you hung out with Chamberlain. So what I really need to know is the last time you had any contact with Chamberlain."

Philip glanced over at Dick who was doing his best to look calm. "It's been years, Detective."

"So if I manage to subpoena Chamberlain's phone records for the last few months, you're telling me your number won't come up."

"Absolutely not."

"Or if I canvass his apartment neighbors, none of them will recognize you as a recent visitor."

"I'm telling you, Detective, I haven't seen or spoken to him in years."

"And you never met Bernie McBride?"

"Wouldn't know him if I tripped over him, Detective. Until a few minutes ago, I didn't even know he existed."

"Can you describe your relationship with Chamberlain when you worked at the Mack place?"

"I think that's over the line, Detective," Dick quickly interjected. "It's none of your business."

"Dick, this is not a formal interview. Philip is free to refuse to answer questions. When he does, or when he lies, it tells me almost as much as when he tells me the truth. Inevitably, the facts will come out. So my advice to Philip is to get in front of this. If he did nothing, he'll be fine.

Turning back to Philip, "So, do you want to tell me about

your friendship with Chamberlain? How far did it go?"

"What the hell is that supposed to mean?" Philip asked, letting his anger show.

"I know this is uncomfortable. You were a young man and you hung out with a known homosexual. It raises questions."

"Maybe it does in your dirty little mind, Detective. I suspect that most normal people wouldn't jump to that conclusion."

"Can you just answer the question without us getting into a social science discussion? Perhaps I can rephrase. Describe what you and Chamberlain did when you spent time together. How's that?"

"We played golf."

"That's all?"

"The usual stuff when you play golf. Maybe a buger afterward."

"Did you ever go to his apartment?"

"No, never."

"Did you ever have any physical contact with him?"

"We shook hands on the eighteenth green. Oh, and we grabbed each other's crotch to show our appreciation for a good shot. How's that?"

"We're not going to get anywhere with that attitude, Dr. Sarkis."

"I told you it was just golf, but you don't seem to want to accept the answer. You want dirt, so I'll shovel as much as you like if it will satisfy you and get you off my case."

Scotty rose from his chair and stretched his back. He picked up his trench coat and pulled his suit jacket closed as he stared down at Philip. "All right, Dr. Sarkis. Here's what's going to happen from this point. I'm going to try to find Jimmy Chamberlain. I have a number of friends around the country who owe me favors, and although I can't put out an official bulletin, I can ask my buds to be on the lookout for those two. I've done this successfully before. It's not easy, but it's feasible when you know where relatives live and stuff like that.

"While I'm at it, I'm also going to go through everything he left behind that I can get my hands on. And I mean everything. Bank records, phone logs, work documents, the whole banana. And then I'm going to do the same thing for Bernie. All I need is something small and seemingly insignificant that ties them to you or to Sonny, you know, recently. Just to give you an example: I was going over photos from the accident scene the other night and I happened to see someone who looked an awful lot like our boy Bernie up on the hill. The photo was taken by a biker on the path across the river from the accident, but he focused in pretty good with a telephoto lens. He was hoping to get famous and put it up on the web. It's amazing what our crime people can do with digital photographs these days. I expect we might be able to make a positive ID, which would mean that Bernie was there when the truck exploded. Pretty cool, right, Dr. Sarkis?"

"Bully for you, Detective."

"Right, bully for me. I know that this sounds like a pretty big project, to pull all of the loose ends together, doesn't it? Yup, it's going to take me a long while because none of my superiors is willing to allocate resources at this point. They think it was just an accident and don't want any more publicity about the case. I'm going to do this in my spare time, like a hobby, and I'll have to do it by myself. All alone. What that means for you is that this thing is going to hang over your head for many years to come. Because I'm not going to let go. Not in my nature. The guys at the precinct call me the bulldog because I never let go of a bone once I suspect there's meat on it."

"Lou," Dick began.

"Save it, Dick. I don't need your bullshit," Scotty said, turning back to Philip who sat expressionless. "Because, I'm convinced as I can be that you're a bad man, Dr. Sarkis.

You've been involved with too many cases in which people have been killed to be a coincidence. I never should have let the Hamlin case go so easily. That was a mistake I'll go to my grave regretting because what you did in the Poconos to those nurses and to that guy Robinson in Boston wouldn't have happened if I had nabbed you for having the Hugh and Bonnie killed and chucking their car into the river years ago.

"See, I believe that Chamberlain and McBride did you a solid by killing Sonny. I don't know exactly why they went to all that trouble yet. Maybe Jimmy liked you or maybe you threatened to out him and Bermie. It doesn't matter because if you're lying to me about not seeing either of them recently, it will be a sure-fire indicator that my theory is true, and then the motive won't matter as much. It will be easy to fill it in. And then I'll have you, and you'll never again be able to dispose of people you regard as evil. You're the evil, Dr. Sarkis, and I'm going to prove it this time, once and for all."

Dick watched Philip carefully during Scotty's scary soliloquy. While Dick himself squirmed as he listened to Scotty's resolve, Philip sat stone-faced, not reacting to any part of Scotty's emotional summary. And what frightened Dick most of all, and what he was working hard not to transmit non-verbally to Scotty, was that he had arrived at exactly the same conclusion. But for the sake of his sanity and his family, Dick had decided to push it all aside. Scotty would do no such thing. The game was on and his granddaughters were in jeopardy.

Scotty donned his trench coat, said his goodbyes and departed. Dick sat, elbows on the desk, his face in his hands for a minute or two, trying to gather his thoughts. When he finally summoned the courage to look up to confront his grandchildren's father, Philip was gone.

Exactly why he died that awful day two weeks later became a matter hotly debated not only within the police department, but also in the papers, which ran front-page stories about the incident. No one could say for sure why this brave and distinguished senior police detective was sitting in a liquor store parking lot in North Philly that rainy Tuesday afternoon, far from his office and his ordinary beat. Had he been lured there or was he following a lead in one of his cases? Was it just a coincidence that he happened to arrive when the parking lot was empty, in the middle of the afternoon? Did he know why he had been summoned? And why did he sit quietly in his car for several minutes? Was he waiting for someone to meet him?

Clues in the case were hard to come by. No customers were in the store or in the parking lot when Scotty's car exploded. Security cameras covered the store and the front of the parking lot but not the area where Scotty had chosen to park. The clerk, the only person in the store, was sitting in the back having his lunch when the explosion destroyed the car and took out the store's front windows.

Scotty, as was his custom, was working alone and had not told anyone in the precinct where he was going when he left his desk abruptly around noon that day. One of his office neighbors thought he heard Scotty talking on his cell phone just before he departed, and had the impression that someone was giving him an address. Was it the address of the liquor store? Could have been, but the other detective wasn't paying close enough attention. When Scotty's phone records were eventually retrieved, the last call was from an untraceable cell phone and lasted just a couple of minutes.

As good a detective as he was, Lou Scotty was never known for his record keeping. Combing through his files only corroborated that foible and provided no hint of why, in the middle of a busy business day, a veteran detective drove north on Broad Street to a hole-in-the wall liquor store.

News of the car bombing spread fast on social media that afternoon. Ordinarily, Dick would have been clueless, uninformed until he tuned into a TV or radio news station at the end of the day. But this piece of information caught the attention of his tech-savvy administrative assistant, who wasted no time barging into Dick's office.

"You had better go on-line to CBS3.com, Dick," she advised. "They're covering a live story that you'll want to hear about."

Dick smirked, "Really? What's so damn important?"

It didn't take long for his rhetorical question to be answered. For the next hour, he watched as news of the detective's slaughter, covered by a herd of reporters, developed on the local news station. Dick sat transfixed, staring at his computer screen, muttering over and over to no one in particular, "Philip, what the hell did you do this time?"

Chapter 29

Over the next several days, news of the policeman's dramatic killing reached its usual din in the papers. The first term the scribes used was "possible terrorism," a sure-fire way to get the public's attention. That possibility was quickly minimized by the police investigators who let it be known that Scotty had nothing to do with terrorism investigations, and thus was an unlikely target of an extremist group. Next came an attempt to prove that the bombing was in retaliation for some yet-to-be-discovered offense against the black community. Once again, cold hard facts ruined a great story as cooler heads pointed out that Scotty had, in the past, partnered up with African Americans who loved him dearly, and that none of his recent arrests had any racial overtones whatsoever. Despite an intense scrutiny of every phase of Scotty's life, nothing even remotely resembling race discrimination could be unearthed.

In fact, anything that anyone could discover about Scotty only served to make him shine more brightly as an individual, as a husband and father, and as a police detective. He earned a half-page obituary in the *Philadelphia Inquirer* that Dick read with interest. Scotty had grown up in the Northeast section of Philadelphia in a solid blue-collar neighborhood and attended college at Penn State on a ROTC scholarship. Following college graduation, he had been deployed to Germany where he served honorably, paying back his debt to the Army. In Berlin, he met his wife Greta, who worked as a translator for the American consulate. They eventually married and moved back to Philadelphia where Lou Scotty joined the police force.

Lou Scotty performed well in his job and moved up steadily within the ranks. He was described by nearly everyone on the force as quietly competent, never flashy, and fiercely loyal to the department and to his colleagues. His good work was recognized by promotions he truly deserved. He eventually sat for and passed the detective examination. Though he occasionally partnered with several other detectives, who had nothing but praise for his work ethic, Scotty strongly preferred to work alone, summoning help only when he needed an extra hand. Solo detective work was not favored by the police administration, mainly for safety reasons, but Scotty's captains routinely made an exception and allowed him the latitude to decide when he needed to be alone. They even forgave him his most deplorable habit, not mentioned in his glowing obituary: an unwillingness to keep his records up to date. His 90 forms routinely were left blank until an entire investigation was completed, at which time he would fill them out grudgingly, though entirely able to recall all of the facts down to the minutest detail without the benefit of notes.

Lou Scotty had left behind his wife, employed as a German teacher at Rosemont College, his mother, aged 88, an older brother and younger sister who resided in the Philadelphia area, and two teenaged children, a boy, Louis, and a girl, Meghan, all of whom grieved intensely for the fallen lawman. As did the police force and the city government, which put on a public funeral at the Basilica of Sts. Peter and Paul complete with eulogies by the Mayor and the Police Commissioner.

The attention focused on Scotty only made Dick squirm all the more. He had rationalized his decision to remain silent and not divulge what he knew about the case to Scotty, Dorothy, or anyone else by repeating the mantra: "Sonny was a bad man." Which he clearly was. And any inkling that Dorothy and Philip had a hand in Sonny's death would cause the childcare agencies to pull the plug on the adoption. Dick simply couldn't let that happen. Ursula, Dick's oracle, had agreed with that decision. But Scotty's death upped the ante considerably. An innocent man had been killed. The police were reluctant to declare the case a murder, but it was going to be difficult to arrive at any other conclusion. And what frightened Dick most of all was the amazing resemblance this crime had to Sonny's demise. Car explosions were not as common an occurrence in the United States as they were in the Middle East.

Which brought Dick back to Jimmy Chamberlain and Bernie McBride. Had Scotty discovered their whereabouts, and if so, had they decided to dispose of the detective the same way they had removed Sonny Cardinelli? Or had Philip once again intervened and somehow convinced the Romanos to work their particular brand of magic? In either case Dick once again had to decide if he wanted to divulge all that he knew and suspected to the authorities. Yet again, he was stuck and needed help from Ursula.

Though anxious, Dick waited for Ursula's next weekend visit. After much discussion, they had decided to introduce Ursula to Dorothy and Philip. They hit it off immediately, Ursula enjoying the grandparent experience and getting to know Dorothy and Philip about whom she had heard so much. Dinners with Philip and Dorothy became an occasional part of the weekend plan to which both looked forward. Such a dinner was on the agenda for the upcoming weekend.

But first, they would have their Friday evening together. Dick managed to control himself and stuck to the usual routine of drinks and conversation. His patience was rewarded with a pleasant dinner followed by passionate lovemaking and his first decent night's sleep in quite some time. He rose early, awakened by the sound of rain falling on the patio roof just outside his bedroom. He organized his thoughts as he prepared French press coffee. He sat on a comfortable sofa in front of the large picture window in his living room, surveying the south side of the city from eight stories up, watching the people and traffic navigate through the rain, organizing his thoughts.

An hour later, Ursula joined him after pouring her cup, clutching her robe around herself, snuggling up against him, enjoying his warmth.

"I love it here, Dick. Your apartment is so cozy. There's something about a rainy Saturday morning. Maybe just knowing we don't have to go anywhere."

Dick laughed. "We actually don't. In fact, I didn't plan anything for us until dinner tonight with Dorothy and the kids."

"And Philip."

"Yes, and meathead."

"Dick, you have to stop thinking about him so negatively. It's going to ruin your relationship not only with him but with Dorothy and the children."

"Ursula, you have been telling me that for months, and I agree fully. I've tried hard to keep an open mind about Philip, but then something else always seems to happen to upset the applecart."

"And has there been a new development?"

"Ursula, did you happen to hear about Detective Scotty?"

Dick anticipated the negative reply. Despite her sophistication in the arts, Ursula was usually unaware and uninterested in current events. She assiduously avoided television, radio, and newspapers, and except for truly earthshattering events like 9/11, remained blissfully unaware of the woes of the world, her country, or her city. "I simply don't know what difference it makes," she would say apologetically. "I can't influence what happens, so why worry about it constantly? If it's truly important, I'll hear about it without listening to the constant cackling."

Dick, the polar opposite when it came to public issues, understood Ursula's logic, but her attitude made some of their communication difficult at best. Dick liked to talk politics, for example, but every discussion with Ursula was necessarily prefaced with an explanation of who the players were, their background, and a myriad of facts that almost anyone else in the country would know by heart.

"Let me start from the beginning, then," Dick said, feigning patience. He went on to explain the entire situation starting with some of the facts Ursula had already heard, like the adoption conundrum and Sonny's untimely death. Ursula nodded, waiting for Dick to get to the most recent events.

Ursula was shocked to hear of Scotty's death. "That poor man and his family."

"I know, Ursula. He was a good person, which is why I'm distressed. I don't think I can keep what I know to myself any longer."

"Explain, please."

"I know that Philip and Chamberlain had a connection. I also know that Chamberlain's friend Bernie McBride had experience with explosives. Scotty was just beginning to get to the bottom of things when he was killed."

"So were you, Dick," Ursula said, concern in her voice. "Are you in any danger?"

"I don't think so. If there is a bad guy here, they know I'm not the threat. Too much to lose if I open my mouth. The detective was far more dangerous to them."

"Surely the police will have Scotty's records. Won't they be able to follow-up on the leads he was developing?"

"He mostly worked alone so I'm not sure what his superiors know about the details of the case."

"No, Dick. I don't agree. The police won't let this one fall in the cracks. If what you say is correct, one of their own was assassinated. They'll be highly motivated to find the answer."

"Then there is even more reason to do what I think I need to do next."

"Talk to Dorothy."

"Exactly. I know that Philip hasn't leveled with her. She

has to be concerned about Scotty's death, but she can't put it into proper context without knowing all about the goings-on at the Mack place."

"Then make some time to fill her in. Getting her perspective will also make you feel better. Holding this in hasn't been good for you."

"She's been my confidante ever since she was old enough to understand," Dick replied, tears welling up.

"Call her now and set up a time this afternoon. Invite her to lunch. I have some heavy shopping to do anyway, so you don't need to worry about entertaining me."

"Thanks, Ursula. I can always count on you to steer me right."

"And vice versa, Dick. Now let's get this day going in the right direction."

They spent the rest of the morning with a leisurely breakfast and some reading and lounging. Dorothy was able to free herself for lunch. Philip was only too happy to take the girls for a "hangburger" as Erin called her favorite sandwich, and a Muppet movie they were craving to see.

Dick picked a tavern on Walnut Street that he knew would have low traffic at lunchtime, even on a weekend. Most of the patrons were either nursing their Friday night hangover or preparing for a late afternoon jump start on Saturday night activities. The food was decent, nothing notable except the clam chowder, but privacy assured for what would be a deep conversation.

Dick met Dorothy outside the joint. The rain had stopped and the sun was just beginning to break through the cloud cover. They were greeted by a hostess and were quickly escorted to a booth where they situated themselves and made do with small talk as their ice teas were delivered. Dick waited until their soup arrived before diving into the conversation he was dreading and looking forward to at the same time.

"I need to go over some things with you regarding a case

I've been tracking lately."

"Happy to help. You know that, Dad."

"I do, honey, but wait until you hear about the case. You might not be so agreeable."

"It's the Cardinelli case, isn't it?"

Dick looked at Dorothy with amazement. "How on earth did you know that?"

"Come on, Dad. You're a detective. If it weren't important, you wouldn't have dragged me out to lunch on a Saturday when Ursula is in town. And you obviously had to vet whatever you're going to talk about with her, which is why we're meeting the day after she arrived from New York. And what case is more crucial to all three of us than Sonny's death?"

"You got me. I was hoping I wasn't going to have to bother you with the case again, but there's some new stuff you need to know about."

"Relax, Dad. I knew this was coming. You weren't about to let the case go without looking into it further. You don't want to risk losing Emily and Erin so you had to make sure all of the holes were plugged. And they aren't, right?"

"You could say that," Dick said with true disappointment.

"It's not your fault, Dad. I'm sure you did whatever you could, just as I did when I went back to the Romanos."

"Yes, I've been trying to figure things out, and Ursula has been helpful."

"But the Scotty murder threw a monkey wrench into the case, didn't it?"

"I'm glad we're having this conversation, Dorothy. I've been worried sick about the case and Scotty's death made me frantic."

"So tell me what you know, and let's see if we can put your mind at ease a bit."

"What I'm going to tell you isn't pleasant, I'm afraid."

"Is Philip part of the saga?"

"Integral, you might say."

As their salads arrived, Dick dove into the back story of Philip's employment at Mack Trucks, Jimmy Chamberlain, the truck service, and his relationship with explosive expert Bernie McBride. Dorothy listened intently, asking a few clarifying questions along the way. She bit her lip occasionally, which Dick knew to be reflective of surprise or unhappiness, but otherwise she remained expressionless, letting the information soak in before making any reply. As Dick finished his private-eye-like summary of events, he paused, waiting for Dorothy's reaction. As usual, she asked the question at the crux, the question that worried Dick the most.

"Dad, tell me what you believe to be the nature of the relationship Philip had with this guy Chamberlain."

"I don't know, Dorothy. I asked Chamberlain and Philip and got the answer I expected: golfing buddies."

"But you obviously suspect there was more to it," Dorothy half asked and half concluded.

"Philip was young and impressionable. A lot of young people experiment with things they later reject."

"That's not my concern, Dad. I'm not worried about Philip's sexuality. I have first-hand evidence that he's at least partially heterosexual. What I am worried about, and I know you are too, is that Chamberlain had strong enough feelings to persuade him to kill Sonny, or at least to arrange to have his partner do it somehow."

"And their disappearance and then Scotty's death just make the theory more plausible."

"Did Scotty know about Philip's relationship with Chamberlain?"

"If Belrose told Scotty the same stuff he told me, he would have wanted to look into that idea further. But I don't think he got the chance. I believe Chamberlain took off before Scotty went back and explored that idea like I did. My interview probably spooked Chamberlain and convinced him to get lost."

"So Scotty was a few steps behind you."

"Yes, but catching up fast, which may have gotten him killed."

"And since he worked alone and kept crappy records, we

aren't sure if the police will pick up the thread."

"Right. I'm sure they'll go back over the cases he was investigating to see if they can come up with some theories. The fact that his car was blown to pieces has to take them to the Cardinelli case. And if they find out about Bernie McBride, they'll intensify their investigation. But they have no physical evidence, and they have no Chamberlain or McBride. Unless they can pull a rabbit out of their hat, I suspect they won't be able to come after Philip... or you."

"I wish I found that reassuring, Dad. But it's not the cops I'm worried about."

"It's Philip."

"Yes, once again, it's Philip."

"And once again, it isn't just Philip."

"No, it isn't. If he's involved, he again managed to convince someone to take out a bad guy. Except this time, we suspect the killers did it not for vengeance but for love, or because Philip threatened Chamberlain with exposing his affair and sexual preference."

"And to cover tracks, an innocent and good person was sacrificed," Dick added.

"Pretty big differences, Dad."

"What are you going to do, sweetheart?"

"You mean besides talking to Philip? What are my options?"

"You only have two, darlin'."

"Stay or leave. Sounds familiar."

"You've decided to hang in with him the other times. Why?"

"Because I couldn't be sure he was the culprit."

"And you're sure now?"

"No, but how many times can I dismiss these terrible events as coincidence? It's getting a bit absurd, don't you think?"

"I guess so."

"And this time, an innocent person was killed. Scotty had a family, and he was a good man. If Philip had a hand in his death, I couldn't bear to even look at him, let alone cohabit."

"So unless Philip can convince you he's innocent, that's the end?"

"Come on, Dad. You know there's a very big issue on the other side of the ledger. The same issue that has been driving you to absolve Philip and keep the authorities at bay."

"The girls."

Dorothy nodded and smiled. "Almost any scenario will jeopardize them: the police find enough evidence to make him a suspect or a person of interest; you or I go to the police and tell them what we know; I leave Philip for any reason. Any of those would cause CPS to yank the kids."

"They wouldn't let you raise them alone?"

"Tough to say but there are several things working against us. First, we aren't married. They were concerned about us not staying together especially because there are two kids. Their assumption is that one person would have a hard time taking care of both, so they grilled us on that issue and made it rather clear that the stability of our relationship was a critical factor in letting the adoption go forward. Second, if Philip were labelled as a criminal, I would necessarily be tainted. All of the stuff from our past would be on the table, and it would be hard for me to dissociate myself completely. And finally, they just hate bad press. They get so much of it any-time something bad happens to a child that has been under their authority. So if Philip made it to the news, there would be many questions as to why the agency let two children re-main in the home of a criminal or criminals, as the case may be."

"I see your point."

"If I want to keep Emily and Erin, and I do as much as I want to keep my right arm, walking away from Philip or co-operating with the police is probably not an option."

"Do you want me to explore this further with anybody at City Hall?"

"No, Dad. Not for now. Let me think about this, talk to Philip and then I'll decide what to do."

"You know my vote."

"Of course I do. You've been pining away for grandchildren, and I've seen the way you've bonded to Emily and Erin. You want me to do anything except jeopardize their adoption."

"Puts you in a tough spot, lassie."

"I'm a big girl, Dad. I'll figure it out. And you'll be the first to know what I decide."

"I trust you, daughter. Just remember, I'll back you no matter what. I love those girls, but you're still the most important person in my life."

Dorothy reached across the table and grabbed Dick's hand. "Thanks, Dad. I appreciate that more than you know. But before I get all weepy, would you mind if I go? I have a few errands to run. It'll help me keep my mind off this for a little while at least. Will we see you and Ursula for dinner this evening?"

"Don't see why not, but that's up to you."

"Let's do it. I promise to keep silent until tomorrow and not upset everybody this evening. I know the kids are looking forward to seeing you guys. After everybody is asleep tonight, I'm going to pour myself a cognac, sit with my doggies, and try to process everything and make a decision about what to do."

Dick and Dorothy stood and hugged. After a long embrace, a peck on Dick's cheek, and see-you-laters, Dorothy walked briskly away, leaving Dick to contemplate his daughter, his life, his future... and finally whether to pay the check with cash or a credit card.

Chapter 30
Dorothy's Epilogue

Here I am, sitting on our sofa, staring into a cold, dark fireplace, surrounded by our three Portuguese water dogs, Meeko, Buffy and Rocky. They followed me out to the living room from the bedroom, confused as to why I would interrupt their rest and mine. I'm glad they did; I'm happy for their company and consolation. It's well past midnight. Philip is sleeping soundly as he usually does, and he thinks I am too. Sleep doesn't come easy for me anymore, even with a cognac, and it certainly isn't possible for me tonight. I have a lot to think about before the sun comes up, and now is the perfect time.

I need to sort out how on earth I found my way into this terrible mess. Locked in a relationship with a nutty man with whom I've fallen hopelessly in love. Literally imprisoned by circumstances and people and feelings I never could have anticipated. How did it all happen?

I never wanted to have a serious relationship with anyone—except my father, of course, and I don't believe I was
given much of a choice there. Mom died when I was very
young. I don't remember Mom as much as the shock of not
having her around. I think that was because I saw my father
come apart after she died. They were so close. It took a long
time for him to recover, and I know I was a large part of the
reason he was able to pull himself together. He would have
to snap to, or I was going to live somewhere else, and he
wasn't going to let that happen. Too much pride.

Anyhow, we bonded during my childhood and adoles-
cence and beyond. We did everything together. He made me
into a sports fanatic; even got me to root for the Eagles and
the Phillies, and it's an understatement to say the teams
weren't very good back then. He didn't care; he watched
every game on television, and he dragged me along to attend
many of their debacles in person.

Dad encouraged me to join school clubs and teams and
came to every function. He never missed one, even when I
didn't want him there and told him to stay away. I did well in
high school and could have gone almost anywhere, but he insisted that I stay local for college and law school. I caved because I knew he would be crushed if I wasn't around. I know
some teenagers grow to hate their parents. That didn't happen
to me. I never went through a period of rebellion. He adjusted
to me and my silly moods. We never had a knock-down, drag-
out battle. A lot of minor skirmishes, but that's no surprise. A
lot of times we would end up laughing about our arguments.
I knew he loved me totally and unconditionally. How can you
fight that?

Dad was such an all-encompassing presence that I knew
it was going to be hard to find a husband who matched up to
him. So I didn't look very hard. Instead, I focused on my career, determined to please my father by not only becoming a
great lawyer but also a skilled detective. "Not many women

have that skill combination, Dorothy," he would say. It wasn't until I was actually practicing law that I began to wonder how valuable my talent truly was. Granted, it helped in a few cases, but it was a lot of work that sometimes yielded little advantage. Ironically, it was Philip's incredible malpractice cases that brought out the best of my talents, at his urging, and subsequently got us into enormous trouble. More on that later.

It was all pretty simple in the beginning of my career. I was working hard, building a practice, living high in a nice apartment in town, hanging out with my father. I went from one short-term relationship to another, using men more for sex than companionship. I had no trouble attracting the opposite gender. I don't spend a lot of time making myself beautiful because I don't have to. I have my mom's looks and body. All I had to do when I was younger was go someplace where there were a lot of men, show off what I had, and they would flock to me. I could afford to be picky, and I was. And my detective training helped me size them up quickly and discard most after one night or less. I used the keepers for whatever I thought I needed at the time, like someone to accompany me to a social function or a wedding, but they too were dispatched, eventually, inevitably.

Then came Philip, and oh my God, it really was the lightning bolt. Just like in the movies. I used him as an expert witness in a case I was working on. He had an excellent reputation nationally as a legal consultant, for his expertise and honesty. He really understood how to take care of patients and had a good idea of what the standard should be in the community, not necessarily in the ivory tower, where he spent most of his time. All of the lawyers I spoke to who had used him told me he wouldn't steer me wrong or pad his bill with long meaningless reports or tell me what he thought I wanted to hear, as some experts do. I was immediately impressed with him on the phone, but I was bowled over when I saw him for the first time. We met at his office to discuss the case I had sent him. It was a friggin' thirty-minute meeting that literally changed my life.

To this day, I still haven't been able to figure out what there was about Philip that flicked my switch that day. It certainly wasn't his looks. Don't misunderstand: he's far from ugly. Dark features, decent body, nice hair and expressive brown eyes, but no one would call him handsome. He was polite and considerate but his personality was anything but sparkling. There was just something about him. Highly intelligent, inquisitive, aggressive, confident.

But most of all, Philip was intensely interested in me. Not my looks, or my figure, but me. When he asked me a question or wanted my opinion, he looked me in the eye and really listened to what I had to say. And he didn't bullshit me the way other men did, telling me how wonderful my research or my assessments were. He told me the truth, in a nice way, of course, but with complete honesty.

But if I had to use one word that explains my attraction to Philip, it would be respect. Philip Sarkis grew to love me, I know that, but that love was fostered and nurtured by the respect he had for me as a person, as a woman, as a lawyer, and now as a parent. Respect is what has sustained us through so many difficult circumstances. Which is exactly why I'm so worried right now. Has what happened caused me to lose respect for him? And he for me?

I knew from the beginning that Philip was married. I had promised myself that I would never date a married man, not under any circumstances. My attraction to Philip was so strong that I violated my principle and went after him. I tried to rationalize my impulsive behavior with the usual "he's unhappy with his wife and his marriage," but that wasn't true—not when I first met him. Fact is, I didn't know enough about his personal life to make any judgments about his marital satisfaction. I completely ignored the fact he had young kids. I trapped him into having sex with me that first time. I felt so guilty afterward, and I know he did too. We broke it off quickly, as we should have.

And then Hamlin happened. Philip was bushwhacked by a conniving couple who had colluded to kill Hugh Hamlin's wife and then tried to make Philip the culprit by accusing him of malpractice. He found himself in a terrible situation and he came back asking for my help in his defense. I don't think our affair would have been rekindled otherwise. I took pity on him, started helping him sort out that terrible case. We spent time together, and we fell in love. I didn't drag him away from his family. His wife deserted him when he lost his job and his standing in the medical community, and he almost killed himself. Is all of this a rationalization of my reckless behavior? Should I have turned him away when he needed help, or made it clear that we weren't going to do anything other than work on his case?

Maybe the strange and dangerous cases he dragged me into over the years have been punishment for my sins of tempting adultery and fornication. Is that my Catholic guilt showing? For whatever reason, through it all, he and I have had a difficult time keeping out of trouble. I guess the easiest to understand was the Hamlin case. Bonnie and Hugh had to be punished for what they did to Moira, Hugh's wife, and to Philip. I just wish the court had done its job, and the Romanos hadn't intervened in the end. After I spoke with the brothers, I had a pretty easy time believing that Philip was innocent, that Detective Scotty was wrong, and that Philip really didn't help the Romanos kill Hugh and Bonnie.

But then came the Adolphus Agency in Wilkes-Barre. A group of neo-Nazi nurses who got what they deserved, Romano-style, for having euthanized dozens, or maybe hundreds, of World War II veterans who had the audacity to fight against the Motherland. I almost got myself killed, and that really set Philip off. Did it make him angry enough to help the Romanos toast the evil nurses in a hellish fire at their agency headquarters, or was that just another coincidence?

The Boston stabbing of Thaddeus Robinson finally convinced me that there are lots of things about Philip I don't, and probably never will, understand. Like me, Philip had a life before I met him that shaped his mind, his emotions, and his priorities. Having an affair with his best friend's wife, fathering a child with her, and never telling me about it was bad enough. But if Philip actually was the person who attacked Robinson with a knife and deliberately severed his spinal cord, he showed himself to be a person I could never respect and could never trust. Did I let him stay in my life once again because I underestimated how far he had descended? Did I excuse his actions because I couldn't face living without him? Or have I harbored some distorted and ridiculous notion that I could change him, bring him back to being the Philip I fell in love with? How näive is that?

And the most recent bad guy, Sonny Cardinelli, who should have stayed away from our family, and whose death was pretty brutal, even on the Philip scale. He couldn't possibly have known which Philip-button he pushed when he made his move to take the kids away from us. Even if he had bothered to check, he would never have believed that an egghead heart doctor, a nerd he would have disrespected in high school, would not only keep him from cashing in on a juicy malpractice settlement but would figure out a way to take him out completely. He couldn't have realized that Philip had become the black knight, righting wrong and making evil people pay, especially a man he hated for trying to take his newly beloved daughters away. Dorothy, how did you delude yourself into believing Philip didn't get Sonny killed? Just because the Romanos said Philip and they weren't involved? How stupid was that? As your father has told you so many times, they're gangsters who lie for a living. Is this another example of Dorothy putting her head in the sand and pretending everything will be just fine?

I guess all of us, my father included, might have put Sonny's messy death aside for the sake of the girls if not for that damn Detective Scotty. He had to push the investigation until whoever blew up Sonny did the same thing to him. My father's right. Scotty's murder did change everything because now I have to aid in a whitewash that has a pretty good chance of blowing up for multiple reasons.

First of all, what are the chances the police will walk away from Scotty's investigation? Unlikely, especially given how much attention his death has attracted. When they review Scotty's activities, the Cardinelli case will surface. Chamberlain and McBride will become prime suspects and when they are, the search for them will intensify. God help us if the police find them—alive.

On the other hand, the police could discover the Santangelo thread to the Romanos that I did and decide to question the gentlemen. What would keep them from telling the police what they know about Cardinelli's murder, which would put the onus back on Philip? Are you naïve enough to believe they really do like you so much that they would protect Philip and you, if push came to shove?

Nice predicament, Philip, you asshole. Once again, you have placed me in an untenable situation. Tell the police what I know and almost certainly give up my children, or take the chance of being arrested as an accessory to murder. Actually multiple murders, including an honored police detective. No matter what I decide to do, my life has a really good chance of being ruined.

Focus, Dorothy. You have to make a decision. Maybe my doggies have some advice for me. Sometimes I'm convinced they know Philip and me better than we know ourselves. Mitten, bless her soul, always had an opinion and didn't mind sharing it with me.

So what do you think, guys? Help me out here. Meeko,

you're the wiliest of the pack. You know how to process information from your humans. I know you do because I've seen you manipulate Philip and me to get exactly what you want. What's your impression of Philip's behavior?

How about you Buffy? You're our sweetest and most caring creature. I bet you can't even imagine giving up the girls. It would break your little doggie heart not to have them around, so I don't even have to ask what you recommend. Stonewall the police and make them discover the truth, right?

And Rocky, the brightest. The alpha dog. You're a guy. What's in Philip's mind? Did he talk to you and clue you in when he was manipulating me and everybody else? What did he tell you that might help me make this important decision?

No response. I guess it's pretty silly of me to foist this decision on you guys. And very unfair. I'm the one who has to choose. I know my dear father will understand and back me up no matter how I proceed. Philip will never be able to forgive me if I jeopardize our family. He'll leave me, our relationship will be over, and I'll be alone, maybe for the rest of my miserable life. What will that be like? Will I spend my remaining, wretched years wondering what happened to the girls and to Philip? If I think about it that way, I guess I don't really have any choice. Take a deep breath, Dorothy.

Okay, guys, I'm going to make a decision and I'm not going to look back. If you think my choice is nuts, I want you to sit up and bark or at least whine. If you lie there peacefully, as you are now, I'll infer that you agree with my judgment.

I will remain silent. I won't confront Philip; he'll deny everything and insist he's innocent, so why waste the mental energy? I won't confer about this case with my father any further. He's given me as much wisdom as he and Ursula can generate. I won't talk to the authorities. They don't have physical evidence and as long as Chamberlain and McBride stay away, they have nothing to bring them to our doorstep. I'll pray to any god in any heaven to keep the police away. And if they do show up, I will use all of my skills and my intellect, and the Romanos if necessary, to deflect them.

I will try not to feel guilty about Detective Scotty, whose death was collateral damage. Instead, I will use all of my energy to love the girls and to raise them to be wonderful people. I will grow them up to become my best friends, my constant companions, my shopping buddies, and my comfort when I'm old. I'll encourage Philip to be the fantastic father he aspires to be. He has already proven he can be a wonderful parent, and I will not get in his way. I'll make sure my father maintains a prominent place in the girls' lives. And Ursula too, if she chooses.

And I will insist that Philip not take on any more malpractice cases. I don't care if we need the money. I'll never believe him when he tells me he'll remain emotionally isolated. We will de-complicate our lives and concentrate on the important things, just as we told our bosses we would. We'll find a wonderful place to live with the girls, with a big backyard for you guys to run around in, and we'll try to lead normal lives—whatever the hell that means.

What do you think, doggies? Am I making a catastrophic mistake? If you think I am, please jump up now and let me know. Otherwise, I shall assume from the fact that you're all lying quietly next to me that you're content with my decision. One last chance, guys. All right. I understand. You're probably not in love with my plan but you can live with it, is that fair to say?

It's late, my pets. Let's go to bed. On the way in, I'll stop in the girls' room and make sure they're tucked under their covers, sleeping hard, dreaming nothing but sweet dreams. Then, I will crawl under the covers and snuggle up against that maddening man I love so much and try hard to make peace with what I know about him. I'm going to need you to join us on the bed, as you usually do, so I can feel your warmth, hear your heart, and sense your love. I need to fall asleep knowing that your souls are melding with mine. I need your strength. I need it so much.

Acknowledgments

Every time I have tried to thank people who have helped me with my books, I have failed to convey how important each of them is to whatever success I have achieved. I don't think I will do much better this time, but here goes.

I can start with my wife, Dorothy (no, not Dorothy Deaver) who has not only encouraged me to write, but has listened to the rants and raves that are the natural part of giving birth to good fiction. She likes the idea that I exercise my right brain as she does when she creates beautiful pottery. Most importantly, she has not resented the time I have taken from our relationship to pursue this silly passion of mine. Although I have to say that a lot of my writing occurs while most normal people, including Dorothy, are unconscious.

Then, there's my best friend from high school, my golfing buddy, and all around good guy, Jim Kaufmann. Jim is a retired medical science editor. However, I think "edit" doesn't do justice to the contribution Jim has made to the quality of my books. His thorough review of my work and his thoughtful and erudite suggestions have had a major impact on every aspect of the story and the writing craft. The tales of Philip and Dorothy simply wouldn't be the same without Jim.

I am frequently asked how I find the time to write creatively. Time management is the key, and my ability to juggle many balls is made possible by God's two most amazing administrative assistants, Donna Simonds and Roe Wells. Dorothy calls them my secret weapons. I guess that secret is no more.

And once again, thanks to my patients. Not only do you fuel the engine of my imagination, but you inspire me daily with your courage and perseverance in the face of some pretty amazing and scary illnesses. Many of you have become my fans, but it is yours truly who should be asking for *your* autographs.

PETER R KOWEY MD

Dr. Peter Kowey is a cardiologist and an internationally respected expert in heart rhythm disorders. After college at St. Joseph's University in Philadelphia, he attended medical school at the University of Pennsylvania and trained in cardiology at the Peter Bent Brigham Hospital and the Harvard School of Public Health in Boston. For the past 35 years, he has developed a large referral practice in Philadelphia. He is also a Professor of Medicine and Clinical Pharmacology at Jefferson Medical College and holds the William Wikoff Smith Chair in Cardiovascular Research at the Lankenau Institute for Medical Research.

Dr. Kowey's research has led to the development of new cardiac drugs and devices. He has authored hundreds of scientific papers and textbooks and has taught and mentored scores of medical students, fellows, residents and physicians in practice. His most recent venture has been fiction writing. His first three novels, *Lethal Rhythm*, *Deadly Rhythm*, and *The Empty Net* were published in 2010, 2012, and 2014.

Dr. Kowey and his wife Dorothy have three successful daughters and two sons-in-law, all attorneys, and six grandchildren. Their permanent residence is in Bryn Mawr, Pennsylvania, but they spend time throughout the year with their Portuguese water dogs at their Pocono Mountain lake house.

Peter R. Kowey